Lucifer State
A Novel Approach to Rhetoric

Trevor Melia
Nova Ryder
Jean Jones

University of Pittsburgh
Edinboro University of Pennsylvania

Contributing Essayists:

Richard H. Thames: Duquesne University
Richard E. Vatz: Towson State University
Lee S. Weinberg: University of Pittsburgh

Cover Art: *Umedar3*, by Barry Cronin.

Copyright © 2007, 2005 by Pearson Custom Publishing
All rights reserved.

Earlier editions copyright © 1983, 1981 by Kendall/Hunt Publishing Company.

Permission in writing must be obtained from the publisher before any part of this work may be reproduced or transmitted in any form or by any means, electronic or mechanical, including photocopying and recording, or by any information storage or retrieval system.

All trademarks, service marks, registered trademarks, and registered service marks are the property of their respective owners and are used herein for identification purposes only.

Printed in the United States of America

10 9 8 7 6 5 4 3 2 1

ISBN 0-536-45816-2

2006560127

CO

Please visit our web site at *www.pearsoncustom.com*

PEARSON CUSTOM PUBLISHING
501 Boylston Street, Suite 900, Boston, MA 02116
A Pearson Education Company

TABLE OF CONTENTS

Preface v
Notes from the Second Edition vii
Introduction x
Prologue xv

1	A Time to Be Born 1
2	And a Time to Die 13
3	Lucifer 23
4	Security First, Last, and Always 37
5	Jeremy Leventritt, P.H.O. 55
6	D. Date 69
7	All is Well 79
8	Do Not Go Gentle 91
9	Reluctant Lazarus 101
10	Joannah and Quasimodo 111
11	Babel 117
12	Esmeralda and the Clown 131
13	Race with the Sun 137
14	Lucifer's Loose 157
15	Post Natural Death 171
16	Unclean 177
17	Genesis Code 189
18	Knowing Good and Evil 203
19	Race Against Death 217
20	Jekyll Pact 233
21	North Towards Erewhon 239

Epilogue 245
Suggested Readings... 249
From the Therapeutic State to the Lucifer State.................. 267
Metaphors, Allusions, and Allegories in Lucifer State 277

PREFACE

Granted the frankly experimental nature of this text, it is gratifying to be writing the introduction for a new and updated edition of *Lucifer State*. The book, originally intended for an introductory course in rhetoric at the University of Pittsburgh, has found a home in Persuasion and Rhetoric courses all over the United States for over three decades. In many instances, *Lucifer State* has served as an exciting replacement for standard textbooks; in other instances, it has been employed as a supplemental text which brings to life in real and dramatic ways the information standard textbooks in Persuasion and Propaganda seek to present. No matter how it is used, it appears that the text has achieved its purpose. Judging by the reactions of the thousands of students at colleges and universities across America, the book indeed brings theories of persuasion and rhetoric to life.

But what is this book, this novel that acts as a textbook? It is, quite frankly, a bold rhetorical effort in its own right. *Lucifer State* was written because no single textbook could be found that adequately reflected both the spirit and substance of the enterprise of rhetoric and persuasion. *Lucifer State* tells the story of how subtle and unseen societal persuasion functions to constrain us all. It tells the story of an internally consistent society, and shows how government and citizen alike work together to perpetuate the structure that has been created and maintained through rhetorical means. And in its telling, *Lucifer State* confronts the reader with the ways in which we are all persuaded to believe the "truths" of our socially constructed worlds.

As we write these words, our national leaders have decreed that the United States is at war. Our declared enemy is not one of flesh and blood—instead, we are at war against a noun: we are engaged in a "war against terror." Good people can debate the merits of the enterprise and argue about how such an abstract conception of "war" might be filled in appropriately. We are not here in the business of taking sides in such a debate. What we can say is this: the notion of our leaders defining our current international situation in such a way is a persuasive act. Once citizens accept such definitions as the "truth" of the situation, much logically follows. And thereby, such constructions are worthy of examination.

It is in that spirit that *Lucifer State* exists. The book tells a good story, but it does not take sides. Instead, *Lucifer State* works to illuminate how societal persuasion functions. In the spirit of George Orwell's *1984* or Sinclair Lewis' *It Can't Happen Here*, the novel demonstrates how, working together, we all do our part to sustain and maintain THE TRUTH.

One must remember, though, that *Lucifer State* serves a dual purpose. It is a novel, but it is intended as a text for use in college courses. Through its extensive footnotes and by way of the essays appended at the end, the book ensures that the academic points about persuasion and rhetoric will not be lost.

Finally, we would be remiss were we not to note that a book like *Lucifer State* can only come into being with the support of many. The authors are grateful to their academic departments, which have always encouraged serious devotion to teaching and equally tolerated experimental efforts in the classroom. Further, we are grateful to our students—the thousands of young adults who have challenged us and inspired us daily. They are our readers—it is they who have enthusiastically praised the book and offered feedback that has made the book stronger.

Inevitably the ideas that follow have benefited from discussions with a large number of associates. Those who come immediately to mind are Floyd and Ray Anderson, Jeanine Czubaroff, Margaret Diamond, Kenneth Dowst, Kimber Forrester, Dolores Fowler, Robert Friday, Dilip Gaonkar, James Kelso, James E. McGuire, Robert P. Newman, Fred Pearce, Gary Peltier, Richard Roth, Brittany Rowe, Herb Simons, Michael and Jan Smith, Merrily Swoboda, Richard Thames, Audrey Van Meersbergen, Richard Vatz, Tom Wanko, Lee Weinberg, Charles Willard, Bradley Wilson, Ted Windt, Gary Woodward, and George Yochum. We are indebted to our families in ways too numerous to specify.

Trevor Melia,
Nova Ryder,
Jean Jones
2007

NOTES FROM THE SECOND EDITION

The intellectual milieu in which this pedagogical experiment was originally undertaken can perhaps be characterized as one of *doubt about certainty*. With the publication of this second edition, in the humanities, at least, it is *certainty about doubt* that prevails. Though there is a world of difference between these two intellectual postures, rhetoric profits from both. It is the climate of opinion in which Truth is thought to be both available and demonstrable (whether through the manipulation of formal symbolic systems or by empirical operations) that suffocates rhetoric.

Lucifer State was conceived as a means of creating breathing space for the ancient discipline by emphasizing the role of doubt and contingency in human affairs. But, while the text hoped to challenge some of the more pretentious claims to Truth, particularly in the so-called social sciences, it was not intended to derogate the *quest* for truth.

It is said that Frederick Douglass named his newspaper the *North Star* because slaves, escaping from the South, used the star to guide them towards freedom. The slaves did not, of course, expect to reach the North Star and if they hoped to achieve complete freedom in the North they were surely sadly disappointed. Probably the fleeing slaves did not know that Polaris is not a fixed star—that it deviates from true North by a degree or so. Almost certainly they did not realize that the star shares in the general motion of the galaxy and that its steady appearance is the accidental by-product of its peculiar location vis à vis the earth. What the slaves did know is that Polaris led them in the direction they wanted to go. So it is with truth.

It is by now a commonplace that claims to have discovered Truths, which are True here and everywhere else in the universe, True now and forever, are frequently associated with covert claims for privilege and power. This distressing discovery does not, however, warrant the despair and chicanery it appears to have engendered. Amidst the whirling constellations of cultural and historical relativisms there yet remain beacons of truth, good for our place and our time. It is precisely the virtue of classical rhetoric to have acknowledged contingency, particularly of social facts, without abandoning the social realm to chaos. In challenging hegemonic pretensions to possession of ultimate Truth, *Lucifer State* seeks to encourage the *quest* for contingent truth.

Claims to possession of absolute Truth are usually buttressed by appeals to privileged methods, notably science and logic. Attempts to deny the efficacy of these methods in their proper realm are manifestly implausible. Nevertheless, whatever the virtue of scientific and logical explanations, they contribute little or nothing to our search for *meaning*. Moreover, there is plausibility to the contention that these methods, largely the flowers of Western culture, have no *prima facie* claim on the allegiance of humanity generally. It is perhaps for these reasons that theories of narrative understanding are now flourishing. Narrative, storytelling if you will, does appear to be the universal means whereby the brute events of collective and individual existence are given meaning.

A generous interpretation of *Lucifer State* would allow that its narrative anticipates many of the theoretical issues that swirl around contemporary discussions of rhetoric: the power/knowledge equations of Foucault; the linguistic hermeticism of de Saussure; the reflexive impulse of Derrida's Deconstructionism; the strong program in the Sociology of Knowledge of Berger, Luckman, and Bloor; and, of course, the uses of narrativity itself. If there is any truth to that interpretation, the credit should go to Kenneth Burke, who got there "first with the mostest." In any case, experience at the University of Pittsburgh and elsewhere shows that the text provokes discussion of those central issues among undergraduate students equipped neither by disposition nor training to take on first hand the recondite work of the "continentals."

The introductory course at the University of Pittsburgh for which the text was written aimed first of all to convey what it means to hold a "rhetorical point of view." I know of no one who better knows the meaning of that phrase than my friend, and sometimes student, sometimes mentor, Richard Thames. Professor Thames continues to teach his own highly successful version of the introductory course at Duquesne University. It is he who has revised the annotated bibliography for this printing. The bibliography, always an important and integral part of the text, should be helpful in pointing students towards the primary literature with which *Lucifer State* is in continuing dialogue.

Trevor Melia
Pittsburgh, May 1991

INTRODUCTION

The problems of introducing the beginning student to a thoroughgoing conception of the art of rhetoric are considerable. Most students are apt to think of rhetoric at best as vaguely associated with the study of English composition. At worst, they are likely to think in terms of *mere rhetoric*—rhetoric as opposed to *reality*. The honest instructor will wish to acknowledge that rhetoric can be usefully viewed as a *manipulative technique* whose allegiance to truth is frequently doubtful and whose sole objective is persuasion. On the other hand, since the manipulative uses of rhetoric are so widespread, it is obligatory that the instructor convey the conception of rhetoric as an *analytic instrument* designed to dissect persuasive endeavors—shabby or otherwise. Finally, if the full scope of the discipline is to be grasped, it is vital that the idea of rhetoric as a *worldview* with an ancient and honorable tradition also be presented. *Rhetoric: manipulative technique, analytic instrument, world view*—no single class could adequately deal with anyone of these, and yet the introductory course in "Rhetoric" or in "Persuasion" must somehow display all three.

The danger for an introductory textbook is that it will either founder on the rocks of ancient rhetorical theory or run aground in the sandy shallows of contemporary rhetorical practice. A textbook after all must carry a weighty historical and scholarly ballast lest the discipline it represents appear incapable of holding a steady and wise intellectual course. On the other hand, the text, to be useful to the student, must be buoyant enough to be responsive to the light and shifting winds of contemporary culture.

A second and perhaps even more difficult quandary faces the text for the introductory course in "Persuasion" or in "Rhetoric." Rhetoricians are the custodians of two separate and currently quite antagonistic traditions. From its beginning in ancient Greece, rhetoric has been deeply concerned with the practical, political, social, and economic problems of everyday life. Indeed, rhetoric was once the major tool for dealing with what has become the domain of modern social science. But rhetoric is also a humanistic enterprise and as such has always used the linguistic methods of analysis traditionally associated with literature. The current overwhelming concern with theories of *truth* rather than theories of *action* has split the rhetorical enterprise by making a flat distinction between scientific *fact* and literary *fiction*.

Texts exemplifying one tradition, be they ever so methodologically pure and empirically true, have the faintly antiseptic whiff of the social science laboratory about them. The other tradition produces texts more at home in the criticism of fictional art than in the analysis of real life. If the experience of the course for which this book has been written is any indication, students find both approaches discouraging. The one genre which students can be cajoled into reading and which applies literary techniques to social problems is what may be called *social science fiction*.

The obvious criticism of social science fiction is that it is typically neither fine art nor good science. The first criticism is undeniably correct. Occasional claims to the contrary notwithstanding, there is probably no *literary* masterpiece in the genre. Social science fiction is frankly ideological. Its characters carry far too great a didactic burden to serve as the subtle psychological studies required by great literary art. Its artistic limitation aside, however, social science fiction can serve admirably the teaching function that is its true purpose. Whereas social science, which is frequently covertly ideological in its guise as objective fact, is apt to discourage evaluation and debate, its fictional counterpart tends to provoke both. Moreover, social science in its very attempts to convey precise particular facts often produces at the general level a sterile illusion. The best social science fiction is capable of making of its particular fiction an impressionistic general truth.

Such at least are the reasons that led to the use of some of the "classic" works of social science fiction as *supplements* in the introductory course in rhetoric at the University of Pittsburgh. The works of Orwell, Koestler, Huxley, Skinner, etc., raised provocative political and social issues with which a relevant study of rhetoric must deal, but they also serve as a constant reminder of the literary methods available to rhetoric.

As useful as these authors were, however, they themselves needed to be supplemented. First, while students appeared to enjoy reading and discussing such works, they tended to be nonplussed when it came to writing critical reviews of them. Typically students summarized the plot and perhaps identified a couple of key issues. Rarely were they in a position to identify and discuss rhetorical techniques that were implied by the books. Second, while each of these works exemplified rhetorical method, ironically not one saw rhetoric as the prime means of social control. Devices for genetic, chemical, and behavioral engineering abounded, and rhetorical means were distinctly subsidiary.

Lucifer State attempts to address these problems. It is rhetorical both in method and substance. It describes a society that is controlled ultimately by rhetorical means, and technology is distinctly subsidiary. Its allusions are to rhetorical traditions, characters, and sources. The metaphors, allusions, and allegories are identified so that the student should be able to rhetorically "filet" the piece. The combination of footnotes (providing explanations) and italics (drawing attention to especially significant words and phrases) are designed to make available to the student the insights that would be part of an astute, experienced, and informed act of rhetorical criticism. While *Lucifer State* is a work of fiction, every effort has been made to stay within the bounds of what is, if not probable, at least rhetorically and technologically possible. The annotated bibliography at the end provides, among other things, references to factual accounts of much that is presented as fiction here.

Finally, *Lucifer State* tries to acknowledge the fact that rhetoric's roots lie in the relativism of the ancient Sophists rather than in the "quest for certainty" that characterized the work of Plato and Aristotle. Not the least of the epistemic problems of this position—and they are considerable—is what may be called the *relativist fallacy*. In *fact* it is logically impossible to be absolutely certain of uncertainty; in *fiction*, it's a different story.

. . . a deception in which the deceiver is more truthful than the non-deceiver and those who let themselves be deceived are wiser than those who do not.

Gorgias of Leontini

PROLOGUE

P. Goras,[1] Head of State and Master Rhetorician, gazed at the message that had just flashed on the computer screen of the Oval Office.

DATE: 10 JUNE 2192
TO: P. GORAS, WASHINGTON, U.S.A.
FROM: INTERNATIONAL COUNCIL, GREENWICH, U.K.

    I. M. LATOUR HAS BEEN EXILED TO EREWHON III.
    II. REQUEST NOMINEE FOR VACANCY ON INTERNATIONAL COUNCIL.
    III. REPORT EXTENT OF CAPTAIN SEBRING'S PENETRATION OF LUCIFER MYTH.
    IV. REPORT FINAL DISPOSITION OF N. MOLLENSKAYA.

Goras leaned back in his chair and reflected on the events that had led to this cryptic communiqué. That a member of the International Council should have attempted to communicate the *ULTIMATE TRUTH* to an American Lucifer Pilot was almost unbelievable. That James A. Sebring had been able to discover as much as he had was astonishing. It had all begun on the first day of Spring, 2192.

---

[1] ProtaGORAS and Gorgias (cited elsewhere) were two Greek Sophists who might fairly be called fathers of rhetoric. Among other things, they believed that it is impossible to know the truth. Communication for them could not therefore be the process of finding and teaching *the truth*. It had to be *persuading* people to accept one's *opinion*.

1

A TIME TO BE BORN[2]

It was March twenty-first, the first day of Spring. The Lucifer Flight had arrived at Bradley Airstation on schedule, the black box had been unloaded, and there was now just over an hour to go.

Captain James Adam Sebring, a tall man, over six feet, with slightly rounded shoulders and unruly blonde hair pushing out from beneath his flight cap, jostled with the usual Airstation crowd.

There was a scramble of bodies bumping, of luggage and shins colliding, of children of various sizes viewing the world as a pant leg, a belt buckle or a protruding stomach. As the mob moved slowly through the rotunda, an adolescent boy, waving a Red Card in his left hand and shouldering his way through the crowd, stepped squarely on Jim Sebring's toe. Jim cursed volubly, and the lad responded by flashing his Red Card again, while simultaneously making an obscene gesture.

"Get out of my way." The youngster pressed on, shoving and elbowing the people about him. Angry faces turned, but, on seeing the Red Card, the crowd parted silently, almost reverently.

"Good Goras!" Jim Sebring swore again, and this time the angry glances were directed at him. He squeezed his way, oblivious, toward the exit of the huge Airstation.

Outside the air was damp and chilly, the early morning sun just beginning to dispel the night's dew. Sebring separated himself quickly from the crowd

---

[2] The allusion is to the famous biblical passage (See Ecclesiastes, Chapter 3). In general, the *Bible*, the works of Shakespeare, and the Greek classics, having shaped so much of our thinking, are virtually rhetorical sourcebooks in our society. Allusions to these great works in literature usually provide clues about the meaning of the plot or character.

and walked briskly towards the Delta Meter Zone. Moving down the first row of electro-cars and scanning the meters, he saw that the first two cars were less than a quarter charged, and the third slot was vacant. The fourth had been left unplugged.

"Goras!" He swore again and moved on to the next E-car, a bright yellow two-seater bearing the identification number *1984*. The meter read just over three-fourths of full charge. Yanking the plug from its socket in the hood of the car, he let it retract into the power meter and then jabbed at a control and waited while the door slid noisily down into the undercarriage. Glancing at his chronometer, he maneuvered his long body into the driver's seat.

A bearded face appeared at the open door of the E-car.

"Good luck, Jim." Jim stared for a moment. The face was familiar, but he couldn't place it.

"Colin Jeffries," the face volunteered, "Met Comm Section."

"Oh, yes, of course. But how did . . .?"

"Natasha told me. Today is the day, isn't it?"

Jim nodded. "Yes, today's the day—in about fifty minutes actually."

"Well, then," Jeffries thrust his hand through the open door, "good luck and all that." He gave a brief salute, and his bearded face disappeared.

"Thanks," Jim muttered as he ran his finger over a row of buttons on the dash and punched in C-3. He found himself wishing that Jeffries had been Natasha.

The E-car wheeled out of its slot, and a small screen in the center of the dash lit up with a series of lines and arrows showing the most efficient route in prevailing traffic to Sector C-3. Ignoring it, Jim floored the pedal and swerved onto the road, allowing the E-car to reach its top speed of fifty miles an hour. Without releasing the pedal, he drove through a complex system of subsidiary roads until the vehicle finally spilled out onto a major causeway. Along with most of the traffic from the Airstation, James Adam Sebring was headed for Hartford—the city that had once been the insurance capital of the country.

The sun filtered through the windows of the car, and the shadows caused by the tall trees that lined the causeway flickered across his sallow face.

As he approached the city and set about navigating its familiar sequence of interlocking highways, Jim checked his chronometer for a second time.

He thought of Evelyn, his wife, and the drama that was about to unfold. He wondered what it would do to their D. Date compatibility. And he thought of Natasha.

Natasha had agreed with him when he'd suggested to Peter Stoneham, the Airstation Security Officer, that he should let the Lucifer[3] Flight go to the "Living Hell." Ironically, Natasha had been the one to understand that his need on this day was to be with his wife. His wife, Evelyn, on the other hand, had argued that it was not necessary to reassign the Lucifer Flight, that he'd be back from Greenwich in plenty of time, and that he should not let his concern for her override the demands of his job.

It was true that there was nothing he could do, no further contribution he could make. He'd done his bit nine months ago. Still, Evelyn should have understood his anxiety, and she should have wanted him there.

"But I do want you there, Jim," she'd said. "You will be there. There's plenty of time after you get in from the flight."

He shrugged. He probably was behaving unreasonably—erratically, as Stoneham liked to say.

Jim swerved the E-car off the causeway. A "hike" held up the palm of his hand, soliciting a ride. "Goras!" he moaned. "Some lazy bastards won't walk a hundred yards." He passed along the obscene gesture he had so recently received and drove on. He had already reached his destination zone, so he wasn't obliged to pick up a hike in any case.

Jim wheeled the E-car down the east side of the city square, passing as he did the Region 1 Master Medical Facility where Evelyn worked, and where, he sometimes thought, she kept her soul. The yellow electro-car cooled perceptibly as it passed through the shadow of the brooding pyramid-shaped edifice. Jim made a ninety-degree turn, accelerated past the Public Security Building that was situated on the south side of the square, and pulled into a vacant power meter at the end of the block. He slid from his seat, jerked the connector from the meter, and, with a practiced motion, hooked up the now tiring yellow E-car.

---

[3] Lucifer—Satan, the devil, or more broadly the ultimate source of evil, but also the bearer of light.

Suppressing a wave of apprehension, Jim started across the Common toward his destination on the north side of the city square. The Great Clock, Hartford's historic "Sermon in Stone," sat in the center of the Common and dominated the square. Its effect was that of an ancient Gothic cathedral. Taller even than the Master Med pyramid, it towered above the other buildings. The gigantic marble base, which housed the Ceremonial Amphitheatre, supported a huge white stone obelisk. The four sides of the obelisk were carved as four human hands, their long slender fingers reaching upward towards the clock at its pinnacle.

Jim Sebring walked briskly across the red stone pavement which surrounded the Great Clock. He stopped for a moment, tilted back his head, and shaded his eyes against the morning sun to make out the time. It was ten forty-nine a.m. He made his way across the square and towards an oblong, six stories high, semi-glass building, which was surrounded by pleasant-smelling evergreen shrubs.

He entered the rotunda of the Sector-C Life Conservation Unit from the south. This was the curved side, where the huge sheets of solar panels housed more than one million thermoelectric transducers. The unlit signs facing Jim as he entered indicated that to the left, down the main rotunda corridor, lay the FACTOR BLOCK SECTION, and to the right, the CONSULTATION OFFICES. Under the signs stood the route-card decoder. Jim drew a white route-card from his pocket. He slid the card into the decoder, and the indicator above the vertical transporter across from the main entrance flashed on. He stepped into the cylindrical transporter unit and watched through the translucent conduit as the second level slid by. By the time he stepped from the unit, more flashers directed him down two circular corridors and through a variety of sliding glass doors until he stood facing a sign that announced: SECTION F-STERILIZATION READY ROOM.

Jim did not feel ready. Cursing himself for a coward, he rubbed his now sweating palms against his gray and black tunic. Outside, the Great Clock tolled, reminding the world that it was eleven a.m. on this the twenty-first day of March. Twenty-five minutes to go, Jim thought. He stepped forward, and as he did, the door in front of him slid noiselessly open. Simultaneously, a young uniformed orderly, a Green Card holder Jim would have guessed, rose to greet him.

"Captain Sebring?"

Jim acknowledged the query with a nod of his head.

"We've been waiting for you. The rest of your party is already here."

Jim's eyes swept the room in search of his "party." Eight people in all—only two of them associated with Evelyn—Joannah, her best friend, and Noel Baker Smyth, her superior. The rest, Jim judged, belonged to another group. Smyth, busy talking to a medical official on the other side of the room, had apparently not seen Jim enter. Joannah, on the other hand, was already half way across the room, her arms open in greeting.

Joannah Stoneham was undoubtedly the most beautiful woman Jim had ever known. Tall, five feet seven or eight, her body was statuesque, and she knew it. Her wavy, shoulder-length blonde hair framed a classic face—high cheek bones, sparkling myopic green eyes, slightly flared nostrils, generous mouth—a vision, and she knew that, too. The vision threw her arms around Jim's neck and kissed him on the cheek.

"Hello, Joannah."

"It's Esmeralda," she whispered, pushing her lips close to his ear, "but don't tell Peter I told you."

"Esmeralda?"

"Shhh." She grinned at him and glanced around the room sheepishly. "Peter would be furious if he knew I'd told you. He doesn't like me to tell anyone."

"Who's Esmeralda?"

"Me, silly," Joannah said impatiently.

"Oh," Jim nodded.

"But you won't tell anybody?"

"No, of course not."

Joannah beamed. Then, just as suddenly, her face became sober. "Are you nervous, Jim?"

"Yes."

"I am, too, for Evelyn and for you and for him."

"He'll be fine, Joannah," Jim said, realizing that it was he who was reassuring her instead of the other way around.

"Oh, yes," Joannah's green eyes misted. "I know he will, darling, but you see I have been running him through CLEM all morning and I haven't found out who he is yet. I wanted to do that for Evelyn."

Jim nodded, letting her ramble on, savoring the delicate fragrance of perfume that wafted from her, and marveling at the sensuousness of her lips.

"But I will," she said, brightening suddenly. "I will. You tell Evelyn not to worry. I'll find out who he is." And she turned abruptly and left him, stopping half way across the room to glance back and wink conspiratorially.

Joannah always had a way of leaving Jim in a state of bemused confusion. He was never quite sure if he knew, after having talked to her, what he had talked about—or rather, he had the feeling that she had talked about one thing and he about another. Still, she was beautiful; she was startlingly naive, and even if her thinking was chaotic, she was pleasant, giving, and charming to be around. He wondered how Peter Stoneham, of all people, had managed to persuade such a woman to marry him.

From the corner of his eye, Jim saw Noel Baker Smyth approaching. He considered for a moment moving off in the other direction but decided that would be too obvious.

"Ah, Captain Sebring. It's very good to see you again." Smyth's voice was deep; a smile played across his mouth. His thick hand was extended towards Jim.

Jim regarded the steel gray eyes of the Director of Master Med. Smyth was the only man Jim knew who could smile with his mouth and remain detached with his eyes. He took the hand with a deliberate firmness.

Smyth set his feet at parade rest and waited coolly for Jim to say something, as Jim knew he would.

"I'm surprised to see you here, Director. I'd have thought your responsibilities would give you little time for this kind of affair."

"On the contrary," Smyth said, refusing to be needled, "I'm especially fond of Evelyn. I don't know what I'd do without her, and in any case, it's hard to imagine an event of greater social significance."

"She feels the same way about you, Director, and loves her job, but by Goras, we weren't looking to do society any favors." Jim watched his wife's superior closely. He knew Smyth would like neither the sentiment nor the language, and he was rewarded.

A shadow flickered across the Director's face. "I'm sure *you* weren't." Smyth leaned on the pronoun. "I'm equally sure that the social implications didn't escape Evelyn."

"*The social implications never escape Evelyn.*" The words were out before Jim could stop them, and he regretted the disloyalty instantly. "I guess that's part of the job, too," he added lamely.

"It is, and she knows her job. I shall be glad when she gets back to it." Smyth, looking over Jim's shoulder, nodded at someone across the room. "Well, there's not much time," he said, turning his attention back to Jim. "Perhaps we'd both better get moving."

Jim nodded curtly. The most annoying thing about the man, Jim thought, was that he absorbed insults like a lead wall absorbs gamma rays—with no effect. He wasn't exactly sure why he disliked Smyth, certainly Evelyn's hero worship of the man was part of it, but there was something else. Here, Jim reflected, was a man who took himself far too seriously, a man who thought of himself entirely in terms of the eminent position he had achieved. Worse yet, Noel Baker Smyth always treated others in terms of their jobs, as if they, too, were nothing more or less than the social role they had come to occupy.

"Oh, by the way, Jim," Smyth glanced back as he was leaving. "You might want to watch the debate we'll be running on Public Service Three the week after next."

"What debate?"

"Oh, you didn't know? The security question. Peter Stoneham will be presenting our side."

"Our side?"

"Yes," Smyth said, "I arranged it myself. Stoneham's a very good man. His own accident—his appearance—don't you know our officials tend to make him into an object lesson and he knows the homeland security and domestic security fields inside out."

"If Stoneham represents it, I'm not sure *I'm* on our side," Jim said peevishly.

"Yes, I know you and he have collided on the security issue before. But, you might find the debate interesting anyway." Smyth turned to acknowledge Joannah, who was making a bid for his attention.

Jim shrugged his indifference, walked across to the sloping windows, and gazed out. The sun was momentarily hidden behind a fair weather cloud and across the way the large hand on the Great Clock, the figure of a man, pointed at the number five.

"Members of the Sebring party," the strident voice of a female announcer burst through the hidden public address system. "Please prepare for sterilization."

The orderly was already handing Joannah her long sack-like gown and ushering her toward one of the sterilization cubicles at the far end of the Ready Room. When she emerged from that cubicle, on the other side, she would be wearing nothing but a hospital gown. Jim, suppressing the thought, crossed to the orderly, accepted his own larger version of the same sack and headed for the cubicle next to that into which Joannah had just vanished.

Once inside, he quickly stripped and stepped onto the small circular platform in the center of the cubicle. As he did, the platform began to rotate slowly, exposing first one side of his body and then the other to the glowing panel which constituted one wall of the cubicle. As he rotated, Jim eyed his naked torso in the reflecting surface that made up the rest of the sterilization chamber. He noted that his otherwise lean and muscular body was marred by the slightest rounding of his stomach and a tendency toward flabbiness in his rear end.

Perversely, the sight of his nakedness turned his thoughts not to his wife Evelyn, but again to his co-worker Natasha Mollenskaya. During Evelyn's confinement he had made the decision, not yet consummated, to go to bed with Natasha. He was not at all sure why he was so attracted to her. He was certainly not in the habit of having affairs with other women, and while Natasha was a good looking woman, she was not, for instance, to be compared with the veritable Venus who occupied the adjoining cubicle. Jim smiled to himself. Joannah, naked and only a few inches away, was no doubt at this very moment contemplating her own beautiful body.

Somewhere above his left ear a bell rang announcing the completion of the sterilization process, and the glow of the radiating panel subsided to a dull red. Jim reached for his now sterilized gown and stepped towards the panel bearing the exit sign. As he did, it slid upward, admitting him to the Observation Balcony of the D. Date Amphitheatre. Across the balcony in the public section several of the twenty-five or so robed people who sat there examined Jim as he entered. He realized that since Evelyn would not appear, he was now the star performer. People would be watching his reactions with almost as much interest as they would watch the events below.

He walked down the sloping balcony to the front row center seat reserved by tradition for the father to be. As he did he passed the robed figures of several apprentice technicians for whom this event was, no doubt, no more than an assigned lesson. Sharing the front row with Jim were Joannah and Noel Baker Smyth. Some of Joannah's beauty was lost to the voluminous robe she now wore, and Jim noted with satisfaction, Noel Baker Smyth looked a little comical in his sack robe.

Jim had hardly seated himself when the amplified voice of one of the medical team in the pit below addressed itself to him.

"Good morning, Captain Sebring." One of the four robed and masked figures waved at him. "I am Jeremy Leventritt, your wife's Public Health Officer."

Jim acknowledged the greeting. He had met Leventritt only once before and probably would not have recognized him even were he not hidden behind the sterile mask.

The voice continued, "You've been through this before so I can be brief."

Jim swallowed in anticipation of the next few words.

"Your son will be delivered momentarily. All is proceeding well. Both the child and his mother appear to be in excellent condition."

Jim restrained a sigh of relief. So far so good.

Leventritt continued, "As soon as the child is born he will be brought here," the P.H.O nodded towards the curved door which separated the delivery room from the amphitheatre. "Using the equipment you see here," he waved toward an array of dangling tubes, catheters and electrodes, "my assistants and I will try to provide the optimum conditions during the critical period in which the neonate's biological systems are stabilizing."

"Neonate!" Jim thought. "Leventritt sounds like a damn classroom lecturer."

"The console," again a nod toward a large panel with a variety of read-out windows across the top and several ranks of multicolored switches along the bottom, "will provide the data we need. That data and the data provided by Deepscan," the P.H.O. pointed at a rectangular device mounted on tracks above the operating table, "will be telemetered simultaneously to the computers at Master Med."

Jim reflected that in spite of the fact that Leventritt must have given this speech a thousand times before he spoke now as if the information were singular and unprecedented.

"The Master Med computer will integrate the genetic data and calculate the precise life span of the child. As you know, the longevity of the child is determined by its genetic inheritance, by its own unique physical constitution, and to a smaller degree by the efforts of this medical team. The computer, of course, changes nothing; it merely measures. But its calculations, except in the very rare instance of Post Natural Death or death by accident, are always accurate. Those calculations will be displayed on the screen above you." The P.H.O. pointed dramatically to the four-sided screen that hung from the center of the amphitheatre.

All eyes turned toward the readout screen which bore in lights across the top the name SEBRING. Above the two readout windows were the words YEARS and DAYS respectively. The DAYS aperture was blank, but as if immortality were a real possibility, the YEARS window displayed the infinity symbol ∞. Below the readout windows the sex sign of the male ♂ was already displayed.

The light above the door of the delivery room turned from green to yellow, and the amphitheatre dimmed so that all that could be seen was the screen and the operating area. Jim felt his palms sweating again.

"Attention," said a different voice, "the Sebring computation is about to begin. There will be no further announcements. The amplified sounds you hear will be those of the child's heartbeat."

The buzz of conversation in the public gallery had stopped. Somewhere a bell sounded and Jim started involuntarily. Below, the delivery room light changed from yellow to red and the door slid open.

From the adjoining room a thin cry rose in the silence. Jim's second son uttered humanity's universal complaint at losing the blind security of the womb, his woe at the severing of the umbilical cord. Jim winced. The child, shorn of his mother, was now eagerly received by the masked representatives of society and hurried to the center of the amphitheatre where a new stainless steel womb awaited, where feverish hands connected the multitude of wires that made up the social umbilical cord.

"Th'Wump, Th'Wump, Th'Wump, Th'Wump." The amphitheatre filled with the rapid sounds of the tiny heart, drowning the thin wail of the newborn infant.

The shuttling Deepscan began probing for flaws. The technicians battled to provide the optimum environment while the mighty Master Med computers hungrily sucked data through the electronic cord.

"Ready readout?" A terse query from Leventritt.

"Twelve seconds," said the high pitched voice of a female technician, "ten (Th'Wump, Th'Wump) eight (Th'Wump, Th'Wump) six ... five ... four ... three ... two ... one."

Leventritt's right arm and forefinger shot out like that of a conductor. The technician at the center console responded in cadence.

A chime sounded throughout the hall. The D. Date screen blinked once.

Jim gulped, grasped the shining railing in front of him and tried to focus his eyes on the screen. In the window marked YEARS appeared a blur of fluorescent numbers impossible to read and moving too fast.

Jim's eyes watered. 141 ... He thought he saw a number, but it was gone. 128 ... 126 ... 122 ... (Th'Wump, Th'Wump, Th'Wump). Yes, it was slowing ... 118 ... I think. 110 ... 104 ... (Th'Wump, Th'Wump). My Goras, they're moving!

"Get that carbon dioxide level down," Leventritt's voice shouted from the pit below.

(Th'Wump, Th'Wump) ... 99 ... 96 ...

"Damn! The adrenalin is running wild," bellowed the voice of a technician. 91 ... 88 ... (Th'Wump, Th'Wump, Th'Wump). "Get on top of it," barked Leventritt.

94 ... 93 ... Jim could see the numbers plainly now.

"Metabolism is stabilizing," said a technician.

The baby's wail rose momentarily above the amplified sound of his own heartbeat and Jim transferred his attention from the fleeting numbers to the child, wriggling now in the maze of catheters and electrodes like a tiny fly caught in the center of a spider's web.[4]

87, 86, 85, 84 ... (Th'Wump, Th'Wump, Th'Wump ,Th'Wump). Four years slipped by in rapid succession.

"Goras!" It was speeding up. Jim wiped his tongue along the inside of his lips.

83, 82 ... (Th'Wump, Th'Wump). It was slowing again. His mouth was parched. He knuckled the sweat out of his eyes.

81, 80 ... (Th'Wump, Th'Wump). Leventritt was motionless watching the readout.

79 ... (Th'Wump) ... 79 ... That's it ... 78 ... (Th'Wump)...

77 ... 76 YEARS.

The DAYS aperture on the right lit up. A fast succession of numbers, and then slower. It came to rest on 157. A bead of sweat dripped from the end of Jim's nose.

"Seventy-six years, and one hundred fifty-seven days," the official voice.

An isolated hand clap from the public gallery, and then they were all standing, clapping. The technicians acknowledged the applause and Leventritt, removing his mask, turned toward Jim. "Charles Adamson Sebring. Natural Death Date, August twenty-fifth, twenty-two sixty-eight." He was smiling.

"Congratulations!" Noel Baker Smyth stood up and held out his hand. *Society had received its child.*

---

[4]The web is a significant symbol and major motif used throughout this book which is always hinting at the problem of the relationship between the individual and society.

2

AND A TIME TO DIE[5]

Jim Sebring glanced at the digital chronometer in the Meteorological Communications Section of the Environmental Service Center. It read: 21:30 hours. The Lucifer Flight would not be loaded before zero four hundred the following morning, which, Jim thought, would give him plenty of time to do what he had to do.

He looked for Natasha along the long low room that housed the Met Comm Section, but she didn't seem to be around. At the far end of the room Colin Jeffries, the bearded and balding night supervisor, was busy with the bank of video-phones that connected the center with other such centers and with all divisions of the Bradley Airstation. Over on the left, one of the three computer modules was occupied by a cargo pilot and a woman meteorologist whom Jim had never seen before. The main thing for the moment was to be sure of the weather, Jim thought, waving off one of the other meteorologists who approached him. With the extra load he intended to carry, that was crucial. And he had learned a long time ago that when it came to critical weather situations Natasha Mollenskaya was the best meteorologist in Hartford. He considered again how he hoped to make her more than just his personal weather forecaster, but that was a different matter.

As if in response to the thought, Natasha materialized suddenly from behind the massive computer complex that dominated the center of the room. Standing beside it, she looked diminutive, a contradiction to its vast size.

---

[5]The allusion again refers to the famous biblical passage from Ecclesiastes, Chapter 3, providing clues about the meaning of the plot or character.

Her short dark hair fell in half curls across her ears and an unruly wave flopped across her forehead. Her shirt sleeves were pulled up to her elbows.

"Jim." She waved, seeing him, and her round face broke into a smile.

"Hi, Tasha."

This woman was confident and sharp when it came to her work. But there was something more about Natasha that was hard to define. Her weather predictions could be counted on with certainty, but even more appealing was that she was completely unpredictable. She was spontaneous and vital—like no one else he'd ever met.

"What are you grinning at?" she said, sidling up next to him.

"I was just thinking you're contagious."

"Hmm, sounds pretty bad," she quipped, taking a step backward. "What would you say is the Life Consumption Factor?"

"Well," he said, shaking his head with mock seriousness, "I'd say it's at least a thousand."

"A thousand!" she exclaimed. "If I'm losing a thousand days to one, we'd better run out and get me a new I.D. card right away."

"I hate to break up this morbid conversation," Jim said, "but talking of cards," he grimaced, "there's one approaching now."

Jim nodded toward Peter Stoneham who was making his way across the Center with his odd, lopsided gait, stopping for a minute to chat with Colin Jeffries, offering some advice to the cargo pilot who was just leaving the computer module area, but bobbing his way inevitably, Jim knew, towards Natasha and him.

The Homeland Security Officer seemed oblivious to the disfiguring leer stamped on his face, which made his smile curve and slope down grotesquely. He seemed unaware of the drooping left shoulder that topped his twisted body. And yet Jim knew he couldn't be unaware of it, and at that moment, in spite of his contempt for Stoneham's official function, he felt a surge of admiration for the man. Stoneham had survived an E-car accident that would have wiped out a less determined man. He had, much to everyone's amazement, wooed and won Joannah, his wife, who was as beautiful as he was ugly. And there was no doubt, as Noel Baker Smyth had intimated, Stoneham was a walking security sermon—especially when he appeared with Joannah. Unfortunately, Jim reflected, he was also a talking security sermon.

"Congratulations, Sebring, on your son's D. Date," Peter Stoneham said. Jim smiled his thanks.

"Of course, Evelyn deserves a successful pregnancy." Peter's head nodded as if agreeing itself. "Evelyn deserves the very best." He went on, seeming to stare at Natasha with his glass eye, while looking at Jim with his good one. "She consumes her own time wisely and I'm sure she'll teach your son . . ."

"Aaaachoo!" Natasha's sneeze interrupted the sermon from Stoneham and the Security Officer glanced at her suspiciously, wondering if the sneeze was real or if it was a deliberate attempt to shut him up. "We were just on our way to check the weather for tomorrow's run."

"Yes, I noticed," Stoneham said. "You're taking care of the briefing, Miss Mollenskaya?"

"Yes," she smiled. "That's what I'm doing."

"Yes . . . of course. Good." His head nodded more vigorously. "Good." His face took on a perplexed look, as if contemplating the wisdom of his own remarks. "Well, then," he added finally, "don't get distracted and remember, security first." He turned abruptly and loped away down the aisle.

"Would you believe my wife thinks of the Stonehams as her best friends?" Jim shook his head at the retreating figure.

"Come on," Natasha grabbed his arm and pulled him towards one of the briefing modules. "I've already gone over the route for you."

"And you," Jim relented, "since when does a mere meteorologist sneeze at a Security Officer?"

"It's an allergy." Natasha rolled her eyes.

"Don't give me that," Jim laughed.

"O.K., I won't. I'll give you the weather instead." Her demeanor changed abruptly.

"The Bermuda high is just right," Natasha said, all meteorologist now. "It's dominating the entire North Atlantic and there's a small low over Iceland."

Jim sighed and sat down at the briefing desk.

"Greenwich is socked in at the moment," Natasha went on.

"The hell it is."

"Temperature thirty-seven, dew point thirty-six. That's ground fog. It'll burn off before you arrive." Natasha reached for the high altitude readouts and Jim caught the faint trace of perfume as she leaned close to him.

"Passenger job picked up some moderate C.A.T. at thirty thousand, south of Greenland an hour ago," she said.

That got his attention. Clear air turbulence. It was a totally invisible menace, difficult to forecast and capable of tearing his light, high-speed jet apart. He frowned. "Don't worry about it; you'll be well clear at fifty thousand," Natasha said.

"You can never be that sure about C.A.T."

"I can be sure about this C.A.T.," she said, reaching for the console and swiveling to face the satellite screens behind her. "Number three screen," she said.

His eyes focused on the screen's message: SECURITY FIRST, SECURITY LAST, SECURITY ALWAYS.[6]

The standard sermon dissolved into a picture of the North Atlantic. Natasha was pointing. "As you can see, it is clear as far south as the Azores."

She had remarkably smooth skin and a little snub nose. Her black hair glistened.

"There's ground fog covering the South of England." She fiddled with the control panel and a circle appeared on the screen around the Greenwich area. "Want to take a closer look?" She turned to face him.

"No, it's the wind I'm worried about. Let me look at the low." Jim was concentrating on the small patch of cloud covering the North of Iceland.

Natasha once again poked at the control console. Twenty-three thousand miles out in space a satellite camera switched coordinates. The screen filled with a close-up of Iceland. "It's typical anti-cyclone and it won't intensify. It's slow moving at about twenty knots northeast-nominal."

---

[6]Social science fiction (a genre distinct from science fiction) normally uses exotic or futuristic settings to offer up its main object of criticism. Social science fiction always seeks to critique the status quo in the here and now. The strangeness of the setting no doubt serves to disarm the reader rhetorically. Arguments readers would resist were they applied to their own situations may be accepted when they refer to an alien society. In this work, the current overwhelming emphasis on "security" in both government policy and in the personal lives of citizens comes in for continuing criticism.

"I'll need to hit the chute. What have you got on wind progs?"

"It's tail winds all the way. You know that!" She looked at him quizzically.

"Yeah, I know. The question is how *much* tail wind?"

"Jim?"

"I've got to off-load a hundred and eighty pounds of fuel," he said, trying to sound casual. He didn't feel casual. In the old days, they'd have used a hundred and eighty pounds taxiing out to the take-off pad. With new conservation technology he was talking about an eighth of his total fuel capacity.

Natasha whistled. "What are you up to, Jim?"

He glanced around the room. Jeffries was still busy at the communications bank. The woman meteorologist was across the room alone now, but staring at one of the unused screens seemingly mesmerized by its blinking message: HE WHO DIES BY ACCIDENT DIES ALONE.

Stoneham seemed to have disappeared. Jim lowered his voice, "I'm taking Charlie with me."

Natasha's eyes widened perceptibly. "Taking your Uncle Charlie on the Lucifer Flight? Goras, Jim, I know how you feel about him, but that's damn risky! They'd ground you for good. Why?"

"Charlie taught me how to fly the old Chariot." Jim was speaking rapidly, too rapidly. "He taught me a lot of things really. He never had a chance to jockey a jet and always wanted to." He swallowed hard.

Natasha glanced sharply at him, "What is it, Jim?"

"I told you," he sounded almost angry, "I owe him. He taught me to fly, and besides," Jim turned away, "and besides..."

"And besides, Charlie is up for his Red Card. That's it, isn't it, Jim?" Natasha had reached for Jim's arm, "Oh, Jim."

"Good Goras!" He was almost shouting, "Don't make so much of it. Charlie knew it was coming. I knew it. Everybody knew it! D. Dates aren't secret."

"Yes," Natasha was speaking very softly, "but it still comes as a shock. I should know." Jim, still fighting his own emotions, didn't hear her.

Natasha tried to relieve his embarrassment, "O.K., Captain Sebring, me lad, we'd better take a closer look at the progs. You really will need those tail winds." She was busy with the console again. "There's the area of the chute right now."

The satellite camera had shifted its attention to the interface between the high and the low—the "chute" where the westerly winds barreled between the two systems almost like water through the narrows in a river.

"Eighty knots at fifty thousand and south of your great circle route . . ."[7]

The technical information sliced into Jim's mood like a knife. He turned to face Natasha.

She was an eager conspirator now, just as he had guessed she would be.

"It's moving though. Let's see where it'll be at zero four hundred E.S.T." The fingers of her right hand moved deftly among the console buttons. The computer took over from the satellite camera, recomposing the picture in terms of its own predictions for the next twelve hours. Natasha pointed to the now moving picture.

"The chute's moving northeast with the low. It will cross your route at zero five hundred."

She nodded toward the constantly changing time reference flashing in the right hand lower corner of the screen.

"Here's where it will be by the time you get there." Natasha stopped the whirling numbers at zero five thirty E.S.T. "Forty nautical miles north and the wind will have dropped to sixty knots at fifty thousand feet."

Jim nodded his approval, "That's plenty if I fly a little north of the route." He paused, "Who's on security in the morning?"

"Our friend, Peter Stoneham."

Jim laughed grimly. "When it comes to security matters, Stoneham has no friends. He'd nail me in a moment. But there's not a damned thing he or anybody else can do to Charlie now." A look of concern then flickered across Jim's face, "Stoneham would guess you were in on it, though. Tasha, I hadn't thought about that."

"Not to worry, old boy," she replied. "There's nothing they can do to me either."

---

[7]Because the earth is spherical, the shortest distance between two points is not a straight line. It is part of a circle which connects the two points, goes around the world, and has as its center the center of the earth—a "great circle."

"What do you mean, Tasha?" Jim's worried face was a plea. A plea not to be told the truth.

Confident the message had sunk into Jim's head, ready to resurface at some other and better time, she replied, "Stoneham might guess, but he couldn't prove anything. He couldn't do anything to me."

"Oh," Jim colluded in the lie, "I suppose that's true. Still, I shouldn't ask you to take the risk. Tasha, I owe you."

She shrugged. "I don't play it safe either, Jim. Besides, I figured a grateful pilot is good for a couple of free dinners, et cetera, et cetera."

"Well, you've already had the dinners. How about the et cetera, et cetera?" he said, putting his arm around her shoulders and looking gravely into her eyes.

She smiled and reaching upward kissed him on the cheek. "Call me when you get back," she said.

"I will," he said, "you can count on that." Jim turned and headed for the door. He needed to get a message to his Uncle Charlie.

———

How should she tell him? She was sure she had already planted the seed of suspicion. It was a matter now of cultivating that bitter seed. Natasha Mollenskaya, hurrying home from the night shift at the Met Comm Center, was turning the alternatives over in her mind.

Perhaps she should simply have made a point of allowing him to see her I.D. card. Its color, orange, would have told him immediately.

No, she had seen too many promising relationships founder, shattered on the rock of D. Date incompatibility. And she and Jim, made for each other in so many ways, were certainly incompatible in that respect. But then, she had never married, precisely because she was in that respect compatible with practically no one. Anyway, the glint in Jim's eye had nothing to do with marriage. He was already married. Presumably he shared D. Date compatibility with his wife. Natasha doubted that Jim and Evelyn were compatible in many other ways.

She shuddered and pulled her coat tight against the nip of the early spring morning. The doleful sound of the Great Clock tolling six a.m. wafted across the city, carried by the lightest of breezes.

The sun hadn't risen yet, although there was a hint of lightening purple in the eastern sky that suggested it would only be a matter of an hour or so before it did.

She passed the dark clumps of shadows that would soon materialize into trees and stared through the black clusters atop them that would shortly become leaves. She thought somberly of the movement of time—her time—and she thought again of Jim.

She could take the bull by the horns, "Jim, old boy, I'm well into Orange already. Let's get on with it." Natasha laughed aloud. That was not her style and it certainly wasn't his.

What she would like to tell Jim, what she knew intuitively he would understand, was that she wanted to use up what time she had left in the most fulfilling way possible. It was how she had always lived from the time she had first known, from the time when she was a very little girl, when her father had first described to her the dramatic sequence of events that had sealed her fate.

It had seemed so good at first, her father had told her. From the minute the D. Date countdown had begun everything had seemed favorable. The years had slipped by from the beginning at a slower rate than average. A steady drop from infinite D. Date. Not sporadic, not threatening at all, her father had said. A nice smooth readout. And then more slowly the years had clicked by, until finally she had been vouchsafed seventy-three years. The flying digits had actually stopped. The Public Health Officer had turned to congratulate her father. And then, unbelievably, the numbers had started to move again. Some new factor—some unexpected datum—had entered the computer. The machine had not liked the taste of what it sampled and its unerring prediction had become more ominous. The years had skidded by. They had plummeted . . . sixty, fifty, forty and still down. The technicians had been paralyzed, taken completely by surprise, until finally, almost before they could comprehend it, the verdict had been rendered: thirty-six years and eighteen days.

So she had known, since she could understand, that her life would be short. And back then as a young child of eight, she had decided to take everything she could. And those things which society, because of her early D. Date, had refused her, she had achieved on her own. Music and art, which she could not choose as a vocation, she had chosen as an avocation. Ineligible for an extended university education, she had gone to auxiliary classes. From the limited number of careers available to her, she had chosen meteorology and performed her job with zest.

Above all, she had resolved that if she had only half as much time as other people then she would live with twice the intensity. In a society which had developed an almost pathological emphasis on physical security, she had resolved to take psychological risks. Jim Sebring was one of those risks. Whether he would bring pleasure or pain she did not know. What she was certain of was that a relationship with him would bring intense feeling, and that was what counted.

She stopped across the street from a brilliantly lit E-car barn and stared, as she often did, at the neat, deserted rows of multicolored electro-cars lined up and awaiting maintenance. The mixture of hues shone and sparkled in the artificial light and she found something compulsively beautiful in that disorganized array of colors.

Glancing up, she contemplated the unlit window of her own apartment on the second floor above the barn. Inside there, too, she had scattered colors about with indiscriminate zest. Jim would like the colors—would like the apartment in fact. And he'd be bound to search out her D. Date calendar. It would tell him in plain figures how much . . . how little . . . time she had left.

Her eye caught a sudden movement in the barn below. Through the long Lucite doors she imagined she had seen something move. She had not imagined it. Something passed quickly—a shadow or a form from between one row and another. She thought she may have been dazzled by the lights, hypnotized by their brilliant reflections. But no! There it was again! Something had flitted quickly across an aisle.

Instinctively the thought flashed into her mind, a P.N.D.[8] The recurring nightmare, full of shadowy soulless creatures, pale and hollow human forms, erupted from her subconscious. She had never seen one, except in a nightmare. Indeed, she had never met anybody who had seen one. Some even argued that they didn't exist. She was sure they were wrong. She pulled her coat tightly around her and glanced quickly at the flight of stairs on the right

---

[8] P.N.D.—abbreviation for Post Natural Death

side of the building that led up to her apartment. The entrance was well lit and silent; there were no shadows, no place where a P.N.D. might hide.

Moving slowly across the street, she kept her eyes upon the rows of E-cars. No, she told herself solidly, it is not a P.N.D. A P.N.D. would never put itself in a place where the light would fall on its loathsome face. Nature's errors hid themselves well, even from each other. Neither did they flit and scamper but kept their bent, crooked forms in dark obscure places, moving only at night and only alone, moving from no place to no place. No, she told herself, that was not a P.N.D.

She straightened her back and walked with her head up almost smiling at her own silliness but keeping one eye on the bright cars as she walked.

Who was she, she told herself, to be so illogical about the P.N.D.'s, who were, if they existed at all, completely physically harmless, unaggressive freaks of nature who sought only to hide themselves from human eyes? Natasha shuddered and walked more quickly as she passed the large Lucite doors. She stared defiantly down each vacant aisle as she passed by.

Suddenly an unshaven face appeared at a large window and peered at her with an open grinning mouth. She stopped, frozen in her place, and stared into a glinting, lustful eye.

Another face appeared beside it, and then another—a mob of faces clustered behind the window to stare at her.

"My Goras, Natasha, you fool! You fool!" she murmured.

She began to run toward the steps, her face set in determined effort.

"Gorasdamn. It's Senile Delinquents."[9]

---

[9] Senile Delinquents are those in Lucifer State who have received their red cards and therefore feel they have nothing left to lose. Obviously, they are the counterpart to juvenile delinquents and gangs, and serve as a vehicle for commenting on and criticizing attitudes toward youth and old age in our contemporary society—another theme in this book.

3

LUCIFER[10]

The main exit of the Bradley Airstation Launch Center slid closed behind Charles Mortimer Hazlitt for the last time. Charlie Hazlitt had worked as a Launch Controller at the center for twenty years. Almost daily for twenty years he had left the underground center through this same exit. For twenty years he had nodded to the security guard as he walked through the gate in the chain link fence that surrounded the Airstation. Now he nodded for the last time. It was one of many "lasts" that he'd experienced since his first "last" a couple of days ago. Two days before, he had gotten his last monthly medical and received his Red I.D. Card.

Now Spitfire, dutifully released exactly seventeen minutes ago by Charlie's housekeeper and roommate, Martha, came bounding along the chain link fence to meet him. The big German shepherd had greeted him thus almost daily for eight years. This was another last. Charlie reached in his pocket for the dog biscuit he habitually carried and fed it to the panting dog. He patted Spitfire and, turning his coat collar up against the late evening chill, set off walking slowly toward the main terminal located on the north side of the Airstation. As he did, he watched Flight 231 rocket down Runway 26. Charlie had set up that rocket-assisted takeoff just before he'd left the center. Now he watched ruefully as Flight 231 arched steeply into the star-strewn spring sky. Another last.

---

[10]Lucifer—Satan, the devil, or more broadly the ultimate source of evil. But also the bearer of light.

By the time he had reached the main terminal, the jaunty swagger of Charlie's walk and the confident swing of his arms had returned. The terminal lights showed Charles Mortimer Hazlitt to be a stocky man, about five feet eight inches tall and weighing perhaps a hundred and eighty pounds. The cheeks on his weather-lined red face bulged in response to the jovial upward turn of his mouth. Set above the round, high, red cheeks his hazel eyes sparkled. The medical people no doubt took Charlie's face to be merely that of a typical hypertensive. Charlie's friends knew his face to be obvious evidence of an irreverent fellow who, his penchant for practical jokes aside, was invariably good company.

Charlie, closely followed by Spitfire, made his way briskly across the rotunda of the main terminal to the row of bright blue console booths that adorned one curved wall. He paused in front of the first booth, grinned broadly at its departing occupant, and stepped inside. As the panel closed behind him, he took the shiny new Red Card from his back pocket and slipped it into the small I.D. slot of the console.

As he waited for the console to come to life, Charlie reflected on the bygone days of text messaging and cell phones. Identity theft had destroyed the freedom of easy cellular phone communication, or so the authorities claimed. Charlie had his doubts. He wondered if the authorities were using "identity security" as an excuse for greater government control and less personal freedom, but he also knew that every time he mentioned these doubts to others, they dismissed him as a conspiracy theorist.

"The government could care less about what you or I are up to, Charlie," argued Martha. "And what's more, even if they did care, they could listen in to us all they want. Our lives are dull as ditchwater and they'd find nothing in our messages but my reminders to you to bring home a gallon of milk."

"That's not the point, Martha," he responded. "It's about the loss of freedom. It's about what we don't know. We should never just trust everything that the authorities tell us and we should never just give up our freedoms."

"Oh, Charlie, you are being ridiculous!" she would respond, and Charlie would just give up. He couldn't find the words to express his concerns convincingly and Martha was right about their lives. They did live quietly and without consequence. And ultimately, if the government wasn't fudging on the reasons for the elimination of cell phones and if they were telling the truth about the dangers of identity theft, then getting rid of the phones was a small price to pay for identity security. It was just a minor inconvenience to stop in at the console to check messages.

The console was ready, so he punched the MAIL button and looked up at the message screen.

The first message was cryptic: GO TO THE DEVIL. 03:30 F GATE. J.A.S.

Charlie squinted, trying to make out the message, and as its meaning gradually became clear to him, his face split into a wide grin. "Ah ha!" He rubbed the palms of his hands together and danced a little jig. "Go to the devil is it?" he muttered gleefully. Quickly he punched the PRINT OUT button—he should be able to remember the message, but lately his memory had taken to playing tricks on him. The machine disgorged the instructions on paper, making Charlie's memory, or lack thereof, irrelevant. Charlie read the message again, emitted an exclamation of delight, and stuffed it into his pocket.

He pressed the CANCEL button and Jim's message disappeared both from the screen and from the console's data bank. Now it was the machine's memory that was wiped out. Charlie smiled at the thought and pressed the MAIL button once again. A second message appeared. This one was from Martha, who sent him each day some small message as a token of her apparently inexhaustible affection: BE CAREFUL. TAURUS IS TROUBLE TODAY. LOVE, MARTHA.

Martha had always been taken with horoscopes and he supposed she always would be. When he was a Gemini, before his blasted D. Date had sneaked up to Taurus,[11] Martha's messages had not been quite so ominous. Oh, well, this was her way of giving him hell for the way he lived, and heavens knows she had the right.

---

[11] In Lucifer State, horoscopes are based on death dates rather than on birth dates. This reversal provides another clue to a theme in the novel, as it causes the reader to consider the persuasive impact of "birth dates" in our society.

He punched the REPLY button and then tapped in a brief response: TAURUS WILL BE AWAY FOR A COUPLE OF DAYS. NOT TO WORRY.

He hesitated, then added: DON'T FORGET TO FEED SPITFIRE. LOVE, CHARLIE.

With that Charlie slid open the console booth door and commanded his waiting dog, "Home, Spitfire, home!" Spitfire hesitated a second and then loped off obediently. Charlie watched his German shepherd successfully break the photo-electric beam that operated the exit doors of the terminal and vanish into the night. Martha wouldn't appreciate having the dog underfoot for two days without Charlie there to care for him, but with Spitfire in the house, there'd be no danger from the Senile Delinquents.

Charlie returned to the console. He pressed the MAIL button once more. A third message appeared on the screen:

REF. PUB. ANN. CH. 17. END MESSAGES.

He scrutinized the third message for a moment puzzled. The computer had found some reference to him on the Public Announcement Channel. He hit the button marked P.A. and then the number 17. The message screen blinked back into life.

APRIL 1
NOTICE OF IMPENDING DEATHS

ANSELM, R. O.	APRIL 22
BROWN, J. H.	APRIL 27
CHAMP, R.	APRIL 20
EVANS, G.A.	APRIL 21
FONDLEMAN, R.W.	APRIL 26
GODFREY, L.W.	APRIL 27
<u>HAZLITT .C.M.</u>	<u>APRIL 26</u>
HOCHBERG, J.M.	APRIL 26

He stared at the screen and then, as if to confirm the brutal public announcement, he withdrew his Red I.D. Card from the console and examined it:

CHARLES MORTIMER HAZLITT
NATURAL D. DATE: APRIL 26, 2192

The card, which he'd gotten two days ago, only told him what he already knew and what he had known more or less from the beginning. Issued a Blue Card at birth and then a Green, a Yellow, and then an Orange, he'd been ready, at least as ready as anyone could be to get his Red Card.[12]

With each change of color he'd become a bigger deal and gotten a few more privileges—not that he gave much of a damn about those things. This was especially the case since the more privileges he got, the less time he had to enjoy them. Well, he wasn't bitching now, not even about the time he'd lost. To hell with "optimum living"! He'd called the tune and he'd pay the piper. Even when Leventritt had handed him the Red Card and told him to get ready for his Terminal Rites, Charlie had managed to make a crack about being able to do what he damned well pleased from now on.

But, now, looking at the cold public announcement and realizing that Martha would see it too, something stirred in Charlie. He felt deep in his chest an almost palpable sensation—not a pain, he'd had plenty of those these past couple of years—but this was different. "An ache," he muttered. "Galloping Goras! Who'd believe Charlie Hazlitt would get a heartache?" He grimaced because he knew that, unlike his various aging pains, this ache would be with him to the end.

Charlie glanced back at the screen. He was moved this time to notice that Fondleman and Hochberg, whoever they were, would share his day.

"Twenty-five days," he muttered. "Twenty-five days." He abruptly hit the CANCEL button. "I don't know about you Fondleman and Hochberg, but

---

[12] The colors are those of the rainbow arranged in order.

I've got a lot to do in twenty-five days." He activated the door of the booth and left.

Jim Sebring quickened his pace as he approached the swing-wing jet. He couldn't see his Uncle Charlie yet, but he knew that he wouldn't be standing out there in the lights, and Jim couldn't see into the shadows.

He wondered if Charlie had run into any trouble. Any Red Card holder these days was likely to be suspected of being a Senile Delinquent. The Delinquents, however, tended to travel in gangs and Charlie's being alone should allay any suspicion on that count. Anyway, Charlie was a charming miscreant, and if he had run into anything, he would have weaseled his way right out of it again.

He began to whistle loudly as he neared the plane. He still couldn't see Charlie, but intuitively he knew he was there. He waited. Then he saw the short, stocky figure walk jauntily out of the shadows, looking as if he owned the supersonic jet.

The two friends stood looking at each other, grinning. Charlie was wearing a pair of overalls Jim had borrowed for him from a mechanic who was even shorter than Charlie.

"You look ridiculous," Jim said.

Charlie snorted. "I'd have thought you could have done better than this." He hitched up his pants to exaggerate their shortness.

Jim laughed and, putting his arm around the shoulder of his Uncle Charlie, turned him around to face the jet. "What do you think of her, Charlie?" The polished black swing-wing star-jet shone in the cold purple light of the ramp. She looked for all the world like a sleeping panther.

"*Winged Chariot* is one helluva plane," Charlie gulped, "but this is something else." Charlie was referring to his own antique aerobatic biplane.[13] The plane in which he had taught Jim to fly.

"Yeah, the old *Chariot* would still out-maneuver this job," said Jim, "but when it comes to speed, that's something else again."

"What'll she do?" Charlie's face was radiant.

"Better than two thousand at altitude. Slow by old time standards, but those old war planes really slurped fuel. This thing is efficiency in motion."

Charlie nodded appreciatively. Jim looked quickly around. "Come on old friend. Let's strap her on. The security boys will be here with Lucifer any minute now, and you'll never pass for a brass ass from Master Med in that outfit."

Jim activated the door mechanism and let the steps swing down into position. Charlie took the steps two at a time, and Jim followed.

"Hey!" Charlie stopped abruptly and surveyed the interior of the plane. "This," he said, sweeping his arm across to indicate a set of curved leather seats in the ample cabin, "this is the style fit for a Red Card holder. But where the Hell are you going to hide me?"

"On the john."

"On the john? Goras! Did you say on the john?"

"Don't worry, Charlie. It's an executive john, accustomed only to executive asses."

"On the john," Charlie muttered. He entered the tiny toilet compartment with an exaggerated display of dignity.

Jim reached over to close the compartment.

"Respect," Charlie said turning to face Jim.

"What?"

---

[13] Charlie apparently borrowed the name of his airplane from the famous poem, "To His Coy Mistress," published by Andrew Marvell in 1681. The poem presents a young man attempting to seduce a young woman by arguing that life is too short for them to postpone sexual pleasure. With its focus on living in the moment, the poem provides a clue to Charlie's personality and summarizes a variety of themes so well that the second half is worth citing in its entirety:

> But at my back I always hear
> Time's winged chariot hurrying near:
> And yonder all before us lie
> Deserts of vast eternity.
> Thy beauty shall no more be found:
> Nor, in they marble vault, shall sound
> My echoing song: then worms shall try
> That long-preserved virginity,
> And your quaint honour turn to dust,
> And into ashes all my lust.
> The grave's a fine and private place,
> But none, I think, do there embrace.
>
> Now, therefore, while the youthful hue
> Sits on thy skin like morning dew,
> And while thy willing soul transpires
> At every pore with instant fires,
> Now let us sport us while we may;
> And now, like amorous birds of prey,
> Rather at once our Time devour,
> Than languish in his slow-chapt power.
> Let us roll all our strength and all
> Our sweetness up into one ball
> And tear our pleasures with rough strife
> Through the iron gates of life.
> Thus, though we cannot make our sun
> Stand still, yet we will make him run.

"Respect," Charlie repeated, "that's what it says on the back of my Red Card. It's one of my privileges." He pushed his face into a frown and shook his head slowly. "It definitely says I should be treated with RESPECT, and it's signed by P. Goras himself."

"Yes, well, the best I can do right now is a padded can," said Jim, giving his stocky friend a little shove. He closed the compartment and retreated toward the cockpit, grinning. From the toilet came the sound of Charlie's muffled laughter.

Jim was busy with his cockpit preflight when the orange Security Van slid to a silent stop by the star-jet a few minutes later. He watched as one of the two guards jumped from the front seat and walked to the rear. The rear of the S-van slid open and a third guard offered his waiting colleague a hand into the S-van. Jim had watched the ritual scores of times. It never varied and he was counting on that this time. The two uniformed guards emerged from the back of the van each gripping with one hand the handle of a pair of giant tongs. Suspended between the jaws of the tongs was Lucifer.

Lucifer was perhaps eighteen inches long, a foot wide, nine inches deep and jet black. It was clear from the exertion of the guards that the box, though not extremely heavy, was not light either—perhaps a hundred pounds. The guards, leaning slightly away from each other to maintain the pressure on the jaws of the giant tongs, walked the five steps to the star-jet. Jim felt the jet lurch to one side as the two guards and Lucifer added their weight to the steps. Then the nose of the plane tilted slightly as the men carried their load forward to the cockpit. Jim swiveled in his left seat, as he always did, to greet the guards.

"Good morning."

One of the guards grunted an acknowledgment as he maneuvered Lucifer through the narrow door separating the cockpit from the cabin.

From close up Lucifer looked to be a rectangular slab of solid lead. There were no handles and to the casual observer no means of access to the black slab. Actually, very close examination would reveal the faintest suggestion of a line running around the slab about a third of the way down from the top. That line was the only evidence of the point where the parts of Lucifer were mated by finely milled surfaces. In spite of its solid appearance, the black slab contained a small carrying space at the heart of it. The nature of its contents were testified to by the ominous orange warning printed across the top: CAUTION! RADIOACTIVE MATERIAL.

Jim knew that the RADIOACTIVE MATERIAL was in fact Cobalt fifty-seven, a substance apparently vital in a variety of ways to modern nuclear medicine. Because it was radioactive, the production and transportation of Cobalt fifty-seven was strictly controlled by the International Commission on Fissionable Materials. Cobalt fifty-seven was produced only at the Cavendish Laboratories in Cambridge, England, and its world-wide distribution was recorded meticulously by the International Bureau of Standards at Greenwich.[14] The job of transporting the vital, though dangerous, material was assigned to special aircraft—the so-called "Lucifer Flights." In this country all such flights originated and terminated at Hartford.

The guards, breathing heavily now, lowered Lucifer into the specially built orifice that was located in the floor between and below the two cockpit seats. Once in position, only three or four inches of Lucifer protruded above the cabin floor. One of the guards leaned forward to fasten the hasp that held Lucifer securely in place. The other guard, producing a sealing caliper from his voluminous pockets, pressed it against the hasp overlap and triggered it. The Seal of State, to the smell of molten metal, flowed into place ready to testify against anyone foolish enough to meddle with Lucifer.

The ritual was almost over. Jim contributed his part, "What do the people at Master Med think I'm going to do, give Lucifer to the Gorasdamn Martians?"

One of the departing guards threw back over his shoulder, "If they could carry it, they'd be welcome." He laughed and was gone.

Jim glanced again at the metal slab. It always looked less ominous somehow on its outbound journey, though, of course, Lucifer's appearance never changed. The radioactive potency of the Cobalt fifty-seven decreased by half every two hundred and seventy days until eventually it became useless for medical purposes. The disastrous world-wide practice in bygone times had

---

[14]A major argument in this book is that, particularly in an affluent society, *time*, not *money*, should be the standard of universal value. Greenwich is significant here because it is the site of the zero degree meridian and it serves to establish time standards (Greenwich Mean Time; Universal Time: astronomy; Zulu time: navigation) all over the world.

been to dump the weakened, though by no means spent, Cobalt and replace it with a fresh supply. Levels of radioactive contamination had risen to critical points and the supply of fissionable material—a potential source of nuclear weapons—had gotten out of hand. Now, each nation returned its supply of weakened Cobalt to Greenwich for regeneration at Cambridge. World supplies of the material were therefore almost stable and every gram of the stuff, whatever its potency, was accounted for. Its transportation was rigorously controlled.

Jim continued the ritual. "Ground Control, this is Triple Six Lima ready for the Lucifer check."[15] There was a pause. He glanced at his chronometer: 03:55. The boys on Ground Control would be half asleep at this time in the morning.

"Triple Six Lima, this is Ground Control. Proceed with the check."

Jim glanced at a dial high up on the right side of the cockpit. It showed a steady green light and a flickering needle. "I'm indicating only normal background radiation." He leaned forward and flicked the lowest switch on the left side of the panel, "And here's the emergency signal."

"Roger on the normal radiation, Triple Six Lima, and we're receiving the emergency transmission five by five, loud and clear."

Jim flipped the red Lucifer switch off again. It was another ritual, the details of which, he recalled, he'd first gotten from Evelyn. It was when he had received his promotion from Captain to Senior Captain and had simultaneously been transferred from the big subsonic job to this much smaller supersonic swing-wing star-jet. He'd been called to the Master Medical facility, where he met Evelyn for the first time. She'd been efficient, slightly pompous even back then, but it seemed to him that he'd guessed it for a cover-up—female coyness. A bad guess. But, in any case if he'd gotten any bad impressions, they'd soon given way to the excitement he'd felt when he'd discovered their D. Date compatibility.

Jim selected a card from the rack above his left ear and slid it into the autocontrol computer on the right side of the cockpit.

---

[15]Triple Six Lima—possibly an allusion to 666, the mark of the beast (the devil). See Revelation 13:18.

"On occasion you may be called upon to transport Master Med executives. You'll usually be informed of this ahead of time," Evelyn had told him.

Obviously executives impressed the hell out of her.

"But your principal mission will be to transport Lucifer safely and promptly."

In fact, he'd been called upon only three times to ferry executives. Once he'd flown P. Goras himself. Nobody had told him who this passenger was, but there was no mistaking that huge moon-shaped face. In any case, he much preferred cargo to "geese." Inanimate objects trumped living things in his book. Charlie, of course, was an exception. At the thought, he swiveled to call through the cockpit door.

"Hey, Charlie, get your ass up here."

By the time Charlie's cheery face popped into the cockpit, Jim had the twin jets winding up and was talking to Ground Control. "Triple Six Lima, I.F.R. Greenwich, England, taxi instructions." He motioned to Charlie to secure himself in the right seat.

"Roger, Triple Six Lima, cleared to Runway Two-six for R.A.T.O. departure. Wind two eight zero at niner, and the 'window' is clean."

Jim eased the jet out of the floodlit ramp area and turned to Charlie, "I guess this makes you copilot of a star-jet."

Charlie was busy running his fingers over the host of dials, switches, and knobs that made up the controls of the supersonic jet. "Don't distract the copilot while he's checking out gauges."

He was half serious. The seat Charlie sat in had at its command all the controls necessary to fly the jet. The right side also contained the autocontrol equipment which made a copilot quite superfluous. This plane could be flown, if the need arose—take-off to landing—from the ground. In an emergency, even the pilot could be dispensed with. With his "manual override," Jim retained control, but he wondered how long before the pilot became backup for the auto-control rather than vice versa.[16] He smiled ruefully to

---

[16] Jim's speculation here introduces another major theme. It is what might be called the problem of *technological idolatry*—the tendency of humans to surrender their decision-making capacity to the tools of their own creation. An obvious and simple example of this is the "spell-check" function on computers. Humans have developed the computer and the spell-checker, and now have come to depend upon it, forgetting how to write and spell without technological aid.

himself as he recalled the old chestnut, "In case of emergency break glass and take out pilot."

"What'll we cruise at?" Charlie interrupted Jim's thoughts.

"Around fifteen hundred knots at fifty thousand feet. We'll be at Greenwich in less than two and a half hours."

Charlie whistled.

"And then my friend, you and I and a fun French woman Lucifer Pilot, Michele LaTour, are going to turn old London town upside down."

Charlie chuckled.

"Triple Six Lima. If you're ready for R.A.T.O. hook-up, switch to launch control on one eighteen-point-seven."

Ground Control was anxious to get rid of them and go back to sleep. "Roger." Jim twirled the number two radio to one-eighteen-point-seven as he wheeled the jet off the taxiway on to the threshold of Runway Two-six. "Bradley Launch Control, Triple Six Lima is in position for R.A.T.O. hook-up."

"Roger, Triple Six Lima. Stand by one." The voice of Launch Control.

"Well, Charlie, how does it feel to be on the receiving end of R.A.T.O.?" In twenty years as a launch controller, Charlie had provided Rocket Assisted Take-Off for literally thousands of planes.

"The boys better do a good job with this one." Charlie smiled.

The "job" was, in fact, vital. In the old days, jets had handled their own take-off requirements. This meant carrying and using enormous loads of fuel just to clear the airport and gain altitude. Now, a rocket engine running beneath the runway and connected electromagnetically through a pedestal to the plane provided the power for take-off and climb to ten thousand feet. Fuel and weight conservation was enormous and take-off noise was minimal. As a bonus, take-off accidents, almost always the result of power failure, were virtually unheard of now.

Jim felt the star-jet "squat" on the pedestal and then lift clear of the runway. A second later, Launch Control confirmed, "We are showing 'hook-up'."

Jim hit the gear retract and glanced at the row of green lights on the launch panel. "Roger on the hook-up and Triple Six Lima is go for R.A.T.O." He shot a sidewise glance to confirm that Charlie was secure in his contoured seat. Charlie was licking his lips, obviously a little nervous about being on the firing end of a "launch" for the first time. "Don't worry, Charlie; it's all automatic from here to ten thousand."

"Triple Six Lima, the 'window' is clean and we're counting." Good! No clouds in the star-jet's trajectory. Charlie would get a good view. Jim was not required to acknowledge. "Three . . . two . . . one . . . Launch!"

Jim felt his contoured seat close around him as the runway lights turned into a blur. From below came the muffled thunder of the subterranean rocket engine, then the magnetic disengage with the control column moving steadily back as if pulled by some unseen hand, and at last the star-jet was streaking upwards. As the rate of acceleration decreased, the contour seats relaxed their grip and Jim turned to look at Charlie. Charlie was a little pale; he had felt the tremendous acceleration despite the fact that most of the forces were absorbed by the seats.

"You okay, Charlie?" Jim was reaching for the wing retract lever.

"The copilot's fine." Charlie's face was beginning to glow again.

"All right then, I'll tell the boys in Launch that we're passing through eight thousand while you see if you can get us under our own power." Jim activated the audio while Charlie gingerly advanced the jet thrust levers until at ten thousand feet the plane, pushed by its own twin jet engines, was climbing steeply. "Want to take the stick?" Jim waved at the control column in front of Charlie.

"You bet I do." Charlie grasped the column and the jet lurched slightly. Jim suppressed the urge to give his old teacher some instruction. Charlie would figure it out for himself. Jim dialed in 135.85 on number two radio. "Hartford Departure, Star-jet Triple Six Lima is with you out of ten thousand heading two six zero, squawking one one two two."

"Roger, Triple Six Lima, radar contact. Come left to zero eight zero. Climb on course; report twenty thousand."

Jim acknowledged the instructions while Charlie banked the plane left, reaching for zero eight zero. Below them, the flashing apex of the Master Med pyramid set amid the multicolored lights of Hartford that receded steadily.

"Jim, I know you're risking your neck for me." Charlie's face was intense now. "I've only got twenty-five days. I'll never be able to repay you for all this." He paused and waved his hand at the glowing panel and beyond to the twinkling lights that lay embedded in the rich velvet of the night sky. "I don't know what comes next," Charlie's husky voice betrayed his profound emotion, "but I'll tell you this, Jim lad, *if there's a life after death and you ever need me, the Devil himself won't keep me...*"

"I believe you, Charlie," Jim interrupted, "but you owe me nothing. I seem to remember that it was *you* who taught *me* to fly, and a man never had a better teacher."[17]

Jim was lost for words. He and Charlie were not used to talking about the mutual bonds of affection and respect that connected them. Jim blinked away the moisture from his eyes and fell silent.

Triple Six Lima climbed steeply. Jim looked past the radiant face of his old friend and out into the night where the red giant Betelgeuse kept position in Orion.

---

[17]Flying is used throughout to symbolize being free, and especially free of the limitation (the web) of social control.

4

SECURITY FIRST, LAST, AND ALWAYS

The nursery was bathed in pulsating orange light as Evelyn Sebring walked in, bent on bringing the aversive conditioning period to an end. Evelyn knew that her baby could only profit from the lesson. The association of the strident sound of the klaxon with the internationally recognized sign for danger—the color orange—would serve young Charles Adamson Sebring for the rest of his life.

Nevertheless Evelyn was distressed at the baby's wailing response to the lesson. She was relieved when her jabbed instructions to the conditioning control panel replaced the sound of the blaring klaxon with the reassuring Th'Wump, Th'Wump of the human heartbeat. The aural stimulus quieted the baby almost instantly. Evelyn, searching for a corresponding positive visual stimulus,[18] poked the control panel once again and the ceiling above the child lit up with the universally recognized and beloved symbol for Unity in Death.

The symbol—the abstracted figures of a male and female, hands interlocked, heads inclined each towards the other, joined in eternal sleep—flicked on and off in cadence with the soft sound of the heartbeat. Evelyn smiled, partly because of her own warm response to the symbol, partly because she knew that the visual lesson would soon be lost to the baby. Young Charlie's

---

[18]Obviously, this society has incorporated some of the principles of behaviorist psychology into its childrearing practices. B. F. Skinner's *Walden Two* offers a fictional example of a behaviorist "Utopia" and provides an interesting comparison with the more rhetorical approach to social control exemplified in *Lucifer State*.

eyelids were already drooping. He would soon be enjoying a brief and shallow version of the eternal sleep.

She sighed and turned her attention again to the baby. She resisted the temptation to lean over and stroke his fine wisps of blond hair, wanting to do nothing to distract from the conditioning the baby was experiencing. She had learned well the parenting standards of Lucifer State in her prenatal courses and was convinced that the experts were right to say that children first and foremost needed to be trained in the rules of security and community. She'd read about the old days when children were the centers of the family universe and she could see precisely why earlier parenting practices had come to be debunked. In the old days, children were little narcissists who believed the world revolved only around them.[19] Contemporary childrearing practices, based in science, provided wisdom and guidance to raise strong, independent, and responsible children.

Lost in thought, she sat down and contemplated the slowly flashing Unity in Death symbol that flashed above the baby's head. She closed her own eyes momentarily and found her thoughts drifting back once more to Jim and to the phone call she'd received earlier from Noel Baker Smyth. The smile faded from her face. Jim's actions were unreasonable as far as she could see. Jim did what he did; he was what he was; there were never any explanations.

Evelyn remembered that after her first meeting with Jim she had felt an intuitive sense of certainty about their D. Date compatibility. As executive assistant to Noel Baker Smyth it had been an easy matter for her to check Jim's medical record and confirm that their natural D. Dates were no more than six months apart. In the subsequent Lucifer briefings she had come to like the gangling, somewhat diffident pilot more and more. Inevitably her thoughts had turned to marriage and she had set about letting Jim "discover" their compatibility. First she had contrived to flash her I.D. card in such a way that she was sure he could not have failed to see its color—Blue at the

---

[19] We see here recognition of the fact that attitudes toward children and childhood vary across cultures and over time. Our conceptions of "childhood" suggest that children deserve great amounts of family attention, and this seems <u>normal</u> and appropriate to us. Readers of *Lucifer State* may find their ways of treating children as odd, but it must be remembered that the reverse is also true. Citizens of Lucifer State would find odd our parenting practices, seeing those practices as producing dependent, selfish, fearful and narcissistic individuals who focus only on empty consumerism and who lack a sense of community or global responsibility.

time. At a subsequent briefing, she had pretended to be studying the population extrapolations for the year in which both of their natural D. Dates fell. Jim, waiting for her attention, had allowed his gaze to follow hers to the readout display and she had casually commented that this was "her year."

Jim had tried to conceal his surprise at the "discovery," but she knew by the look on his face that he knew. Knowing that the idea of marriage had occurred to him, too, it was only a matter of waiting for him to reveal his "discovery" to her. It was almost too simple.

The short, uneven waves of her light brown hair fell forward across her wide forehead as she leaned down to look one more time at the baby. She still felt awed by the miracle of his life, by the fact that she and Jim, despite their disparities, had produced a son with such a future. But then she had always been awed that out of the infinity of possibilities she and Jim, inhabiting earth at the same time and the same place, were also destined to pass into eternity together. It seemed to Evelyn to be evidence that the universe intended their union.

But Jim's behavior had contradicted everything. Her mind drifted back to the beginning. The marriage ritual had been almost gratuitous. She was vaguely aware that she had been born before Jim—that was of course unimportant.[20] What sanctified their marriage was the knowledge that they could hope to live their lives together and then pass into eternity as one. It would take some effort, but at the beginning things had looked almost perfect. Evelyn's natural D. Date, little more than four months before Jim's, looked superficially to be a little problematical. She could expect to lose at least two months if she had a single child, a second child would cost a further four or five months. Thus, unless a couple decided to remain childless, a seven month discrepancy in favor of the woman was regarded as ideal at the time of mar-

---

[20]The social construction of "marriage" in *Lucifer State* revolves around compatible D. Dates, and the understandings of what makes for appropriate pairings is reinforced in all aspects of the society. This mirrors what takes place in our society, where compatible birthdates become a fundamental issue in mate selection. While inhabitants of *Lucifer State* seek D. Date compatibility, our society seeks B. Date compatibility!

riage. But the same medical records that had revealed Jim's D. Date compatibility had also shown that his was a somewhat less than optimum life style.

The records showed that even before puberty Jim had been losing time. Each monthly medical check invariably revealed a loss of at least a day and sometimes more. The pattern, though unusual, was not unheard of, particularly in bachelors. Evelyn had estimated that Jim's profligacy would continue at least until they were married and perhaps for some time afterwards. Still, she had reasoned that Jim would get himself together sooner or later and in the meantime, assuming she bore two children, he could afford over his lifetime to lose at least eleven months.

At first then, she had indulged him in his poor habits—mostly irregular and insufficient sleep and the use of a variety of mood-altering drugs. By indulging Jim's excesses she had known that she would hurry the day when the two D. Date calendars[21] that adorned the wall of the adjoining room— their bedroom—would testify to their absolute unity. Evelyn had dreamed of that day. She had made a point of going to the Terminal Rites of those couples who had achieved perfect D. Date compatibility at the very end. She thought she understood the rapture that such couples showed as they entered eternity united.

Finally, four years after they were married, Jim's monthly medical revealed that his natural D. Date exactly coincided with Evelyn's. She was ecstatic. She had, she remembered, moved the two D. Date calendars from the bedroom and hung them in the living room so that their friends could see the incontrovertible evidence of their married bliss. On the first night they had made passionate love and had melted one into the other, wedded for time and eternity. And so it had continued for a month. Each day, Evelyn removed one leaf from each calendar, almost wishing for the day that the number "1" would appear to announce that they too had achieved Unity in Death.

This state of perfect harmony had survived Evelyn's next monthly medical check. She had always lived at very close to optimum and so she was not surprised that the check had revealed her natural D. Date to be unchanged.

---

[21]The D. Date Calendars indicate not time gone but time remaining and are another instance of the emphasis on *time* and its measurement.

With Jim it was different. He lost one day that month, two days the following month, and two and a half days on the third month. Evelyn had moved the D. Date calendars back into the bedroom. She had watched as month by month the calendars testified to an increasing incompatibility of D. Dates and ultimately of life style and of spirit. Her distress was partly mitigated by the knowledge that a child would remove the discrepancy and by the possibility that Jim was, consciously or subconsciously, encouraging her to bear an heir. Two years later she had in fact presented him with their first son. Her medical check revealed that the birth trauma had cost her a little less than three months. Three months after that, D. Date compatibility was restored. Again for a month it was the most unutterable bliss for Evelyn—a month of passion, a month in which she had reveled in her sense of identity with Jim and in the feeling of security and safety that the oneness brought. From then on Jim's time loss had been nothing short of disastrous.

Evelyn let her eyes focus on the tranquil face of their second child, lulled to sleep now by the Th'Wump, Th'Wump of the heartbeat and the synchronized flash of the Unity symbol. She sighed. Here was the symbol of a unity which seemed now to be out of reach. She had not yet had her post-natal medical check but she doubted that the birth of Charles would remove the eight month and twenty-four day discrepancy that separated Jim from her. The thought angered Evelyn. She knew that most marriages underwent periods of incompatibility; she knew that the struggle for D. Date compatibility was what gave drama to most partnerships, but she knew too that Unity in Death gave marriage its ultimate goal. Jim seemed bent on denying her that goal.

From the front of the house came the sound of the main entrance noisily sliding shut. Evelyn gave her child a last affectionate glance, pushed her slightly squared jaw forward, and rose to greet Jim.

Jim had pulled off his uniform jacket and dropped it on CLEM.[22] The jacket had slid onto the floor where it lay in a heap now as Evelyn entered.

---

[22]CLEM is an acronym—a word made by combining the initial letters of a series of words (in this instance, Computer and Library and Entertainment Module). In *Lucifer State*, home theater technology had been joined with computer technology to create a complete system for the digital transfer of any information.

She glanced at it and then at Jim who was sprawled on the couch with his eyes closed. She hesitated for a moment and then deliberately stepped over the jacket and crossed the room. "I see you're home."

He opened his eyes and smiled at her. "Hi."

She stood looking down at him, her arms folded. "How was the flight?"

He shrugged. "Fine."

"That's good." She sat down across from him and remained silent for a while.

He closed his eyes again.

"Jim?"

"Yeah."

"You look tired."

"I am. I'm beat."

"Did you have any problems?" she asked.

He looked at her again a little quizzically. "Problems, what problems?"

She shrugged. "I just wondered if everything was all right."

"Why wouldn't it be?"

"Oh, I don't know. You look so tired. Maybe the Lucifer Flight's getting to be a strain."

He said nothing.

"It's an important mission, you know," she went on. "I mean it's an important job." Her voice quivered a little in spite of her attempt to keep it calm.

He sighed and closed his eyes again. "You're trying to say something, Evelyn."

"No . . ." she said. "Yes . . . Lucifer Pilots are supposed to be very particular people . . . responsible . . . with a sense of integrity . . ."

"Evelyn," he said without opening his eyes, "you got something to say. Say it!"

"You're so damn smart that you're stupid," she said, suddenly very angry.

He opened his eyes, straightened himself out on the couch, and leaned forward. "All right, Evelyn," he said. "What is it? Spit it out. Out with it."

"Noel Baker Smyth called."

"That's nice."

"You think they don't know?" she said hotly. "You really think they don't know? You think you're smarter than the Homeland Security people, than all of Master Med?" She stopped and glared at him. "You think they don't know you took Uncle Charlie last week?"

"Uncle Charlie?" he said with mock innocence. "Where'd I take Uncle Charlie?"

"Oh, get off it, Jim. You know what I'm talking about. Noel trusted you. It was partly because of my recommendation he put you on the Run. It was because . . ."

"Oh, yes," he interrupted, "I've no doubt you're on very intimate terms."

"Oh, stop it!" she yelled. "You're being ridiculous."

He pursed his lips. "All right," he said slowly, "all right, Evelyn. So they found out about Charlie." He ran one hand through his hair. "How'd they know? How'd they find out?"

"I don't know. I don't even care. That isn't what matters, Jim."

"Oh, I see. You don't care that they found out. You only care that it made a bad impression with Mr. Goras Almighty Smyth. It loused up your image."

"Noel called."

"Oh, I know. Noel called to give you a report on my misbehavior. Why didn't he call me?"

"He did!" she shouted. "He did call you. He thought you'd be back. He doesn't know, you see, that you don't always come straight home to your wife after a FLIGHT . . . NO MATTER HOW BEAT YOU ARE!"

There was a long silence during which Jim relaxed again, letting his back slide into the curved lines of the couch and stretching his legs out in front of him. "I won't dignify that," he said quietly.

She stared at him, feeling that he was deliberately trying to irritate her. "The point is, Jim, that he knows."

"So he knows. What do you want me to do about it?"

"Care."

"I do care. That's why I took Charlie."

"Care about us," she said, "about me and the baby and about your job."

"I don't have to worry about my job. You do enough caring for both of us."

"Jim," she said earnestly, "I'm trying to be reasonable. I want you to care about all the time you're losing living like this. I want you to care about our D. Dates. I don't want it to turn out like it has for Uncle Charlie and Martha."

"Don't nag me, Evelyn. I'm tired."

"Even with what I've given up with the baby," she said ignoring him, "we'll still be incompatible. You're throwing your time away taking risks . . . and lying."

He sighed loudly.

"You're asking me to make an impossible decision," she went on. "You're asking me to throw away my time, too, or to sit by and watch our D. Dates drift completely apart."

"Or get a divorce," he inserted sarcastically.

"No," she shook her head, her eyes becoming moist. "If that's what I wanted, I would never have had the baby."

Jim stirred. "I know Evelyn," he said. "You're right. I'm a bastard."

"That's not the point, Jim," she said, "But surely, I'd hoped you would try for our sake. We were almost nine months apart before the baby."

"Evelyn, it just isn't that bad. I'm watching my time. I won't let it get out of . . ."

"Watching your time! Do you know what your last Life Consumption Factor was?"

"My L.C.F.? No, I don't remember, but I bet I'm about to find out."

"One point one! That's what it was. That's losing almost three days a month. With an L.C.F. like that and being still incompatible after I've had two children—that's grounds for divorce."

"So divorce me. "

"I don't want to."

He stared at her in a long silence.[23]

"So if you don't want to live without me," he said finally, "why can't you learn to live with me . . . or at least, learn to let me live?"

---

[23]For all the changes in Lucifer State, one constant remains. Marital squabbles, rooted in poor interpersonal communication, sound much the same as they do in our society.

She felt defeated. Nothing could penetrate. "I just wanted you to know," she said lamely.

"Goras, I know!" he yelled. "Don't you think I know?"

"Well then, if you know so much, what are you doing pulling a stunt like that? Why in Goras' name would you take Uncle Charlie on a Lucifer Flight? You know that kind of tension isn't free."

"Because I care about him. You wouldn't understand about that."

"Yes, that's obvious!" she yelled. "He's more important than me. Everyone seems to be more important than me."

"And what does that mean?"

"I know you're careless, Jim, about security and about tensions, but it doesn't account for it all." She bit her lip. "There must be more deceptions than I know about to account for all the time you're losing."

"Evelyn, you're talking in riddles again."

"All right," she said. "All right, I'll tell you what I think. I think you're trying to hide your own guilty conscience."

"Galloping Goras, do you always have to be so obtuse? What are you getting at?"

"I'm getting at this," she said, her voice breaking now, "I think you've found yourself an outside interest, and I think you feel guilty about it and I think that's causing some of your D. Date attrition."

"Oh, I see," he snorted. "And do you have anyone in particular in mind?"

"What about the meteorologist woman?" she snapped. "What about her? Is that where you were when Noel couldn't reach you?"

"Yes," he said sharply. "That's where I was, with Natasha Mollenskaya."

Evelyn felt herself choke up and turned away from him abruptly. "For once in your life you're honest," she whispered.

"Most things in your mind, Evelyn, are pure fantasy."

"But apparently not this Natasha Mollenskaya." She swung on him. "Apparently my pure fancy was right about her."

"Wrong!" he flung back viciously. "You're dead wrong, Evelyn."

She stared at him. "You just admitted. . . ."

"Natasha was attacked by Senile Delinquents last night. Did you know that? No?" His eyes widened in mock surprise. "Well apparently, Evelyn, you don't know *everything* after all."

"Attacked?"

"Yes, attacked, outside her apartment—a pack of them was hiding in an E-barn."

"Oh, dear." Evelyn's hands covered her mouth. "Was it . . . was she . . .?"

"She fought like a wild cat," Jim said soberly. "Apparently all the blood on her was not her own."

"Oh, dear," Evelyn repeated, shuddering. "How bad?"

"She'll be all right," Jim said. "She lost some time, of course."

"The poor woman."

"Scratches and bruises and a broken big toe, when she hauled off and kicked one." He grinned. "I bet those Gorasdamned bastards got a shock of their lives when they found out what they'd tangled with."

"She got away then?" Evelyn said.

He nodded. "She managed to lock herself in her apartment and called Security. Peter Stoneham told me about it when I came in from my flight."

"A VISITOR—JOANNAH STONEHAM." CLEM's metallic voice announced suddenly.

Evelyn caught her breath. "Jim . . . "

"Forget it, Evelyn," Jim said. "It's just a matter of a simple misunderstanding."

"I'm sorry, that's all," Evelyn muttered.

"It's not your fault, Evelyn. In fact if anyone's to blame . . . "

"A VISITOR—JOANNAH STONEHAM," CLEM repeated.

Evelyn turned slowly and crossed the room. She ran her hands across her wet cheeks. "I wish I knew what I was supposed to think, Jim," she said.

"For Goras sake, Evelyn, it's not what you're supposed to think. It's what you really do think."[24]

Evelyn depressed the activating button on the console to allow Joannah to enter.

---

[24] A crucial issue: how able are we to truly think for ourselves? How much does societal pressure persuade us to think in appropriate societal terms? How often are thoughts we have really rooted in what we are "supposed" to think?

Joannah's lovely face was bright, her eyes smiling. If she'd noticed that she'd interrupted a heated domestic squabble or if she had sensed the tension in the flashing glances exchanged between Jim and Evelyn, it was not apparent.

Joannah, radiant, bubbling, threw her arms around Evelyn. "I'm really excited, Eve," she said. "I can't wait to see Peter. I just barely made it. The debate will be coming on any minute now." She swiveled toward Jim. "Adam, aren't you excited?"

Jim, repressing his irritation at the use of his middle name—a habit with Joannah—nodded his reluctant agreement. The nod was all that Joannah needed. She enveloped him in her embrace.

As he saw the perfection of her smooth, pale skin and the cascade of chestnut blonde hair on her shoulders, as he felt her lips gently brush his cheek and her body press against his, he wondered for the umpteenth time how Peter Stoneham had come to marry so lovely a creature, and why she stayed with him.

"It's time," she was saying, swinging herself away from him and gliding over to CLEM. "What's the channel, Evelyn? Oh, I remember—P.S. Three. Peter worked so hard to be prepared."

"Please be reminded," the handsome face of Ella Soames, the Public Moderator, filled the screen, "that your vote may be cast at any time until eight p.m. The resolution reflects the public concern generated by the increasing incidence of senile delinquency in the public parks of our city and by the unprovoked sexual attack on a young male citizen last week."

Joannah had seated herself between Evelyn and Jim on the couch. She had crossed her legs and was bouncing her right foot impatiently.

"Specifically it provides that the municipal parks shall henceforth be closed between the hours of sunset and sunrise. Vote totals will be, as always, continuously registered on the upper right hand corner of your screen. As you can see, a number of citizens have already voted and at this moment, the proposition is carrying by forty-two thousand four hundred and sixty-three in favor, thirty-three thousand one hundred and thirty-seven against."[25]

---

[25] In keeping with its emphasis on rhetorical means of social control, this society has, with the help of technology, perfected democracy to the point where every citizen votes on every issue.

"Oh!" Joannah bounced up and down and clapped her hands like a small child. "We're winning already," she squealed.

"Probably because Peter hasn't opened his mouth yet," Jim muttered.

Evelyn threw a threatening glance at him, but Joannah seemed oblivious.

"We have heard from only thirty-five percent of the total eligible voters so far. The proposition calls for a simple yes or no vote. Each voter should therefore place his or her I.D. card in the receptacle and depress either the plus for yes or the minus for no on the remote control. You are reminded that once registered, your vote cannot be changed."

Even seated, it was obvious that Ella Soames was a tall woman. She held her head high and her shoulders straight as she spoke. Her high cheekbones gave her face a sculptured appearance, which was further complemented by her dense, black wavy hair. Her smooth dark face was intense as she carefully articulated the words.

"Debates on the proposition will continue throughout the day and the preceding lecture, 'The Psychological Bases of Senile Delinquency' by Professor Chaim Heinsohn, can be retrieved and reviewed merely by pressing the P2 button on the D.R. portion of your remote."

"When is she going to introduce Peter?" Joannah complained.

"... in the next segment, the third of today's debates, in which Peter Stoneham ..."

A tiny squeal from Joannah.

"... will take the affirmative side of the proposition, and, a visitor to our country, Francois Ahmed Levec, will argue the negative ..."

Levec was a mountain of a man, dwarfing both his opponent and the moderator. He was wide but not fat, with broad square shoulders and a big-boned, firmly padded athletic frame. His round black face was surrounded by heavy wads of steel gray, tightly curled hair. As he offered a half smile to the audience, the nostrils of his nose flared.

"He's a brute ... a positive brute," Joannah giggled.

"... with a very brief statement of the general grounds for his position on the proposition." Ella Soames nodded towards the man on her right. "Ladies and Gentlemen, for the affirmative, Mr. Peter Stoneham, who is Security Officer for the . . . ."

"Oh, there's my Peter," Joannah breathed, nudging Evelyn with her elbow.

Evelyn nodded.

"People don't laugh at him now," Joannah went on. "People listen to him now. They respect him."

"Oh, no one ever laughed at Peter, Joannah," Evelyn objected.

Joannah's pale brow wrinkled. She shook her head solemnly. "Oh, yes, Evelyn, they did that. They did that and much worse."

"Joannah . . ."

"But never mind." Joannah's face brightened suddenly. "That's all over now. That was over hundreds of years ago."

Jim cast a quizzical glance at Evelyn.

Joannah tossed her head back defiantly and smiled broadly at Jim. "Now they respect him. They admire him and listen to what he has to say." She turned to Evelyn. "Peter cares about people, you know. That's his thing; that's why he's so interested in security. He always cared about people—even back then."

"Ladies and Gentlemen," Peter Stoneham cleared his throat and leaned forward. The E-car accident had all but destroyed his right shoulder and the reconstruction job had left it almost hunched. A related injury to the neck caused Stoneham's chin always to be inclined towards the misshapen shoulder. His left eye moved continuously while his right eye, the glass one, stared fixedly ahead.

"Doesn't he look nice?" Joannah murmured.

Evelyn frowned in concentration.

". . . since that momentous day in the nineteen hundred and eighty-fourth year of the Christian Era when medical and genetic technology conferred on us the ability to predict Natural Death Dates.[26] This has led inevitably to an increased concern for safety and security. Nothing is more traumatic than injury and premature death brought about by failure to take proper precautions." He glanced down at his notes. "Those of us who have dedicated our-

---

[26] This allusion, of course, is to George Orwell's dystopian novel, *1984*.

selves to homeland security are, justly I think, proud of the fact that such injuries and deaths have gradually been reduced to the point where the statistical threat to any individual is almost negligible.

"Added to that is the fact that crime and terrorism all over the world has been virtually eliminated because of D. Dates. Citizens worldwide, because they now know their precise life-spans, rarely commit unlawful deeds that will shorten their lives. Raised from infancy with an understanding of the true value of life, citizens worldwide now protect it. Still, as P. Goras reminds us, 'The price of security is eternal vigilance.' Senile Delinquents, while still rare, are the one exception. Here and elsewhere, these misguided individuals have hitherto confined themselves to acts of harassment and vandalism." He paused dramatically. "Last week, however, there was, as you all know by now, a shocking case of sexual assault." Another pause. "And just last night a mob of Senile Delinquents attacked an innocent woman."

He shook his head and cleared his throat. "Next week could produce even greater tragedy. These regrettable events have taken place always after sunset and most frequently in our public parks. Prohibiting the use of the parks after dark would greatly reduce this threat to public security." He fixed the camera with his good eye. "All public-minded citizens should therefore support this legislation."

"Thank you, Mr. Stoneham." If the moderator was impressed, her face did not show it.

Stoneham nodded soberly.

Joannah applauded loudly. "Bravo, Peter! Bravo!"

Jim flinched and cast his eyes up at the ceiling.

"That was a fine opening statement," Evelyn commented.

Joannah grinned broadly. "You really think so?"

"Let's listen to the other guy, all right?" Jim said irritably.

"... Stoneham seeks to save you in the name of security from yourselves." Levec's voice was deep and sonorous and he spoke with a thick French accent. "I shall seek to save you from Monsieur Stoneham. I beg you to remember that this country owes its existence to people like Columbus, the Mayflower voyagers, the early pioneers... people who were willing to move outside of the bounds of security and take a risk."

"I can hardly understand him," Joannah complained.

"Sh...h...h..."

"It was perhaps inevitable that when man perfected the ability to compute natural life spans—when we came to know how much time we had coming—we became acutely conscious of risk."

"He's saying nothing noteworthy here. This has nothing to do with the park," said Evelyn.

"We learned to value security almost above all else."[27]

"Of course, that's obvious," Evelyn nodded her head in emphatic agreement.

"In the name of public security, armies have been raised, battles have been fought, people have been killed, and individuals have found themselves arrested and locked away without recourse under the law.[28] In the name of public safety and homeland security the most basic human rights have been restricted. If you take the time to think about it, you will see that where and by what means you travel, the privacy of your personal, medical, financial, and even library records—all these activities and hundreds more besides—are restricted in the name of safety and security. It is not too much to say that *there is a most fundamental conflict between safety and freedom.* The proposition before you, ladies and gentlemen, like many before it would sacrifice the latter on behalf of the former. I urge you for the sake of liberty to reject it."

"You cannot believe that citizens should remain exposed to the danger of brutal attacks from Senile Delinquents?" Stoneham's tone was incredulous.

---

[27]Levec here is identifying "security" as what rhetoricians might call a contemporary "God term." These terms designate concepts so seemingly holy or self-evidently good as to put them beyond question. To disagree or to challenge a "God term" is to risk finding oneself outside the bounds of "normal" society, and therefore, open critique of "God terms" is rare. "Devil terms" perform the same function but for the opposite reason. See Richard Weaver's *The Ethics of Rhetoric*.

[28]The notion of "killing" in the name of "security" is an instance of *irony*. Compare the unintentional irony of such phases as "peacekeeping forces" and "heavy fighting in the demilitarized zone."

"I certainly do not believe that those who wish to avoid such attacks should be exposed to them," Levec responded calmly.

"Then you must support this piece of legislation."

"Not at all, Monsieur Stoneham. Prohibiting citizens from enjoying their public parks will do nothing to eliminate senile delinquency. In fact, your plan to remove citizens from the parks at night will make the parks safer for Senile Delinquents. No one will be watching them."

"That's absurd!" said Stoneham.

"In reality, the principal effect of this proposition will be to provide employment for people like you. Bureaucrats, Monsieur, make regulations and regulations make bureaucrats."

"Right on," Jim said loudly.

"You would feel differently about bureaucrats and regulations had you been the victim of last week's attack in the park." Peter Stoneham's one good eye narrowed, "That I can assure you, Monsieur Levec." His head twitched convulsively towards his right shoulder.

"Au contraire, Monsieur Stoneham, I cannot know how I might feel because I have never had my honor attacked in precisely that way."

Jim sniggered.

"And in any case, it is not clear, had I been in the park, how I would have been saved by your proposed regulations. Is it that these monsters—these Senile Delinquents—would have been repelled by an eloquent reading of your rules? Would I have—how do you say it—hit my assailants on the head with a copy of the municipal regulations?"

The snigger erupted into laughter. "Oh, I like this guy." Jim reached around Joannah and tapped his wife on the shoulder.

"That man is not who he appears to be," Joannah exclaimed.

"Make light of a serious matter if you wish, Levec;" the Security Officer's voice was a little higher pitched. "The fact is that the victim would not have been in the park!"

"To be sure of that, Monsieur Stoneham," Levec interrupted, "we would have to know why he was in the park in the first place."

"He was in the park because there was no regulation prohibiting it. There ought to have been a law."

"Oh, no, Monsieur, *there ought almost never to be a law*. Perhaps the victim went into the park seeking the possibility of sexual encounter . . ."

"Ridiculous!"

". . . or perhaps he felt he could defend himself against possible attack, especially since he would assume that other upstanding citizens would be in the park as well. In either case, there is no good reason to restrict his freedom. Why is he the one to be prohibited from the park? Why create a regulation to make the park a *safe and secure* place for criminals?"

"Ah, Mr. Levec," said Ella Soames, "as it happens, the victim has already testified that he *thought* senile delinquency is restricted to vandalism of public buildings. He was ignorant of the danger."

"Ah, one is sorry then that this young man should have had his body—how do you say it—vandalized. Still, if he was ignorant of the danger, then he would perhaps have been equally ignorant of your regulations prohibiting the danger."

"I think I know who he is," Joannah said, leaning forward to scrutinize Levec's face.

"Ignorance of the law is no excuse," Peter snapped.

"Forgive me, but perhaps Monsieur means *there is no excuse for laws against ignorance.*"

"He's being deliberately naive," Evelyn said.

"No, no! I mean ignorance about official security regulations is intolerable." Peter turned in exasperation to Ella Soames. "He's deliberately confusing the issue."

"I think perhaps you are, Monsieur Levec," she said.

"Perhaps so, but if I am confused and if the poor young man with the vandalized body is ignorant, then we should be educated, not regulated."

"Oh, come now, Monsieur Levec." Ella Soames frowned. "Some regulation is justified and surely security is important."

"Ah, yes, Madame, sometimes regulations must regrettably be passed. But this regulation, saying that I cannot walk in the park at night, proposes to make me secure at the cost of reducing everybody's freedom."

"That man makes good sense." Jim was nodding vigorously.

"Such freedom is not safe," Stoneham objected.

"*Freedom is never safe.*[29] Still, Monsieur Stoneham, God, who in his wisdom gave you such strong feeling of self-importance, gave to the rest of us a strong sense of self-preservation."

"Insult is a cowardly method of debate," Evelyn said hotly.

"I think he's dead right," Jim grinned at his wife.

"You would."

Joannah was shaking her head. "I should have known," she muttered. "I should have known who he was."

"Well apparently, Monsieur Levec," Ella Soames was saying, "the voters don't agree with you. I see that the vote is running in favor of the proposition: sixty-one thousand three hundred and forty-two for, to forty-three thousand four hundred and sixty-four against."

"See, they agree with Peter." Joannah tossed her head indignantly. "The people know who is concerned for their safety and security. They do, Peter; they do."

"Ignorance is bliss," Jim muttered.

"I think that's a particularly appropriate remark coming from you," Evelyn said coldly.

"Monsieur Stoneham, no one is more secure than the animals in your local zoo, and no one is more concerned for their security than the local zookeeper," said Levec.

"Score one for the French!" said Jim, getting up and inserting his I.D. Card into the receptacle. "As for me, I'm convinced." He punched the minus sign emphatically. "I vote no!"

Evelyn calmly walked over and registered a YES vote. Joanna quickly followed suit, glancing disapprovingly at Jim as she brushed past him.

"All we like sheep have gone astray," Jim said, shrugging and grinning at the two women as he stretched out on the sofa.

---

[29] The explicit reference here is to physical freedom. But Levec's conclusion likewise applies to psychological freedom. How often does each of us "play it safe" and fail to take the risks that would lead to richer and fuller lives?

5

JEREMY LEVENTRITT, P.H.O.[30]

Dr. Jeremy B. Leventritt poked the digits 1 ... 8 ... 3 onto the keyboard of the modest computer console that sat on the left side of his desk. He slid his thickly padded chair into a reclining position and, with his hands cupped behind the back of his head, stared grimly at the smiling face of Charles Mortimer Hazlitt which now completely filled his large office telescreen.

Leventritt knew himself to be a first-rate Public Health Officer. He did not look the part. A pleasant face framed by light and tightly curled hair, set on a short and fat body, he was not at all distinguished. But Leventritt was bright, perhaps even damn bright, and superbly trained for his job. His deep brown eyes communicated to his patients not only his own sense of self-confidence, but a genuine concern, altogether without piousness, for their welfare. These assets combined to produce the sort of results that had made Leventritt perhaps the most highly respected and valued P.H.O. in the territory. Nevertheless, he reflected ruefully, with Charlie Hazlitt he had failed miserably. How? Why?

He closed his eyes and reviewed in his mind the responsibilities and duties that came with his prestigious position. His first obligation, of course, was to help each of his patients to come as close as possible to achieving his or her Natural D. Date. Discharging his obligation was a matter of providing for both the psychological and physical health of his patients. The second of

---

[30]The reader will notice that in this chapter Jeremy Leventritt is setting up a classic "brainwashing" session.

these was almost completely dependent on the first and, in point of fact, he relegated matters of merely physical health to the team of surgical and dietary technicians who assisted him.[31] Hazlitt, it was true, had lost some time because of the physical trauma associated with an early aircraft accident. Otherwise, his longevity, having been initially established at birth, was inextricably linked with Leventritt's ability to maintain Hazlitt's sense of social and psychological integrity. It was in these areas that the real failure had occurred.

Leventritt, seeking to relieve himself of the doubts that now assailed him, reflected that he had not taken over Charlie Hazlitt's case until about a decade ago. A P.H.O. long since deceased had presided over the birth ceremonies. Axel Flagstadt, now practicing somewhere in the Southwest, had handled both Hazlitt's Puberty Rites and the Terminal Rites of Hazlitt's parents.[32] The latter had achieved perfect D. Date compatibility and almost optimum longevity. Whatever Flagstadt's reputation, and Leventritt had heard some less than complimentary rumors, he could not have been totally incompetent. Still, it was true that Charlie Hazlitt had begun to lose time immediately after his Puberty Rites and had been losing time ever since.

Leventritt surrendered to the temptation to replay for the third time the teletranscripts of those rites. The pudgy forefinger of his right hand moved clumsily among the computer keyboard and the faintly archaic Puberty Ceremony once again flitted across the telescreen. Leventritt leaned forward, killed the sound, and scrutinized the silent drama. He noted again the slight hesitation with which young Hazlitt, those many years ago, had removed his ceremonial robe. Except in cases of physical deformity, such hesitation was, in Leventritt's opinion, invariably indicative of poor pre-ceremonial preparation. He jabbed at the keyboard once more and froze the action.

The teletranscript showed that Hazlitt's physical preparation had been more than adequate. The nude body, though slightly on the stocky side, had

---

[31] Whereas the behaviorist tends to reduce the symbolic "mind" to nothing more than the physical and biochemical "brain," (what Kenneth Burke calls a metonymy), Leventritt, a rhetorician, here treats the physical body as subsidiary of the mind. (See bibliography.)

[32] By now it is clear that this fictional society has ritualized at least four important transitions: Birth, Puberty, Marriage, and Death. These rhetorically potent rituals have characterized many if not most societies in the past. The implication is that the de-emphasis of such ritual in contemporary society is a mistake from a rhetorical point of view.

been in splendid condition; the musculature was magnificent; the sexual development impressive. Why then had Hazlitt been reticent to present himself to the ceremonial audience? Obviously it was a question of psychological preparation. Unfortunately, in those earlier days, the practice of teletranscription had been restricted to major ceremonies and to such monthly medical examinations as were immediately perceived to be problematical. Thus Leventritt lacked the pre-puberty teletranscripts which he believed, had they been taken, would have contained clues to the origin of Hazlitt's problems.

Jeremy Leventritt sighed as he eased his corpulent frame out of his chair. He wondered if his own P.H.O., the redoubtable Maria Montenez, ever found herself gazing at his, Leventritt's, puberty teletranscripts. Leventritt shuddered at the thought; he had been no Adonis then and now, he glanced ruefully at his slightly bulging belly. He was a positive wreck. His eyes wandered back to the stilled picture of his naked patient and he sighed again. He envied that body, but he did not envy Charles Hazlitt his premature death.

The question was how much Leventritt had contributed to the unfortunate outcome. He had had ten years to get behind that smiling face to the man who lay beyond but he'd never really reached him. Hazlitt could not, in any case, get back the time that had been lost previously, but in fact Leventritt had never succeeded in slowing the pace of Hazlitt's D. Date attrition.

Charles Mortimer Hazlitt had lost more than seven years during his lifetime. Two years had been lost to the aircraft accident. Flagstadt was perhaps responsible for three more years. The remaining two years, Leventritt reflected bitterly, were his. He must not allow himself to rationalize away his failures. Above all, his one remaining responsibility to his patient must discharged flawlessly.

Leventritt reached reflexively for the intercom button on the keyboard. "Klaus, get me the best damn Ops. team you can lay your hands on, and make it fast."

———

Klaus Koehler preceded the three Operating Theatre Technicians into Leventritt's office. He exchanged a brief nod with his superior, and then, standing just inside the entrance, he motioned the others in. "Dr. Leventritt, you know Ian McCloud from Optics."

Leventritt had made a quick appraisal of the group as they had entered the room. McCloud, he knew well. Although the Scotsman hadn't worked on Leventritt's team recently, they had worked together on several occasions in the past, and Leventritt had always been impressed with the man's artistry. Ian McCloud loved his job and tried to make each ceremony more effective than the last. The result was that McCloud's name was associated with several classic displays of optical wizardry. Leventritt was pleased. Above all, he felt it necessary to have a good optics man on the team because he recognized in himself a certain lack of sensitivity in that area.

"Of course." He leaned across the desk to shake McCloud's hand. "Ian, this is a tricky one; glad you weren't tied up with anything else."

McCloud nodded. "Honored to be on your team again, Dr. Leventritt."

Leventritt knew he meant it.

"And I believe you also know Francesca Dascomb—Olfactics and Tactilics." Klaus nodded towards the sexy blonde who had by now made herself comfortable in one of the seats opposite Leventritt's desk.

"Francesca and I are old friends." This was a bit of an overstatement, but it was true that she and the P.H.O. shared a keen interest in the historic forerunners of contemporary Ritualistics. Francesca had done an impressive study of an early snake handling cult, and Leventritt had made that the opportunity to congratulate her. They had gone on to exchange esoterica about early religious revivals, sports spectaculars, political rallies, rock concerts, and the like.[33] Now he walked over to accept her proffered hand, noticing, as he did, the almost imperceptible fragrance of a semi-sweet perfume. He resisted the temptation to make some clever comment and contented himself with, "In any case, Francesca's reputation precedes her everywhere."

"Now, Jeremy," the smile of pleasure belied the protest, "let's not stand on ceremony. Introduce me to our charming young colleague here." She

---

[33] It is worth considering the ritualistic elements at work in public societal events like religious revival meetings, rock concerts, and sports events. Rituals influence behavior, induce conformity among participants, and even persuade participants to act in ways that are not part of their normal way of being in the world. They are, therefore, fundamentally persuasive.

turned to face the strikingly handsome young man who had entered the room last.

Leventritt looked askance at his aide. Klaus reddened slightly. "Allow me to introduce Carter Donnerly; he's new to the staff...er...came to us directly from the Training Academy."

Donnerly turned rather stiffly to acknowledge Francesca. Leventritt meanwhile shot a reproachful glance at his aide. How the hell had Klaus allowed the Center to assign him a new graduate for a case like this? Klaus shrugged his shoulders and rolled his eyes in acknowledgment of his superior's irritation.

"Dr. Leventritt, Mr. Donnerly is a specialist in Sonics."[34] The explanation was unnecessary, and Klaus knew it.

"Glad to have you, Donnerly. Someone must think highly of you to give you an assignment like this fresh out of training."

The sarcasm was lost on the young Sonics man. His face broke into a practiced smile. "I'm sure it will be a pleasure to work with you, Dr. Leventritt. I'm aware of your reputation, and I've had the privilege of observing some of your ceremonies."

"Observation and actual performance are vastly different matters, Mr. Donnerly." Leventritt disliked obsequiousness. He felt in no mood to waste time on idle flattery and he was slightly annoyed that this novice would presume to make judgments one way or the other about his, Leventritt's, performance.

"Now, now, Jeremy," once again a protest from Francesca, who now leaned over to give Donnerly a reassuring pat on the arm. Leventritt smiled. Donnerly had recoiled, almost imperceptibly, from the physical contact—the reaction would not be lost on Francesca who was, after all, an expert in such matters. A flush had crept into the tanned, almost Spanish, face of the Sonics man; his pale blue eyes had hardened slightly.

Leventritt, feeling guilty about his own impatience, extended his hand and offered a warm smile. He reminded himself that the first ceremony was

---

[34]Between them, the "team" had expertise in manipulation of each of the five channels to the central nervous system—hearing, sight, touch, taste, and smell.

an auspicious occasion for a Blue Card holder just out of training and, in any case, it was vital that he get the best out of this novice. "I'm sure we're going to find your assistance invaluable." Donnerly appeared to be reassured. "And now, colleagues, I suggest we get to work."

McCloud and Donnerly seated themselves, and Klaus Koehler turned to leave.

"Thanks, Klaus," Leventritt called to his retreating aide. Klaus waved his acknowledgment and the door slid closed behind him.

Leventritt once again depressed the digits 1 . . . 8 . . . 3 . . . and the screen lit up. "The face you see, ladies and gentlemen, is that of Charles Mortimer Hazlitt," he paused. "Five days from now he will die." Donnerly leaned forward as Leventritt continued. "It is our job, as you know, to help the patient accept if not welcome the transition." McCloud looked merely professional; Francesca Dascomb, almost indifferent. Leventritt was irritated. "Hazlitt will be reaching his D. Date seven years prematurely." The P.H.O. leaned on the last three words.

That got them!

There was an audible intake of breath from Donnerly. "Goras," he muttered.

McCloud leaned forward in his chair, all ears now.

Even Francesca began to scrutinize the face of Charlie Hazlitt with renewed interest. "How the hell did that happen?" she asked, not taking her eyes from the screen.

"Charles Hazlitt is, and always has been a loner," Leventritt was warming to his subject. "He has little regard for social conventions or attitudes; he has never been successfully integrated into society."

"That's an effect, not a cause surely." The Scotsman was tugging at the lobe of one of his large and protruding ears.

"Precisely, Ian." Leventritt was pleased that he wasn't being allowed to get away with sloppy analysis. "He lost a couple of years to physical trauma."

"Chalk that up to the Security people," Donnerly interjected.

"More important to us," Leventritt didn't pause, "his Puberty Ceremony appears to have been mishandled." The P.H.O. resisted the temptation to disclaim personal responsibility for that ceremony, "And in spite of my best efforts, the loss has been chronic since that time." Leventritt refused to spare himself.

"Three guesses as to who blew the Puberty Rites."

Francesca had guessed the truth and was eyeing Leventritt evenly.

"That's scarcely the point, Francesca." Leventritt refused the alibi. "Ten years of my monthly counseling sessions have done nothing to relieve the problem, and now we are faced with a very difficult Terminal Ceremony—complicated by the fact that, as you would expect, Hazlitt has to make the transition alone."

"No sexual ties, eh?" Francesca was disappointed. To the chagrin of some of her colleagues she tended to think of sexual activity as largely a matter of touch, taste, and smell, and, therefore, properly a part of her domain.

"Looks like Olfactics and Tactilics may have to take a back seat to Optics this time," McCloud said, enjoying Francesca's discomfiture.

"Don't jump to conclusions, Ian," the P.H.O. spoke a little more sharply than he intended. "I don't know whether we want to reduce sex to olfactics and tactilics, but Hazlitt is no celibate."

"Damn! I can *see* it in his face...." Francesca leaned on the word "see." "What sort of an optics man are you, Scottie?" Francesca's body shook with suppressed mirth.

Leventritt pressed on. "This woman," he fiddled with the console and Hazlitt's face was replaced with that of a woman whose youthful characterlessness had apparently not given way to mature beauty, "this woman is Martha Straun, Hazlitt's roommate and housekeeper. There was never any legal spouse, but Hazlitt's attachment to this woman is clearly substantial."

"Not very intelligent, I'd guess." The Scotsman was gazing at the screen and tugging at his ear again.

"But sensuous. Look at that mouth and the nose." Francesca enjoyed qualifying her colleague's estimate. "One hell of a sexpot, I'll bet."

Donnerly was a little taken aback. This wasn't textbook stuff.

"What would you say, Carter dear?" Francesca reached to her right and squeezed Donnerly high up on the left thigh.

Donnerly jumped and stammered, "She ... er ... er ... I agree with Mr. McCloud. She doesn't look very intelligent."

Leventritt looked at Donnerly with annoyance. He'd have to get over these sensitivities or he'd be no damned good.

"My dear man, we're talking about sex, not intelligence." Francesca squeezed again. She was unmerciful.

Donnerly squirmed.

Leventritt met Francesca's eyes, trying to decide whether she hoped to break Donnerly up or break him in. Her even gaze told Leventritt that it was the latter, but damn it, she was also trying to get a rise out of her superior by teasing him.

McCloud rescued Leventritt. "I take it that the D. Date incompatibility is considerable."

"Yes, Martha Straun has better than five years left. Breaking this tie is going to be particularly difficult." Leventritt saw the opportunity for a homily. "I don't need to tell you that the ceremony has to be as therapeutic for her as it is for Hazlitt."

"She'll be in the Inner Circle then," Donnerly had finally found something unexceptionable to say.

"Of course, along with several others—relatives—of whom only one appears to have any very profound psychological connection with Hazlitt." Leventritt fingered the console again. "This man is Hazlitt's nephew, James Adam Sebring, a Lucifer Pilot."

"A good-looking man." Francesca murmured.

"Yes, no doubt, but like Hazlitt, something of a problem. Indeed, the two cases are in some respects very similar. The uncle has had a great deal of influence on the nephew, who has become something of a rebel. It would be something of a bonus if we could get some behavioral changes in Sebring at this ceremony."

"Sebring a patient of yours, Doctor?" McCloud asked.

"No, but this woman, his wife, is." A profile view of Evelyn Sebring flashed onto the screen. "You'll need to watch for some animosity between Evelyn Sebring and Charles Hazlitt. She resents his influence on her husband. I don't need to tell you if such animosity breaks out, don't suppress it. Use it." Leventritt was staring directly at Donnerly.

"We are taught that such outbursts can have unexpected effects on the audience." Donnerly ventured a mild protest.

"Mr. Donnerly. It is our job to anticipate those effects that can be anticipated and incorporate smoothly and flexibly those that can't. Any fool can follow a script; I make it a practice not to use the things. You must be prepared to deal with what really happens, not with what you hope will happen." Leventritt took the edge off his voice and added, "You may find it useful to stop thinking of the public gallery as *audience*. In fact, they are a special kind of participant and should be thought of in that way."[35]

"Do we have any idea what the composition of the audience—er—public gallery will be?" Donnerly was persistent.

"That's a good question, Mr. Donnerly." Leventritt did not want to discourage his novice Sonics man. "The only special case so far as we know is an aunt on Hazlitt's mother's side who will have become a Red Card holder herself. She and her husband will be celebrating their own Terminal Rites eight days later. She is, therefore, of course, prohibited from the Inner Circle but apparently intends to be in the public gallery. Her presence, I am sure, will be of no great consequence to Hazlitt. I cannot be sure that the reverse is true."

"The theatre will be packed," Francesca observed.

Donnerly raised his eyebrows in query.

"Yes, Francesca, it will be. This sort of ceremony does not provoke joy like those in which Unity in Death has been achieved, but the drama is likely to be greater, so people will come. In any case, many P.H.O.'s will be encouraging their patients to attend. This Terminal Ceremony offers a great opportunity for people to get rid of negative emotions—pity, fear, hate, and the like.[36] I remind you, too, that we have a chance to present an excellent object lesson. Very few of those in the public gallery will be using their time as badly as Hazlitt has, but there will be some who are living at less than

---

[35]The role of the audience members as full participants at ritualistic events is worthy of notice. The Superbowl, without the audience, becomes a backyard football game.

[36]Leventritt apparently understands the importance of the emotional outburst that frequently accompanies "crisis" persuasion and is variously referred to as: abreaction (psychiatry), catharsis (drama), conviction (religion). He also seems to agree with Eric Hoffer (see bibliography) that it is the purgation the "negative" emotions (fear, anger, hate, frustration) rather than the "positive" ones (love, compassion, etc.) which play the crucial role in these "conversion" experiences. In political movements, a symbolic "God" (a source of all that is good and the appropriate object of the positive emotions) is rhetorically desirable; a symbolic devil (a source of all that's evil and the appropriate object of "negative" emotions) seems to be rhetorically mandatory.

optimum. Our attempts to reassure Hazlitt should not be allowed to conceal from the public the costs of his sort of life style."

"You're not implying that Hazlitt has been involved in senile delinquency, are you?" The Scotsman got no further.

"No, no, not at all," Leventritt interjected, "we have absolutely no evidence of that and, in any case, the time loss pattern, though chronic, has been very even—none of the ups and downs you'd expect with senile delinquency. No, Hazlitt is not antisocial; he's asocial—and that, of course, is in many ways a good deal worse."

"There's no danger of P.N.D.?" Francesca sounded serious.

"I don't think so. Post Natural Death, as you know, is extremely rare, and Hazlitt exhibits none of the symptoms. No, I think we are looking at a case in which what used to be called the social construction of reality has failed—very probably, as I've said, in connection with the stresses of puberty.[37] Hazlitt lives in a world of his own construction. We've got to get into that world, both for his sake and for the sake of those he leaves behind."

"His susceptibility to the audience will be low then." Francesca had hit the point that had been worrying Leventritt.

"Yes, Francesca, that is precisely the problem. Initially at least, we must expect to work through Martha Straun and Jim Sebring. If we're successful, the reactions from the public gallery will begin to get to him. Obviously we'll be relying more than usually on Metabolic Remote Scan. M.R.S. is your bailiwick, Ian. What about it?"

The Scotsman winced. "We've been having trouble, as you've heard, breaking in a new technician. At a wedding ceremony last week, the idiot had the scanner poorly aimed. He missed the groom and we were reading the P.H.O.—though we didn't know it. We thought we had the coolest groom in history—heart rate and blood pressure were both subnormal. Adrenalin was practically nil. Sonics 'synced' with the wrong heart rate, of course, and start-

---

[37]The P.H.O. is alluding to the theory that what each of us takes to be "real"—particularly about such puzzling matters as life, death, dreams, God, etc.—are in fact socially generated "truths" designed to produce what is agreed-upon appropriate behavior and to allay our deepest fears about the unknowns of the universe. Society, according to the theory of the *social construction of reality*, acts to create, sustain, and enforce the socially constructed "truths" we all take for granted. (See bibliography: Berger and Luckmann.)

ed hyping up the P.H.O. Looked for a while like the P.H.O. and the bride would get it on and leave the groom watching..."[38]

Francesca's blond hair began to bounce as her suppressed chuckle burst into a voluble laugh. "I take it, Jeremy, you weren't the P.H.O. in question?"

Leventritt smiled, "I'm glad to say, no." In fact he'd taken part in an unmerciful ribbing of Gossage, the P.H.O. in the case. "In any event, we can assume with Ian watching over things, I'll suffer no such fate in this ceremony. Mr. Donnerly, I expect you to coordinate with Ian and with M.R.S. very closely—and be particularly careful not to hype the metabolic rates too quickly. If you get too far ahead, you're likely to get no response."

Donnerly nodded, acknowledging the instruction seemingly without resentment. "The music is going to be difficult. I take it that Hazlitt has no strong religious background."

"He doesn't appear to have much reverence for anything really..." noted McCloud.

Leventritt intervened, "Colleagues, no one is totally irreverent; it is a matter of identifying where the reverence lies. If it is not in religion, then in science or philosophy, art or nature. Hazlitt is no exception."

The P.H.O. fingered the keyboard and the screen displayed a picture of Charlie Hazlitt standing next to his antique biplane. "This, ladies and gentlemen, is where his heart is. Hazlitt speaks of flight the way other men speak of God. I will not presume to tell you how to use that fact, but it is a fact, and I expect you to make use of it."

Leventritt glanced at his three assistants and added, "I've instructed Klaus to provide you with all the information retrieval codes you'll need. I suggest you study the complete teletranscripts on Hazlitt and as much as you can on the other principals and get back to me with your proposals." The P.H.O. rose from his seat.

"How about a computer trial?" McCloud had obviously forgotten Leventritt's well known bias against computer mockups of such ceremonies.

---

[38]The Scotsman's marvelous machine is, of course, nothing more than a means of providing a continuous report on those psychological functions that affect, and are affected by, persuasive messages. The principle is the same as that of the so-called "lie-detector" but with additional cybernetic features built in.

"Ian, I've always believed that the staging of these ceremonials is a matter of art, not science. You will be provided with enough data to support everything up to and including a computer-generated dramatic hologram. You may prepare as you please, but my experience is that such computer projections predict the obvious and miss the vital."

"Dramatic hologram?" The question escaped Donnerly's lips almost before he knew it.

The Optics man was on him immediately. "What in God's name do they teach in the Academy these days?" McCloud's voice was heavy with sarcasm.

Leventritt was more gentle. "It's merely an extension of the dialogue capability of the ordinary home computer, Mr. Donnerly. CLEM can project a reasonable three-dimensional facsimile of a single character and even generate a plausible dialogue. The Academy's equipment, I believe, can create three-dimensional images of up to four subjects but the dialogue between them is a little wooden..."

Donnerly nodded his confirmation.

"...but you should see our latest model." McCloud could hardly wait to bring the new man up to date. "It can handle up to ten three-dimensional figures as well as project how each will react with the others in any given situation. We can program an entire Inner Circle and let the machine predict the action."

"The problem is..." Leventritt did not want Donnerly to buy McCloud's presentation uncritically, "...the problem is that the computer merely extrapolates from what it already knows about each subject. It cannot predict reactions in novel situations and it does not attempt to account for the input from the participants in the public gallery. As I was saying, it predicts the obvious and misses the vital, and..."[39]

"...In any case," Francesca interrupted in an effort to head off the standard sermon, "Carter will need to be familiarized with our technical set-up." She again applied a suggestive squeeze.

---

[39] Leventritt is merely hinting at the complex issues that separate the humanist-linguistic-qualitative approach to the study of humans from the social scientific-technological-quantitative methods. The former approach is that of classical rhetoric; the latter is more typical of modern social science.

"Yes, he will," Leventritt responded dryly, "and I have no doubt, Francesca, that you'll be pleased to perform that service."

The three assistants had risen and were walking towards the door. Francesca turned, grinned at Leventritt and shot back, "You bet I will—a technical orientation and maybe some post-graduate work in tactilics." She reached for Donnerly's arm and guided him through the door. The door slid closed behind them.

"Damn that woman!" Leventritt poked at the intercom key. "Klaus, get in here right away."

6

D. DATE

It was eight o'clock in the evening of April twenty-third. Jim Sebring sat at a table by the front window of the Cracked Atom and gazed up at the majestic statue of Admiral Nelson. The Admiral was a solitary but secure remnant of the earlier Christian Era.

London's Trafalgar Square was bathed in a blue-white artificial light, intense but diffuse, so that neither the gray stone column nor the bronze figure perched atop it cast a shadow anywhere. The rotary causeway that surrounded Nelson's column was alive with gliding E-cars making their way through the Saturday night traffic.

Inside the establishment, seated across the table from Jim was a tall, stylishly thin woman whose once jet black hair was now flecked with gray. She had all the beauty that comes to a woman who has lived her life well. The wrinkles that surrounded her remarkably expressive hazel eyes bespoke a person whose sense of the whimsy of things had frequently expressed itself in smiles, chuckles, and outright laughter. Her rounded cheeks and generally solicitous manner combined to give Michele LaTour a warm image. It was that warmth that put Jim at ease when he unburdened his worries to her, as he frequently did, during these friendly meetings at the Cracked Atom.

Jim knew there was another Michele—the Michele who, as her uniform testified, had fought her way up the ranks to become a French Lucifer Pilot and the woman who was capable of expressing a sense of self-reliance, authority, and dignity born of many successful battles with the elements at the controls of her supersonic jet. But that Michele—the one who liked to rendezvous here at the Cracked Atom and talk shop—was somewhere else tonight. The woman who faced Jim Sebring looked pensive and troubled.

The table attendant appeared and Jim ordered two Cannabis cocktails without consulting her.

Michele remained silent.

"Where are you, Michele?"

"Well, I'm here, of course." She had a deep, husky voice, surprisingly sensual, and a slight French accent.

"No, you're not."

She shrugged.

"Something wrong?"

"No . . . no, Jim. I'm fine." She smiled again, a fleeting smile, but she was staring out of the window. She wasn't really paying attention to him.

Jim thought about the two days that Michele and Charlie had spent together. He had known intuitively when he had introduced them that they would hit it off immediately, and he'd been right. He was immensely grateful to Michele for the good time she'd given Charlie. Like Charlie and him, she loved to fly and she loved to talk about it. He supposed that other than Charlie and Natasha, she was the best friend he had. But this wasn't the Michele he knew, and he wondered now as he watched her if he had really done a favor by letting her get to know Charlie. Perhaps they'd gotten along too well.

"I'm grateful to you, Michele," he hesitated. "Charlie, he has so little time . . . and that was a good time . . ."

She nodded. "It was for both of us." Her attention was still occupied somewhere else outside the window. Her brow wrinkled slightly.

Jim turned to follow her gaze. The rotary causeway was a mass of moving E-cars. Unlike their American counterparts, the English electric mobiles were all one color, a conservative dark green, except for those used by the Security people, which were a bright fluorescent orange. Across the square in front of Nelson's Column, an orange E-car had stopped without pulling completely off the causeway. Two green E-cars had come to a stop behind the Security car. The driver of the second one emerged waving a clenched fist.

Jim turned away from the window grinning. "Those Security guys. They'll do it every time."

The table attendant had returned and was observing the scene. He shook his head as he set the Cannabis on the table. "Arse 'oles, bloody arse 'oles," he muttered.

Jim nodded in agreement.

Michele leaned across the table as the attendant left. "Jim . . ." She was looking directly at him. "There's something I want to ask."

He sensed it was about Charlie. "Sure."

"I was wondering about the Terminal Ceremony. Is it the same in America as it is in France?"

So she *was* brooding about Charlie. "I suppose so," he said.

"Who takes part in the ceremony?"

"Anybody who wants to."

"No, no," Michele shook her head impatiently. "That's not possible. I mean there must be something special for the family?"

"Oh, you mean the Inner Circle?"

"Yes, the Inner Circle—if that's what you call it—who's part of the Inner Circle?"

"Mostly family and a few friends . . . whoever Charlie invites . . ." The puzzled expression evaporated from Jim's face. "Oh, why didn't you say something? I'm sure Charlie would want you to be there if he knew . . ."

"NO!!" Her sudden vehemence startled him, but she continued more quietly. "No, Jim, you misunderstand. I don't want to be there. I'd just like to know how the ceremony is conducted. Do you have a communion wine as we do?"

"Oh, you mean Aqua Vie?"

"Yes, Aqua Vie, that would be it. Who drinks the water of life?" she laughed dryly.

Jim stared at her, puzzled again, "Everybody in the Inner Circle."

"And your priests, what you call P.H.O.'s, do they drink this Aqua Vie?"

"Yes, of course." It was Michele's turn to look puzzled. "I see." She thought for a moment. "Well, then who *doesn't* sit in the Inner Circle?"

Jim looked down at his untouched Cannabis cocktail and then across at hers, also untouched. "Why not a toast to Charlie?" he said with a forced grin. "To the good life he . . ."

"Who doesn't sit there, Jim?" she asked, cutting him off. "Who's missing?"

"Missing?" He shook his head. "No one is missing, Michele. Everyone's there who's important to him." What did she want him to say? "Well, yes, except, of course, for the other Red Card holders."

"Other Red Card holders . . ." It was a thoughtful statement, not a question.

"Naturally. You know, they're so close to their own ceremony . . ." He left the sentence unfinished.

She nodded slowly and sank again into silence. Jim took a sip of his Cannabis.

"When is it?" she asked suddenly. Her deep husky voice was trembling.

"Michele . . ."

"When is it, Jim?"

"The Terminal Rites are at midnight the day after tomorrow."

"Jim." She glanced out of the window again. "Jim, there's something you don't know . . . something you need to understand . . ."

Jim reached across the table for her hand. "Michele, I do understand, and I'm sorry now that I brought him over."

She shook her head. Her mouth opened as if to say something then closed again and finally, "I have to go, Jim. I'm sorry." And she turned and fled. At the door, she glanced back at him once and then was gone.

Jim stared after her. He should have known. He should have guessed. She and Charlie were so much alike.

———

It was eight o'clock in the evening of April twenty-third.[40] It was a fine evening—an evening to be alive—James Sebring thought. There was a spring in his step and from time to time a half smile flickered across his face. He was headed towards East Hartford, towards the Electric Mobile Barn and one of the little apartments that sat above it. He was headed towards Natasha.

---

[40]Again, the *time* motif is stressed. Thanks to the speed of his star-jet, Jim has experienced "eight o'clock in the evening of April twenty-third" twice—once in London and again in Hartford.

His hands were stuffed in his pants pockets and his uniform jacket was unbuttoned and thrown back so that the warm southwesterly wind blew against his shirt front and tossed his wide black tie over his left shoulder, where it waved a perpetual greeting to whoever might follow him. He held his head high and let the wind whip at his face because it felt good and because he felt good.

This was the first really warm wind of the year. He could smell its sweet-scented dryness and he could visualize its sweeping journey across the sun-baked lands to the south. This was the same warm wind that had stirred up the hot, dry sands of the southwestern American deserts and transformed the air above them into a parched, blinding confusion of yellow dust. It was the same wind that had bent the rubbery stalks and scattered for miles the black-podded seeds of the tropical flora of the Mexican lowlands. This was the same wind, Jim mused, that had blasted against the nose of his star-jet as he'd whistled at thirty thousand feet across the mid-Atlantic just a couple of hours earlier. The street on which he walked was bright, bathed in a pale blue mixture of fluorescent and incandescent light, which made it seem neither night nor day, but some strange other time—a man-made time. A solitary passing E-car slowed, the driver waved and beckoned him to the vacant passenger seat, but Jim shook his head and waved him on. He turned off the main street which led onto a smaller lane and the hum of the E-car receded. He was glad for the quietness of the evening.

Less than two hours ago, he thought, he'd been sitting transfixed for perhaps the hundredth time at the controls of his star-jet, watching the blue-black of the night give way to deep, deep purple. As his speeding jet had slowly brought the sun back up from behind the western horizon, the purple had changed to violet and then to crimson red until when he landed, the sun was just clear of the horizon but sinking again.[41]

Normally Jim would have tried to shake off the euphoria that gripped him. Normally he'd be preparing to meet Evelyn, not Natasha. Evelyn, he reflected, would never understand his need to fly. "Down to earth"—the phrase summed up perfectly Evelyn's virtues and her vices. Literally and

---

[41]Obviously Jim's jet travels faster than the sun—a fact which is responsible for the above anomalous effect.

metaphorically, Evelyn was down to earth, sensible, sober... sanctimonious? Jim played with the idea guiltily. He dismissed it. If Evelyn disapproved of him, it was because there was much to disapprove of.

Jim's spirits dipped a little. At this very moment he was engaging in deceit. He had lied to Evelyn, telling her that his E.T.A. at Bradley was two-thirty a.m. He had lied so that he could keep this rendezvous with Natasha. What was worse was the fact that the lie would not be possible had Evelyn not recently presented him with a son. It was she who controlled his flight itinerary and who therefore, when she was on the job, knew exactly where he was and when. How much more of his life Evelyn controlled Jim hesitated to guess.

An E-car appeared at the far end of the street. It whined slowly and rhythmically past him until it was a faint hum in the distance, and then nothing. Silence again.

Why, Jim wondered, was his world so fragile—so illusory that its truth had to be defended by deception? Evelyn's world, he was convinced, was illusion, too. But everyone cooperated in that illusion until it appeared as solid as concrete.[42] He shook his head bitterly. *He had to defend a truth with lies; Evelyn sustained a lie with truth.* He'd have to try that line on Calderoni, his P.H.O., if he decided to cut his D. Date attrition, decided to unburden his conscience by confessing the details of his relationship with Natasha.

But what did he have to confess? His respect for her—respect that had grown to admiration—admiration that had become fascination. Nothing scandalous really. Well after tonight, if he had his way, there'd be more to confess to—a lot more!

He crossed the street slowly and stood for a moment in front of the E-car barn, the second story of which contained Natasha's apartment.

He walked slowly along the front of the building and peered through the long Lucite doors. The place was brightly lit and he could see the rows of multi-colored electro-cars parked in long, neat ranks, all awaiting periodic maintenance.

---

[42] The notion that Jim is introspecting about here is sometimes called by rhetoricians CONSENSUAL VALIDATION—the idea that what is "true" is so because, and only because the majority says so.

He thought about the night Natasha had made this same walk and looked through these same doors. She was alone, too, and they must have been waiting and watching her, their eyes lusting after her. It could be that they were back there again now, hiding behind the E-cars. But they were not likely to show themselves tonight. He was a more formidable target. The Senile Delinquents usually attacked women and young boys. They went for the vulnerable and the weak.

Shielding his eyes, he stared intently through the bright lights, almost wishing to see some movement. For Natasha's sake, he'd like to teach them a lesson. But there was nothing.

Reaching the end of the building, he glanced down the side and saw the broad staircase, which led to Natasha's apartment. It was flanked on either side by antique railings.

He took the stairs two at a time, stopping at the top as he heard from inside the faint sound of keyboard music. Above the door, a large thermo pane emitted a flickering light. To the right of the door the Plexiglas indent screen glowed steadily. He pressed the palm of his hand against it and immediately the door rolled open, bottom to top.

Jim grinned, realizing that Natasha must have programmed CLEM to open the door to his palm print without further query. She had given him the key to her apartment.

The music was louder now, though it was the sights rather than the sounds that commanded his attention as he stepped through the doorway and into Natasha's living room. At the far side of the room, next to the door that obviously led to her bedroom, CLEM was projecting a series of three-dimensional pictures. The first was a modernized Renoir depicting nudes bathing; it was followed by a contemporary abstract of the same theme, a Kabe, Jim judged, and then an extremely provocative example of ancient Chinese erotica. Jim laughed volubly and turned toward her. She was seated at the keyboard rippling effortlessly through a familiar Chopin etude. He was taken back. They had talked about music occasionally, at her instigation he now remembered, but she had never mentioned being a keyboard musician—and a damn good one at that.

Tasha turned her head briefly, smiled at him and, without stopping, waved one hand casually towards the table in the center of the room. For a moment he did not move, entranced at the gay charm of her playing, and then he crossed over to the table and poured two goblets of amber-colored wine from the decanter sitting there. Crossing back he slid the flickering candelabra back from its spot at the end of the keyboard, making a place for her goblet of wine. Natasha ran a rippling cadenza from the bottom of the keyboard to the top and, in a single motion, swept up the goblet in her left hand and held it towards him. Their glasses came together.

"I had no idea, Tasha."

"Oh, I was hoping you'd have all sorts of ideas." She had risen to her feet.

"I mean I had no idea you played so well."

"I don't. My left hand is weak."

Jim, ignoring the self-deprecation, stepped back to admire her, gazing first at the sheen of her dark hair as it caught and reflected the candlelight and then moving down to the angular line of her cheek and to the gentle curve of her shoulder.

"Keep going. It gets better as you do." She was laughing at him.

"You're a brazen wench." He pulled her toward him, but she ducked under his arm, reaching instead for the decanter.

Natasha refilled their glasses, led him to the sofa and, curling her legs under her, demanded: "Tell me about your trip. What was the flight like? What did you do in London? Who did you see?"

He saw from her eyes that the breathless series of questions were provoked by genuine interest, so he told her of the euphoria of his outrunning the sun in its westward flight. He described the sights and sounds of London and told her of his strange meeting with Michele LaTour at the Cracked Atom. She in her turn talked to Jim of her music and art, taking particular pride in the oddly antique candelabra which she had made herself out of odds and ends. Finally, their mood turned somber as Jim described Michele's concern over Charlie's Terminal Rites.

When he finished talking, Natasha gazed in silence for a moment at the amber wine in her half empty goblet and then walked slowly over to the keyboard. Without looking at him, she said almost in a whisper, "Jim, I want to play something for you."

He crossed the room and stood behind her as she struck the first melancholy chords of Beethoven's *Pathetique Sonata*. Her hands seemed strangely powerful to him now, and he listened, puzzled, as the sadness of the opening gave way to the explosive anger of the "Allegro" movement. The music did not speak of love as he had expected, and he thought for a moment that she, too, was thinking of Charlie. But something in her manner, her complete absorption, the passion with which she played suggested that her message was more personal. And then, as the sonorous tones of the "Adagio Cantabile" began to sound plaintively from the keyboard, understanding came. She was speaking to him not of love but of death . . . no, more like it, of both. Suddenly he remembered her reaction when he had first told her of the imminence of Charlie's D. Date, remembered her empathic response when he had spoken of Charlie's desire to fly a jet just once before he died. Jim had guessed from the relatively modest job she held, from her whole attitude in fact, that Natasha was not destined for a long life, but this was a far more urgent message. What an insensitive fool he'd been!

Natasha struck the final resigned chord and, after a pause, lowered her hands to her lap but continued to stare at the keyboard in front of her.

Jim spoke first. "When, Tasha?"

"Soon," she said, turning her face towards him, her eyes now glistening with tears. "Very soon, Jim."

He swept her diminutive form, now shaken with sobs, from the keyboard bench and guided her gently towards the bedroom. As he did, his eyes rested for the first time on the calendar which had been hung in the obscurity of the shadows above CLEM. He read the numbers: 45 days—June 7.

7

ALL IS WELL

A steady stream of robed figures filed up the broad red-tiled pavement that led to the Great Clock Tower. Only one of the four clock faces was visible from the southern approach and since the giant obelisk that supported it was obscured by the late evening darkness, the enormous, illuminated orb seemed suspended in the sky. The figure of the woman pointed dramatically straight up at the number twenty-four and stood facing, and seemingly awaiting, the expectant male now ninety degrees away and moving perceptibly toward her. Once an hour, pointing to each number in sequence, the two figures locked in ecstatic embrace only to be torn apart moments later. Fifteen minutes from now, at midnight, the conjugal pair would finish their day united again. The great bell would announce their achievement—and it would also mark the end of the last full day of life for Charles Mortimer Hazlitt.

Those who had come to witness and participate in the Terminal Rites were fleetingly revealed by the floodlights that illuminated the gigantic base of the Tower. All of the celebrants, except the holders of the Red Card, wore traditional black ceremonial robes and each clutched a small white leather-bound Book of Liturgy.[43] The bands of color which trimmed the black robes announced in general terms the D. Date of each wearer. Most of the children wore blue, or occasionally green. The robes of the adults were trimmed in

---

[43] The little book is presumably analogous with the little Black Book (*The Holy Bible*), little red book (*Mao's Thoughts*), little blue book (John Birch Society doctrine), Hitler's *Mein Kampf*, etc. Such books almost invariably accompany fervent belief systems. They vary from the sublime (*The Holy Bible*) to the ridiculous (*Mein Kampf*) in content; they are almost always "best sellers;" they are usually not only read but also memorized and quoted as ultimate authority. Their size and shape allow them to be carried easily.

colors ranging from green, for those who looked forward to remarkable longevity, to yellow and orange for the less fortunate. One couple was noticeable for obvious signs of difference in maturity, the man having already lived much longer than the woman. Still, their union, like that of all the other couples, had been made possible by D. Date compatibility so they wore gowns trimmed in like colors—orange in this case. Holders of the Red Card, of whom only two were in evidence at the moment, wore robes entirely of scarlet.[44]

Jim and Evelyn Sebring joined the slowly moving, murmuring throng as it made its way toward the massive marble doorway that was the main entrance to the Tower. Evelyn Sebring was dressed in a robe trimmed in bright yellow. The color that framed Jim's neck and ran down the front of his robe was orange, which presented an incongruity that drew more than one furtive glance of disapproval from passersby. Evelyn, acutely conscious of the disapproval, reflected her discomfort by disengaging her grip on Jim's arm. Jim, for his part occupying another world, seemed oblivious both to the crowd and to his wife.

Once inside the Tower entrance, the congregation split in two, half turning down a corridor to the left and heading for the west entrance to the amphitheatre, the other half turning right and circling toward the east entrance. Jim and Evelyn, as participants in the Inner Circle, walked straight ahead and, in accordance with tradition, entered by the South portal.

The arena they entered—used exclusively for the rituals accompanying puberty, marriage, divorce, and death—was capped by a huge dome. Its floor sloped downward on all sides towards a small circular stage in the center. The slowly rotating stage was sparsely furnished. Close to the center was a simple Romanesque, backless bench with curved arms and an upholstered seat. In front of the bench and at the periphery of the stage stood a small lectern supported on wrought iron legs. Two or three feet to one side of the lectern, a decanter of amber colored Aqua Vie, the ceremonial wine, was surrounded by fourteen goblets. The decanter and glasses rested on a silver tray, which in its turn sat on a simple circular marble table.

---

[44]This society obviously understands the powerful socializing force of uniforms.

Surrounding the stage and on the same level was the single row of armless red velvet seats that made up the Inner Circle. The Inner Circle was itself encircled by a dark mahogany rail which separated it from the three banked rows of white seats reserved for the Chorus. Beyond the railing that divided the Chorus from the general public rose fourteen tiers of seats upholstered in green velvet.

Between the center stage and the broad flat walkway that rimmed the amphitheatre radiated four aisles, one for each cardinal point of the compass. Jim and Evelyn made their way slowly down the south aisle toward the Inner Circle. Behind them, on the other side of a dark polarized wall, was the observation gallery. In that gallery, viewing the procedures from obscurity, were a variety of intern-technicians and an occasional Public Health Officer.

The other three galleries that surrounded the arena housed the arrays of panels which controlled the sights, the sounds, and the smells that permeated the amphitheatre. In those galleries, already busy at the control panels, were the bearded Scotsman, Ian McCloud; his now serious associate, Francesca Dascomb; and the neophyte Sonics man, Carter Donnerly. The three chief technicians and their various assistants watched as Jim and Evelyn Sebring seated themselves in the Inner Circle.

McCloud identified the other occupants of the Inner Circle for the technician who operated Metabolic Remote Scan apparatus. Seated across the stage from the Sebrings was Charlie Hazlitt's unnaturally young and unintelligent-looking roommate and "housekeeper," Martha Straun. On her left was Charlie's brother, John, and John's wife, Marianne. On Martha's right, across the north aisle, was Sandra Hazlitt, Charlie's unmarried sister, and to her right, Kay and George Kuhn, respectively sister and brother-in-law to Charles Hazlitt. Seated between the west and south aisles with Jim and Evelyn Sebring was Alicia Kuhn, Hazlitt's niece. Across the south aisle on Jim Sebring's right were three males all unrelated to Charlie Hazlitt. Jonah Ball, a taciturn New Englander, was a flight instructor friend who had been involved in an aircraft accident with Hazlitt years ago. Next to him, craggy-faced and white haired, Tobias Kopelnick, once Charlie Hazlitt's teacher, and though presumably much older than Charlie, now his friend. Finally, seated to the left of the east aisle, Llewelyn Price, a tall, dark, cadaverous man who had been Hazlitt's co-worker at the Airstation for nearly twenty years. McCloud also pointed out to his assistant a distinguished-looking couple, clothed entirely in scarlet and seated halfway back in the southwest quadrant. The woman was Agatha Strang, Charlie Hazlitt's aunt on his mother's side. She would normally have sat in the Inner Circle except that she and her husband were eight days away from their own Terminal Rites and therefore restricted to the public section.

High above the now filled amphitheatre, the reaching figure of the pursuing male achieved his purpose and the sound of the huge bell reverberated through the Great Clock Tower. The lighting around the base of the arena dimmed, and a hush spread contagiously across the congregation. The great dome was transformed into a perfect replica of the early summer sky except that the stars composing the constellations of the zodiac were slightly emphasized and their westward revolution was perceptibly accelerated.[45] As the great bell sounded the twentieth stroke, the center stage and the north aisle were urged from the darkness by the diffuse glow of bluish-white light. When the reverberation of the twenty-fourth and last stroke of the bell had vanished into eternity, the hush was broken by a ruffle of tympani. The north portal was suddenly illuminated and standing there, clad entirely in scarlet, eyes screwed up against the light, was Charlie Hazlitt.[46] The crowd sucked in its breath as one person.

From the darkness beyond the north portal stepped the figure of Dr. Jeremy B. Leventritt. Looking somewhat less portly in his own orange trimmed ceremonial robe, Leventritt grasped Charlie Hazlitt by the elbow and guided him down the north aisle to the illuminated stage. Charlie seated himself stiffly at the center of the Roman bench and looked expectantly at Leventritt who stood now, Book of Liturgy open on the lectern in front of him, gazing into the darkened amphitheatre.

"To everything there is a season, and a time to every purpose under heaven . . ."[47] Leventritt's sonorous voice appeared to emanate from the starlit dome.

---

[45] The careful design of the amphitheater bespeaks understanding of a central principle of so-called "brainwashing," conscious and relatively complete **CONTROL OF THE ENVIRONMENT**.

[46] We may assume that Charlie, faced with imminent death, is likely to be in a state of **PHYSICAL AND MENTAL FATIGUE**—thus exemplifying two more conditions for "brainwashing."

[47] This line and those that follow are from the Bible—Ecclesiastes, Chapter 3.

"UNDER HEAVEN..." The low-voiced chorus echoed the last two words of the opening line of the ancient rite.

"A time to be born and a time to die, a time to laugh, a time to cry..." Leventritt did not look at the Book of Liturgy—he didn't need to.

"TO LAUGH, TO CRY, BE BORN AND DIE..." The chorus spoke the words swiftly fading to a whisper on the last elongated syllable. From half way back in the southwest quadrant came an audible sob. Leventritt ignored it.

"A time to plant, a time to pluck up that which is planted. A time to get and a time to lose..."

"TO GET...TO LOSE..." The chorus in perfect cadence and unison.[48]

"A time to keep and a time to cast away..."

"KEEP AND CAST AWAY..." The chanting chorus was louder now.

"A time to rend and a time to sew..." Leventritt paused; the chorus was silent.

"A time to keep silence," again a pause, "and a time to speak."

"SPEAK!" The command from the chorus was loud and urgent.

Charlie rose and, replacing Leventritt, stood grasping the lectern with white knuckled hands as the stage slowly revolved.

"I, Charles Mortimer Hazlitt, having no further use for this world's goods," Charlie's voice was soft, almost a whisper as he delivered the traditional preface, "do, with certain exceptions, hereby give and bequeath such possessions as are legally mine, to my beloved," Charlie paused, "housekeeper, Martha Straun."

As he pronounced her name, a spotlight momentarily played on the housekeeper, plucking her pallid face out of the otherwise darkened Inner Circle. Across the north aisle from Martha, Sandra Hazlitt, Charlie's sister, had greeted the announcement with an audible intake of breath. Charlie appeared not to notice. "To my sister, Sandra," he continued, "I bequeath those family heirlooms that were left to me by our parents, Christopher and Sarah Hazlitt." The figure of Sandra Hazlitt was suddenly bathed in light.

---

[48]The chorus is frequently used in a variety of persuasive situations. Usually it speaks for the group or the society generally. For an electrifying example of its use, see Leni Riefenstahl's classic film dealing with the Nazi Nuremberg rallies, Triumph of the Will.

Her face, which bore a marked resemblance to her brother, showed no sign of gratitude. Charlie remained oblivious.

"To my friend, Llewelyn Price, I leave the portrait of Charles A. Lindbergh that he has always admired." The stage rotated to the point where Charlie's back was turned toward his gaunt co-worker so that he did not see the nod of approval that greeted his bequest. "I hope that my nephew, Jim Sebring, will accept and care for my dog, Spitfire." By this time, as the probing spotlight picked out Jim Sebring, Charlie was facing his nephew. Their eyes met for an instant and Charlie's expression softened as he read the tacit assent in Jim's face.

In this manner, Charlie continued, dispossessing himself, one by one, as tradition dictated, of everything he owned, down to the very ceremonial robe in which he stood—that, Charlie bequeathed to his teacher, Tobias Kopelnick. At each bequest, the spotlight flashed on so that the hushed crowd could lean forward and identify the beneficiary. Finally, Charlie intoned the ritual closing, "There being no objections to this my last will," he paused, "I do affirm myself to be neither creditor nor debtor to any person and herewith I sever the material bonds which have bound me to transient life."

A ruffle of tympani marked the end of the will.

"The airplane." In the darkness Evelyn Sebring plucked urgently at her husband's sleeve. "He's forgotten *Winged Chariot*," she whispered.

Jim Sebring responded by putting a restraining hand on his wife's arm. He was leaning forward, intent on hearing his friend's Final Testament.

Charlie's normally florid face was pale now. The irrepressible smile surrendered to approaching death. He leaned forward on the lectern, "This is my Last Testament." His voice was tremulous. "I am not a learned man, like my friend, Tobias." Tobias Kopelnick's white hair was caught for an instant in the spotlight. "I guess I haven't lived an optimum life." From the audience again came a murmur of assent; from the chorus, in unison, a keening sound.[49] "Still," Charlie raised his voice in defiance, "I've been mostly happy; I've loved a good woman." The spotlight sought out Martha, who

---

[49]Keening—a ritual wailing, used in some funeral ceremonies.

was now weeping. "I've had few friends, but they were good friends." Kopelnick, Ball, and Price were instantly framed in light. Charlie twisted his head, looking for his nephew, and quickly the light picked Jim Sebring out of the darkness, too.

"GOOD FRIENDS." The chorus echoed.

"I've been slowing down lately, but I've sent a good many planes on their way in my day." The night sky that canopied the amphitheatre gave way to a silent, three-dimensional replica of the Hartford Airstation. "And I learned to fly myself."

"TO FLY." The chorus echoed Charlie's pride, and the Hartford Airstation dissolved into *Winged Chariot*, the antique airplane in which Charlie had taught Jim Sebring to fly.

"I didn't choose to be born," Charlie's voice had dropped almost to a whisper again. "A man ought to make his own choices."

"CHOICES?" The chorus breathed the question.

"We ought to make our own choices." Charlie's voice shook with vehemence, and then became more subdued. "A man's gotta take responsibility for his choices, too." He paused. "I've made some bad choices."

"BAD CHOICES?" The chorus encouraged Charlie.

Sensing that Charlie was about to make his Confession, the congregation tensed.[50] The canopy was filled with storm clouds now. The odor of ozone permeated the amphitheatre, and the tympani began to beat softly and slowly.

"I've made mistakes."

"MADE MISTAKES?"

The rotating stage glided to a stop. Charlie peered into the darkness in front of the lectern. Gradually the figure of Martha Straun—still weeping—was illuminated. She turned her tear stained face toward him.

"I was not always," Charlie gulped, ". . . not always . . . faithful."

"NOT ALWAYS FAITHFUL!" The chant stabbed the darkness.

"It didn't mean anything," Charlie pleaded.

Martha's chin had fallen to her chest. She muttered something inaudible.

---

[50]In **CONFESSING**, Charlie meets another requirement of "brainwashing," that of deprecating the old identity before exchanging it for a new one.

"I knew about it." Martha was sobbing quietly.

"SHE KNEW!" affirmed the chorus.

"I . . . was very hurt and . . ." Martha's voice trailed off.

AND?" The chorus queried.

"And I was unfaithful, too."

"SHE WAS UNFAITHFUL, TOO!" The chorus raised its communal voice above the now louder and more insistent tympani.

"Martha!" Charlie reproved. His shocked expression softened. "Well," he paused, "I guess it's only fair."

"ONLY FAIR," the chorus affirmed.

"I don't mind going by myself," Charlie pressed on, "I'm ready . . ." Martha's glistening eyes were turned toward him again, "but I don't like to think of you left alone."

"LEFT ALONE."

Martha nodded her understanding and sympathy and then faded into darkness as the stage again began rotating.

The invisible, probing fingers of the Remote Scan detected increased metabolic activity somewhere in the southwest quadrant of the Inner Circle. The tense figure of the New Englander, Jonah Ball, was illuminated and the orbiting stage glided to a stop. The tympani sounded a ruffle again and then resumed its steady, though somewhat quickened, beat.[51]

"Jonah, my friend." Charlie was again leaning forward over the lectern, peering myopically at the flight instructor.

Jonah Ball cleared his throat, "Charlie, I was thinking about the accident." Ball licked his lips. "I mean the investigation and all."

Charlie Hazlitt nodded. "Yeah, Jonah, we really wiped that plane out."

"It was you the security people grounded, Charlie."

"That's right, Jonah. They clipped my wings for two years. Negligence, they said—and falsifying the records." Charlie shook his head as if rendering his judgment on their judgment.

---

[51]The tympani is just one constituent of that part of the brainwashing formula which calls for **SUPER-STIMULATION**. Music of some kind almost invariably accompanies fervent rhetorical situations. There are reasons for supposing that the rhythmic element (exemplified in military marching, rock concerts, hypnosis, etc.) has physiological effects that render one more susceptible to persuasion.

"It was me that did it. I was the one who cooked the maintenance records." Jonah ran shaking fingers across his sweating forehead. "It was me they should've grounded."

"That was a long time ago, Jonah," Charlie interrupted, "besides, I knew it wasn't me. I guessed it was you. But what the hell? If the security people gotta hang somebody, Old Charlie was as good as anybody. Besides, you'd've lost your job."

"I'm sorry, Charlie. It wasn't right." The flight instructor's head was bowed now.

Charlie nodded. "It's all right now, Jonah. It doesn't matter any more."

"DOESN'T MATTER ANY MORE." The chorus echoed as Jonah Ball vanished in the darkness.

From across the stage out of the darkness came a muffled sob and the spotlight picked out the pinched face of Sandra Hazlitt, Charlie's unmarried sister. The pace and intensity of the beating tympani increased perceptibly as the rotating stage brought Charlie face to face with the now openly sobbing woman.

"I hate you, Charlie Hazlitt; I hate you!" Sandra Hazlitt leapt to the stage and began pounding Charlie's broad chest with clenched fists.

Charlie stood his ground, face waxen, making no attempt to defend himself. In the darkness, Leventritt half rose from the Roman bench and then, as Sandra's fists fell to her sides and her sobbing subsided, he sat down again. Charlie had grasped his sister by the shoulders and, holding her at arm's length, pleaded, "It was so long ago, Sandra." Her tear-stained face tilted upward towards his.

"LONG AGO?" The chorus inquired mercilessly.

"I was just a boy."

In the darkness Leventritt tensed.

"JUST A BOY." Reiterated the chorus.

"You were a man; a brutal man." Sandra screamed her refutation.

"HE WAS A MAN, A BRUTAL MAN!" the chorus affirmed.

"You got what you wanted in a man's way," she hissed the words. "You molested me, Charlie Hazlitt!" Her voice rose to a scream. "Molested me, your own sister! That's what you did!"

"HE MOLESTED HER!" The chorus repeated the charge.

"I really did wrong." Charlie's head was bowed, hiding his stricken face, his voice a whisper.

"HE DID WRONG." The communal voice rose toward the arched dome, which now displayed a hologram of Charlie as he had appeared nude at his Puberty Ceremony.[52]

Charlie fell to his knees, sobbing now, "Forgive me, Sandra, forgive me."

"FORGIVE! FORGIVE!" the chorus urged.

"To err is human; to forgive, divine." The sonorous voice of Leventritt emanated from the great dome.

"FORGIVE! FORGIVE!" Again the chorus was keeping time with the now racing tympani.

"Forgive!" A voice rose from the otherwise hushed congregation.

"Forgive, forgive . . ." The rest of the crowd in the amphitheater took up the chant.

Sandra Hazlitt took a step toward her kneeling brother and the crowd fell silent. The furious throbbing of the drums continued. Leventritt was standing now, one arm outstretched pointing toward the penitent Charlie, the other toward his sister as if urging their reunion. From all sides of the arena came the sound of sobbing.[53]

Finally, Sandra took the last two steps toward her stricken brother and reaching down gently, lifted his bowed face upward and uttered the ritual phrase, "All is well between me and thee now and forever."

"ALL IS WELL." The chorus exulted.

"All is well," intoned Leventritt as he urged Charlie from his knees into the arms of his sister.

"All is well," the congregation echoed.

Leaving Charlie and Sandra clinging to each other, Leventritt turned to the silver tray which bore the ceremonial wine—Aqua Vie. Slowly, deliberately, he raised the decanter of amber fluid and filled each of the fourteen

---

[52]Presumably here is the biographical fact that has eluded Leventritt for so long—and has led to chronic loss of time for Charlie.

[53]The audience, of course, is an integral part of the ritual and what is **SUPER-STIMULATING** for Charlie is **RE-STIMULATING** for them. According to the brainwashing formula, it is necessary that the believer be regularly re-stimulated (re-subjected to the conditions that prevailed at the moment of crisis, abreaction, conversion, indoctrination, etc.) lest the original belief be lost.

goblets that surrounded it. He moved to the periphery of the once again slowly rotating stage and, as he drew abreast of them, handed a glass of Aqua Vie to each of the Inner Circle celebrants. When only three goblets remained, he gently separated Charlie and Sandra and handed a goblet of Aqua Vie to each of them. Finally Leventritt guided Charlie to the periphery of the stage so that he stood facing Evelyn Sebring.

Evelyn stood and, tears of ecstasy running down her cheeks, touched her goblet to that of Charlie's so that the tiny tinkling sound was audible throughout the now hushed amphitheatre. "All is well between me and thee now and forever." Charlie and Evelyn repeated the ritual phrase in unison.

They stood for a second thus gazing at each other until a single muffled stroke of the tympani urged Charlie counterclockwise to repeat the ritual with Jim Sebring and with each of the other celebrants of the Inner Circle in turn. As Charlie moved around the Inner Circle, forgiving and being forgiven, the great dome of the amphitheatre radiated the changing colors—the oranges, the violets, the crimsons of a late autumn sunset as it might be seen from above the clouds. In the background sounded the slowly rising choral anthem, "All Is Well—Hallelujah," set to the ancient music of Handel. The chorus and congregation, now standing with hands and arms interlocked, swayed to the rhythm of the Great Anthem.

Finally, having come full circle, Charlie turned to face Leventritt, who had by now raised his own glass. "Charles Mortimer Hazlitt, All is Well." Leventritt's voice blended with that of the chorus. The two goblets came together and then fourteen glasses of Aqua Vie were emptied as one at a single draught. Charlie Hazlitt stood now at the very center of the stage, his face calm, almost ethereal,[54] as the tympani roared and circle after circle of swaying, ecstatic singers joined the chorus in affirming, "ALL IS WELL! ALL IS WELL! HALLELUJAH!"[55]

---

[54] Charlie is experiencing the state of **EUPHORIA** called for by the formula.

[55] The tenth and final point, the act of **PROSYLETIZING**, is missing, but we may assume that the participants in this ceremony will go out and "spread the gospel."

8

DO NOT GO GENTLE[56]

The sky was already beginning to darken and a large cumulus thundercloud drifted slowly overhead completely obliterating the sunshine. In the distance the Great Clock tolled as Jim Sebring walked briskly up to the entrance of the Environmental Service Center. The tolling clock did not register on his mind, and neither did the first cold heavy drops of rain that had begun to fall. He glanced toward his wrist, conscious of the fact that he'd been compulsively looking at his chronometer all morning. He was aware that knowing the time could not tell him what he really wanted to know, but he did not seem able to check his reflexive behavior. The final farewells had been said, and Charlie's earthly ties had been cut. What real difference did it make, he asked himself, what precise moment Uncle Charlie would die?

It was a matter of official policy that after going through their terminal rights ceremony, each person had the right to spend what time remained as they wished. Charlie had chosen to spend his last day privately. Jim could see how this fit Charlie's personality, but he also wished that Charlie had chosen otherwise. In any event, though, the choice was Charlie's and Jim knew he needed to respect his uncle's decision.

As he entered the building, Jim nodded briefly to a pilot who was just leaving and then made his way, slowing his pace a little, towards the Meteorological Communications Section. He told himself once again as the door to Met Comm slid open in front of him that he must remove all thoughts of Charlie from his mind. He told himself Natasha was right; it was

---

[56]An allusion to the poem by Dylan Thomas.

the only sane thing to do. But then he wondered, would she expect him to do the same thing when it was her time, when she'd made all her farewells, performed all her duties, received her rites?

Yes, she would. That's exactly what she would expect, or at least that's what she'd want. Well then, perhaps he wasn't sane at all because he could not wipe Charlie from his mind. And the thought of Tasha leaving him was incomprehensible. He smiled a dry smile. He'd only just found her in time to lose her. No—he didn't want to deal with that thought. It made him feel deserted.

He entered the Met Comm Section, shaking off these things. They were selfish, useless thoughts.

The room vibrated with activity. Two or three videophones buzzed, sometimes alternately, sometimes simultaneously. The Aircraft Communications Radio blurted into life sporadically with pilot reports and queries.

Colin Jeffries, the section supervisor, bounced between the readout consoles, videophones, weather display, and microphones. Jeffries, as always, ignored Jim Sebring in favor of an exaggerated display of interest in the tools of his trade.

Jim looked around the room, nodded, and smiled at a few familiar faces and finally saw Natasha seated in front of a readout console. The console clicked busily and she was reading off the data and punching the keys of a computer on her left. The large screen above her head blinked its interminable security message: HE WHO DIES BY ACCIDENT DIES ALONE.

"Hey, Tasha!" he called.

She looked up and grinned at him.

"Come on. Time for a break." He motioned with his hand.

She nodded. "Stand by one minute," she said, as she turned to call across the room. "Colin, I'm taking a break. Can you live without me?"

Jeffries crossed towards her and shook his head soberly. "It's not going to be easy, lover," he said, grinning at Jim as he slid his arm around her hips.

Natasha shrugged. "Well, after all, Colin," she said, patting his hand on her hip, "nothing comes easy, does it?"

"I'll meet you in five," she yelled to Jim and then turned and tapped away with renewed energy at the computer keyboard.

"Screw the weather. Make it three." Jim was glaring at Jeffries.

"Right," she threw back. "I'll be there in three."
Mollified, Jim grinned and left.

———

Jim sipped at the synthesized mixture that passed for coffee at the Nutrition Center, and then he sat with his hands wrapped around the mini-urn and let the warmth penetrate his fingers. He stared down at the black abyss of his coffee and tried consciously to erase his mind into a blank. Across from him on the table sat a mini-urn of vitamix coffee in front of a vacant chair.

After a while, he shifted his gaze to the vacant chair and reflected futilely on his morbid frame of mind. His preoccupations had kept him awake most of the previous night and now, aided by his sleeplessness, they had grown almost obsessive. He glanced across at the entrance expectantly when he heard it slide open but returned to his somber thoughts when he saw that the newcomer was not Natasha.

The thought nagged at him that any one of these moments that he was idly whiling away could be Uncle Charlie's last. And every moment was one moment less of the forty-two days that Natasha had remaining. But Natasha seemed quite at peace with herself, he reasoned. She seemed only intent on getting the most out of what time she had left. She had asked nothing of him. They already knew now that theirs was just a fleeting encounter. "Written in the sand," she'd said. She'd told him about her D. Date so that he'd know that, too. And no doubt so that he would understand that this one fling would not be a total desertion of Evelyn. Evelyn would not know. It would not hurt her. And afterwards, when it was over—when Tasha was gone—he'd try to settle down, work things out with Evelyn, work for D. Date compatibility. Evelyn was a good person. It was only that she and he were so different.

He wasn't being fair to Evelyn, but he'd live with the guilt—he'd live with it because he couldn't live without Tasha, not at least while there was any time left for them. And afterwards . . .

The door slid open again and Natasha entered.

He smiled as he watched her approach and everything else except Tasha, except for his need for Tasha, left his mind.

"I missed you, Tasha."

"I've missed you, too."

"I've been thinking . . ."

She shook her head and pulled the mini-urn of vitamix coffee towards her. "Don't think, Jim." She smiled. "Sometimes it just isn't a good idea to think. Now, where's the salt?"

"In the brew."

They sat silently for a while. The lighting overhead flickered off momentarily and then on again.

"Overloading," Jim muttered.

"No, I don't think so. A cold front is dumping heavy snow on the solar panels in the hills."

"Oh." He wished the conversation hadn't taken this turn.

There was another pause and they sat looking at each other with solemn faces.

"I take it you find Jeffries interesting?" he said finally.

"I take it he finds me interesting," she retorted.

"Tasha . . ."

"I work with the man," she said.

"Well, he seems pretty familiar."

She didn't speak immediately but paused to take a sip of her vitamix. "He is," she said finally, returning his stare evenly.

Jim shrugged his shoulders and diverted his gaze.

"He's not important," Natasha said.

Jim slouched sulkily in his chair.

"Hey," Natasha said reaching across the table to take his hand, "are you worrying about Charlie?"

He shrugged again without answering.

"Charlie's okay. It was a beautiful ceremony. He was prepared."

"You were there?" he asked surprised.

"Yes."

"I didn't see you."

"I know."

"I can't help wondering, Tasha, if he's gone yet, if he's finally fallen asleep, or if his spirit's already . . . "

"Don't, Jim."

"Maybe Charlie's fighting it. Maybe he's trying to hang on—fighting to stay awake—some people do, you know."

"I know," she said, "some people do, but not Charlie. Charlie's a fighter all right, but Charlie knew what to fight and when." She reached for his hands again. "Charlie knows . . . knew . . . that he'd have to sleep sooner or later, and he wouldn't resist the inevitable."

"I still can't help wondering if he's gone yet."

"Does it really matter?"

"It matters." Jim's voice shook. "Alive is one thing, dead is another."

"Jim, I don't think you understand." Her voice remained gentle. "Can't you see that he was gone already last night? He'd given up his job, surrendered his possessions, cut his ties with society, bade farewell to his friends. Don't you see that except in body Charlie ceased to exist, too?[57] Grieve, Jim, if you must, but not for Charlie; he's gone already and he was prepared to go."

Jim watched her closely for a moment. "Do you think so, Tasha? Do you really think he was ready?"

"He was prepared," she said. "I don't know if anybody is ever ready. Some are not even ready to live, let alone die. I don't know if one can ever be ready, but prepared—yes, I think one *can* be prepared to die and I know Charlie was. His whole life showed it."

"Hell, that's absurd," Jim said. "Charlie Hazlitt lived life like he meant it, not like some Gorasdamn saint getting ready to die."

"That's precisely the point, Jim. You can't live the way Charlie lived if you haven't come to terms with death—prepared for it. Unwillingness to face death—that mistaken sense of immortality—robs life of its meaning. It's a law of economics; what is infinitely abundant has no value. Death is what gives life its poignancy. Charlie knew that—he had to." Natasha was leaning forward now grasping both of Jim's hands. "That's what caused him to wring every last drop out of life and then wring it some more just in case there was something he'd missed." She paused, embarrassed at her own intensity, self-conscious because she knew that *he* knew it was Natasha and

---

[57]Natasha here is raising the issue of the social construction of the "self." If we strip away all links with society, what remains?

not Charlie they were talking about now. "Here endeth the first lesson." She grinned apologetically.

"I'm sorry, Tasha. That was pretty damn thoughtless of me."

"No, Jim . . . no, it's all right . . ."

"Tasha," he said. "I know we've had hardly any time together. And I'll admit, I feel cheated, terribly cheated." He cupped his hands over hers now. "But by Goras, we'll squeeze a lifetime into forty-two days. I promise you that, Tasha, we'll . . ."

"NATASHA MOLLENSKAYA, REPORT IMMEDIATELY TO MET COMM . . . NATASHA MOLLENSKAYA, REPORT IMMEDIATELY TO MET COMM."

The urgent summons over the public address system blotted out his words.

Natasha got to her feet as the message repeated itself. "Something's up, Jim. I've got to go."

He reached for her. "Tasha, wait. Don't go right now. Wait for a minute."

"I've got to go, Jim. Something's wrong. They wouldn't call . . ."

"NATASHA MOLLENSKAYA, REPORT IMMEDIATELY TO MET COMM."

She leaned over and kissed him, clinging for an instant. "Finish your coffee," she said pulling away, "and then come and get me."

He watched her weave her way around the tables and vanish through the exit.

Natasha moved behind Colin Jeffries, who was studying the early morning weather scans, tracing with his finger the diagonal line of frontal activity.

"What's up?" she asked.

"Any update on this?" he said without acknowledging her question.

Natasha glanced at the hieroglyphics at the top right hand corner of the scan. "No, that's it. There should be another update within half an hour."

"How much snow have we got out here in the Catskills?" he said, indicating an area thirty or so miles to the west of Hartford.

"Ground cover?"

"Yes."

"I can only guess. That storm moved in a couple of hours ago. It was a freak. Pilot reports indicate heavy snowfall though—I'd say at least six inches—but it's over now and there'll be no more."

"Good, that'll make it easier for the search team." Jeffries nodded his satisfaction. "And the six inches that's already there could save the poor bastard's neck."

"For Goras's sake, Colin . . ." Natasha was interrupted as the door at the end of the briefing room slid open to admit the gangling figure of Jim Sebring.

Jeffries frowned.

Jim walked quickly over to where they stood and, ignoring the supervisor, addressed Natasha,

"What's the flap, Tasha? When can you leave?"

"She can't." Jeffries' voice lacked the respect due a Senior Captain and Lucifer Flight Pilot.

"Why the hell not?"

Jeffries glanced up at him. "Crash," he said as he turned back to the scanning screen. "Somebody iced up in the storm, or flew blind into the side of a mountain." He turned toward Natasha. "Anyway, Natasha, you'd better stick around till they've found him. It shouldn't take long."

"Of course."

"Iced up in this day and age? Iced up, hell. What kind of an airplane would do that?" Jim's cheeks flushed slightly.

"This one was an antique—a biplane. God knows what kind of idiot would fly into a storm like that in some ancient rattletrap."

"Antique biplane?" Jim turned to look at Natasha, and they stood for a long moment staring at each other.

"Rescue module went out over an hour ago," Jeffries glanced from one to the other. "They may even have him by now."

"What's the ident of the plane?" Jim said. "Did you get a report on the number?"

"No, no word on that yet." Jeffries looked at him quizzically.

Jim's thoughts reached back. Something Charlie had said was pushing into his mind. "I did not choose to be born, and a man ought to make his own choices." "A man ought to make his own choices." Charlie had not mentioned *Winged Chariot* in his will. He hadn't given the plane to anybody. "A man ought to make his own choices"—Goras sake!

Natasha's fingers were rippling across the console keys. "I'll check to see if I can get any word on the aircraft ident."

Jim turned suddenly, crossed the room in three strides and grabbed one of the videophones.

"Give me Airports in Hartford area. I need Officer Tweedmuir in Operations." He spoke deliberately so as not to confuse the audio-directory system, and then waited. Why had he been so stupid? Charlie had as good as told them. That was the message. He thumped his fist on the table.

As if in response, the face of the Operations Officer Tweedmuir flashed on the screen.

"This is Senior Captain James Sebring. I want to know if Charles Hazlitt took his plane out."

"When? Took out his plane today?" The response was impatient.

"Yes, today, last night, anytime?" Jim's voice was quick, irritable.

"I don't know, really." The face on the screen looked disinterested.

"Well, damn it, find out and find out fast. This is urgent."

"All right! All right! I'll call the tower."

"You don't have to call the tower," Jim said quickly. "Slap your glasses on the third stall from the southeast corner of the field. See if there's a big German shepherd waiting there."

"I don't have to do that." The Operations Officer's face grimaced. "That sonofabitch has been howling all morning. Damned if . . ."

Jim abruptly turned the V-phone off. His gaze, vacant at first, focused on the blinking message that occupied an otherwise unused briefing screen: "SECURITY FIRST, SECURITY LAST, SECURITY ALWAYS," he repeated.

Jeffries and Natasha were staring at him.

"I'll be damned!" he muttered, oblivious to them and to the others in the room who were beginning to glance questioningly in his direction. "Charlie, you dog," he said talking to the screen. "You dog, Charlie."

He turned on his heel and walked slowly to where Natasha and Jeffries stood waiting for him. They were murmuring quietly together.

"Jim," Tasha said. "I have the number on the plane. Six Zero . . ."

"I know." He looked at her steadily. "I know the number."

Natasha looked at him. "Charlie?"

"Just got word," Jeffries said, "the rescue module's picked him up already." His voice was more sympathetic now. "They've taken him over to the South Sector Life Conservation Unit. They'll be needing some details for the post mortem report." The supervisor's voice trailed off as he saw the look of impatience flicker across Jim Sebring's face.

Natasha intervened, reaching for Jim's hand. "You'd better get over there."

"Good old Charlie," Jim murmured.

They headed for the exit hand in hand.

9

RELUCTANT LAZARUS[58]

A sharp, high-pitched whistle suddenly pierced the quietness. It continued to emit its shrill wavering alarm at two-second intervals, announcing the arrival of an Emergency Admit to the Factor Assessment Unit (FAU) of the South Sector Life Conservation Center.

The entrance to the FAU slid noiselessly open and a couple of members of the Rescue Shuttle entered, deftly guiding a medical transporter which bore the inert figure of a man. Two medical technicians relieved the rescue people smoothly enough so that the transporter never stopped moving.

"This the crash victim we got over the wire?" The interrogator was the taller of the two technicians, a slim, smooth-faced youth.

"Yep, tried to move a mountain with an antique airplane." The respondent was a squat, burly rescue man whose ruddy face bespoke much exposure to the elements. "The mountain didn't budge." The rescue man snickered.

The slim one, busy steering the transporter around a sharp curve in the white marble corridor through which they were hurrying, did not acknowledge the humor.

"You guys telemetered the vitals and forgot the I.D. I'm holding a line open to Master Med and Master Med wants the line back. They're unhappy, very unhappy,' the young medical technician admonished.

---

[58] *Lazarus* is the character in the Christian *Bible's New Testament* whom Jesus raised from the dead. Its use here foreshadows what is to happen to Charlie in the chapter to come. The name is frequently used in modern literature and is almost always an allusion to the biblical story. Sylvia Plath's poem, *Lady Lazarus*, in which she writes of being revived after having attempted suicide, is an excellent example.

"Well, they're going to be a lot more unhappy." The second rescue man, about the same height as his colleague but fatter and now out of breath, joined the debate. "We don't have an I.D." The rescue man continued, "I went through his duds twice. There was no Card, no nothin'." The trio was slowing down as the entrance to the Factor Assessment Theatre loomed in front of them.

"Damn!" The smooth-faced technician swore as he stepped aside, allowing his fatter colleague to wheel the transporter through the door, which had rolled quietly open as they approached. The two rescue men had come to a halt, recognizing the limits of their jurisdiction.

"Well, I guess if I were going to rearrange the landscape with an airplane I wouldn't want the Security people to know who I was either," the ruddy rescue man volunteered.

"There'll be hell to pay," said the slim medical technician, finding no humor in the situation. "Make sure your report shows that we didn't get a positive I.D.," he growled, swinging on his heel and following his colleague into the Factor Assessment Theatre.

Senior Medical Technician David Briles rubbed his smooth face and frowned as he watched his junior colleagues busily hooking up multiple sensor units to the battered, now nude, and still inert body of his unidentified patient. Briles' job, always important but also relatively simple, had suddenly become complicated. His morning, routine and routinely pleasant to this point, had suddenly gone sour.

He nodded his head by way of acknowledging that his blood-splattered colleague had finished placing the last sensor. Briles turned with trepidation towards the massive array of switches, dials, lights, and screens that covered one side of the theatre. He was not awed by the complexity of it all; indeed, he relished his mastery of it and even coveted a few more instruments with which to make the array even more impressive. But now, because some idiot had violated the cardinal rule—the rule which required every citizen to carry his D. Date card at all times—now he, Briles, was going to have to try to cheat his machine. He was not confident.

Normally, those probing sensors would relay to Master Med a continuous record of no less than thirty-seven biological variables. The Master Med computers would retrieve the patient's records, carefully compiled from the data supplied by routine monthly medical examinations, and compare the data Briles sent with normal parameters for the patient. Consulting its vast storehouse of medical knowledge, the computer would then provide Briles with an L.C.F. readout, a diagnosis, and instructions for therapeutic intervention. Only the first of these, the Life Consumption Factor, concerned Briles directly; the diagnosis and therapy instructions he merely relayed to the appropriate units.

The L.C.F. readout indicated the rate at which the patient was losing time and consequently the seriousness of his illness. On the basis of that readout Briles could determine to which of the four major units within the Center the patient should be sent. Unit I handled patients whose L.C.F. readout was less than ten. These patients, usually picked up at monthly medical exams, were temporarily losing not more than ten days of life each calendar day. Somewhat more critical were patients whose Life Consumption Factor lay, again temporarily, between ten and a hundred; these people were dealt with by Unit II. Unit III handled L.C.F.'s between a hundred and a thousand—regarded as critical. Life Consumption Factors above one thousand, where a patient was losing at least a thousand days for each calendar day, were Priority One Emergencies, handled by Unit IV. Those who didn't get out of Unit IV fast graduated to the Morgue.

Briles, reaching for the master switch, glanced toward the battered patient. His practiced eye told him that here was a Unit III case at least—perhaps worse. The decision, however, lay not with him but with the computer—thank heavens. The Senior Medical Technician, using both hands, switched on a whole row of yellow switches and watched as thirty-seven monitoring lights turned green—one intermittently. Briles motioned to his junior colleague to adjust the offending sensor and opened the line to Master Med. The Master Med computer simultaneously acknowledged the transmission and complained about the intermittent reading, one in the hematology group. Briles' fingers moved across the console, deftly acknowledging the complaint; he did not wish to offend the mighty Master Med computer.

"Change that bloody sensor, will you, Johnson!" Briles was less concerned about the feelings of his junior colleague. The order was gratuitous, as Johnson was already completing the task.

"That does it," the junior technician said. "She's quit winking at us." The offending light was indeed now registering a solid green.

Briles merely grunted and tapped his first request into the console—one which he was quite sure would be denied:

L.C.F.?

The computer responded immediately:

SUBJECT IDENTITY?

Briles' hand went reflexively to his smooth chin as he glanced at the problematic request. The elapsed time chronometer had begun measuring the efficiency of his performance the moment the patient had entered the Factor Assessment Theatre, and he knew that time was slipping away. "Well, here goes nothing;" he said, addressing himself as much as his junior colleague. He went to work on the console again.

SUBJECT: MALE CAUCASIAN, 5' 8", 180 LBS.
L.C.F.?

Again the response was instantaneous:

SUBJECT IDENTITY INADEQUATE. ENTER D. DATE CARD.

Briles sighed. He'd given the machine only information which it could have, and no doubt already had, deduced for itself—he knew it, the machine knew it, and judging by the look on his face, even Johnson knew it.

"Don't just stand there, you idiot, get a P.H.O. on standby," Briles snarled at his assistant. He played his last card:

SUBJECT: PILOT. CRASH VICTIM. HARTFORD. L.C.F.?

Accidents of any sort were rare these days, so if the aviation people had reported this one, the computers might have identified the aircraft and, through it, the pilot. The Master Med computer was no doubt querying its subordinate computers at this very moment, but with negative results:

SUBJECT IDENTITY INADEQUATE. ENTER D. DATE CARD!

This response was identical to the last except for the exclamation point, which Briles recognized as a reprimand, a mechanical reprimand, against which there was no appeal.

"Okay, signal the P.H.O., dammit." The senior technician stared balefully at the lapsed time chronometer again—four minutes thirty-seven seconds already and no solution in sight. Under normal circumstances he would have had the patient on the way to the appropriate therapy unit in three minutes or less.

"Dr. Montenez is on her way down." Johnson's voice made it clear that he did not share his superior's discomfort at this admission of defeat. Before Briles could think of some way of making Johnson pay, the door slid open and the willowy figure of Dr. Maria Montenez swept through.

"What's the problem, Briles?" She did not wait for a reply but rather crossed immediately to the patient, one hand searching for a pulse and the other pressing back his eyelids. Releasing the eyelids, her gaze swept across the monitoring section of the readout display.

"Good Goras!" she exclaimed. "Why isn't this patient on his way up to Unit IV?"

"We don't know who he is, Dr. Montenez." Briles' voice took on a distinct whine.

"In a few minutes it will be a matter of supreme inconsequence who he is, for he will certainly be dead."

Johnson was already wheeling the medical transporter toward the Factor IV Delivery Port.

"But, Dr. Montenez, Master Med couldn't give me a Life Consumption Factor readout until I give them an ident, and this patient came in without his I.D. Card," Briles protested.

"Mr. Briles," the P.H.O. brushed a stray wisp of her auburn hair from her eyes, "in the first place, you should not be so dependent on the computers that you can't spot an L.C.F. obviously in the thousands. In the second place, you could have done no harm had you risked over-estimating the seriousness of the patient's condition and sent him directly to Unit IV as soon as the hitch developed." She paused to acknowledge Johnson's signal that the patient had been dispatched and then went on. "In the third place, diagnosis may depend upon the patient's genetic and medical history and therefore upon his identity, the Life Consumption Factor certainly does not."

"Someone should tell that to Master Med," Briles grumbled sulkily.

"I intend to do just that, Mr. Briles, but in the meantime I expect you to demonstrate that this machinery is your servant—not your master." She paused and said, "Now, get the Director of Master Med on the line."

"Noel Baker Smyth?" The senior technician was obviously taken aback.

"Yes, Noel Baker Smyth himself." She pivoted on her heel and made toward the exit. "I'll take it up in Unit IV," she called over her shoulder as the exit slid closed behind her.

Dr. Mitsuo Tamaka gazed at the three blank readout apertures and repeated the expostulation a second time, "No L.C.F., no diagnosis, and no recommended therapy. I'm a doctor, not a bloody computer. What do they expect me to do?" Tamaka raised his hands helplessly.

"They expect you to save this patient if that's still a possibility. That's what they expect, *Doctor*." Maria Montenez was fuming.

"Maria, Maria," Tamaka protested, "if the computer would do its job and give me some instructions," he waved at the empty readout apertures, "I'd be happy to save the man."

"Very well, Doctor, I will be your computer." Montenez was studying the elaborate electronic display of the Unit IV Therapy Section. She deliberately mimicked the metallic "voice" of the computer's audio mode. "Life Consumption Factor is above one thousand and rising astronomically." She shifted her gaze to the cardio-vascular display. "B.P. differential is very low . . . correction: has just become zero." Again her glance shifted. "The central nervous system is severely depressed . . . the E.K.G. is nearly flat . . . and . . . there is clear evidence of renal insufficiency . . . no broken bones . . . exterior wounds are superficial. Doctor, I'd say you're looking for cerebral trauma and kidney damage and I'd say if you don't get this patient on life support pretty damn quick it won't matter what you're looking for."

Tamaka looked at her hesitantly.

"Pretty damn quick," she repeated in a firm voice.

Tamaka motioned to his two assistants, who without a word went to work on the catheters. Tamaka himself turned to the panel behind him and began rapidly throwing switches and positioning controls. Maria Montenez divided her attention between the comatose figure of Charlie Hazlitt and the E.K.G. readout. Tamaka's assistants had finished with catheters and turned to help their chief with the maze of switches and dials that operated the Life Support System. The machine began sucking Charles Mortimer Hazlitt's blood.

Montenez glanced from her patient's face to the E.K.G.—this time merely to confirm her diagnosis—the electroencephalogram was flat. "Gentlemen," she addressed their backs, "your patient, whoever he is, is dead."

Tamaka did not turn. "No, Doctor. I don't think so," he paused. "Your patient may be dead; mine is just coming to life." He gestured toward the bubbling column of blood, Charlie's blood, and then to a second E.K.G. Whether the blood now belonged to Charlie, or was that of the machine, or perhaps a mixture of the two, was impossible to tell, but it was indeed beginning to dance. Montenez stared across Charlie's inert body at the backs of her busy colleagues and at the dancing E.K.G., mesmerized. Perhaps the machine had given the patient back his life or perhaps the patient had given the machine life—she could not tell.

Tamaka adjusted one of the controls. "You're right," he exclaimed, "the central nervous system is severely depressed, but the scan shows no cerebral damage." Tamaka's plump face wrinkled, like the top of an overripe tomato, in puzzlement. "Odd, the kidneys seem okay, but something's getting through that's not getting past full dialysis." He brushed back his close-cropped thick black hair. His eyes never left the readout display.

"That is unusual in an accident case," Montenez allowed. "It could account for the low cerebral activity, though." She was intently examining the patient. She looked up at Tamaka and his colleagues, deciding that life, if it existed at all, had flown from her patient into the bowels of Tamaka's machine. Her ruminations along that line were interrupted by a clanging ring of the videophone. The smooth face of the technician, David Briles, flashed onto the screen.

"We got a fellow down here who may be able to give us a positive I.D. on the patient."

This time Tamaka didn't hesitate. "Send him up pronto, and open a line to Master Med."

He was obviously relieved at the prospect of assigning the problem and the responsibility to the Master Med computer.

Jim Sebring emerged from the Sterilization Unit and followed the tall hurrying figure of the Senior Medical Technician past the corridor which led to Unit III, turning rather toward a door marked UNIT IV THERAPY. He'd expected to find Charlie already in the morgue, but as far as he'd been able to gather from the close-lipped senior technician, Charlie had still been alive, though unconscious, when they'd dragged him from the wreckage of *Winged Chariot*. Jim was glad that Charlie had not been conscious—it was too bad that a freak blanket of snow had robbed him of his last choice. Still, mercifully, Charlie couldn't know that.

The chief technician had stopped and turned to motion Jim into the Therapy Unit. Jim dutifully preceded the smooth-faced medic into the room.

"This is Captain Sebring," Briles announced without further ceremony.

Jim's eyes swept the room—six people altogether. Three were busy working at the technical array that dominated the far side of the Unit. Two more advanced to greet him, an Asian man and a tall, attractive woman. Between them in the center of the room—seemingly suspended in a jungle of wires and tubes like a fly caught in a spider's web—was the inert form of his Uncle Charlie.[59]

---

[59] As noted in footnote 17, flying is used throughout to symbolize being free, and especially free of the limitation (the web) of social control.

"Captain Sebring," the dark-haired Asiatic held out his hand, "I am Dr. Tamaka. This is my colleague, Dr. Montenez." She inclined her head in his direction. "I understand that you may be able to identify our patient." Tamaka's demeanor was suitably sober.

Patient! Jim stared at Tamaka. These idiots had actually been trying to save Charlie. For Goras' sake! Save him for what? But of course they didn't know.

Jim gave a grim chuckle. He became aware that the two doctors were staring at him, puzzled by his behavior and also anxiously awaiting a positive identification.

"Perhaps you would like to step a little closer." Tamaka motioned Jim toward the spider's web.

"No!" Jim was aware that his voice was too loud, too emphatic. "I mean, it's not necessary. That's the body of my uncle, Charles Mortimer Hazlitt."

Tamaka turned instantly to the chief technician. "Get that off to Master Med right away," he said. Maria Montenez put her hand on Jim's arm. "You don't understand, Captain Sebring. Your uncle—" she glanced uncertainly at Tamaka, "your uncle is not dead."

"Oh, good heavens, no!" Tamaka exclaimed, gesturing past Charlie's immobile body to the dancing wave forms and the flickering needles. "As you can see, he's really doing very well, all things considered."

Jim stared first at Tamaka and then at the battered, shriveled body of his friend at the center of the spider's web. "You must be joking." His voice reflected his incredulity. "Charlie Hazlitt's Terminal Rites were last night."

"Good Goras!" The ejaculation had come from one of Tamaka's assistants, all of whom had turned from the display panel in astonishment.

"It can't be!" Maria Montenez' face registered her disbelief.

Tamaka's mouth dropped open in dismay, and then, shocked into action, he lunged at the control panel, switching off the master switch of the Life Support System. The eyes of the five people were riveted on the E.K.G. as Jim followed their gaze. The dancing lines subsided a little; the symmetry and rhythm were gone, but a grotesque pattern remained—the bizarre dance of living death.

From the center of the web came an unearthly moan. Charlie's left leg twitched; his eyelids fluttered once and then opened.

Jim walked woodenly forward and bent over his friend. He was transfixed for a moment by Charlie's breathing, and by his wide, vacant, uncomprehending stare, and then, weeping, he turned and shouldered his way toward the door.

10

JOANNAH AND QUASIMODO[60]

"Eve, you're my best friend," Joannah said. She brushed a hand across her cheek. "I know you think I'm strange. I know everyone thinks I'm strange, but you're my best friend."

Eve nodded sympathetically. She had her mind on other things. Jim was very upset by the *thing* that had happened to Uncle Charlie. He didn't talk about it much to her. He didn't talk about anything much to her anymore. Evelyn suspected that he was being consoled by the Mollenskaya woman. And then there was her monthly physical which was scheduled for this afternoon and there would be her new D. Date and she knew of course that the birth of the baby would have cost her time—but how much time?

"I've never told anybody else how it is," Joannah said, "except Peter, of course, and he's forbidden me to ever tell anyone."

Evelyn put her arms around Joannah's shoulders. "Joannah, perhaps you shouldn't tell me things between you and Peter. No matter what, you should be loyal to him."

"No, no, no," Joannah protested, "you don't understand, Eve. I would never say anything bad about Peter. There is nothing bad to say."

"Whatever it is, Joannah," Evelyn glanced at the two D. Date calendars on the wall of her friend's apartment, "whatever it is, it can't be too impor-

---

[60] Quasimodo is the name of Victor Hugo's gentle misshapen hero in *The Hunchback of Notre Dame*.

tant." The calendars indicated that Joannah and Peter had a long time to live, and, what was more important, that they would die together.

"If Peter would just let me tell people who he is," Joannah said as she wiped another tear from her pale face, "if he wasn't so modest . . ." Her voice trailed off. "But he gets so angry, you see . . ."

"Joannah," Evelyn said softly, "Peter knows who he is. We all know who he is—the area Homeland Security Officer, and a very good one, too."

"Oh, no," Joannah protested for the second time, "that's not right at all. You must let me explain to you."

"All right," Evelyn said, finally giving in to Joannah, "but you mustn't take too long explaining. I have an appointment with my P.H.O."

Joannah heaved a sigh of relief and pulled Evelyn beside her as she sat down on the couch.

"You see, Eve, I love Peter," she began. "I have loved him from the moment I discovered that he was really Quasimodo."

"Quasimodo?"

"Yes. Oh, yes," Joannah exclaimed excitedly. "Isn't that a surprise?"

Evelyn nodded dumbly.

"Oh, don't feel badly, Eve," Joannah soothed. "Even I didn't recognize him before the accident. Then, he was so handsome—so debonair, more like the guard from *The Hunchback of Notre Dame*. I would never have known who Peter was then, because, you see, I knew the story, and besides our D. Dates were wrong. Even when he had that wreck in the E-car and crushed his shoulder and lost an eye, even then I didn't recognize him immediately—even though I had watched *The Hunchback* almost everyday on CLEM. But you see, Eve, because of the accident, Peter lost twenty-eight months from his natural D. Date and I discovered that he and I had the same D. Date."

Evelyn patted Joannah's hand gently. "Joannah, dear, you're getting things muddled up. Peter is Peter."

"No, Eve," Joannah was shaking her head, "You must let me tell you so you'll understand. You see, I knew who Peter really was because I knew his story and I understood about the transmigration of souls and about reincarnation. I loved my father so very much, but he died in an accident while I was still a child. And my mother explained to me about all that, that my father was not really dead but that his soul had gone to find another body. And the body, you see, the one he found, would belong to a new baby born when he died. It was only later that I realized what could happen." She leaned forward, grasping Evelyn's hands intently. "You see, since souls have to find a new body very quickly, sometimes souls get into the wrong body. But I can always tell when this happens, and I could tell about Peter."

"And so you think Peter is Quasimodo?" Evelyn avoided looking at Joannah.

"Oh, yes, he is Quasimodo. But you see, Peter gets so angry. He's afraid that I'll tell people who he is."

Evelyn smiled at her friend sadly. "Well, I guess it doesn't really matter who you think Peter is. But I can understand Peter's problem. You see, you simply can't go around telling people that Peter is Quasimodo. What would they think?"

Joannah shook her head impatiently. "Eve, listen. You won't understand until I tell it all to you. I'm not really strange—people all over the world and for much of history have known that reincarnation is *true*. But you're the only one who will know about Peter and me after I tell you—except, of course, for Peter.[61] You see, one day when I was watching *The Hunchback of Notre Dame* on CLEM, I suddenly realized about me. You see, Eve, a long time ago I was Esmeralda—the gypsy dancing girl who was saved from the mob and protected by Quasimodo, the Hunchback."

"Oh, no, Joannah . . ."

"Yes, yes. You see I proved it. I wasn't absolutely sure myself at first, but I asked CLEM to give me the names of all the people whose D. Dates were on the day she was born. It turned out that in my last body I was a famous and very clever Italian mathematician. I was a man then, you see. And anyway he—that is I, when I was him—was born on the D. Date of a beautiful,

---

[61]We now see that Joannah has a coherent life narrative that under girds her thoughts, her actions, and her communication. The problem is that her life narrative does not mesh with the consensually validated understandings of her society. In fact, we cannot know if reincarnation is *true*, just as we cannot know that other explanations of what happens after death are *"true."* These are matters of *belief*. Yet, when belief structures come to be seen by the faithful as *matters of fact* beyond dispute, they influence greatly the lives of believers. *Perhaps the strongest persuasion occurs when "beliefs" become "truths."*

wanton, woman spy—and so on until I came to Esmeralda. Of course, when I was Esmeralda I loved the handsome guard who was really a villain in the wrong body. As Esmeralda, I didn't realize that Quasimodo, the one-eyed hunchback, was a great lover in the wrong body and that he had wanted to be with me all the time, but had never tried to seduce me, because I was so beautiful and he was so ugly."

"I see," Evelyn said, staring at her friend in disbelief.

"You do understand now, don't you?" Joannah said, smiling at Evelyn. "I knew you would if I just explained it all to you."

Evelyn nodded slowly. "I understand, Joannah."

Joannah, the tension dissolving from her face, threw her arms around Evelyn. "I knew you would. I knew you would understand, Eve."

Evelyn hugged her friend and stroked her soft golden hair. She swallowed back the impulse to cry. "Of course I understand, Joannah."

Joannah pulled herself away and clutched Evelyn's arms, beaming with happiness. "Of course," she went on, "after his accident, when our D. Dates had become the same and I recognized Peter was really Quasimodo, well then, I told him that I knew who he really was and I tried to make it up to him. I made love to him every chance I got. He didn't seem to mind that I knew who he was. But now, you see, he gets upset when he thinks I might tell somebody who he is. I think it's because he's so modest."

"Joannah," Evelyn said quietly. "I think he's right. You must not tell people who Peter is."

Joannah stared at her friend, puzzled. "I don't understand. *I don't know why everyone shouldn't know who they are* and why everyone shouldn't know who everyone else is, too."

Evelyn shook her head. "No, people don't want to know who they are, Joannah. You must tell Peter that you're not going to tell anybody who he is either."

"Not tell anybody that Peter is Quasimodo?"

"No. After all, it doesn't really matter as long as you know, does it?"

"No, I suppose not. But I don't understand why not."

---

[62]There is a tradition in literature that clowns and madmen, in spite of their idiosyncrasy, see and tell the truth.

"Joannah, just tell Peter that you won't tell anybody, and everything will be all right. Don't even tell him that you told me."

"But I didn't tell you—that is, I only told you about Peter being Quasimodo. I didn't tell you about..."

"No, no!" Evelyn raised her hands in protest. "Please, Joannah, don't tell me who anyone else is."

Joannah stopped abruptly and stood looking at her friend, her eyes filling with tears. "I just don't know why nobody wants to know who they are," she said.

Evelyn patted Joannah on the arm and, gathering her coat, prepared to leave. "Joannah dear," she glanced again at the calendars, "you do know something... something more important than a lot of the rest of us."[62] She grimaced, "Talking of which, I'm late for my appointment with Dr. Leventritt."

11

BABEL[63]

"Post Natural Death is something of a puzzle to us, too, Evelyn, and of course, it is always distressing to the family and friends of the victim. Fortunately it's a rare phenomenon." Jeremy Leventritt was seated on the corner of his desk looking down at Evelyn Sebring. "It is only natural that your husband—that Jim—is upset, and I must say that as Charlie Hazlitt's P.H.O., I feel some responsibility."

Evelyn was barely listening. She had just emerged from her monthly physical examination, and ever since the baby had come, she'd worried about it. The baby would have cost her time and the trauma of giving birth could easily have disturbed her normally close-to-optimum Life Consumption Factor. The technician had taken the new readouts, the new D. Date, and L.C.F. an hour ago and for some reason withheld them. Evelyn started, guiltily aware that Leventritt was looking at her quizzically. She wracked her brain and remembered that he had been talking about Jim's uncle's situation.

"Oh, I don't think you had anything to do with it," she said. "Charlie is . . . was . . . that sort of a person. One never knew what he was going to do next."

"I should have anticipated his behavior all the same." Leventritt looked troubled.

"I've tried to explain to Jim that the Master Med computers could do nothing without an I.D., but he refuses to understand." Evelyn sighed.

---

[63] The biblical account claims that all the people of the earth spoke a single language until men tried to build a monument that would reach heaven itself (the Tower of Babel). God, displeased by humanity's hubris, brought the attempt to an end by causing the builders to speak in different languages.

"I think I can understand his chagrin. After all, without medical intervention, Charles Hazlitt would have died at the natural time if not quite in the natural way. As it is we are now faced with Post Natural Death—a condition we do not fully understand and which therefore simultaneously fascinates and horrifies us. Jim must be made to understand that some of the lurid tales about the so-called P.N.D.'s derives from our superstitions and is probably without foundation. In any case, he will have to face his fears."

"Jim is not the superstitious type. He doesn't believe in the Devil, so I don't think he thinks of Charlie's body as having been taken over or anything like that. It's just that he's heard about how the body continues to live even though it's decaying. I've told you how he loved his Uncle Charlie—it's hard for him to think of Charlie that way. He's terribly upset, angry and afraid. I'm afraid that . . . that . . ." Evelyn's voice trailed off, close to tears.

"And you're afraid that this will make things even worse between you and Jim," Leventritt urged.

Evelyn took a tissue from her purse and dabbed her tear-filled eyes. "All that anger, fear, and frustration can't be good for him. It will cost him time and God knows the situation is bad enough already."

Leventritt nodded in sympathy. "Last time we talked, the D. Date discrepancy had risen to eight months . . ."

". . . and twenty-four days," Evelyn replied.

"Chronic D. Date incompatibility is grounds for divorce. You know that."

"I don't want that." Evelyn was emphatic. "What I want, I guess, is to turn back the clock and to have things the way they were once. I want for Jim and me to share life AND death together."

"The birth of young Charles will have reduced the discrepancy somewhat, but I doubt it will have removed it altogether," Leventritt said tentatively.

It occurred to Evelyn that if today's readout had been disastrous, then obviously, Leventritt hadn't been told about it. "I know," she said.

"Another child, a third child, almost invariably costs twice as much time as the second. That would remove the discrepancy."

"I've thought about that, but Jim's not working at it." Her voice rose. "He doesn't give a damn. Why should I? I can't keep trading away my life. It's not reasonable. He's not reasonable. Why can't he live closer to optimum?"

Leventritt regarded her thoughtfully for a moment. "You know as well as I do, Evelyn, what causes D. Date attrition other than illness, accidents, and special situations like this Hazlitt affair."

"I know, I know," she said. "I know what but I don't know why!"

"People do physical damage to themselves with drugs. They're deceptive, dishonest, even violent. All these take their toll."

Evelyn stared steadily at the floor. "I've warned Jim about drugs and he's warned about his diet at every monthly medical, but he ignores the recommendations. Still, he's never had a high factor illness," she raised her head and fixed Leventritt with a defiant stare, "and Jim's not violent, dishonest, or deceptive." She paused. "At least he never used to deceive me." She spoke more quietly.

"Do you believe he's faithful to you now?"

"Yes!" Evelyn threw the reply back instantly. She was angry again. It was irrational, she knew. She waited for Leventritt to wait, as she knew he would. "I'm not sure," she said finally. "He's away so much ... you know ... his job—the Lucifer Flights. Anyway, I believe he still loves me."

"And you? Do you still love him? No regrets?"

"Of course," she said.

Leventritt remained silent again. It was a predictable habit of his. But the silence was long this time.

She understood suddenly.

"Of course I still love him," she said, "but I get angry sometimes."

"You mentioned your colleague, Mr. Smyth, last time." Leventritt changed the subject abruptly. "He seems to have impressed you as an intelligent and attractive man, and apparently he's attracted to you."

"He's not my colleague. He's my boss," Evelyn said blushing slightly, "and what does he have to do with anything?"

Leventritt didn't answer.

"He's a very kind, understanding and responsible person. I have never thought of him in any other way."

"Maybe you should."

"Look, Dr. Leventritt . . ." She felt her anger rising.

"Jeremy . . ." he interrupted.

She ignored him. "I know it's your job to explore the possibility of divorce in cases of chronic D. Date incompatibility, but Jim and I and the kids . . ."

"I understand." Leventritt smiled reassuringly. "Don't despair, Evelyn. I'm sure that Jim's P.H.O., Dr . . ." his left hand slid unobtrusively to the desk console and he glanced at the computer screen, "Dr. Calderoni is working with him. In any case, you know D. Date compatibilities often do fluctuate. It's a rare partnership that doesn't develop incompatibility at some time. Most manage to work it out."

Evelyn, unsure that Leventritt's prognosis was correct, avoided his eyes.

"Well," Leventritt paused, "let's make sure of our facts first. Klaus should have the new readout by now."

Evelyn wanted to ask Leventritt why she hadn't been allowed to watch her new D. Date and L.C.F. as it registered. That was the normal procedure and she could not understand why things were different this time. She restrained the impulse.

Leventritt was busy with the computer. The face of his assistant, Klaus Koehler, flashed onto the screen.

"Klaus, have the figures on Mrs. Sebring come through yet?"

"I'll check right away."

Leventritt prodded the computer once again and Koehler's face was replaced on the screen by a score of medical hieroglyphics. Leventritt studied them intently. "Hmmm. The dieticians are reasonably satisfied—want you to cut down on caffeine, as usual. The iron deficiency seems to be chronic."

Leventritt was talking more to himself than Evelyn. "Calcium's off, but that's because of the baby. It's temporary. Your uric acid is a bit high, but the prescription will take care of that. You did stop by the dispensary on the way up?"

"Of course."

Leventritt was filling time now, trying to relieve the tension of waiting for, quite literally, the fatal figures. Stopping by the dispensary for the "pill" was an invariable part of the monthly ritual. Thanks to the computer's analysis and prescription, Evelyn could be sure that whatever the deficiencies and excesses described by the medical hieroglyphics on the screen, the capsule would take care of them.

"Anyway," Leventritt continued, "provided the readouts are acceptable, I see no reason why you can't return to your job. In fact, it would be good for you." He poked the console impatiently and the face of his assistant reappeared on the computer screen. "Got those figures yet?" he said.

"Yes, they're on the line," Koehler responded without hesitation.

"Okay, patch them through now if you will."

Klaus Koehler nodded his assent and his face vanished, leaving the screen blank.

"Shall we have a look at your L.C.F. first?" Leventritt again gave Evelyn a reassuring smile.

Her mouth was dry and she felt her heart thumping. Stupid, she thought; she'd gone through this monthly ritual countless times, and yet, she was more nervous than ever. She licked her lips.

"Oh, I am sorry, Evelyn." Leventritt was looking at her closely. "Of course, you're wondering why you weren't allowed to watch the readout as it came in. That was really thoughtless of me." Leventritt looked genuinely stricken.

Evelyn decided once again that she really liked the man.

"We've been having trouble with unstable Life Consumption Factor readouts, especially in post-natal checks. But you have nothing to be concerned about, I'm sure."

Evelyn's doubt on that point obviously reflected on her face.

Leventritt hastened to explain, "As you know, the L.C.F. reflects conditions at the moment the reading is taken. In cases such as yours, where the subject has reason to suspect that there may have been substantial change, there is, understandably, a good deal of anxiety."

Evelyn nodded.

Leventritt continued, "The anxiety itself becomes part of the L.C.F. It raises the readout. The subject sees the elevated L.C.F. and this increases the anxiety, which raises the L.C.F. even more, and so on—regenerative feedback we call it."

Evelyn frowned, partly to hide her relief and partly in irritation at her own stupidity. Her job at Master Med demanded intimate understanding of the regenerative feedback phenomenon. Why hadn't she guessed?

"Well, you can be as nervous as you want now; you're not connected to the computer, so you can't affect this readout." Leventritt poked at the console and turned toward the screen.

SUBJECT: EVELYN SEBRING
L.C.F. 1.0020 (+.0015)

Evelyn breathed a sigh of relief. 1.0000 would have been perfect optimum living; consuming one day, and only one day for each calendar day. It would be too much to expect.

Leventritt was less pleased. "Good, but not as good as it was. Your last reading was 1.0005. As you can see, you're up a little. You've been worried over the Hazlitt affair, no doubt."

Evelyn wasn't listening; she was waiting for what came next—her new D. Date.

Leventritt smiled at her sympathetically. "Are you ready?"

"Yes." Her throat was tight so that the word, to her annoyance, came out thin and high pitched.

Leventritt prodded the computer. "This will merely be a video replay of the readout they took an hour or so ago," he observed.

Evelyn, watching the screen intently, said nothing.

SUBJECT: EVELYN SEBRING

The identification flashed on momentarily and then was replaced by a picture of the three, D. Date apertures—all vacant. Evelyn tensed as the numbers began to flash.

2222

The aperture on the left stabilized at 2222. That was the year. The other apertures lit up in sequence.

12.................21

The numbers returned her stare-unblinking: 2222-12-21. It was over and that was it. December 21st, 2222.

She said it aloud, "December 21st, 2222." She'd lost a year. Not really... but it was a different year. Her old D. Date had been 2223—May 3, 2223. She tried vainly to perform the subtraction in her head.

Leventritt solved the problem. "Four months and fourteen days or one hundred and thirty-four days to be precise—not bad for a second child." Leventritt looked genuinely pleased.

Evelyn said nothing, angry that he could be pleased at her loss. One hundred and thirty-four days. Men should bear children, she thought bitterly.

Leventritt did not notice. He was prodding the computer again. "That reduces the incompatibility to four months nine days," he observed. "Jim's D. Date is August thirteenth." He glanced toward her and added hastily, "But of course you know that."

Evelyn didn't respond. She'd thought about it a thousand times. As things stood, and with Jim things never stood for very long, he would be gone at the end of that summer. She'd be faced with the fall and winter alone. The idea of the winter she'd particularly dreaded. Well, now she wouldn't have to face that—just the fall. December 21, 2222; December 21st, the last day of autumn. Good heavens! The last day of autumn 2222—that was Noel's D. Date. She remembered having been surprised at the relatively close proximity of their D. Dates because he was a good deal older than she, and she recalled his explaining that his was on the longest, darkest night of the year—the last day of autumn.

Evelyn started laughing. Jim wouldn't like that. She and Noel Baker Smyth now shared perfect D. Date compatibility. She was laughing volubly now.

"Evelyn, what is it?" Leventritt was staring at her, embarrassed. "I'm sorry, Jeremy. It's just that... that..." Suddenly she was sobbing—sobbing uncontrollably, her frame shaking with emotion. It was too much. Jim and Uncle Charlie... and a hundred and thirty-four days... and the longest night of the year... and Noel. It was just too much.

Embarrassed at the emotional outburst, Evelyn had risen and made for the door. Leventritt crossed quickly over to her. Uncharacteristically, he grasped her hand.

"Evelyn," he said, "perhaps as your P.H.O. I ought not to say this, but I know how important D. Date compatibility is to you and how defeated you feel." He was gazing intently into her eyes. "Marriage, you know, is the state's method of insuring that two people conduct their private relationship according to social rules. Those rules may have very little to do with the real bonds that hold a couple together, but because they have social consensus behind them, they are very powerful weapons. One partner or the other may be tempted at any time to appeal to social consensus to change the behavior of his or her mate. But appeals to societal rules, when used against one's mate, often results in private defeat."

Evelyn lowered her head, uncomfortable, but Leventritt reached over and lifted her chin, insisting on eye contact.

"D. Date compatibility, as you recognize, Evelyn, provides a profound psychological bond between two people. Our society teaches that both partners must live at optimum levels in order to preserve that bond. That is our social rule. It is a rule that Jim continually violates, and it could be used as a weapon against him."

Again Evelyn averted her eyes.

This time Leventritt did not intervene. He continued, "There is another way. If you wish to die with Jim perhaps you have to live with him. Live with him even if that means losing time with him. Optimum living is, after all, quantitative and not qualitative. It measures how long we live, not how well." Leventritt raised her chin once again. "Evelyn, I'd like you to think about that," he paused, "and perhaps we can discuss it next month."

She stared at him for a moment completely at a loss for words, and then, cheeks burning with embarrassment, turned and left.

———

When Evelyn left Leventritt's office, she discovered it was a beautiful, bright afternoon. The spring sunshine warmed everything it touched and gave Evelyn a renewed sense of calm. It was like the dawning light after a night of dark and ominous dreams. Everything was movement and activity—the electric cars as they whirred quietly by her, the people walking, not too fast, chatting, enjoying the sunshine, the leaves—yellow-green, spring leaves, swaying, rustling, almost inaudibly. The sun, Evelyn thought, had stirred in everything a sense of life and living that made thoughts of death and dying unreal.

Evelyn paused at the top of the flight of steps that led up to the entrance of the Master Medical Building. In her reluctance to relinquish the spring sunshine, she turned and took time to reexamine the city square on which stood the massive pyramid-shaped building in which she worked. Evelyn had been coming to this historic square almost daily for ten years. She now realized that during the couple of months away occasioned by her pregnancy, she had come to miss the place.

Most of the buildings on the other three sides of the square were old enough to give a reassuring sense of continuity to the city. The function of the buildings had changed over time. Most had originally housed the old insurance companies—companies which had made immense profits by statistically predicting mass mortality and accident rates and playing odds that couldn't lose. D. Date technology had wiped them out, of course, but the huge buildings survived, sound as ever. Even they, however, were overshadowed by the obelisk of the Great Clock Tower that rose above the Common in the middle of the square. Its function, Evelyn was sure, would never change.

She turned and gazed upward at the sloping sides of the Master Med Building. The giant base of the pyramid occupied a whole city block. The rest of the building rose twenty-one stories from its base, narrowing as it reached for the sky, until at its apex it contained a single suite that housed the offices of Noel Baker Smyth.[64] Evelyn's destination, toward which she now hurried, was one of the seven offices that lay one floor below on the twentieth level.

Passing through the portals of the building, she made her way with easy familiarity through throngs of workers to the express transporter in the Great Concourse. She entered the transporter and watched through its translucent sides as it accelerated nonstop toward the twentieth level.

---

[64] Besides being reminiscent of the Tower of Babel, the shape of the Master Med building is generally suggestive of the social hierarchy it contains. For a discussion of hierarchy and rhetoric, see the work of Kenneth Burke.

She was speeding, as it were, through the brain center of the Northeast Region of the country. Here in microscopic magnetic metal cells were stored all the data vital to the well-being of the society. Here the genetic and medical history of each individual in the region was known to the Master Med computer. Here were computed not only all individual L.C.F.'s but the Aggregate Life Consumption Factor—a measure of the health of the whole community. Here vote tabulation was carried out and regional resources and demography were monitored. Here Noel Baker Smyth presided and Evelyn was his principal assistant. Evelyn Sebring relished the prospect of returning to her job.

The doors of the transporter rolled open, announcing the twentieth level, and Evelyn found herself surveying the familiar scene. The offices of the six Associate Directors of Master Med lay three on either hand, and at the end, directly across from the transporter, was a seventh office, which was her own. Evelyn's office straddled the short flight of stairs which led to the suite occupied by Noel Baker Smyth, and so the only access to Smyth was through Evelyn. It was she who decided who could or could not see the Director. It was she who decided what problems were serious enough to merit his attention. She made many decisions that bore the singular authority of his final word, some of which he was hardly aware. In general, Evelyn was really his woman Friday, although she would have been the first to repudiate this label. She regarded herself as, and was in fact, much more than that.

Indeed, the importance of her function was at this moment testified to by the fact that, as soon as her arrival on the twentieth level was noticed, she found herself surrounded by the six Associate Directors who were anxious to welcome her back. Evelyn was pleased with the reception, even though she knew that most of the group of three men and three women resented her. Each of the Associate Directors was an expert in and directed one of the major functions carried out on the floors below. Evelyn, though she lacked any such expertise, nonetheless coordinated the operations of all.

Evelyn's power derived both from the nature of her relationship with Noel Baker Smyth and from her intimacy with the Master Med computer. Each of the Associate Directors had access to the computer at the highest level in his or her own division. None shared all the information available to the others. Evelyn's level of access vouchsafed to her all the information available to all of the Associate Directors. The only level denied to her was that reserved to the Director alone.

As soon as she had acknowledged the greetings of her colleagues, Evelyn entered her office bent on the much more important task of reestablishing her bona fides with the computer. To do this it was necessary for her to switch the computer to its audio mode and address it in Basic Beta Language—BABEL for short. BABEL was a semantically pure language, devoid of ambiguities and, therefore, of puns, of humor generally, and of all traces of poetry.[65] Evelyn read aloud the Rainbow passage, a short paragraph containing all the sounds of BABEL in every conceivable juxtaposition. Her voice, as was required, was flat and metallic, offensive to the human ear but apparently pleasing to the computer, which immediately confirmed its qualified obeisance to her.

By way of confirming her access, Evelyn queried the computer about the schedule of Senior Captain James Sebring. Dutifully, the computer announced in a voice not unlike Evelyn's BABEL voice that Captain Sebring had departed Greenwich, England, thirty-seven minutes earlier on the return leg of a Lucifer Flight—a fact that Evelyn knew to be accurate. Satisfied with the response, she switched the computer to its video mode and requested the latest A.L.C.F.'s (Aggregate Life Consumption Factors) for the various subareas within the Hartford Region. Her eye fell immediately on the figures for northwestern Massachusetts and she chuckled. The current A.L.C.F. was 1.0019, up three points from two months ago and still rising.

"That'll teach him," she murmured. Governor Orville would no doubt pay a fair political price for that error. Noel, she knew, had been quite upset with Sam Orville because of an overly ambitious flood control project which the latter, a man of considerable rhetorical talent, had "sold" to his constituents. The enormous project involved the construction of a series of dams and channels, massive bulldozing and earth removal, and the erection of huge concrete structures. The whole project was to be called the Orville Dam, a title which the Governor had come up with at the last minute, and

---

[65] One language tradition seeks to make language semantically pure so that, like mathematical symbols, each word would refer to one and only one thing. Such a language would be optimum for computers. Humanists, in opposition to this view, are generally persuaded that the metaphoric, ambiguous, poetic functions of language cannot and should not be eliminated.

which served further to convince Smyth that this whole thing was to be a monument to a monumental ego. However, the people of northwestern Massachusetts had voted to proceed, and that was that. Policy dictated freedom to choose without restraint, and the people had chosen to go ahead with the project, despite warnings from Master Med about possible environmental side effects.

And now, here it was—an increase in the Aggregate Life Consumption Factor for that identical area, obviously more than coincidental. By now, the people were beginning to face the consequences of their ill-advised decision, and it was D. Date attrition; as a group, the people of northwestern Massachusetts were losing more days than they had prior to the project. No other circumstance would so quickly and absolutely change public opinion. No doubt, as the figures became known, the project would quickly be abandoned and most certainly Sam Orville would be voted out.

Evelyn chuckled once again and crossed to her computer console; the information on Orville would be as good a way as any to announce her return. She rapidly pressed several buttons on the console and all the data on the screen, but that from Northwestern Massachusetts, vanished. It was her habit to isolate any data important enough to merit the Director's attention and simply transfer it, flashing on and off, to Noel's own readout display upstairs. This she did now, all the while watching the screen. Within seconds an exclamation point appeared on the screen—Noel's standard manner of acknowledging information. After a couple of seconds the screen went blank and Evelyn waited:

* * * * * * * * * * * * * * * ↑

She smiled. The row of asterisks were the standard, though unofficial, symbol for kisses. The upward pointing arrow was Noel's invitation to come upstairs. She took the stairs two at a time.

As Evelyn reached the top stair a massive door slid open, admitting her to a spacious room whose single large window provided a spectacular view of the City Square and the Great Clock Tower. Inside, the room was surprisingly archaic. Noel Baker Smyth had indulged his passion for antiques when he had furnished his office. Apart from the standard computer console, littered with assorted microfilm canisters, and the oversized computer monitor and videophone, which occupied most of the right side of the room, there was virtually nothing to distinguish it from a twentieth century American business office. Furthermore, Evelyn knew that all traces of modernity were removable by the flick of a switch, which slid an ornately carved mahogany panel over the computer display.

The room offended Evelyn's sense of efficiency, but even she had to admit that there was a certain warmth about it. The heavy leather-upholstered chairs complemented the huge mahogany desk very nicely. The wall to the left, almost completely covered with those most inefficient relics of historic culture—books—gave the place perhaps too much the air of a museum for Evelyn's taste. But the Holy Bible that invariably lay on the desk, from which Noel was fond of reading little homilies, was a nice touch. It was also, Evelyn had guessed, the source of Noel's computer access codes, an ironic gesture so typical of him. The only concession to convention was the standard portrait of P. Goras that hung above the bookshelves on the left. That concession, Evelyn had decided, could hardly be avoided since, although Smyth reported directly to the Elite Council, it was P. Goras to whom he was ultimately responsible.

"Eve, my dear." Noel Baker Smyth crossed the room to greet her. "What a relief to have you back." Noel's face was wreathed in smiles as he hugged her.

She knew Noel Baker Smyth to be a master of appearances, but the twinkle in his steel gray eyes told her that his pleasure was genuine. "I'm delighted to be back, Noel," Evelyn's response was genuine, too, "though I'm sure you managed quite well."

Smyth smiled at the little appeal for reassurance but acknowledged it nonetheless. "You don't know the half of it," he said. "Vote Tabulation made a mess of Peter Stoneham's Park Security Referendum and on top of that, they are faced with Goras' annual referendum tomorrow. That'll be a massive vote, of course. And now, we've just posted the second highest rate of Senile Delinquency in the country. The Elite Council is very unhappy about that and, to top it all off, the damn computer won't talk to me."

Evelyn laughed. Noel's failure to master BABEL was a standing joke between them. His naturally deep and well-modulated voice just wasn't suitable for producing the metallic monotone for Basic Beta Language. Besides which, try as he might, he couldn't clean up the richly metaphoric, even poetic, language that salted his speech. The computer always reacted to these obscenities by throwing a tantrum. This breakdown in communication was normally not serious since Evelyn's BABEL was flawless and she handled the bulk of Smyth's computer work. The very small percentage of material so confidential as to be withheld even from Evelyn, Noel punched in using the computer keyboard. In her absence, however, the situation must have been chaotic.

"I'm afraid my little spats with the beast have left it sulking. Thank God for our . . ." he paused, "for our compatibility." He smiled warmly and then he turned back toward his desk.

Evelyn eyed his retreating figure quizzically. She wondered if it were possible that Noel was already aware of her new D. Date. She decided against interrogating him, choosing rather to query him about another matter.

"You heard that our people fouled up a diagnosis on my husband's uncle?"

"Yes," he grimaced ruefully, "I was very sorry, doubly so when I remembered that Hazlitt is Jim's uncle."

Evelyn ignored the veiled reference to Charlie's illegal flight to Greenwich with Jim.

Smyth continued, "Maria Montenez has already given me hell about the whole affair."

"Charlie Hazlitt and my husband were very close. I'm worried. Jim's extremely upset."

"Yes, I'm sure he is." Smyth shook his head, "And I can imagine when he gets back from Greenwich and is greeted by the latest news he'll really be distressed."

"News?" Evelyn stared at Noel Baker Smyth.

"Good heavens! You mean you haven't been told? Oh, Eve, I'm awfully sorry. Mr. Hazlitt came out of his coma, and then got out of the Unit somehow late last night. He's reported to be very weak and critically ill, but he hasn't been seen since." He lapsed into silence, and from across the square came the doleful sound of the Great Clock tolling the hour.

12

ESMERALDA AND THE CLOWN[66]

"P. Goras is not a clown!"

Joannah cowered. Peter Stoneham was livid with rage. He snatched the picture from the wall above CLEM and smashed it to the floor in front of her.

"P. Goras is not a magician; he is not a gypsy; and he is certainly not a clown!"

"He is too a clown. I know he's a clown." She looked at the picture lying in front of her and began to cry. It was a beautiful portrait of a clown that she had found in one of the most exclusive city stores that very afternoon. She had known immediately that it was P. Goras, even though someone had cleverly attached an engraved brass plate to it bearing the legend: *The Jester*.

"What on earth do you think people would say if they saw that?" Peter was pointing at the shiny new brass plate that Joannah had had engraved and attached to the frame herself. It read: *P. Goras*. Peter's good eye was glaring fiercely down while his other eye, his glass eye, stared steadfastly ahead, giving him the grotesque appearance that endeared him so to Joannah.

"Oh, please, let's keep it, Peter. Please!" She was on her knees now, picking up the portrait and pleading with him through her tears.

---

[66]Esmeralda is the name of Victor Hugo's heroine in *The Hunchback of Notre Dame*.

"This is for your clown!" Peter's foot came crashing down on the clown, knocking it out of her hands. Joannah let out a scream as if she herself had caught the blow.

"Oh, Peter, how could you? How could you?"

"Don't you know I have a position to uphold?" His head, cocked as always toward the high shoulder, was twitching now.

Joannah turned her tear-stained face upward toward him. His head always twitched that way when he was angry. It was at moments like this that Joannah could see, could be absolutely certain, who Peter really was and she knew how much she loved him. "Don't be angry with me, Peter. I'll throw him away." She looked at the battered portrait longingly. "I'll throw the portrait away."

"Joannah!" Peter screamed at her in a fresh paroxysm of rage. "How many times do I have to tell you that P. Goras is not a clown?"

Really afraid of him now, she jumped to her feet and rushed through the doorway at the far end of the room. She activated the door as she passed through and it closed behind her. Peter gazed for a second at the closed door and then turned and walked over to CLEM.

On the top of the computer lay several feet of printed readout paper that CLEM had been disgorging when Peter had arrived home from work a few minutes ago. He picked up the sheet and examined it carefully. At the top it bore the date:

MARCH 21, 2192

Below the date ran two parallel columns of names, thousands of them, headed respectively by the words:

BIRTHS
DEATHS

Peter fed the long readout sheet through his hands, peering intently with his one good eye until he came to the entry that was circled in the BIRTH column:

CHARLES A. SEBRING

He shook his head in disgust, dropped the sheet to the floor, and turned toward the window.

The apartment overlooked Central Park. It was raining so that Peter could not see the Great Clock Tower that sat on the Common in the city square beyond the park.

He heard the bedroom door slide open behind him and turned.

"Ta-daa."

Joannah stood framed by the circular portal wearing only a green felt hat. One hand was resting on her left hip, which was thrust to one side. Her right hand she held behind her head. The green felt hat was cocked to one side and slightly forward. Joannah's blonde hair cascaded over her shoulders framing her breasts which—miraculously, considering their size—thrust straight forward toward Peter. The triangle of crisp pubic hair, having a decided reddish cast, contrasted slightly with the ringlets that tumbled from under her hat.

"Ta-daa." She undulated across the room towards him. Peter said nothing.

Joannah slid her right arm around his neck and drew him towards her.

His looked into her eyes. "You are not Esmeralda. You are Joannah, and sometimes you disgust me!" He slid from her embrace and stormed into the bedroom.

Joannah stared after him, tears again coursing down her cheeks. Something was wrong; something was very wrong. They'd argued about this sort of thing before—many times. She always made up with him by offering him sex. He had never before refused.

———

The following evening at eight o'clock Joannah stood by the entrance to Central Park waiting for him. It was Wednesday, and on Wednesdays, Peter always drove in from the Airstation, picked her up there, and took her out for dinner. He never missed.

The Great Clock tolled eight and Joannah knew that for the first time he would not come. Peter was never late.

She tucked the square, gaily-wrapped package she was carrying under her left arm and turned slowly into the park headed for their apartment on the other side.

The gathering dusk hid from her the newly erected billboard at the entrance to the park. The billboard proclaimed a notice—a notice signed by her husband, Peter Stoneham—which forbade use of the park after sunset.

Inside Joannah's package was a picture of Dimitri Geller, the Decathlon champion in the Olympic games of 2188. His magnificent body was clad only in the briefest of loincloths. Joannah had carefully removed the original nameplate from the famous portrait and replaced it with one bearing the inscription: *P. GORAS.* Actually she had salvaged the nameplate from the ruined picture of the clown. Joannah knew that P. Goras was not an athlete. She knew he was in fact a clown before he became head of state, and before that he was a gypsy, and before that, a magician.

But Peter had never before failed to make love to her when she came out wearing the green felt hat. There was something about the hat, she didn't really know what, that got to him. Obviously Peter could not bear the idea that Goras was really a clown. So today Joannah had bought the picture of the beautiful athlete and attached Goras' name to it. It was all wrong, of course, but Peter was not very clever about these things. He wouldn't know the difference and he'd be very pleased that she had given Goras a beautiful body.

From overhead on her left came the plaintive sound of a night hawk. Joannah turned right toward the little footbridge that led across the ornamental pond. The ducks, hidden in the darkness, tittered nervously at the hollow sound of her footsteps on the wooden bridge. She walked on obliviously.

Joannah knew that what people looked like on the outside didn't count for anything—she'd learned that when she was Esmeralda. But she could understand Peter's love for beautiful bodies. After all, he was the one who had been trapped in Quasimodo's body, and now with his accident and what it had done to his present body, she could understand that about Peter.

She could see now, just past a set of dark bushes and beyond a wide path leading out from them, the first twinkling of lights from the windows of the apartment house where she and Peter lived. She walked a little faster. Oh, yes, she would make it up to Peter and try to be more understanding. She smiled. Peter would be pleased with her new portrait of P. Goras and everything would be fine again. They'd make love like they always did and they'd be happy. And she'd try to take Evelyn's advice and she wouldn't talk anymore about who Peter was. And some day, when their D. Dates came—her walk took on a little skip—someday, she thought happily, she and Peter would leave their bodies behind. And when people found them, they would be two skeletons, clutching each other just like Quasimodo and Esmeralda. And their souls would find two new bodies with identical D. Dates and they would go on that way for ever and . . .

The Senile Delinquents grabbed her from behind. They did not realize that P. Goras was a clown. They knew they were about to die; they knew she was very beautiful; they knew it would cost nothing and they had nothing to lose. And so, the Senile Delinquents dragged her into the woods and stripped her clothing from her, and when they could no longer abuse her body, they stabbed her with their knives. And as she whimpered, "Quasimodo, save me," they bludgeoned her to death.

13

RACE WITH THE SUN[67]

Jim sat in their usual place by the left front window of the Cracked Atom where he could contemplate the statue of his old friend Admiral Nelson.[68] Tonight the Admiral seemed more like an old friend than usual, no doubt because Jim hadn't had much else to do for the last hour but admire his bronze majesty. He wondered again why his other old friend Michele LaTour hadn't turned up. They'd had no specific arrangements to meet, but each knew the other's schedule and they gravitated to the Cracked Atom whenever they chanced to be in London at the same time.

He glanced at his chronometer. It was after eleven and he realized that if Michele didn't come soon it was unlikely that she would come at all. He drained his second Cannabis cocktail and stared moodily at the empty glass, debating whether to order a third. He wondered if possibly Michele had found some romantic interest and was otherwise occupied. He smiled. If she had, then that was good; it would mean she was beginning to get over Uncle Charlie. Well then, maybe she'd left him a message. He pushed his chair away from the table and crossed to a row of white console booths in the back of the room. He entered the first, pulling his orange I.D. Card from his pocket as the panel slid closed behind him.

He pushed the card into the narrow I.D. slot, pressed the MAIL button and concentrated on the screen, only half expecting it to respond.

---

[67] See the last two lines of Andrew Marvell's poem, referenced in footnote 13.
[68] The statue of Admiral Nelson, "Nelson's Monument," dominates Trafalgar Square in London.

The screen blinked into life and a brief message flashed on:

MUST SEE YOU 2300 HOURS. URGENT!   M.L.

His shoulders stiffened. Urgent! What could Michele find so urgent about seeing him? He examined his chronometer again. It was already 11:22. Odd! He exited the booth and looked carefully around the room. Michele had not arrived. Why would Michele want to see him urgently and where was she?

He ordered a third Cannabis on the way back to his table. The Admiral didn't have any ideas at all. He had discussed the matter thoroughly with him and neither of them could come up with a reasonable solution. Of course, the Admiral may have had a little too much Cannabis. For one thing, he'd grown so that now he was about twice the size of his stone column.

Jim decided to think it out by himself. Maybe Michele had found a lover. No, that would not lead her to send an URGENT message. Maybe she'd forgotten she'd sent the message. No, that wasn't reasonable. People don't leave URGENT messages and then forget about them one hour later. Perhaps she'd had some sort of accident. That was possible, but unlikely. He wasn't thinking coherently. That was probable. No more Cannabis cocktails! He'd have to take a stabilizer to sober up before his Lucifer Flight as it was and that was always such a walloping comedown.

He wished it were already the next morning in Hartford so he could be with Natasha. He hadn't seen her for two days and June seventh was now only thirty-three days away. He felt a longing surge through him. How could he ever survive without Tasha?

A protective inner voice responded. "Don't think about it. Call her. That's it. Call her."

He waved to the table attendant.

"V-phone, please."

The attendant nodded and disappeared briefly. It would be great to see Tasha and hear her voice, even if only by phone.

The attendant reappeared with the videophone.

Jim depressed the ACTIVATE button and spoke slowly, "USA... Northeast Region... Hartford—Mollenskaya, Natasha." He waited, tapping on the table.

"The residence of Natasha Mollenskaya. Oh, hello, Jim! Hardly recognized you. You make a lousy image." A male voice!

Jim stared at the blank screen. The voice was familiar. A sudden tightness gripped his throat.

"I assume it's Natasha you want."

It was Colin Jeffries! It was the Gorasdamn condescending voice of Colin Jeffries!

"Jeffries, your video's out" Jim muttered, still not quite comprehending. Had he called the Met Comm by mistake? He was trying desperately to remember. No, Jeffries had said, "the residence of Natasha Mollenskaya." No mistake. He felt anger rising in him, flushing his face.

"I'll get her for you. Hold on one minute." Jeffries was still talking.

Jim slammed his fist against the DEACTIVATE button. "You bastard!"

"We're receiving the Lucifer signal five by five, loud and clear." The voice of Greenwich Tower was unmistakably British.

Jim Sebring reached for the lowest switch on the left side of the panel and turned off the emergency transmitter. "Roger," he said, "Star-jet Triple Six Lima is ready for R.A.T.O."

"Triple Six Lima, go for R.A.T.O.," the tower confirmed. "Ten seconds and counting...seven...six...five..."

A shaft of light burst through the windscreen and Jim looked up from the panel to see the first rays of the rising sun ricocheting off the sleek black surfaces of the silent Lucifer jets lined up on the west side of Greenwich International Airstation. He glanced at his chronometer. It was precisely 6:00 a.m. Greenwich Mean Time.

The variegated emblems on the fleet of sleeping Lucifer jets identified them as belonging mostly to western European nations. The Lucifer Flight for Russia, China, and exotic lands of the Far East would have departed hours ago. This fleet of planes, with much shorter trips, would not leave for another couple of hours.

"three...two...one...take-off." The controller's voice was precise but laconic. As the subterranean rocket began its muffled roar, Jim reflexively tensed his body against the G forces of the take-off and allowed his mind to wander. From the ground to ten thousand feet everything was automatic. He wondered who would be flying the Lucifer jet that sat in the middle of the line just opposite the tower, the jet bearing the tricolor of France. Michele LaTour had never turned up last night at the Cracked Atom. Something was wrong. He felt it intuitively.

"We have you passing through five thousand on course, Triple Six Lima."

Jim, still pinned to his contoured seat by the g-force of the takeoff, was not required to acknowledge the tower's transmission.

Had Michele met him at the Cracked Atom, he would have talked to her about Colin Jeffries. Colin Jeffries at Natasha's apartment. Gorasdamn! He began to feel the anger arising again.

"Triple Six Lima, prepare for power pick-off." The controller's voice.

That transmission had to be acknowledged. "Roger, Greenwich." Jim leaned forward. Grasping the control column with his left hand and hitting the manual override switch with his right, he felt the tension come into the column and eased the twin jet thrust levers forward. The plane was under its own power and the bonds with Greenwich had been cut. Jim savored the sensation. He was, he reflected whimsically, in control of the aircraft now if not in control of his life.

The plane climbed effortlessly through ten thousand and Jim relaxed in the solitude of his cockpit. Maybe Jeffries had simply stopped by to pick Natasha up, as both were on duty at midnight. No, that wouldn't do. He'd called at 7 o'clock Hartford time, five hours before their shift began. And there was the blank video, as if Natasha didn't want her guest identified. But then, why let Jeffries answer the videophone at all?

It didn't matter anyway. Natasha would do as she damn well pleased and she wouldn't bother concealing it. Natasha and Jim didn't have an agreement—she was a single woman and she was within her rights. But then he remembered that she'd said that Jeffries was unimportant! Jim's mind whirled.

His left thumb curved around the horn of the control column to depress the mike button. "Greenwich Departure, Star-jet Triple Six Lima is at flight level three-two." Then without waiting for an acknowledgment, he pushed forward the yoke and lowered the nose. The airspeed began to build. After a few seconds, he pushed the wing retract control over one notch and the wings slid back ten degrees.

Triple Six Lima was a swing-wing star-jet. It was so called because its wings were capable of retracting backwards a total of thirty degrees, giving the jet a sleeker configuration and enabling it to fly at greater speeds. However, as the wings were swung back in ten-degree increments, the reduction in effective wing area also reduced the plane's lift. Therefore, each time Jim moved the wings back ten degrees it was necessary for him to build up greater airspeed. He continued the wing retraction and speed increases until his instruments indicated an appropriate match. A slight bump in the aircraft announced that he had reached a stable speed and now the star-jet moved on at its cruising speed.

Below, the English coast just north of Liverpool slid past. Jim headed the jet out across the Irish Sea into the blackness of the northwest sky. Behind him, the sun was slowly sinking in the east. His jet was outrunning the sun. Shortly, Jim knew, the sun would set and the stars would rise in the west as the great celestial clock ran backwards. When he landed at Bradley at 4 a.m. he'd have gained two hours.

He smiled to himself. He, Jim Sebring, was gaining time, living at better than optimum. The thought would please Evelyn, but he doubted that she ever looked upward to read the celestial clock.

Time gained, time lost, he mused. Tasha's time was very short now, only thirty-two days. If only the clock, the remorseless clock, could be turned back for her. But she was spending her time with Jeffries. Damn Jeffries. Damn Natasha!

He began to feel the chill of the air surrounding him and leaned forward to turn up the cockpit temperature five degrees. The star-jet sped into the darkening night.

What would it be like to be without Tasha forever, separated from her by an eternity? That loneliness he could not conceive and he didn't want to. He pushed the thought from his mind. Under the left wing of the star-jet, barely visible in the darkness, thin white streaks of stratus clouds, looking like the streaks made by a piece of chalk laid on its side and scraped across a blackboard, began to appear. He glanced at the jet's synchron. It read: 17° 21' west longitude, 62° 40' north latitude. He was south of Iceland, where the low level stratus had been predicted.

Jim pressed the mike button and put in a call to Reykjavik with a position report and a request for a weather update. As he expected, fog was forming all down the coast of the mainland. St. John's, Boston, and New York all lay under a coastal fog, but Bradley, further inland, was still open. The winds across the Davis Straits were adverse but diminishing.

He remembered his last trip back from Greenwich to Hartford with Charlie. Charlie had been elated to find that he would gain two hours. Jim had been amused because Charlie had either forgotten or ignored the fact that they had lost two hours on the trip in the other direction. Well, Charlie's gained time all right, not hours, but weeks, months maybe, who knows? Charlie could not have imagined that he'd end up a P.N.D. He had used *Winged Chariot* to cheat death, but in the end death had cheated him.

A glimmer of light appeared off the right wing of the star-jet. It was the southern tip of Greenland. The cloud layers had gone. Jim triggered the mike.

"Erewhon Three radio, this is star-jet Triple Six Lima, IFR, Bradley, do you read me? Over."

Erewhon Three, he thought. It had always struck him as an odd name until Tasha had mentioned to him one time that the name was borrowed from a famous Christian era novel about a Utopian society.[69] "Erewhon," she had said, "was 'nowhere,' spelled backwards, very nearly, anyway." Well, Jim thought, it was an appropriate name. Greenland, which wasn't green this time of the year even at its southernmost tip, was exactly that—Nowhere.

The voice from Nowhere spoke: "Triple Six Lima, this is Erewhon Three." It was a woman's voice, self-assured, deep, husky and sensual.

Jim frowned and thumbed the mike again. "Erewhon Three, I'd like a position report confirmed and relayed to Boston." He listened again carefully.

"Roger, Triple Six Lima. Confirm your position." He thought he heard a trace of a French accent.

The transmission was too short, but the conviction was growing. He glanced at the synchron. "Triple Six Lima is at flight level three-two, 45

---

[69]Samuel Butler's famous satire, *Erewhon*, uses the device of an imaginary land to critique the customs of contemporary England.

degrees 48 minutes west longitude, 59 degrees 5 minutes north latitude. Estimating Boston at zero-three-five-five Eastern Standard, zero-eight-five-five Zulu." He hesitated. Needing a longer transmission to establish whose voice he thought he was hearing, he asked an obvious question. "Would you give me the weather for the Davis Straits?" he said.

There was a brief pause. Jim waited.

"Roger, Triple Six Lima. Winds in the Straits are generally..." The voice from Erewhon droned. But it was now a different voice, a male voice. Jim frowned. That first voice had been Michele LaTour. He was sure of it... almost. What the hell would she be doing at Erewhon? She was supposed to have been at the Cracked Atom. She was supposed to be at the Greenwich Airstation. She was a Lucifer Pilot, not a voice from Erewhon—not a voice from Nowhere. But why the sudden switch of controllers?

Jim's left thumb hooked around the horn of the control column ready to query Erewhon and then he thought better of it. He'd be busting procedures relaying a personal message. It would be reported and he just wasn't certain. Instead he acknowledged the Davis Straits' report with a curt, "Roger, Triple Six Lima. Out."

Perhaps he had let his imagination run away with him, an easy thing to do alone at thirty-two thousand feet over the North Atlantic. He glanced at the plane's chronometer—0704 ZULU—a little before 3 a.m. at Bradley. This was a slow time for Tasha, he thought, not much traffic. She'd be taking a break—with Colin Jeffries no doubt!

He tried to shake thoughts of Tasha spending an evening with Jeffries at her apartment. Would she do that? If she wanted to, yes, she would. And if she did, would she ... would she go further? If she wanted to, yes. Jim felt a knot in his stomach. Why shouldn't she? She had only thirty-two days left. Why not grab what she could, while she could? It made sense. The knot in his stomach tightened. He wondered if she'd told Jeffries how little time she had left—told Jeffries the way she'd told him, by playing the piano. No! That moment was theirs—hers and Jim's—to hold on to forever. She wouldn't; she couldn't share that with anyone else.

Jim glanced at the fuel gauges and noted that not much time was left on the starboard tanks. He switched to the port tanks. Not much time.

Jeffries wouldn't have to be told. He'd have seen the ominous date, June 7, on the D. Date calendar, and the bastard would know how to use that information. He'd understand that Tasha would be desperately trying to make up for anything she'd missed in life, knowing that she'd already paid the price—her fate sealed. He'd know that there were for her no more consequences; so eat, drink, and be merry, for tomorrow, almost literally, she would die. Oh, the bastard would know that, and use it he would.

Jim's stomach turned. What was he doing for God's sake? He'd just described the psychology of a Senile Delinquent. Tasha wasn't that. She hadn't turned against society, bitter and frustrated as they did. It was just that she had escaped society—broken out of the web—she was flying.[70]

Jim gazed over the nose of the hurtling jet. The sun behind him had sunk well below the eastern horizon now. The moon, a nearly full moon, had risen in the west. Thirty-two thousand feet below, the iceberg-littered Davis Straits sparkled and flashed in the moonlight.

He ruddered the star-jet around five degrees to the south to compensate for the earth's curvature. The inevitable excitement of his approaching first contact with North America merged somehow with the excitement of his recollection of Tasha and him that first night.

"Triple Six Lima, this is St. John's radio. Over." The stark, clear voice interrupted Jim's reverie.

He was vaguely aware that the call had come in several times. "Damn," he muttered. He'd busted St. John's airspace without calling first. "St. John's radio, this is Triple Six Lima. Over."

"Triple Six Lima, we have you one hundred nauts inside the zone."

A gentle rebuke. The guys at St. John's must be used to enraptured North Atlantic pilots failing to report penetration of their zone.

Jim glanced at the synchron. "Roger, St. John's, estimate your station in zero-six minutes."

When Uncle Charlie had been with him he had reminded Jim that St. John's had been the place Alcock and Brown had left from on that first per-

---

[70] As noted in footnote 17, flying is used throughout to symbolize being free, and especially free of the limitation (the web) of social control.

ilous nonstop flight across the North Atlantic so many years ago.[71] Charlie was an aviation history buff and his eyes had gleamed as he had described the navigator crawling out of the open cockpit of that ancient biplane—out of the cockpit, onto the wing, ten thousand feet above the North Atlantic—to chip ice out of the air intake of one of the engines. The flight had crashed in Ireland, but they'd survived.

"Triple Six Lima." A decided edge in the voice this time. "We had station passage a minute ago."

"That's affirmative, St. John's. Sorry." Jim shook his head violently as if to shake loose the nostalgia which plagued him, but it was useless. His thoughts drifted back now to his first flight lessons with Uncle Charlie in *Winged Chariot*. Charlie had severed "the surly bonds of earth" for him, taken him all the way from orientation to basic aerobatics.

Jim decreased his heading a further five degrees as the brilliant patch of light to the right of the airplane's nose signaled the huge hydroelectric station on the Bay of Fundy, many miles to the west.

The day he'd soloed, Uncle Charlie had taken him out and gotten him smashed—first time ever for Jim. Uncle Charlie had become just "Charlie" sometime that night, as if Jim's first solo had been some rite of passage . . .

Suddenly, the jet lurched violently, bringing Jim immediately back to the present.

The clear air turbulence hit him without warning like a thunderbolt. The star-jet acted as if it had tried to ram through a brick wall. Jim grabbed for the throttles, reducing power and simultaneously sucking back on the control column.

A second and more severe shock shook the star-jet. Jim glanced instinctively at Lucifer. It was still secure. His thumb reached for the mike button. No question, this was clear air turbulence, an unseen disturbance in the air mass that could rip his high-speed plane apart. Jim withdrew his thumb from the mike without saying a word. Time to report later, better get the airspeed down and change altitude.

---

[71]Charlie apparently knew that John Alcock and Arthur Brown first successfully flew the Atlantic in 1919—eight years before Charles A. Lindbergh's famous flight. Ironically, what Charlie probably did not know is that Lindbergh was the co-inventor of one of the first artificial life-support devices (the heart pump).

Powerful natural forces, acting like a hidden fist, struck the left wing on the underside throwing the jet into a steep right roll. He countered with full left aileron and the roll slowed to a stop at ninety degrees of bank. The lights from the hydroelectric station swung onto the nose. The left wing started down towards straight and level.

A sledgehammer blow struck this time at the underside of the right wing. The jet rolled violently to the left. The hydroelectric lights described a complete circle in the windscreen and then disappeared. The nearly full moon flashed across the windscreen once . . . twice . . . three times. Triple Six Lima plunged, spinning vertically to the left. Jim stamped on the right rudder, fighting vertigo and nausea, as the vertical speed indicator slid off the bottom of the scale, pegged at ten thousand feet per minute. The swing-wing star-jet was spinning out of control towards the icy North Atlantic, now four miles below.

"Get the power off and stop the rotation." It was a voice . . . a voice from the past . . . Charlie's voice.

Jim hauled the throttles back. Suddenly he was in *Winged Chariot* in his first spin, fighting the controls desperately while Charlie beside him, cold and remote, gave terse instructions.

"Feed in aileron against the spin, lad."

Jim jerked the wheel to the right and watched fascinated as the spin rate decreased very slowly and the airspeed began to climb from the green into the yellow—Caution! His hands tightened on the yoke.

"Keep the stick forward until the spin has stopped." Charlie's voice again.

Jim resisted the temptation to pull back on the yoke. The increasing airspeed would increase the effect of the right rudder and aileron, which now jutted out into the air that hissed past the otherwise streamlined airframe of the plane. The mad left gyration had distinctly slowed now, but the speed had risen through the yellow into the red danger zone.

The jet was now less than two miles above the water and hurtling downwards at better than 1500 knots. The rotation slowed to a stop. Jim neutralized the controls and stared in dismay at the airspeed, indicating a ludicrous 2000 knots. He pulled the yoke backwards until the wings groaned under the stress.

"Easy now, lad, easy," he heard Charlie warn. If he pulled any further on the yoke, the wings would fold upwards like a blown out umbrella, but if he didn't, he'd hit the water still going at better than 1000 knots.

"Don't run out of altitude and ideas at the same time. Think, lad, think."

Jim's head stopped spinning. He went ice cold. There was nothing he could do. The star-jet was already streaking through 5000 feet still doing 1700 knots. It was all over.

"Think, lad, think." The urgent whisper melted into the whistling wind. The jets were silent. If only he could slow down.

"Think, lad, think." Jim felt Charlie's icy breath brush across his right cheek.

Four thousand feet, 1300 knots. If only he had air brakes like the old dive bombers. Three thousand feet, 900 knots.

"Think, lad, think."

Brakes. Brakes—that was it! Jim lunged at the throttles, releasing the safety catch, which prevented the jets from being inadvertently thrown into negative thrust. Reverse jet thrust was used to slow the plane down once it landed. It was never used while in flight, but it might work, and he had no choice. He hauled the throttles back through the detente, as the plane hurtled through two thousand feet, and the twin, fuselage-mounted jets wound up from first a howl and then a scream. Every ounce of their power was now being exerted forward against the motion of the aircraft. Jim's body shot forward pressing into his shoulder harness as the plane, its speed now rapidly decreasing, curved through one thousand feet. Pinned forward in his seat, against the yoke, Jim raised his feet off the rudders and braced them on the panel. The star-jet sank through five hundred feet. It was now or never! He clung to the yoke and pushed backwards with all the power his legs could muster.

He heard a loud crash.

An auxiliary oxygen container broke loose from its mounting bracket and slammed across Lucifer. The hasp had broken off and, striking Jim's right knee a glancing blow, disappeared under the instrument panel. The oxygen container careened off Lucifer into the panel on the right side of the cockpit. Jim fought to retain consciousness as the g-forces sucked the blood from his brain downwards toward his feet.

The wings groaned again and the star-jet leveled off, barely one hundred feet above the phosphorescent whitecaps of the waves. The plane then started to climb. Jim, pressed back in his seat and fighting the blackout that threatened to overwhelm him, struggled to reach the jet thrust levers; for now, under the combined effect of a climb and reverse thrust on the jets, the plane was losing speed so fast that it threatened to stall and fall back into the ocean below.

Jim's right leg, bloody from the blow to the knee, came back from the dash towards the throttle quadrant. With a quick kick of his right foot, he pushed the levers well forward. The star-jet skidded upwards in response to the asymmetric thrust of its twin jets. Jim leaned forward and equalized the levers. Triple Six Lima responded with a shallow climb. For the moment, she was under control.

He resisted the temptation to raise the nose of the star-jet to a normal angle of climb. The wings of the plane were still in the thirty-degree swept-back high-speed configuration—abnormal for a climb from low altitude. In this configuration, the stall speed of the plane was high—280 knots.

The moment the star-jet's airspeed fell below that figure, the plane would cease to fly. The normal climb speed of 180 knots was out of the question. Jim trimmed the plane for 350 knots, a steady and safe climb speed. The altimeter inched through 3000 feet and he tried to assess the damage.

The engine instruments indicated all was well with the twin jet power plants, which made sense. There was no reason why they should have sustained any damage. The oxygen container had taken out most of the instruments on the right side of the cockpit, but they were mostly duplicates. The container was now rolling around on the floor on the copilot's side.

A steady hiss told Jim that one of the vacuum instruments on the right side was leaking, meaning his own vacuum instruments would be unreliable—a nuisance, but not at this point dangerous. The inertial guidance system had been wiped out and with it any possibility of the star-jet being brought in from the ground, but that was okay with Jim. He preferred to handle it himself anyway.

His eyes swept to the Geiger counter just above his head, over the left side of the windscreen. Its green indicator light shone back reassuringly. It was working and, thankfully, giving no indication of abnormal radiation.

Jim scrutinized Lucifer. "Goras," he mumbled. The thing was sitting in its receptacle all right, but restrained by nothing more than gravity. It had sustained a tremendous blow from the oxygen container. A huge dent in the side of the receptacle was mute testimony to the power of that blow. The retaining hasp literally had been sheared right off. Had the jet gone into a negative-g configuration any time after the container had torn loose and done its damage, the lead box with its ominous contents would have slid out of its receptacle.

Jim glanced again at the Geiger counter for reassurance—again the steady green. "Damn lucky," he muttered.

The plane skittered through 8000 feet. He reached for the mike. A position report to Boston Center was overdue. If they'd been watching the scope, they'd probably seen him vanish as he fell below the radar coverage. Jim managed a grim smile. He could see the guys clustered around the scope trying to make sense of the cavorting blip that was Triple Six Lima. He activated the mike

"Boston Center." He deliberately worked at a low-pitched and leisurely style. "This is Triple Six Lima. Do you read me? Over."

The familiar click of the mike relay was absent. He'd wasted his impressive efforts at voice control. Number one radio was dead. He switched to number two. The cockpit came alive.

"Six Lima, I repeat; seventy-seven hundred if you are receiving me."

"Six Lima" had to be Triple Six Lima. Boston was already calling him. Seventy-seven hundred was the emergency code to be set on the transponder of any plane experiencing serious difficulty. It created a distinctive pattern so that all radar receivers within range could easily identify the distressed aircraft.

Jim decided against 7700; he'd try transmitter number two first. "Boston Center." Again the well-modulated voice. "Triple Six Lima. Do you read me? Over."

"Triple Six Lima, this is Boston Center. We read you five by five. What is your situation?"

"Boston Center, Triple Six Lima has encountered severe clear air turbulence and sustained light damage." The Center would recognize the understatement traditional with professional pilots.

"Roger, Triple Six Lima. Can we be of assistance?"

Jim glanced at the altimeter, now moving towards 15000. He leveled off and thumbed the mike. "Boston, Triple Six Lima is level at one five thousand. Can you give me a position report and vectors to your station?"

Boston was almost directly on route to Bradley, Jim reasoned, and if he had any further trouble it would provide an alternative landing place.

"Roger, Triple Six Lima. We have you two-three-three nautical miles northeast. Come left to heading two-four-zero degrees. Over."

Jim eased in the left rudder and glanced at his chronometer. It was 3:39 a.m., Eastern Standard Time. Judging by his position, that first encounter with C.A.T. occurred no more than ten minutes ago. Sometimes ten minutes could seem like a lifetime, Jim reflected, and no doubt vice versa.[72]

"Triple Six Lima, come right to two-four-five degrees."

Jim sighed with relief. Boston Center was going to shepherd him all the way in. He was suddenly aware of an intense sense of fatigue. His right knee, though no longer bleeding, was throbbing violently. He leaned forward to add some right rudder trim against a small but persistent left turn. He found the trim removed the turn all right, but his instruments indicated that the plane was now skidding very slightly.

"Keep the bloody ball centered."

Jim could hear Charlie now and see him jabbing his finger at the instrument, which indicated when their antique training plane was skidding. Charlie hadn't needed the instrument then; he could feel the skid in the seat of his pants, just the way Jim could now. Jim fiddled with the rudder trim again—no use, he couldn't both hold his course and get rid of the skid.

"Whatever you do, hold your course."

"Triple Six Lima, come right a further five degrees and be informed that Logan is zero-zero."

The coastal fog had reduced the visibility at Boston to nothing, just as predicted.

"Triple Six Lima, we could crank up the F.D.E. for you." Logan, like most major airstations, was supplied with Fog Dissipation Equipment.

---

[72]Again the "time" theme, but here Jim is contrasting *clock time* and *psychological time*.

"Negative, Boston. If Bradley is still open, I'll proceed to Hartford." Jim reflected that the F.D.E. would give him a mile visibility and a five hundred foot ceiling at best. He'd still have to let down through several hundred feet of "soup" with unreliable gyros. Besides, Tasha was, he hoped, waiting for him at Bradley Airstation in Hartford.

"Roger, Triple Six Lima. We have you crossing the station now, and Bradley is C.A.V.U."

Ceiling and visibility unlimited at Bradley. Fifteen minutes and he'd be on the ground.

Jim throttled back to five hundred knots, just below the highest permissible speed for a reduction from thirty degrees of wing sweep. He reached to his side and jerked the wing activation lever up once and waited for the ten-degree change to show up on the indicator dial in front of him, but nothing happened.

He glanced backward out of his side window to confirm visually that his wings remained at full sweep. He tugged at the lever—nothing! The fog dispersal equipment of his mind cranked up, and thoughts of Tasha and of the apartment dissipated instantly.

"Fat, dumb, and happy." Charlie's mocking voice reverberated through Jim's head. That persistent left bank—the skid and that last pullout—had damaged one of the wings. One of the wings was jammed at full sweep. Which wing? Left bank meant probably the right wing. Jim loosened his shoulder harness and leaned across the right seat to stare at the right wing. No noticeable difference, but of course, all it would take would be a degree or two of upward bend. It was too little to see, but enough to increase the lift slightly on that wing and plenty to jam the wing at full sweep.

Jim reached for the red knobbed auxiliary lever that would back up the wing hydraulics with an explosive charge of CO^2.

"Wait! Think!" Charlie's voice again.

Jim thought. That CO^2 back-up assumed a minor malfunction in the hydraulics. It probably did not anticipate one wing free, the other wing physically distorted and completely jammed. The CO^2 charge might activate the left wing, but it could not possibly budge the right. Goras! The extra wing area on the left would send the star-jet into an irretrievable wing-over. The plane would corkscrew to the right out of control.

Jim eyed Lucifer. His right hand, sweating now, moved convulsively from the red knobbed CO^2 lever to the coding switch on the transponder. He set in 7700 and dialed in 133.55 on his number two transmitter.

"New York Center." His voice was no longer under control. "This is Triple Six Lima. I have a MAYDAY!"

The response was immediate. "This is New York Center. All aircraft clear this frequency. Go ahead, Triple Six Lima."

"New York, Triple Six Lima has suffered structural damage. My wings are jammed at full sweep."

Jim grappled with rising panic as the ominous implication of his situation penetrated his mind.

"Roger, Triple Six Lima." The voice was calm. "New York is zero zero, but F.D.E. is operating at Kennedy. We have three-quarter mile visibility, hour hundred feet ceiling, and no wind. We can give you Runway Two-Four, straight in, niner five hundred feet."

Jim rubbed his sweating palms against his pants. New York understood the nature of his problem, but not its extent.

"New York, this is Triple Six Lima. My gyro instruments and inertial guidance systems are out. And be informed, Triple Six Lima is a Lucifer Flight."

This time there was a pause. "Triple Six Lima, stand by." The voice of New York sounded shaken now.

Jim's mind reeled. With the wings retracted, the wheels couldn't be lowered. No wheels, no wheel brakes. He wiped his hand across his sweating forehead and licked his parched lips. Wing flaps would be useless, too. He'd have to belly-in doing a full 280 knots. He could still use reverse jet thrust if he could keep the star-jet going straight ahead. Ninety-five hundred feet might be enough, but just barely.

"Triple Six Lima, this is New York Center. You're instructed to land at Bradley, Runway Two-six. Bradley is C.A.V.U., wind two-five-zero at seven."

Land at Bradley! They must be mad! Runway 26, the longest runway, is only 6500 feet.

"Triple Six Lima, come right heading two-eight-zero and contact Bradley approach on one-three-five point two-zero. And good luck, Triple Six Lima. New York out."

"New York! Do you realize there's only six five hundred feet at Bradley?" Jim almost screamed into the mike.

"Affirmative, Triple Six Lima." The voice was sympathetic. "New York doesn't want a Lucifer Flight terminating in the metropolitan area with a no-gyro approach. I'm sorry."

The logic was unassailable. Jim switched to Bradley Approach. Anger and dismay filled his voice. "Bradley Approach, Triple Six Lima is with you." He glanced at the altimeter. "Descending through five thousand feet."

"Roger, Triple Six Lima. Radar contact. Come right heading two-eight-zero degrees."

Jim pressed the right rudder and the mike button simultaneously. "Give me a long straight-in approach. I need time to get set up."

"Roger, Triple Six Lima. You'll intercept the I.L.S. twenty miles out, and two-six is foamed."

Jim grunted. That foam would reduce the risk of fire, but it would lengthen his final slide.

"Triple Six Lima, come left to two-five-niner degrees and contact the tower on one-two-three point seven."

Jim, ice cold now, ruddered the plane around to 259 degrees as he dialed in the tower.

"Bradley tower. Triple Six Lima is with you at three thousand feet."

The Airstation swung into the windscreen, a riot of color. An alternating green and white rotating beacon atop the still invisible tower shone over a host of blue lights indicating a maze of taxiways. There were the dim parallel white lights of Runway 26, and at the far end, the rotating red lights of the emergency vehicles waiting for the inevitable crash. At the threshold of the runway, a row of green lights glittered and, leading up to them and to the center line of the runway, a brilliant moving fireball of stroboscopic light. Presiding over the scene was the bright yellow star Arcturus, just about to slip below the horizon, slightly south of the Airstation.

Jim looked at his chronometer . . . 4:08 a.m., May 6th. This then was to be his D. Date. He thought of Tasha down there, probably watching. "Gorasdamn," he murmured beneath his breath, and then out loud, "Gorasdamn it to hell."

"Triple Six Lima, this is your final controller and I have you seventeen miles out on the center line."

Jim broke into a hollow laugh. What could the final controller do now, beyond direct him to his death, at the appropriate time and place?

"Damn all controllers, everywhere,"[73] he muttered. He reached over and shut off the radio. He gazed over the nose at the runway hurtling toward him. Why bother? 6500 feet just wasn't enough. They'd have to go into the next sector to scrape him up. He looked at Lucifer and groaned.

"Altitude one-five thousand feet, speed three-five zero knots." He felt the frigid air on his cheek. Charlie was beside him again. "Get the speed down to just above stall, lad."

Jim was making his first landing in *Winged Chariot*.

"Flatten the approach and nurse her in."

Jim eased back on the yoke and reduced the power.

"Speed three-two-zero knots. Altitude five hundred feet," the voice whispered. "Speed three hundred knots. Altitude two hundred feet. Flatten the approach."

Jim nursed the yoke back.

"Two hundred ninety knots and one hundred fifty feet. Don't get the nose too high."

The green threshold lights hurtled out of the darkness to meet him.

"Two hundred eighty-five knots and one hundred feet. Power off. Get ready for reverse thrust."

Jim blinked the sweat out of his eyes.

"Speed two hundred eighty knots. She's settling. Give it power, a touch of power. You can do it, Jim. You can do it." The voice faded.

The green lights flashed by. The star-jet was gliding like a swan on a river, but way too fast. Jim activated full reverse throttle.

"Onto the rudders... Keep those jets forward... She's slowing... By God, she's slowing," he said, praying that his words would guide his actions.

"The end of the runway and she's turning over! I can't stop her!"

Jim chopped the jets just as the right wing dug in, slamming him, harness and all, against the left side of the cockpit. He watched helpless as Triple Six

---

[73] If flight metaphorically stands for freedom, then a flight controller limits freedom.

Lima entered her last wing-over. Jim heard the sound of Lucifer's lead container smashing into the instrument panel, and then, overhead, the steady green light turned to flashing red. The star-jet completed her wing-over, shorn of one wing.

Outside, Jim heard the oscillating wail of emergency vehicle sirens. Inside, there was silence except for the steady shriek of the Geiger counter responding to a barrage of gamma rays. Head spinning, Jim groped in the darkness for the lowest switch on the left side of the panel. As the spinning black vortex of the panel sucked him in, he threw the switch and groaned, "LUCIFER'S LOOSE."

14

LUCIFER'S LOOSE

With his one good eye, Peter Stoneham surveyed the bank of scanner screens that lined the wall of his office. Six separate silent pictures gave him a view of strategic locations around the Airstation. There was at the moment very little activity anywhere. It was 4 a.m. on the morning of May 6th and it had been one of the worst nights that Peter could remember.

When Joannah had failed to come home Wednesday night, he had assumed that she was retaliating because he had missed their regular Wednesday evening supper date. Moreover, he had been sure that she had stayed overnight with her friend, Evelyn Sebring. He could have confirmed that fact by calling Evelyn, but such a call would, he decided, be an admission of defeat. He did not intend to be defeated in this matter. Joannah's delusions, harmless enough, even pleasant at first, were threatening to get out of hand. They had to be dealt with.

Unfortunately, Peter's change of shift occurred Thursday so that he had all day to brood alone undistracted at the apartment. By early Thursday evening, he had persuaded himself that Joannah would by now be repentant and would make amends, as she always did, by seducing him. Having built himself up to a fever pitch in anticipation of that outcome, he'd finally called Evelyn. Joannah was not there, indeed had not been there. Frustrated, angry, and embarrassed, he had videophoned all their other friends and acquaintances to no avail. By the time he had left for his midnight shift at the Airstation, he was beginning to be worried.

Since midnight Peter had tried repeatedly to engross himself in the responsibilities of his job. The problem was that things were so quiet he had found it impossible to take his mind off Joannah. Nothing, absolutely nothing of significance showed up on the scanner screens. All the runways were vacant. The Airstation tower contained a skeleton staff, most of whom at the moment were pretty unoccupied, other than keeping an eye on the radar screens.

As the night wore on, visions of Joannah standing there nude in her silly green hat began to haunt Peter. His feelings of embarrassment at the more threatening aspects of her delusions were increasingly replaced with a renewed sense of wonder at her incredible beauty and the old sense of his enormous good fortune in being married to her. Finally, he had called his friend, John Murphy, Chief of the City Security Force. Murphy had assured Peter that he would run the standard checks at the various Life Conservation Units and get back to him. That had been nearly an hour ago.

The videophone buzzed loudly, and Peter, reacting instantly, swiveled to face the screen. He found himself looking at the image, not of John Murphy, but of Noel Baker Smyth dressed modestly in an elegant dark robe. The Director of Master Med stared intently at Peter with his piercing gray eyes. His normally immaculately placed white hair was not disheveled but was short of perfect with a wide thick wave flopped across his forehead. He leaned forward as he spoke. "We have a flight in trouble, Triple Six Lima," Smyth said abruptly without pleasantries.

The fact that the Director of Master Med was relaying this information could mean only one thing. Peter reached across and depressed the yellow alert button as he continued to listen. He felt himself tense.

"Triple Six Lima is a Lucifer Flight," Smyth continued. He spoke quickly, directly, "This is top priority. Divert all aircraft." Smyth's voice took on a tone of urgency. "Stoneham, in the event of a crash, the plane is to be cordoned off and you will await the arrival of the security people from Master Med."

Peter's head twitched as he waited for Smyth to finish. He resisted the impulse to jump into action. He knew his job well enough and these instructions were an unnecessary waste of time. He forced himself to remain still.

"The security people will be equipped to handle radiation problems," Smyth added abruptly.

"I'll keep in touch."

The videophone screen went blank. Peter reached for the tower button. "You boys working on Triple Six Lima?"

"Yes, the call just came in."

"You're diverting other aircraft?"

"Yes, not much coming in anyway."

"What runway?"

"Two-six. We're having it foamed."

"Okay, I'll be back to you." He was already typing into the computer console on his desk:

TRIPLE SIX LIMA?

The readout screen on the right of his desk lit up instantly:

TRIPLE SIX LIMA, LUCIFER FLIGHT,
SWING-WING STAR-JET.
DEPART GREENWICH SIX A.M. (GMT) ONE A.M. (EST),
ETA BRADLEY—FOUR A.M. (EST)

The readout screen flashed blank for an instant then returned:

CONTACTS:
REYKJAVIK, TIME 0652 ZULU
EREWHON THREE, TIME 0743 ZULU
ST. JOHN'S, TIME 0801 ZULU
BOSTON, TIME 0836 ZULU
NEW YORK, TIME 0850 ZULU

At this juncture the telescreen began flashing in red letters in its lower left quadrant:

0851 MAYDAY DECLARED

The information poured onto the screen:

WINGS JAMMED—THIRTY DEGREES SWEEP,
AUTO CONTROL OUT,
INERTIAL GUIDANCE OUT,
VACUUM GYRO SYSTEM OUT.

Peter jabbed again at the keyboard of the computer console:

PILOT?

The telescreen made the identification without hesitation:

PILOT: JAMES ADAM SEBRING
RANK: SENIOR CIVIL CAPTAIN
D. DATE: AUGUST 13, 2222
TOTAL TIME: 7437 HOURS
TIME IN TYPE: 1574 HOURS

"Jim Sebring, of course . . . of course," Peter muttered, "that's Sebring's run." That's bad luck for Evelyn, he thought, but then with 1500 hours plus in a swing-wing job, Sebring would be as good as anybody to handle the problem.

He crossed quickly to the videophone.

"Sebring, Evelyn."

A high-pitched buzz announced that he had connected with the Sebring household, but the videophone remained blank. He waited, impatiently drumming his fingers on the side of his desk.

Finally, the videoscreen flashed into life. Evelyn was sitting up in bed, quite inefficiently clutching some bedclothes around her. She was half asleep, and Peter watched, fascinated by her unguarded and simple humanity as she reached across to fumble with her own videophone. Abruptly the picture on the screen disappeared.

"Peter?" Her sleepy voice jogged him back to the situation at hand. "Peter, what's wrong?" There was a short pause, then he heard Evelyn's voice again, "Peter, is it Joannah?"

"It's Jim," Peter said, all efficiency again. His voice conveyed the urgency of the moment. "Jim's in trouble, Evelyn. He should be coming in any minute now."

"Jim?"

"Evelyn, you'd better come right down." He didn't wait for a reply but returned immediately to the tower video monitor. He flicked on the audio and listened.

"Triple Six Lima, this is your final controller." Inside the tower control room, a balding, hawk-faced controller was crouched over the radar screen flanked on either side by intent observers. "I have you seventeen miles out on the center line."

Peter turned up the audio. There was some fast conversation between the controller and his supervisor, who leaned over his left shoulder. The hawk-faced one returned to his mike, "I repeat, this is your final controller. Are you receiving me, Triple Six Lima?" The controller ran his hand across his balding head and turned again to his supervisor. "Looks like his radio is out, Linda."

"Continue to give him his position," she said tersely.

The controller returned to his mike, "Triple Six Lima, I have you ten miles out on the center line, low, ground speed three-five zero knots."

Peter turned down the audio and walked quickly across to the observation window, which constituted one wall of his office. His gaze swept the length of Runway 26. It was brilliantly lit and the foam looked like a fluffy layer of stratus clouds when viewed from above. As yet he could see nothing of the incoming aircraft and he reflected briefly on the nature of Jim Sebring's situation. It would have been difficult for any plane to make a belly landing under such circumstances, but with the cargo of a Lucifer Flight—Cobalt 57 at full potency, Jim's situation was dire indeed. Peter found himself analyzing the situation almost mathematically, and he reflected with satisfaction that his feelings for Jim Sebring—whatever they were—didn't impair his objectivity.

His thoughts were interrupted by the scream of tormented jets and suddenly Triple Six Lima came thundering out of the night. She was coming in very fast, nearly twice the speed of a normal approach, but even at that speed she was settling.

Peter heard the engines cut off and watched tensely as the shining black star-jet whistled across the threshold lights. There was a brief spurt of the engines again, and then silence except for the whistle of the wind around the streamlined fuselage. Ironically, she looked more beautiful now than ever with her wings swept back and cleared of dangling wheels and flaps.

And then, she was on the foamed runway and sliding.

"Beautiful!" Peter breathed. It was as soft a landing as he'd ever seen. Whatever Sebring's shortcomings, they did not include anything to do with piloting an airplane.

"Beautiful!" he repeated. But Triple Six Lima was moving unbelievably fast. The sudden thunder of the reversed jets startled him. The speed of the airplane slowed noticeably, but she continued to slide down the runway. The plane was getting close to the end, very close! Peter could see she was not going to make it. The star-jet lurched off the end of the runway and tipped violently sideways. Her left wing found a drainage ditch and then she somersaulted over, breaking off the wing. The plane came to a standstill, right side up and minus one wing. It was 4:11 a.m.

Suddenly the red light on the computer console on Peter's desk began flashing. The thin sound of a siren started low and rose slowly up the scale until it reached a steady, insistent whine. Peter went from the window back to his desk in two strides and flicked a switch.

"Rescue!" His voice was urgent. "I want that plane cordoned off immediately. Keep all personnel at least three hundred feet away." He reached almost simultaneously for the videophone.

"Smyth, Noel Baker," he said tersely.

The video lit up instantly. Smyth was waiting, looking now a little drawn, his robe exchanged for a conservative business suit.

"Lucifer's loose," Peter said in a tense voice, his right hand massaging his deformed left shoulder.

Smyth's response was immediate. "Radiation team is on its way. I will be there shortly. Has the plane broken up?"

"No, it looks like it's lost a wing, but otherwise it's intact, about two hundred feet off the end of the runway. I think . . ."

"Okay," Smyth interrupted abruptly. "You know the procedure." The videoscreen went blank.

Peter Stoneham crossed to the observation window and watched as a security van sped from the approach end of Runway 26 to the crash site. The Master Med security people were even more efficient than the Airstation force, Peter reflected.

He watched as the van stopped at the hastily constructed cordon. There was a momentary delay and then the cordon was opened. The security van drove up to the place where the runway ended and the terrain became a ditch. Here it swerved abruptly to the right and detoured round the ditch to reach the plane on the other side.

He watched two figures emerge from the truck, the radiation team clad in sparkling gray metalized fabric suits with integral shoes and gloves. Both persons wore cylindrical helmets with radiation face shields, and each carried on his back a breathing canister that was connected to the helmet. The suits were positively pressurized to insure against infiltration of air contaminated with radioactive dust.

The two radiation people, walking clumsily in their heavy suits, crossed to the star-jet and vanished inside. A minute or so later they emerged supporting Jim Sebring firmly between them. Each holding an arm, they escorted Sebring to the security van where a third figure took charge of him.

Peter breathed a sigh of relief. It was impossible at that distance to determine the extent of Sebring's injuries, but at least he was alive.

As the radiation team retraced its steps to the battered star-jet, Peter returned to the computer console and punched in the words:

LUCIFER'S LOOSE?

He knew that the computer would respond with precise procedural instructions. He also knew he did not need those instructions. The "Lucifer's Loose" drill was a priority item in his training. Even the parts of the procedure that made no sense to him were indelibly imprinted on his mind. Still, one last check could do no harm.

Having read the instructions carefully, Peter punched a button marked: INFIRMARY and swiveled to watch scanner number four. He nodded in satisfaction at the scene. Two medical technicians stood at the receiving entrance, obviously in readiness. Peter switched on the audio and addressed them. "You people are aware you'll be handling a radiation case?"

The technicians turned to face the video sensor and the taller of the two, the senior man, replied, "Affirmative."

"The name is James Adam Sebring," Peter said.

"Yes, we're already getting a read-out from Master Med. We'll have the complete scoop as soon as we get him here and plugged in."

"Okay," Peter said. "Let me know as soon as you do." He switched his attention now to the monitor covering the security office near the main entrance to the Airstation. He snapped off the audio to the infirmary and switched on the security office audio.

"A woman, Evelyn Sebring, will be arriving shortly, probably at the main entrance." Peter's right hand moved quickly among the buttons of the console. "That is her picture that you see on your screen now. As soon as she gets here you are to take her to the infirmary."

He did not wait for a response, but switched back abruptly to the scanning screen close up of Triple Six Lima. A second security van was now backed against the plane and the radiation team was obviously in the process of loading Lucifer into the van.

Peter punched the console and tersely demanded, "Unit One!"

"Unit One here."

"Patch me to the radiation team," Peter snapped.

"Radiation." The response came after only a momentary pause.

"How bad is the spill?"

"Not bad, we've got it all. You'll be clean as soon as we clear out."

"What about the pilot? How bad?"

The answer was quite cheerful. "Oh, he's in good shape. Some minor lacerations—a gash on the head and injury to the right knee—doesn't look serious."

Peter sighed. "And what about the radiation?"

"Now that's another story," the voice was matter of fact. "In that respect, of course, he's a goner. The plane's meters show the poor bastard took a couple thousand Roentgens."[74]

"Damn!" Peter said quietly. He turned the video off but continued to gaze at the blank screen, lost in contemplation.

"Yes, yes, I know about the mild concussion and the knee injury, et cetera." Peter, having hurried to the infirmary, was shaking his head impatiently as he spoke with one of the medical technicians. "What about his L.C.F. and D. Date?" He glanced at the screen that would normally deliver the vital data, but it was blank except for the inevitable homily:

WE CAN'T PREDICT ACCIDENTS;
WE CAN PREVENT THEM!

"The L.C.F. readout is off the scale." The technician shrugged. "His D. Date has stabilized at May 16th. That gives him ten days."

Peter's head, already cocked to one side, twitched convulsively toward his high shoulder. "What are the symptoms?" he demanded.

"There are no symptoms yet," the senior technician replied. "In a few hours maybe there will be some. We're not equipped, but the L.C. Unit will be able to hold down the nausea and diarrhea. Nobody can do anything about the cell ionization. In five days, six maybe, he'll start losing hair and begin hemorrhaging. They'll be able to control the hemorrhaging but beyond that there's nothing we can do." He shook his head. "It's as if he were aging at a fantastic rate."[75]

"I see," Peter said thoughtfully. "Yes, I see. Has he been told?"

"Yes, he knows."

"How is he taking it?"

"He was mad as hell, at first. He's quieted down now though."

---

[74] The "Roentgen" is, of course, the standard measuring unit for radiation.

[75] In fact, irradiation serves here as a synecdoche (part for whole) of the D. Date problem. Jim feels nothing, but he knows that he will die, and he knows when he will die.

"Is it safe to go in?"

"Yes, there's no danger of secondary contamination. He's clean. In fact, he was clean when he came in. He got nothing on him, apparently." The technician nodded toward a door at the rear of the reception room. "In fact," he said, "he has a visitor in there right now. Someone came over from Met Comm."

"Who the hell let him in?" Peter demanded.

"It's not a him. It's a her and why not? It makes no difference. And, besides, the poor fellow . . ."

"It makes a good deal of difference," Peter said, his head twitching. "He is to be allowed no visitors without specific permission from me."

"Why not?" The technician eyed him insolently.

"Don't ask me," Peter said. "Those are the instructions from Master Med. Get that woman out of there!"

The technician regarded Peter sulkily. "All right," he said. "All right, but I tell you he's clean."

Peter walked toward the door at the rear of the room, then hesitating, turned round. "His wife will be allowed in to see him after I've interviewed him," he said. "She's on her way over now."

"What about his P.H.O.? Calderoni will want to see him."

"Don't worry about it," Peter answered. "Master Med is sending a man down who will replace Calderoni. By the way," he added, "Master Med has also dispatched a couple of security people. They will be in charge as soon as they arrive."

"Security people? Why, for God's sake? Don't they know he's clean?"

"Just see to it that you follow their instructions," Peter said curtly, heading toward the entrance to the isolation unit.

As the door slid open, Natasha Mollenskaya emerged, her face pale and tear-stained. Peter paused for a second as if to question her, but then, thinking better of it, passed quickly inside.

Inside the isolation room, Peter moved quietly over to the bed where Jim Sebring lay with a bandage on his head, the color of his face not significantly different from that of the sterile robe he wore. It very quickly became obvious to Peter that Sebring felt better than he looked. In fact, Peter's presence precipitated an outburst from Jim that could be heard outside the room.

"Look here, Stoneham, some Gorasdamned SOB . . ." Jim nodded in the direction of the videophone, "has just informed me that I am to be stuck here without visitors."

"Evelyn is on her way here right now, Jim," Peter said, using his most conciliatory tone.

"I have ten days!" Jim yelled. "Ten days; that's all, and maybe only half of them usable. If some blockhead thinks I'm going to spend them here, he's got another damn thing coming!"

Peter's head twitched in irritation. He was aware that Jim's voice could be heard outside the room and that others, no doubt, were listening.

"Jim, let's discuss that later." His voice was apologetic and his irritation completely disguised. "I've got to get some details," he said a little awkwardly.

Peter felt embarrassed and at a disadvantage. Sebring was beyond the reach even of Peter's powerful security bureaucracy now, and they both knew it. He reached across and flicked the function switch onto RECORD. "You don't mind?" he asked. "We need to record some details."

Jim leaned back against his propped pillows and stared ahead resignedly.

"Well, let's see. We can get the details of the wing malfunction later. We've gotten the basics from the sector controllers. What we need," Peter continued more at ease now, "is your account of the crash."

"Well, damn it, you must have seen that better than I did."

"Yes," Peter said, "and may I say that under the circumstances you did a marvelous job. But, I need to know: did you remain conscious?"

"Yes. No. I was out momentarily."

"But, you did hit the Lucifer button?"

"It's a switch, not a button, and yes, I hit it just before I passed out."

"How did you know there was a leak?" Peter leaned forward with interest.

"Lucifer, or at least half of it, was lodged in the bloody cabin roof, that's how. Besides, the Geiger counter was screaming its head off."

"You say Lucifer broke open?" Peter interrupted.

"That's what I said." Jim's manner was impatient.

"And the contents?" Peter asked.

"I don't know," Sebring said. "I saw two containers. A small metal canister and—I think—a glass container. It didn't break though. It might have been Lucite, maybe a vial."

"Did you come into direct physical contact with either?"

"I don't think so. Something could have hit me, I suppose, but I don't recall feeling anything."

"Where were they?" Peter asked. "The containers, I mean?"

"One was on the floor, right side, by the rudder pedal. That was the metal canister, I think. The other was on the right seat."

"How far away?"

"It's a foot to the seat, maybe two feet to the floor."

"Did you see them spill?

"No. I told you—I don't believe they did spill. It was dark. I was unconscious for a while—not long, I think. I saw them when I came to. The rescue people had the floodlights on. Neither of them looked broken to me. In any case, it doesn't matter. The bloody gamma rays pass through those containers like tissue paper."

"You didn't touch either container?"

"No! Are you kidding? I got the hell out of the cockpit."

"Did you attempt to get out of the plane?"

"No. It was too late. I had a drink."

Peter rolled his good eye incredulously. "You did what?"

Sebring sat upright in bed again. "Look, you stupid SOB, can't you get it into your head? I was a dead man . . . I am a dead man."

Sebring looked down then and examined his hands as if he were looking for some evidence, some indication of the reality of his fate.

"Get the hell out of here," he exploded suddenly and then dropped back onto his pillow and turned away from Peter.

Peter got up abruptly. He knew that there was not much more information to be gained at this point. He nodded briefly at Jim and patted his arm as he turned to go.

Jim snarled suddenly, "And send me a Gorasdamned drink."

"There'll be people here from Master Med," Peter said as he was leaving. "They will want to talk to you."

"The people from Master Med can go to Hell!"

"Evelyn will be here shortly," Peter said in response. The door quickly rolled closed behind him as he left.

Peter felt perplexed by his feelings. His own accident sensitized him. He felt genuinely sad at Sebring's misfortune. Even so, if ever a man had asked for it, it was Jim Sebring. Still . . .

"Mr. Stoneham . . . Mr. Peter Stoneham . . ." The loudspeaker interrupted his thoughts.

One of the medical technicians approached Peter. "I believe City Security is trying to reach you."

"Good grief! I'd completely forgotten." Peter glanced at his chronometer. The time was 5:45 a.m. He practically ran into the small office that was indicated to him by the technician. He crossed the room to the videophone and punched the RECEIVE button. On the small screen appeared the hearty face of his old friend, John Murphy.

"If no news is good news, Peter, I have good news for you." Murphy smiled reassuringly. "Nobody answering Joannah's description has been checked into any of the L.C.U.'s in the last forty-eight hours. City Morgue got three D.O.A.'s," Murphy continued. "Two are regular D. Date cases—died in their sleep. The third, a Caucasian female, was apparently raped, stabbed, and beaten beyond recognition by S.D.'s. We don't have an I.D. on her yet."

Murphy saw Peter's head twitch convulsively and hastened to reassure him, "Not to worry, Peter. This woman got it in Central Park after dark—hardly likely your wife would be there at that time. Strange case though . . ." Murphy rambled on, oblivious to the impact of his words, "first time they've gone that far. They'd stripped her except for this funny green hat, and she had a death grip on a picture of P. Goras, only it wasn't Goras . . . ."

15

POST NATURAL DEATH

James Sebring watched the retreating figure of Peter Stoneham and then slowly shifted his gaze to regard his own hands. He turned them over, looking compulsively for the first signs of his impending fate. Seeing nothing that he could identify as different, he swung himself off the bed and limped across the room to the mirror on the opposite wall. The face that stared out at him was that of a dead man, but the evidence was not in the mirror. The eyes were a little sunken, showing the effect of fatigue, the cheeks pallid, but there was otherwise nothing to testify to the lethal gamma rays that had bombarded his body. Still, Jim knew it would not be long before the effects of the irradiation would be all too obvious. His hair and teeth would fall out, he would go blind, his skin would deteriorate.

"It is as if you were aging at a fantastic rate," the senior technician had told him.

That, of course, was precisely what his off-scale Life Consumption Factor meant. He was aging incredibly at this very moment and death would not intervene in time to save him from becoming just like one of those aged medical monstrosities of the Christian era.

If he were lucky, it would be five days before the deterioration set in, and five days after that he would be dead.

Well, Jim reflected, he'd probably want to hide in some Life Conservation Unit during those last five days. He certainly wouldn't want anyone to see him. But before that happened, he had to get out of here. He had to see Evelyn and his kids and he had to see Natasha.

He stared at his own grim face and broke into a hollow laugh. He'd spent the last weeks worrying about Natasha's imminent death, fretting about the loneliness that would follow, and now the tables were turned. Natasha would live three times as long as he—a lifetime longer it seemed—and she wouldn't go through the horrible transformation with which he was now faced.

Jim shuddered and, turning quickly from the mirror, crossed to the closet at the left side of the bed. He fumbled with the OPEN button and the door responded. Inside, the closet was bare except for his disheveled uniform. He pulled the uniform from its hanger and tossed it on the bed. Discarding his sterile gown, he slipped into his clothes, hesitating only once when a sudden motion sent a wave of pain radiating from his temples. The hesitation, however, was only momentary. The people from Security would be on their way to transfer him to an L.C. Unit and he planned to be gone before they arrived. As he worked his feet into his shoes, the warning light above the entrance to the isolation room lit and the door slid open.

He jerked upright, wincing, his mouth open, prepared to say something but not knowing what to say. He was fully dressed now and his intentions would be obvious.

It was Evelyn who stood hesitantly in the doorway. Without warning, a dog brushed past her legs and bounded into the room. In an instant, Spitfire had his two front paws up against Jim's chest. Jim caressed the dog absently and looked up to meet Evelyn's eyes. She looked ambivalent, embarrassed almost. Finally, in a sudden rush, she ran to embrace him, burying her face in his shoulder.

Jim ran his hand through her hair comfortingly, wondering what words to say. "I've really done it this time," he said finally.

He felt Evelyn's body tense against him.

"Yes," she whispered. "They told me outside." She pulled herself away from him and looked him over at arms length. Her eyes were moist, but her voice was even. "You're dressed, Jim," she said.

"Yes." He wondered whether to admire her self-control or abhor it. "Evelyn, I have to get away, to get out of here—you understand."

"But Jim, you need medical attention."

He laughed dryly "There's nothing they can do for me or to me now but waste my time."

"All right, Jim," Evelyn acquiesced quietly, taking him by the hand. "We'll slip out together. I'll drive you home."

"No," Jim shook his head and gently pulled his hand away. "I can't go home, Evelyn; it's the first place they'd look."

"Where then?" she asked.

Jim could see the torment in her face now. He felt the impossibility of her position. He didn't answer.

"I passed someone, a woman . . . your friend the meteorologist," Evelyn's voice began to tremble, "on the way in." Her voice trailed away into uncertainty.

"Natasha Mollenskaya, she saw the crash and came over." Jim placed his arms around her shoulders and pulled her to him.

"Oh, Jim," she sobbed. "Oh, my God." She wrapped her arms around him and cried bitterly.

Jim felt the tug of his own guilt. He'd not spared much thought for Evelyn and the kids in all this—only for himself and for Tasha. He stroked again gently at her hair. He must try to leave Evelyn as emotionally free as possible. Perhaps he could give her at least that.

"Evelyn," he said quietly. "I guess it was bound to happen one way or the other. I think you knew it all along. You knew it all the time you complained about my D. Date attrition. Perhaps unconsciously you knew this was the way it would end." He sat down on the bed and pulled her to his side. "You've not been happy, Evelyn . . . I mean I've not made you happy. We've drifted apart somehow."

"It's strange," Evelyn said staring straight ahead as she spoke and appearing not to hear him, "but it was because of the Lucifer Flight that I found you, and now it is because of the Lucifer Flight that I'll lose you."

"We've been losing each other for a long time, Evelyn. Maybe I have been losing myself . . . my time, my life. I've been no good for you. You could . . . you should have done much better . . . perhaps now . . ." Jim hesitated, wondering if he should mention the possibility of an alliance for her with Noel Baker Smyth after he was gone. He dismissed the notion, but he felt better, released almost, as he realized these were not just words. Evelyn had been unhappy and would feel better—would be better off—though she couldn't be expected to see that now.

Evelyn opened her mouth to reply, but Jim shushed her. He could just make out the sound of a security van drawing up outside. He took her face between his hands and kissed her.

She embraced him and then reluctantly disengaged as he pulled himself up to leave.

Jim crossed to the door, turning quickly before he left for one final glance at Evelyn. She stood now, in the center of the room, motionless, her eyes riveted on him. It was a pathetic image he knew he would never forget. "Never" forget? Hell, his never was now ten days.

The door slid open as he approached it and he slipped from the room. Spitfire, after a moment of indecision, apparently made his choice and bounded through the door after Jim.

"No, Spitfire," Jim whispered urgently, pointing his finger back into the room. The dog wagged his tail, ignoring the entreaty. Jim heard the door on the far end of the corridor slide open, and with Spitfire on his heels he limped quickly around a corner and out of sight.

Hobbling hurriedly down the corridor, he looked anxiously for an exit. It turned up on the right, almost at the end of the corridor. He gave one final glance back, and then, followed by Spitfire, slipped through the fire door which was on the east side of the infirmary.

As he stepped out, the first rays of the rising sun danced off the row of airplanes immediately in front of him. In the distance the Great Clock tolled six times.

He stopped dead in his tracks awed by the sight. The rising sun . . . the airplanes . . . it was as if his life were a film and some operator had called for a replay. He had seen the same scene at the same time of day a few hours ago in Greenwich. Only the rising sun in Greenwich was a lifetime away, and the film had a very different ending now.

He broke into a crouching run, dodging behind the row of jets until he reached the cover of the Launch Control Building. Spitfire loped along behind him. The east gate of the Airstation was perhaps two hundred yards away, but it was presided over by a security guard. His absence would surely have been noticed by now. Jim didn't know whether anybody would care enough to try to stop him, but he didn't want to waste time finding out. Instead he elected to climb the tall resilient security fence that surrounded the

Airstation. Over the fence, he could head for the trees by the east gate and, using them for cover, walk out to the Southeast Expressway. A mile or so down the footpath that ran parallel to the expressway lay the group of buildings that included Natasha's apartment.

His head ached now, consistently, and his right knee had begun to throb. He looked down at Spitfire. "You'll have to go around, boy," he said, pointing along the length of the fence. The dog wagged his tail and remained contentedly motionless.

Jim shrugged and, turning towards the fence, inserted the toe of his left shoe in a small diamond-shaped space between the wires and hoisted himself up. As he reached the top and pulled himself over for the descent, Spitfire stood on his hind legs, his front paws on the fence, and watched. He made no sound.

Jim let himself drop from the fence from about five feet up. His right knee caved in the instant his feet touched the ground and Jim rolled over in a moment of agony. He lay panting, feeling a sudden overwhelming weariness. The perspiration that covered his forehead ran down into his eyes now, stinging them and misting his vision. A wave of nausea washed over him and he wondered if this could be the beginning of the radiation sickness already.

Jim pulled himself to his feet and followed the fence for a few yards before making for the trees. Spitfire followed him yard for yard along the inside of the fence. Sooner or later the dog would reach the east gate and find his way out.

Spitfire was a familiar sight at that gate, having greeted Charlie there day in and day out for the last eight years, so even if the guard saw the dog he would think nothing of it. And once Jim reached the footpath, he would be just a man walking his dog.

He felt the warm trickle of blood from his right knee run down his leg. His uniform, his shoes, even his face were muddied and wet where he had rolled inadvertently in the muck after his leap from the fence. Jim reflected ruefully that he'd be one hell of a mess walking his dog.

By now he had reached the belt of trees that lay beyond the fence just opposite the approach end of Runway 26. Peering through the trees he could just make out the battered remains of Triple Six Lima, unattended now and looking forlorn and desolate at the far end of the runway.

Inside the fence Spitfire had stopped and had begun to whine and scratch futilely, as if hoping to break out. Finally the dog let out an unearthly howl, and Jim stumbled out of the trees, making toward the point where Spitfire was furiously clawing at the fence.

As he drew closer, Jim saw up against the fence, on the outside of where the dog clawed, a dark form. He stopped, wondering if he were really seeing what he thought he saw, trying to concentrate his blurred vision and focus his mind. He moved a little closer, and then he paused again. He stopped suddenly with his weight resting on his right leg, but this time the searing impulse from his knee did not register in his brain.

There, no more than fifty yards away from the building in which he had worked for twenty years—there, slouched grotesquely against the outside of the fence with his back to Runway 26—was Uncle Charlie. Jim wiped his eyes and stood wavering, transfixed by the apparition.

Charlie's legs were stretched apart out in front of him. His arms were similarly wide open with his palms facing outward, as if in friendly greeting. His head was cocked to one side and back so that the wide vacant eyes appeared to be staring up the invisible sloping approach path to Runway 26. The face was ashen white and gaunt; the skull peering through the skin wore a death's head smile, almost a smile of triumph.

Charlie was dead! Jim sank to the ground, oblivious to the frantic whines of the dog, who sought desperately to reach his former master. Jim saw through a wet haze a vision of old age and of death as it once was, and he saw himself as he would shortly be.

16

UNCLEAN

"You always said that if Jim needed it you'd come back to help and you knew him as well as anyone did. How can I help him to get ready," Natasha hesitated, ". . . to die in ten days?" She addressed the question to the figure of Charlie Hazlitt, who sat across from her in the center of the room.

Charlie's rotund, weather-beaten face screwed up into an uncharacteristic frown. "It's very difficult. Jim's always been one for taking a chance, been willing to lose a few days here and there. But to have only ten days left," he said, scratching his head, "that's something else again."

"You know, Charlie, it's funny." Natasha was still in shock herself and her voice was dull and metallic, scarcely reflecting humor. "It's funny, but yesterday thirty-two days seemed so short, and now it seems like a lifetime . . . a lifetime I'll have to live without Jim. It's hard for me to grasp and it must be worse for him."

"Funny?" Charlie looked at her quizzically.

"I mean strange," she corrected.

Charlie nodded his understanding. "D. Dates are strange things. They remind you how little time you have, but at the same time, they tell you how much time you have, too." Almost mechanically he scratched his head again. "An accident like this is sort of like a broken promise."

Natasha scowled at him. That last line was a paraphrase of a standard security sermon and it irritated her, coming from Charlie.

He ignored her. "You know what else is strange?"

Charlie's voice was as flat as hers. "This radiation thing is just like a D. Date. You don't feel anything. You feel all right except maybe for a couple of extra aches and pains, but you know it's all over just the same." Charlie shook his head.

"You know something even funnier... I mean even stranger... Charlie Hazlitt?" Natasha gave a mirthless laugh. "This radiation thing is just like Post Natural Death, too. At least at the end it is."

"Jim, a P.N.D.? I do not understand." Charlie's face looked blank.

"Well, you ought to understand, Charlie, because that is what you are, or at least what you became." Again the mirthless laugh.

"Correction, I am Charles Mortimer Hazlitt; I am not a P.N.D.—Correction, I am Charles Mortimer Hazlitt; I am not a P.N.D—Correction..."

Natasha snorted her disgust and switched CLEM off. The figure of Charlie Hazlitt dissolved instantly. Natasha could understand how people, lonely and afraid, could seek solace in these computer holograms. CLEM was very clever and could consult its vast data banks and predict what a person might reasonably be expected to say in a particular situation. Occasionally it could produce an intelligent conversation, but something was missing. It was Charlie's BABEL all right, and the image in the center of the room seemed quite real if one didn't look too closely, but Charlie's spirit—that wasn't in CLEM's data bank, and never would be.

Natasha sighed. She had to recover her own balance and get ready to receive Jim. If all had gone well he'd be there shortly. But how could she help? Charlie, or was it CLEM, had provided no useful suggestions.

She wandered across the room to a mirror and gazed at her reflection. She tugged at an unruly strand of hair, and then, turning sideways to the mirror, she addressed her silhouette, "Natasha, old girl, he's a man and you're a woman. He isn't dead yet and neither are you. So get cracking." She turned and headed for her wardrobe in search of the flimsiest dress she could find.

"Good Goras, Jim! Did you crawl here on your hands and knees?"

Natasha had hastened to support the swaying apparition that presented itself at her door. He was covered in mud, blood ran down his face from beneath the bandage on his head, and a crimson stain was spreading down his pant leg. With one arm around his waist and the other grasping his arm around her shoulder, she helped him to a chair.

Jim sank into the chair with a groan and then managing a weak smile, said, "It's not as bad as it looks, Tasha."

"It had better not be, my friend." Natasha had turned and was mixing a drink for him.

She was framed by the light of the apartment windowpane. Jim could see through the diaphanous, pale green gown she wore as if it were nothing, and under the gown he could see there was nothing. He looked down at his disheveled uniform and remembered that a lifetime ago he had left Greenwich bent on making love with Natasha.

"Here, drink this."

The delicate scent of her body penetrated the musty odor of his own clothing.

"It's powerful, so go easy."

Jim took a swallow and then gasped for breath. The Cannabis and cognac brought tears to his eyes.

She laughed. "Stand up while you still can. We've got to get you cleaned up." She reached down to help him up.

He staggered to his feet, still grasping his drink in one hand. "I saw Charlie, Tasha."

She was busy sliding his jacket off. "So did I." Her hands began to work on his shirt buttons.

Jim looked at her puzzled.

"CLEM arranged it," she said waving at the computer console.

"Oh." He nodded. "It was the damnedest thing, Tasha. If I were a spiritual man, I would have believed he had come back to help me out . . . to keep a promise . . ."

Natasha slid his shirt off and ran her hand across his cheek. "And, of course, you aren't a spiritual man, are you, Jim?" She shook her head as if in despair at his inability to understand himself.

"Anyway, he was dead. He's gone."

"Oh, Jim!" Natasha stopped working on his belt to look up at him.

"Spitfire wouldn't leave him," Jim said, "He won't ever leave him is my guess." He took another swallow of the drink and swayed on one leg as Natasha removed a shoe.

She reached up and began to slide his pants down, easing one pant leg over the sticky spot that was his right knee.

The Cannabis and cognac was beginning to do its work. Jim was feeling better. He was standing there nude but unembarrassed as she rolled his clothing into a ball.

"Pour yourself another drink." Natasha wafted towards the lavatorium. "It's the uniclean for these," she waved the clothing, "and a bath for you." As she entered the room, she tossed the soiled clothing into the uniclean receptacle and walked across to the therapy panel above the recessed bath. She selected a mildly anesthetic and antiseptic mix and, setting the temperature for slightly higher than body heat, watched as the therapeutic mixture quickly filled the bath.

"You running us a bath?" Jim was leaning against the portal with a fresh drink in his hand and a lascivious grin on his face.

"I can't tell who you are under all that mud," she grinned back, "and I never bathe with strangers."

"We'll soon take care of that."

He lurched across the room and, still holding his drink, stepped down into the bubbling water.

Slapping his rear end as he passed, Natasha reached for the sulfa-soap.

Jim groaned with pleasure as the warm bubbling liquid went to work on his aching muscles. Natasha relieved him of his now empty glass and rubbed him from head to foot with the sulfa-soap. "I see you're recovering," she said.

Jim grinned sheepishly and reached for her. The gossamer gown floated down to her ankles and she slid down into the bath on top of him.

———

Jim opened his eyes abruptly. He had been sleeping soundly, but his dreams had been haunted by visions of Charlie and of Post Natural Death. The fears that those visions generated were still nestled in his gut.

Remembering slowly where he was and remembering suddenly why his sleep would be terrorized with fears, he shuddered involuntarily. He glanced over to where Natasha had lain beside him, to where he had forgotten for at least a brief interlude the desperateness of his new situation.

He threw back the covers and slid from the bed, determining to himself that his remaining time would be for living, not for moping. He glanced at the clock on the wall and saw that it was 2 p.m. The aroma of ham cooking and something else, mushrooms maybe, wafted into the room.

He looked around for his robe and then, remembering he was not at home, shrugged his shoulders and wandered from the room in his underwear. His right knee felt stiff and sore, but he consciously tried not to hobble. He peered into the kitchen where Natasha was manipulating the buttons on the micronic cooker.

She was dressed in a light blue caftan. The color complimented her black hair and, as she turned to greet him, Jim was aware that she was very beautiful. He stood watching her for a minute, wondering if she had been so beautiful when he first knew her, or if the beauty he saw was in knowing her. Natasha smiled as she saw him but waved him out of the room.

With a show of mock indignation Jim left. He sat down on the sofa in the living room to rest his leg. The National Public Business Channel was on CLEM, but the sound had been turned off. On the screen was the benevolent face of P. Goras—no doubt, Jim thought, acknowledging the overwhelming endorsement of his leadership in the recent national referendum. Jim reached for the remote and turned up the volume.

"I want to express the depth of my gratification at the size of the plurality," said Goras as his huge moon face crinkled into the slightest suggestion of a smile. He continued. "Nothing is more sacred to our democracy than the consent of the governed. That you have again given me your consent is a great honor."

Jim, anticipating the standard sermon about the value of persuasion as the instrument of social policy, thumbed the button on the remote to switch to the Local Public Business Channel. Again there was a talking head, this time that of a local official—but now, instead of sound, there was an L.P.B.C. apology for the loss of audio that was printed across the bottom of the screen. Jim amused himself by trying unsuccessfully to read the lips of the speaker. The picture switched to a close-up of a giant wind generator and then back to the official again.

Jim judged by the official's demeanor that he supported the project. Jim smiled to himself at the thought of people all over the city watching this official's lips move, all trying to decipher his message. He then reached for the remote and hit the feedback control button, raising it to its highest position. The contribution he would make to the motion of the flickering needle that measured audience feedback for the speaker at the studio would be infinitesimal. Still, another wind generator made sense to Jim and the official deserved his moral support. The demand for electricity would undoubtedly rise in the near future, and . . . Jim's thoughts stopped in mid-flight and he shrugged. He reached for the remote's music select button, reflecting that he had no future, near or distant.

At that moment, though, L.P.B.C. solved its audio problems and simultaneously the image of Noel Baker Smyth flashed onto the screen. "You have no doubt heard it rumored, and it was indeed a Lucifer Flight."

Jim leaned forward as Smyth's image was replaced by a picture of the battered remains of Triple Six Lima.

"The nuclear spill was, however, confined to the area of the crash, which has now been decontaminated and presents no danger to the general public." Noel Baker Smyth's voice oozed calm reassurance.

Jim shook his head resignedly at the exaggeration. Lucifer had indeed broken open, had bombarded him with a lethal dose of gamma rays, but the containers had not broken. Nothing had been spilled—not that it made much difference to Jim either way.

Suddenly, however, Jim's muscles tensed as the image of Noel Baker Smyth dissolved and was replaced with a picture of himself. The voice of Noel Baker Smyth was expressing concern for the pilot—James A. Sebring.

Tasha heard the name and came in from the kitchen. She stood behind Jim and leaned over his shoulder to watch the screen.

"Although Sebring was not seriously injured in the crash," Smyth said, "unfortunately he received a lethal dose of radiation. He has subsequently wandered away from the Airstation infirmary. James Sebring," Noel Baker Smyth continued, "is certainly suffering from shock, and possibly, as the result of a head wound, is also the victim of amnesia." Smyth's face became more intense as he paused before going on. "Citizens should be advised that Sebring may be a source of secondary nuclear contamination. It is therefore urgently recommended that anyone seeing this man should avoid any possible contact, or even close proximity to him, and should immediately inform Hartford Security of his whereabouts."

During this last comment, Natasha had let go of Jim's shoulder and taken an involuntary step backwards. After a moment, however, no doubt recalling their recent intimacy, she smiled and returned to place her arms around his neck and her face against his.

"Goras!" Jim yelled in amazement. "That's not true; that's just not true. They said at the infirmary that I was clean. And in any case, nothing spilled. There was no nuclear spillage." He swung around to face Natasha. "Why the hell would they say that, and why should they give a damn how or where I choose to spend my last days?"

Natasha shut off the video and pressed the music select button. "What do we care, darling?" she said returning to Jim. "Anyway, they won't find you here. Come on." She pulled at his arm, leading him towards the kitchen.

Jim became aware again of the smell of ham, and he also became aware, suddenly, of how hungry he was and how long it had been since he had eaten.

In the dining area, thick golden drapes closed off the slanting windowpanes, excluding the afternoon sunlight. Jim smiled. Natasha had spared no effort. The room was lit solely by the light of six candles in the candelabra at the center of a table. It was a small table with one bench at each end. Instead of the usual synthetic stuff, there were natural eggs and ham and mushrooms and small muffins of toast. Steam rose lazily from urns of vita mix and swirled around the dancing candle flames. Jim looked at the array and back at Natasha, appreciating her all the more because he knew how much she disliked domestic chores.

The two sat at either end of the table facing each other. Jim's gaze shifted from her eyes, which he could see were barely restraining tears, to the candelabra which she had fashioned with her own hands. He admired Natasha's hands. He admired the sensitivity with which on occasion they explored his body; he admired the dexterous intelligence they demonstrated at the keyboard; and he admired the grace they had achieved in constructing this crude, but altogether lovely, candelabra.

Her eyes followed his to the candelabra and she smiled. "Don't let the eggs get cold, Jim," she urged.

But he was gazing quizzically now at the candelabra. "Didn't you tell me you got the candleholders from Met Comm?" He waved at the metal canisters she had fashioned into candleholders; his voice expressed puzzlement.

Natasha looked at him with open surprise. "Yes. Why?"

"What are they used for—the canisters, I mean?"

"I told you, Jim," she said, "They're used to hold microfilm spools that we store information on. We use microform and microfilm for any information that we don't trust solely to the computer. It makes the best form of backup."

"I thought so." A note of suppressed excitement crept into Jim's voice.

"I don't understand."

"Lucifer contained one of those canisters." Jim's excitement was more obvious now.

"Yes," she said, puzzled. "You said something about a canister and a vial."

"Don't you see, Tasha?" He gripped her tightly. "It couldn't be radioactive."

"No," she said, "the Cobalt would not have been in the canister. The vial must have contained it."

"No, no, Tasha." He shook her now in his excitement. "It couldn't be." He shook his head. "It just couldn't be."

He got up abruptly and strode out of the dining room and over to CLEM. He typed in a question:

RADIOACTIVE COBALT?

The computer console responded with an instruction after only a brief pause:

STATE ISOTOPE: 57 OR 60

Jim jabbed the response:

57

The screen lit up instantly:

COBALT: 57
HALF-LIFE: 270 DAYS
TYPE OF RADIATION: GAMMA
PRIMARY USE:
  RADIO PHARMACEUTICAL
  GASTRO-INTESTINAL TRACT
  CAUTION! LEAD SHIELDING REQUIRED
  SEE ADVISORY 16 PERTAINING TO GAMMA PROTECTION

Jim stared for a moment at the message and then turned to Natasha, his eyes glistening. His voice was quieter but more urgent now. "Are you sure about the canisters?" he said.

She nodded, "Absolutely!"

"Are they used for anything else?"

"Yes," she said, "by clever people like me to make candelabras."

"Tasha," he said impatiently, "I need to know. Are they used for anything else?"

"No, I don't think so."

Jim stood for a second, seeming to absorb the information, wanting to be quite sure that he wasn't grasping at a delusion. His voice trembled with excitement as he spoke.

"Don't you see? If that were Cobalt 57, and if its radiation were sufficient to give me a lethal dose of gamma rays, it would have also ruined the microfilm."

"Good Goras, Jim!" She stood for a moment, mouth wide open without speaking. "Then you think . . . you think . . . you're not . . ."

"The Geiger counter was going like mad." Jim refused to jump at the reprieve. But Natasha was ahead of him now.

"That could easily be set to go off anytime Lucifer is opened. It wouldn't have to be gamma rays," she said.

"But why, for Goras' sake? Why would anybody go to all that trouble?" Jim shook his head in disbelief.

"Why would Noel Baker Smyth say you are contaminated when you're not?" Natasha's eyes were shining now. "Don't you see? They want you back. They want you back now, and they don't want anyone talking to you."

Jim was looking at his hands, turning them over to inspect both sides. "But then what is Lucifer and why the subterfuge?"

They stared at each other, neither attempting to answer.

"Evelyn!" Jim's voice was so loud and penetrating that Natasha jumped, "Evelyn told me all that I know about Lucifer, and you can bet Smyth knows more than she does."

He shot a glance at the clock and reached for the videophone.

"Sebring, Evelyn," he barked. Even as he uttered the terse command, he turned off the video sending unit.

After a short delay, Evelyn's face appeared on the screen. She looked fragile and weary. Her eyes appeared incredibly sad, and her normally fastidiously placed hair was disarranged. Jim read in the face of his wife hurt and dejection, a reflection of hopelessness, which he had never seen in Evelyn before.

"Evelyn," he said.

"Jim?" She was surprised. "Jim!" she repeated.

"Yes, it's me."

"I don't have your picture, Jim. Your video's off."

"I know," he said. "They're looking for me."

"Yes, there are security people here outside the building."

"Evelyn, there's something wrong about all this."

"I saw the broadcast," she said. "It's strange. You're not contaminated, are you?"

"Evelyn, listen to me. Do you ever handle microfilm at Master Med?"

"Yes, we do sometimes. Not often though. But why, Jim?"

"What happens to Lucifer? I mean, who dispatches it and who receives it?"

"I'm the dispatcher," Evelyn said.

"Yes, I know," Jim said, "but you don't actually handle Lucifer?"

"Oh, no, of course not. I suppose the Master Med section . . ."

Jim stared at the image of his wife intently. "Does Noel Baker Smyth ever receive a canister?"

"A canister?"

"Yes, you know, the small cylindrical containers for microfilm. They're little black canisters, maybe with two silver dots on the cap."

"Yes." Evelyn paused for a minute. "Come to think of it, yes, I think he does."

Jim reached forward as if to grab his wife through the screen. He placed his hands on the case surrounding her image. "Evelyn," he said slowly, "think now, does he get the canister immediately after a Lucifer Flight?"

Evelyn's fingers explored her forehead. "Yes . . . yes, I think maybe he does. But Jim . . . ?"

"What does it contain?" Jim's voice was strained and intense.

"I don't know. It always goes directly to Noel in his office."

"What does he do with it?"

"I don't know."

"Evelyn, listen! Assuming it contains microfilm, what would Smyth want with it?"

"We sometimes transfer the most sensitive video data to an un-networked computer by microfilm."

"Well then," Jim said, "you would enter that data?"

"Not necessarily, Jim. Noel might if . . ."

"Well, you would know if he put it in himself?"

"I may not, especially if he loaded it himself. It would be because it's classified and it would go into the computer at a level to which I don't have access. Only Noel . . ."

"Evelyn, I must know if that canister contains microfilm or not. And if it does, I must know what's on that microfilm. Can you find out?"

"Jim, if it's classified it would be difficult to get, perhaps impossible. Besides . . . why?"

"You must try, Evelyn." He paused. "It's life or death for me."

"Jim, I thought . . . I mean, you're . . . I don't understand. For Goras' sake, you've got to explain . . ."

"I can't explain now, Evelyn," he said, "but I think something's wrong with this Lucifer set-up. Just try, Evelyn. Will you try to find out? I can't explain now."

Evelyn's face stared at him from the screen for a moment. Her voice wavered, "I'll try, Jim. I will try, but you must explain soon. You can't leave me like this."

Jim glanced anxiously at the clock.

"Evelyn, I have to go. Someone may be trying to trace this call. If I'm right about my suspicions, I may have plenty of time to explain later."

He jabbed at the console and Evelyn's worried face dissolved, leaving the screen blank.

17

GENESIS CODE

Frustration—the puzzle of Jim's call, the business of the human watchdogs outside her house, the interrogation of the computer—nothing added up, nothing came through. What could Jim possibly have meant, she wondered, when he said something was wrong with the Lucifer set-up? And how could he translate what was left to him into "plenty of time?"

It was all frustration. Evelyn began to feel the pressure of it jangling her nerves.

Think logically, she told herself, leaning her head into her hands and concentrating her stare onto the dark top of her desk. First, what about Lucifer?

The Lucifer set-up was simple enough. Cobalt 57, which was used medically and industrially around the world, was transported by Lucifer Flights. Its production and distribution were carefully controlled by the International Commission at Greenwich, England. Elaborate precautions were taken to safeguard the material and to protect against its radioactivity. It was all very simple, straight-forward, and, up to now she had thought, pretty much foolproof.

But nothing was completely foolproof and Jim almost naturally would have to be the one to prove that point. And so it had happened to Jim's flight. Unexpected clear air turbulence, she'd been told—just some invisible thing in the heavens. But that invisible thing had attacked Jim's star-jet, wiped out Jim's future—and her future, too, she thought, indulging in a moment of self-pity. In spite of all his faults and regardless of their difficulties, she still could not contemplate the final and total devastation of their D. Date compatibility. She still couldn't believe it.

If only Jim's accident had occurred on his outgoing trip to Greenwich instead of on the return flight, his exposure to the Cobalt would most probably not have been lethal. As it was, he had been carrying a Cobalt shipment that had been regenerated to full radioactive potency.

But what had the canisters to do with all that, she thought, forcing her mind back to the problem. And the microfilm, what was supposed to be on the microfilm anyway?

Jim's erratic call on Saturday could well have been the result of a confused mind reacting to shock and amnesia. But still, she thought, he was right about one thing: there was something odd about the reports of his being a carrier of secondary radiation. Logic told her that just could not be true. It was either a mistake or a deliberately false report. She had seen Jim herself at the infirmary and if Jim had been contaminated, then why had she been allowed to see him? And even if her admittance had been an oversight, a foul-up, why had she not been subsequently contacted?

The security guards, too, who had appeared outside her house—what were they doing there? The two watchdogs had been there when she had returned from the infirmary and the post had not been vacant since. It was understandable, she thought, that they would be anxious to give Jim medical treatment, but their vigilance was a little too much.

In any case, all her attempts to solve the puzzle had only increased her frustration. Her interrogations of the computer had been futile and disappointing. She had discovered nothing she didn't already know. But then, that wasn't unreasonable. If she entered the computer at her own security level, what else would she expect but a replay of the information that had always been accessible to her? If, as Jim seemed to think, the computer held some information important to his case, then access to it, she thought, was not a matter of her BABEL, but of Noel Baker Smyth's *Bible*.

She recalled a long time ago seeing Noel entering something from the *Bible* into the computer, and she remembered thinking at the time that coming from the *Bible* it could hardly be substantive data, so it must be his access code. Obviously, if she was to find anything out, she must get hold of that code.

She raised her head and stared at the clock on the opposite wall. It was 4 o'clock, Monday afternoon—two days since Jim had called—and she had learned nothing yet. Her gaze drifted to a flight of stairs that led from the center of her office up to the massive door which was the entrance to Noel's office. Somehow, if she were ever to solve Jim's puzzle, she had to get through that door.

As if in response to her thoughts, the videophone on her desk suddenly buzzed into activity and Evelyn jumped. She swiveled quickly in her chair and saw on the videoscreen the face of Noel Baker Smyth.

"Evelyn, I didn't know you were in. Security just told me."

"Yes, yes, I'm in," she said almost too quickly. She had the uncanny feeling that Noel had been watching her from the videoscreen, watching her for a long time and listening to her thoughts. She felt as if he already knew what she was contemplating. "I've been in all morning," she said. "You must have arrived while I was out on my morning break."

"Evelyn," his voice was quiet, almost a whisper, "I'd like to say how very sorry I am about the accident."

She nodded, again almost too quickly. "If there's anything I can do?"

"There's nothing. No. But thank you. I just thought—well, there's nothing I can do at home. Every time I go near my kids I start to sob, and our nanny is helping me out, keeping them distracted from our problems. I'm trying to keep things as normal for them as possible. I thought I might as well . . ." She left it hanging.

Stop over-explaining, Evelyn, she told herself resolutely, forcing a fleetingly brave smile. Stop acting guilty. You haven't done anything yet.

"Of course, I understand." He nodded sympathetically. "Why don't you come up and visit?"

Noel greeted her at the door and escorted her silently to a comfortable leather seat. He waited for a minute and then, still speaking quietly, asked, "You haven't heard from Jim?"

"No," she lied, clutching the note pad she had brought with her in her lap and trying not to fiddle with it.

"We're looking for him. We want to help."

"I know," she said. "I'm grateful for that. But the fact is, Noel, I came to work to get my mind off Jim. I need to think about something else for a few hours." She hesitated, judging her position by the compassion in his eyes. "You understand..."

"Of course I do, my dear. Say no more." He crossed the room and began riffling through a sheaf of papers, a bit self-consciously, she thought. He looked up after a moment.

"You may not know that Sam Orville lost the confidence vote in Northwestern Massachusetts, and not without some justification, I might add. In any event, you may want to check with Janet to make sure Vote Tabulation is ready to handle a gubernatorial run-off up there."

Evelyn moved over to Noel's desk and set her note pad down on the corner. Her eyes flicked across the desk and confirmed her suspicion that Noel's *Bible* was not in its usual place.

"The new G.N.P./Energy Consumption ratio for the region is in. It's up two points. The Elite Council will be happy about that. The labor section is revising the Compensation Index upward. You might make sure there are no hitches there."

Evelyn acknowledged the instructions with a smiling nod of her head. Noel was trying to keep her busy, trying to keep her mind off Jim's situation. He knew as well as she did that all workers received the same compensation and that the pay increment would be taken care of automatically. She glanced casually at the antique bookshelves on the left wall, searching for a black leather-covered book with gold lettering.

"The Agricultural Union is renegotiating its contract and it looks like they'll win another forty-five minutes. That will show up all over the place."

Evelyn made a note of that one. Noel was right. Time was the really important variable in these negotiations. If agriculture got forty-five minutes a week more leisure time, manufacturing would be bound to demand an adjustment, too, and so on down the line.

"That'll shake up the G.N.P. and eventually the Compensation Index," she responded. It was too obvious a comment, but Evelyn hoped that it would give the impression that her mind was on Noel's conversation. She was still searching fruitlessly for the *Bible*.

"Yes, you'll want to notify Resource Allocation to be prepared for some quick changes in the next two or three weeks." Noel was obviously absorbed in technical considerations now. "And the Arts Council will have to anticipate a heavier demand."

Evelyn nodded her satisfaction. She agreed with Smyth's analysis, and, more importantly, she had located the *Bible*. It was at the center of the second shelf.

"I don't want you to feel any pressure to take care of these things," Smyth added impulsively, "unless, of course, you think you need to become involved in doing something."

The Great Clock on the Common across the way began tolling. Noel glanced at the wall clock; it was 5 p.m.

"Anyway, for tonight," he observed, "it's getting late." He rose, hesitated for a moment, and then said abruptly, "Would you have dinner with me?"

Evelyn felt unusually grateful for the invitation, although she wasn't entirely sure why. Perhaps, she thought, it was that she needed to escape for a while from the tensions of what she knew she must do. And perhaps also it was that she felt at this moment a great need for the company of someone who knew her situation and who cared.

In any event, she accepted, to his obvious pleasure, and he excused himself to freshen-up before they left.

She watched quietly as he disappeared through the portal in the corner of the room that led to an adjoining private lavatory. Then, seeing her chance, Evelyn crossed quickly to the bookshelves. She withdrew the Bible from its unobtrusive spot on the second shelf.

With shaking hands, she riffled through the antique book from back to front, scarcely knowing what she was looking for. The book was well used. It was old in the first place and Noel referred to it frequently. Finding nothing significant, Evelyn was about to surrender her notion that Noel's computer access code was contained in it. Then, reminding herself of the reasons for her original suspicion, she riffled through it again.

She had seen Noel entering something from this *Bible* into the computer, but she knew that the computer already contained every word of this book—and indeed of all other books. Noel's entry had to be an access code. Finally her eye caught the flash of a different color, red, near the beginning of the book, in "Genesis" or "Exodus" maybe. Simultaneously the nearby sound of running water stopped, and, heart pounding with fear and frustration, she returned the book to the shelf and slipped back to her seat.

Seconds later Noel reappeared. She accepted his proffered arm, noting with satisfaction the pleasure the gesture gave him. As the massive door slid open in front of them, she stole one last guilty look at the middle of the second shelf. The Holy Book was there, but it was no longer unobtrusive. It was UPSIDE DOWN!

For Evelyn, the evening's escape with Noel at dinner had at least temporarily made things seem less catastrophic. She had been aware, of course, that nothing had been resolved. Nothing had changed. Jim's terrible disaster was still foremost in her thoughts, but Noel had been kind, gentle, and understanding. For Evelyn, it had been a long time since she had experienced such devoted attention.

He had asked her about her relationship with Jim and she had confided that lately the two of them had been drifting apart. When Noel had reminded her that he and she now shared perfect D. Date compatibility, she was tempted to confide more. It would have been so easy to trust him, to unburden the whole confusing issue of Jim's videophone call, of the puzzling public statements, and to let Noel explain it all.

But her loyalty to Jim had held her back. She had been torn in two directions, between that loyalty and the guilt she felt about deceiving Noel who obviously trusted her absolutely, but in the end, it was Jim who had the greater hold on her, and so she told Noel nothing of her communication with Jim and nothing of her intentions.

Neither had she told him that Jim was, at this very moment, living with Natasha Mollenskaya, a fact of which she now felt certain. Even on that subject Evelyn felt ambivalent. She was angry and hurt that Jim had not come home with her. As a woman he had diminished her, perhaps even negated her altogether. She sought refuge from that feeling by eliciting signs of sexual interest from Noel and he never failed to respond. On the other hand, her heart went out to Jim in light of the disaster that had overtaken him. He deserved to live his final days in freedom and away from the security guards. And if the Mollenskaya woman could give him some relief from the horror of these last few days, she wanted that for him, too.

After bidding Noel a rather awkward goodnight, Evelyn picked up a vacant E-car and drove across town to where Peter and Joannah's little apartment overlooked Central Park. After the initial shock of Joannah's death had worn off, Evelyn had scarcely had time to spare a thought for her young friend or for Peter. The exception had been two evenings ago when she had received a disjointed and distracting videophone call from Peter.

He had babbled on about his sin, his guilt, about Joannah's affection for her, Evelyn, about his own failure to protect the fragile person that Joannah was. But the thing that seemed to be destroying Peter, and he did appear as a man who had been destroyed, was the nature of Joannah's destruction. Peter's words had painted for Evelyn a picture of his vision of her last horrifying moments at the hands of the Senile Delinquents. And he had clapped his hands over his ears in an attempt to block out his own words. But apparently he could neither erase the picture from his mind, nor deal with the horror of its existence. Evelyn had wept with him when she watched him collapse into sobs and cry out piteously for escape from the haunting vision. She had resolved that she must go to see him, to give him what comfort she could.

She pressed her hand now firmly against the Plexiglas screen outside the door of Peter's apartment. The door of the apartment slid open immediately in recognition of the privileged relationship she had always had with the occupants. Evelyn stepped inside and then stopped in amazement at the scene which greeted her. The floor of the apartment was a foot deep in computer printout tape and CLEM was, at that very moment, busy spewing out more and more of it. At the center of the room, groveling on his knees in the tape, was Peter. His hair, normally immaculate, was completely unkempt; his face, showing several days growth of beard, twitched compulsively as he devoured the tape with his one good eye.

"Peter! Oh, Peter!" She waded across the room and, kneeling, threw her arms around the grotesque form.

He glanced at her for only a second, muttering, "Goras is a magician, Goras is a gypsy, Goras is a clown," and then went back to the task of examining the readout tape.

Evelyn, still holding Peter, looked across at the computer console, hoping to discover what had persuaded CLEM to join Peter in his seeming madness.

The words on the screen instructed CLEM to provide a list of all babies born on the day Joannah had been killed. Again Evelyn groaned his name, "Peter, oh, Peter." She rose to her feet, pulling some of the wretched tape from her arms as she did. "Peter, I'm going to get help."

His head cocked back and his eye blazed at her fiercely. "P. Goras is a magician, he's a gypsy, he's a clown."

Evelyn rushed to the videophone and called the emergency medical services. She waited until they came to Peter's apartment and took him to the hospital. Finally, she returned home, kissed each of her sleeping children, and collapsed into bed, still in her street clothes, where she fell into a troubled and exhausted slumber.

———

Sitting at her desk in the mid-afternoon of the next day, Evelyn found herself unable to maintain her normal professional stance. She put her head on her desk and began to weep. Her tears were not for Jim or even for herself, but for Peter. She had been weeping quietly for ten minutes or so, contemplating what had befallen her friend, and then the phone on her desk demanded her attention. Wiping her eyes, she touched the button on her computer keyboard which connected her to her caller via the videophone.

The call was from Noel. "Eve," said Noel, still gentle, still tentative, attempting not to encroach where it wasn't wanted. "If you're not busy, perhaps you could come up?"

As she walked slowly up the seven stairs that led from her office to Noel's, she pushed from her mind thoughts of Peter and Joannah and tried to steel herself for concentrated effort. Somehow she must find the opportunity to get what she needed.

"I need a printout on Jeremy B. Leventritt," Noel said. "I would like a complete file of all the information in our computer on him. I want to take it home tonight and do some reviewing."

For a second, Evelyn was mildly curious. She knew that Noel had received a message from the Elite Council that morning and wondered if his request had something to do with that confidential communiqué. But her mind quickly wandered. She stole a brief glance at the *Bible*. It was still upside down, painfully obvious to her but, she reasoned, not noticed by

Noel. How was she to get a second chance to examine that *Bible*? A thought clicked in her mind—an outside possibility. She rested her head for a moment against the back of her chair, eyes closed.

Noel reacted instantly. "If you're not up to it, Eve . . ."

She shook her head. "No, it's all right. I'm just a little tired."

"It was thoughtless of me," he said apologetically. "Of course, I can do it myself."

"It's not that," she said. "I find when I'm alone I tend to brood. Perhaps we could do it together?"

Noel grabbed at her suggestion. "Yes, of course."

Evelyn rose wearily. "I'll just run down and pick up Leventritt's I.D. Code."

"Stay seated, Eve." Noel's words were so intense they were almost a command. "You stay," he said motioning with his hands. "I'll get it."

Evelyn smiled gratefully.

She remained motionless as she watched him leave and listened for his footsteps down the stairs. Then, hands wet with perspiration, she crossed to the bookshelves and removed the black leather-bound *Bible*. She took a second to examine the book edgewise, noting with satisfaction that a single section at the beginning showed signs of being used much more frequently than the rest. She slid her thumbnail into the worn section and flicked the book open. She found herself staring at parts of the second and third chapters of "Genesis," marked in red. The number 17 was circled in the second chapter. Across the page, in chapter three, the text of verses 4 and 5 was clearly underlined in red. She spent a few seconds absorbing the information and then riffled once again through the book to confirm that there were no other markings and then returned the book to its place on the second shelf. This time she was careful to replace it right side-up. Before Noel returned, she found time to dry her perspiring palms and slow her breathing, though her hands were still trembling.

Noel entered smiling, I.D. Code in hand. "I should compliment you, Eve," he said. "Your office is immaculately organized. Mine should be so neat."

Evelyn had some trouble in addressing the computer in Basic Beta Language. She found that there was a tremor to her voice and it was difficult for her to maintain the monotone. She was relieved when the computer took over the conversation, and then, as it began methodically to print out the information on Leventritt, she found time to compose herself.

She hoped that her hands were no longer trembling, although she dared not look. She felt triumphant at having accomplished this much of her mission but also dejected at the way in which she had tricked Noel, betraying both his confidence and his concern for her.

Although it took no more than two minutes, it seemed to Evelyn an eternity until the computer had regurgitated all the information it contained on Jeremy B. Leventritt. Fortunately Noel seemed anxious to be on his way. He accepted the Leventritt folder with a smile of gratitude and escorted Evelyn back to her office.

After Noel vanished into the vertical transporter, she forced herself to wait five minutes and then slid her chair to its position in front of her own computer console.

She took a deep breath and switched the mode control to BABEL AUDIO, simultaneously depressing the READY button on the console. The "on-line" light flashed on. She hesitated for a second and then switched back to MANUAL MODE. Perhaps it made no difference, but Noel, because of his inability to master Basic Beta Language, would type in all his operations on the keyboard. She decided to do likewise.

She hit the ENTER key and the computer screen immediately lit up with the words:

USER IDENTIFICATION?

Evelyn entered her I.D. Code and then, responding to a further request from the computer, her password. The machine devoured the information and, satisfied with it, responded promptly:

REQUEST?

Evelyn stared transfixed at the keyboard. She hesitated again, wondering if she should stop at this point, do no more, forget the whole thing. But even as she wondered, she knew her decision had already been made. She was just postponing what she must do. Finally, she punched emphatically at the keyboard:

GENESIS 2:17?

The computer responded instantly:

BUT OF THE TREE OF THE KNOWLEDGE OF GOOD AND EVIL, THOU SHALT NOT EAT OF IT: FOR IN THE DAY THAT THOU EATEST THEREOF THOU SHALT SURELY DIE.[76]

Evelyn stared at the screen, mesmerized for a moment by the ominous warning.

Yesterday she had gone to some pains to borrow a copy of the *Bible* from the Municipal Museum, but she did not bother to consult it now; there was no reason to doubt that what she read on the screen was an accurate quotation of Genesis 2:17.

She felt vaguely disappointed. The computer was treating her interrogation as a normal request. Nothing at all unusual.

She turned again to the keyboard and this time punched in:

GENESIS 3:4?

The computer responded:

UNKNOWN

Evelyn looked at the response with a growing sense of excitement and disappointment. The reply was certainly abnormal. It was inconceivable that the computer did not know a part of the text of perhaps the greatest book in Western literature. Thinking she might have incorrectly typed her request, she tried again.

GENESIS 3:5?

---

[76]This is God's warning to Adam and Eve in the Garden of Eden.

The computer responded again:

UNKNOWN

Evelyn leaned forward in her chair and cradled her head in her hands to think. Why was the computer not responding to her request? And, if this was in fact Noel's entry code, why had the machine not accepted it as such? She was sure that she had the correct *Bible* references. As she visualized what she had seen in Noel's *Bible*, it suddenly occurred to her where her mistake was. The number 17, indicating that verse of Chapter two, had been circled in red ink, whereas, she recalled now that in Chapter three, verses 4 and 5 of the text were underlined. The whole quotation had been underlined; the verse numbers were not circled.

Noel was a careful, precise person. Of course, then, the markings indicated that the chapter and verse number only be given in Genesis 2:17, whereas Noel had indicated the actual text should be used for the references from Genesis 3.

Evelyn reached into her desk for her borrowed copy of the sacred text and swung around to the keyboard again. She was trembling now, certain she had the answer. Opening the Bible she carefully entered the text of Genesis 3, verses 4 and 5:

AND THE SERPENT SAID UNTO THE WOMAN, YE SHALL NOT SURELY DIE: FOR GOD DOTH KNOW THAT IN THE DAY YE EAT THEREOF, THEN YOUR EYES SHALL BE OPENED, AND YE SHALL BE AS GODS, KNOWING GOOD AND EVIL.

As the text unfolded on the screen, Evelyn felt the hair at the back of her neck stiffen. She ran her hands across the goose bumps on her arms. She shivered involuntarily at the vision of the Devil calling God a liar, but she knew she was on the verge of penetrating, if not the mind of God, at least the ultimate regions of the computer. And she knew the Director of Master Med well enough to know that this was just the sort of barrier he would erect.

God promised death, the Devil knowledge.[77] Well, Jim was dying anyway, and he needed to know why. She pressed the ACTIVATE button. The computer responded:

REQUEST?

She was in! Suddenly the feeling of guilt was gone, replaced by the euphoria of achievement. Suddenly she didn't care about what was proper, about what was right. She gloried only in her victory. She attacked the computer keyboard with ferocity:

WHAT ABOUT LUCIFER?

The computer surrendered. The screen began to fill immediately. Evelyn, uncomprehending at first, rapped out another question and then stared at the answer in disbelief. As the full implications of what she was reading began to dawn on her, she fired a barrage of queries at the compliant machine. Again she watched in amazement and terror as the mighty Master Med computer disgorged its sinister secrets. Finally, after a few moments of stunned silence, she reached for the videophone console. "Mollenskaya, Natasha," she said in a flat voice.

There was a short click, a brief whir, and then a woman's voice: "Natasha Mollenskaya here."

The videoscreen was blank.

Evelyn spoke again in a steady voice, with no trace of emotion, "Tell Jim he's all right; he's not going to die. Tell him . . . "

There was a single click and the line went dead.

Tears coursing down her cheeks, Evelyn swiveled to face the door and waited.

---

[77]And, of course, *Evelyn* is seeking forbidden knowledge to pass on to James *Adam* Sebring— she is playing exactly the same role as the biblical Eve.

18

KNOWING GOOD AND EVIL

Noel Baker Smyth was in a mild state of shock. Not that the communiqué had been entirely unexpected—one was supposed to be prepared to receive "the word" at any time. But he had supposed, quite reasonably he thought, that he would still have a few more years. He was not, after all, showing any obvious signs of physical or mental deterioration.

He paced the floor of his modest apartment, pausing occasionally to gaze at the computer into which he must sooner or later tap out his response to the message he held in his hand.

The message read:

> FROM: THE NATIONAL ELITE COUNCIL
> TO: NOEL BAKER SMYTH, DIRECTOR
> NORTHEAST REGION, HARTFORD.
> SUBMIT NOMINATION FOR A SUCCESSOR TO
> YOUR POSITION AS DIRECTOR IMMEDIATELY.

The message, Smyth mused, was terse and to the point—a typical Council communiqué. Still, he was puzzled and both disturbed and relieved. He was ambivalent. He had never been sure in the past exactly how he would feel when he received "the word." And now that it had happened he still wasn't sure how he felt. On the one hand, he was not sorry to relinquish the enormous responsibilities which had been assigned to him in his position as Director, responsibilities which he had neither sought nor expected. On the other hand, he would have been less than honest with himself were he not to admit that he enjoyed the power and prestige which had come with his position and which he must now relinquish.

He knew, of course, that ultimately a demand for his resignation and exile was inevitable. It went with the job. And yet, at his age, one would not have expected it. It seemed reasonable to suppose, therefore, that the Elite Council must disapprove of the manner in which he had discharged his duties. The Sebring affair, Smyth conceded to himself, was a bit of a mess but one not entirely of his own making. He sighed as he laid down the communiqué and examined his synopsis of the Leventritt file.

The obvious choice for his successor, he thought, was Maria Montenez. She had performed with considerable skill the function of P.H.O. to other P.H.O.'s—including Leventritt. It was no mean accomplishment, Smyth reflected, to socialize, integrate, and rationalize the existence of these people who themselves understood all, or almost all, the tricks of the trade. In most respects, Montenez was the obvious nominee. But she was married and that was a considerable disadvantage. More important was the fact, Smyth believed, that here was a woman who treasured her own illusions far too much to survive their destruction.

No, Smyth shook his head slowly, Leventritt would be a better choice. Leventritt's own skill was beyond question. His handling of the Charles Hazlitt affair, where Leventritt ordered that Charlie be allowed to "escape" the hospital and meet his end, was a bit macabre for Smyth's taste. But, it was also creative and brilliant. Moreover, Smyth had no doubts about assuring the Council of Jeremy B. Leventritt's ability to handle THE TRUTH.

Smyth doubted that Leventritt would enjoy the responsibilities that the revelation would bring and no doubt he would be less than grateful for Smyth's recommendation. Nonetheless, Smyth thought, Leventritt could handle the job and that's what counted.

Suddenly, the Director of Master Med was startled from his ruminations by the shrill alarm of the computer access security system.

"Good Goras!" he exclaimed.

Comprehending the situation in an instant, he swung around to view the videoscreen. The image that met his eyes caused him to stop and stare in the most profound dismay. The expression of shock and disbelief on Evelyn's face left no room for doubt about what had happened.

"Oh, Eve, Eve, what have you done?" he muttered.

He saw her sink back into her chair and swivel to face the door. He stared for a moment longer at the back of her head and then abruptly turned to key the videophone.

"Central Security. This is an Alpha Code. Evelyn Sebring is in her office on the twentieth floor of the Master Medical Facility. She is to be detained there incommunicado until I arrive."

A plague of circumstances—not circumstances but near catastrophes, it seemed, had tumbled down upon him. But precipitated by what? As the transporter unit in the Master Medical Building sped him from the Great Concourse to the twentieth floor where Evelyn waited, Noel Baker Smyth gazed through the glass panel and watched the floors flash by. He might have been formulating in his mind what he would say to Evelyn, but he wasn't. He was still trying to trace the course of events that led to his current difficulties. The Hazlitt affair had no doubt helped to precipitate his own removal from office and possibly it had been an instigating factor in James Adam Sebring's erratic behavior, but the Lucifer accident, that had been pure and simple fate. It had been the whim of the elements. A maelstrom in the heavens had spawned this storm of events, and the violent, erratic winds had whisked Eve from her feet and set her down in a new, unfamiliar, terrifying place. He saw the culmination of it all not in his own dismissal but in the sad rending of the canopy of ignorance that had protected Eve, the sacred canopy which he personally had always contrived to protect.

The Director of Master Med stepped from the vertical transporter and strode across the twentieth floor to where a guard stood in silent vigil outside of Evelyn's office.

"You can go," he said.

The guard shuffled his feet hesitantly, as if not comprehending the command.

Smyth waved his hand impatiently. "That's all. You can go," he repeated.

The guard nodded, offered a mirthless smile of deference and left quickly.

Eve was sitting where he had seen her last on his telescreen, still facing the door. It was as if she hadn't moved. She probably hadn't, he thought. She looked at him with cold, unfamiliar eyes, offering no real acknowledgement of his presence.

He crossed the room to her side and spoke quietly. "I think perhaps in my office, Eve," he said. He touched her arm tentatively.

She rose immediately. He had not expected such a sudden reaction. She stood looking at him now with a slightly puzzled expression. Then she turned slowly and, walking stiffly, preceded him up the stairs to his office.

He waited until she was seated and then, sitting directly opposite her, he leaned forward and spoke.

"Eve, I'm sorry this happened."

She sat watching him but made no response. Under the circumstances, Smyth knew his words sounded ridiculously inadequate.

"I know you must be terribly shocked. I would have done almost anything to prevent this."

"All this time you've known." Her voice was flat but controlled, and she looked away as she spoke.

"Eve . . ."

She turned to face him now. "You've known that Death Dates are an illusion," her voice became more intense, "a fabrication, a monstrous lie."

"Yes, I've known it, I've believed it, and I've perpetuated it," he said calmly.

Her voice rose and her eyes flashed the accusation. "But it's genocide!"

He spoke sternly now. "Don't pass judgment, Eve, on what you do not understand."

"Understand? What is there to understand?"

"Understand," he fixed her with his eyes and his body stiffened slightly, "understand that D. Date is not a gratuitous hoax; it's an essential myth.[78] Understand that the originators at the end of the Christian era were faced with the collapse of the original myth—belief in a benevolent creator." He leaned forward again. "Understand that humankind was faced with an exploding population, diminishing natural resources, global warming, deadly pollution, terrorism, unsecured nuclear weapons, and that the

---

[78]The idea of promulgating such a myth as a means of social control is advocated by Plato in his *Republic*.

Apocalypse—war, pestilence, famine, crime—threatened to engulf humanity. Understand that humankind, who had wrested from God's hand control of birth and of longevity, was forced ultimately to seize control of death, too."

"Not humankind," she said viciously, "but you, Noel Baker Smyth. You have seized control. You have played God."

He shrugged. "If God refuses to play God, then someone must; the people insist on it. The originators of D. Date, and those of us who have followed, have had to endure a soul-freezing existence outside the sacred social canopy so that the rest could enjoy the illusion of peace and security."[79]

"And people like me," she said staring at him incredulously, "have been dupes, stage hands, helping you maintain the illusion."

Smyth sighed at the hopelessness of his situation. How could he expect her to understand and sympathize with him? He did want her sympathy, but there was so little time and so much to understand. He shook his head in resignation.

"Yes, Eve, until now, helping me to sustain The Truth while I maintained the illusion for everyone else has been your vital, if unwitting, function."

"Until now?" She looked at him uncertainly. And then defiantly, "Yes, what will you do with me now?" Her voice had developed a slight tremor. "You can't let me live knowing what I do."

The words hit him like a blow struck from the inside. He understood the profound shock and disillusionment she felt at the loss of the D. Date myth, but he was dismayed at the extent to which her feelings seemed to be directed at him personally.

"Eve," he strained to control the deep sadness that he felt, "can you have worked with me for so long and still suppose that I would . . .?" He left the sentence unfinished as he saw the tears well up in her eyes.

"Oh, Eve." He wanted to wrap his arms around her and comfort her, understanding now her fear. She had translated her discovery into her own

---

[79] It is worth here reflecting on how we elect people to represent us and give them the right to withhold information from us through the use of a system of "security clearances." Like Evelyn and the citizens of Lucifer State, we build a "sacred social canopy" of peace and security over ourselves by willingly choosing to advance a system of laws that leads to most of us being denied the right to information about the real dangers of our world.

death warrant. "Eve," he said gently, "you know how we abhor violence, how P. Goras has always emphasized persuasion."

She spoke quietly now. Some of the hatred was gone from her eyes, replaced with weariness. "And how am I to know that," she said, "or anything else? It's all been a sham—all of it."

Smyth hoped now that the rest of it would not be an added burden for her but a relief. "You must leave," he said. "You must go to a place where you cannot tell what you know."

She stared at him still shocked. "Exile! Me?"[80]

"You were physically exiled the moment you violated the computer. You did that to yourself, Eve. Believe me, you could not be happy here now. If you were to go out to the street corner right now and shout out what you know, you'd be perceived as a lunatic. You must go to a place where you will live with others who, like you, have penetrated the Lucifer Myth."

"And if I refuse?"

Smyth looked at his feet. "You cannot refuse, Eve," he said.

She nodded with tired resignation. "So much for persuasion," she said. And then, "Where is this place?"

"Greenland."

"Greenland?"

"Yes," he said. "You will go to one of three different societies there, known as Erewhon One, Two, and Three. You will be told all about each and be allowed to choose."

She looked at him bewildered and then, hands trembling, she reached into her pocket and pulled out her yellow D. Date Card. She turned it over slowly in her hands, trying to comprehend the ramifications of all she was just coming to understand. Could it really be that everything she'd ever been taught to believe had been false?

"Who will choose my D. Date there?"[81]

His heart went out to her.

---

[80]The biblical allegory is continued: Adam and Eve, having "eaten of the tree of the knowledge of good and evil," now come to know good and evil—and are exiled from Eden (Utopia).

[81]The stories we are persuaded to believe about the "real" meaning of life do not die easily. Even as Evelyn now knows that D. Dates are false, she still clings to the myth.

"And what about my children and Jim?" she added suddenly.

"No one will choose your D. Date. Understand, Eve, that our best information suggests that you will have begun to deteriorate by . . ." he did not need to read the date on the card; he knew it by heart, ". . . by December 21, 2222."

The realization hit her suddenly. "But that's your D. Date, too!" she paused trying to assimilate the new meaning of that fact. "Does the best of your information suggest that you will have begun to deteriorate by then?" The sarcasm in her voice was heavy.

Smyth averted his eyes, fingering the black-covered Bible that lay once again in its accustomed place on his desk. "My own D. Date has no technical significance. It's a matter rather of personal preference. Actually, Eve . . ." his voice took on an apologetic note, "actually, the date is an expression of my notion of personal compatibility. I'm sorry; it was presumptuous of me."

"You mean . . . you mean you would have allowed yourself to be put to . . ."[82]

"In certain circumstances," he interrupted her, "I'd have been allowed that option, but more likely I would be instructed to go to Greenland and, unwisely I think, use everything known to the Erewhonian science of geriatrics to prolong the process of dying. You will have the same option."

"You mean," her voice had softened noticeably, "I'll become a P.N.D. in a society of P.N.D.'s?"

"If we . . . if you choose, you will suffer what we would call Post Natural Death. Yes, everyone has that option there. That doesn't mean that there aren't any young people, though."

"The children!" she started as a new tension vibrated through her. "What will happen to my children?"

Smyth hastened to reassure her. "You may take them with you, Eve, or you may leave them here. They will be provided for."

She shook her head in despair. "How can I choose? I don't know anything about Greenland, about these Erewhon places."

---

[82] If the state would have permitted it, Smyth would have willingly gone to his death with Evelyn on her D. Date.

"I haven't seen these societies either." He hesitated. "I may do so shortly. But one can learn something," he nodded towards his bookshelves, "by the study of the history of previous societies."

"You know I'm no historian."

He could sense her feeling of helplessness, her utter confusion. He wanted to sound reassuring, but he also wanted to be meticulously honest with her now. She must at least be able to rely on that.

"Two of the societies, Erewhon One and Two, are based, I believe, on the predominating political systems at the time D. Date was instituted."

"Capitalism and Communism," she ventured.

"Precisely," he said. "They are, from our point of view, very similar to each other, although the inhabitants don't appear to think so. Both hold in common the notion that economic factors—money, profit, and the like—are the fundamental determinants of human behavior, though they disagree on the methods of distributing the economic rewards."

His voice had become businesslike, cool almost, as if he sensed that Eve needed something firm and factual on which to replant her feet.

"About the third society I know very little except that, like our own society, it is predicated on the belief that time is the universal and fundamental unit of value for human beings. But, whereas we control individual and social behavior by relating it directly to time consumption, they do not."

"But that, too, is a fraud. The whole optimum living idea has to be an illusion." Some of her anger returned. "You've been robbing Jim of his life and I've been nagging him about his D. Date attrition. Oh, that's rich." Her voice was bitter.

"A fraud? No!" Smyth shook his head. "If Jim has consistently lost time, it is because the computer estimates that certain of his activities are not ultimately good for him, or for you, or for society. We have every reason to believe that such activities do in fact reduce the natural life span. What the originators did was to replace an artificial and often corrupt system of rewards with a simple, just, and, above all, *natural* system."

"Natural!" She stared at him in amazement.

"Yes, natural." This point almost above all he wanted her to understand. "Nature rewards certain activities and punishes others by giving and withdrawing life. The computer merely speaks for her. It punishes individually, socially, and ecologically unsound behavior."

"I've no doubt," she said, "but nature did not program the computers, you did."

"That's true, Eve, but you must understand that *someone always programs the computers. Some elite or other always makes the decisions and persuades or compels the rest to acquiesce.* In our own pre-D. Date American capitalistic society, the elites hid their interests behind a complicated system of laws and a dual system of penalties. The laws dealt largely with crime against property because the elites had disproportionate ownership of property. They invented a dual penalty system, which sent the poor to prison while it legitimized a system of bribery, called 'fines,' for the rich."

"It was at least an unjust system democratically agreed upon," she retorted. "Now apparently democracy and freedom are just a delusion."

"Democracy is *always* a delusion." The Director smiled grimly. "Control of the masses by elites is always accomplished by persuasion, by force, or by both. Democracy was and is merely the most rhetorical system—the most dependent on persuasion. And as for freedom, well, FREEDOM IS WANTING TO DO WHAT YOU MUST DO."

"They had to vote, and the voting system, unlike ours, wasn't a fraud and a sham!" she said.

Smyth was pleased. Evelyn was becoming engrossed in the debate. He felt sure that if he could overcome the emotional shock, if he could provoke her to intellectual combat, she would begin to understand. And with understanding would come the first step in her rehabilitation.

"The vote, my dear," he said, "then as now was the principle item in the rhetoric of a free society. It did not measure the will of the people; it measured the persuasiveness of the elite. The vote in our system is scrupulously honest, I can assure you. What the masses decide, the government executes. D. Date technology merely causes the people to want—to vote for—the policies the Elite Council has already decided are most naturally beneficial."[83]

---

[83] An example of this governmental policy can be seen in Chapter 11, where the people were persuaded to vote to abandon the Orville Dam project.

"And the Elite Council, I don't remember being asked to vote on its membership," she said sarcastically.

"Eve, you share the delusion that afflicts the citizens of Erewhon One—the Capitalist Society. They apparently believe that democracy is measured not by what sort of government they get, but by how they got it. They are said to tolerate a vastly privileged government, with elected politicians living in the lap of luxury. The only thing they insist on the right to determine who shall get the privilege. Erewhon One greatly resembles the Christian era in the United States," he noted, going over to take down from the shelf a book on American history.

"The citizens of Erewhon Two—the Communist Society, on the other hand, do not choose their government. They believe that it is not how you get a government that makes it democratic but rather whether those who govern share the economic lot of the people. Our own system," Smyth paused, fixing Evelyn with his intense gray eyes, "the system you call a fraud, combines the best of both. The Regional Directors, the Elite Council, and P. Goras himself live exactly as you and your neighbors do. Indeed, with respect to the one commodity we do distribute unequally—leisure time—they have less, not more, than those whom they govern. And while it is true that the people are made to want P. Goras, they are carefully persuaded to believe that he is the best possible leader, it is also true that he is elected in a genuinely free election with no fraud."

She remained silent for a moment. He waited for her to fly back with an answer. He did not want her to be defeated.

"And P. Goras," she paused thoughtfully, "Goras the magician, or is he a clown? Does he really share our situation? Is he put to death mathematically? Does anti-social behavior shorten his life?"

"Unfortunately, Eve, in that respect he cannot share the situation of the masses." Smyth's voice was more subdued. "The comforts of delusion are denied him. Like me, and like you now, he must face exile and ultimately Post Natural Death."

She looked at the Director for a moment, slowly shaking her head.

"Eve," he said, "when you get to Greenland and experience first hand the problems—the crime, avarice, terrorism, physical decay, juvenile delinquency in the form of gangs—problems that we have largely solved here—perhaps you will judge me less harshly."

"Crime? Juvenile delinquency?"

"Yes, in our system we appear, thanks to D. Dates, to be subject to natural law. We don't complain about or evade our social laws any more than we complain about the laws of gravity. Certain activities have certain consequences. That's all. In the Greenland societies, the law is obviously human-made. The laws therefore are disputed. There are endless debates about morality. The laws are frequently violated."[84]

Evelyn laughed bitterly. "The Senile Delinquents have just raped and murdered my best friend. They have destroyed her husband and you talk as if our . . . your . . . system is perfect."

Smyth nodded his head sympathetically. "It's true that the Senile Delinquents commit anti-social acts. It's the flaw in our system. We seem to lose our grip on some of our older citizens. On the other hand, in the Greenland societies, it is the young who get out of control."

She frowned at him, puzzled, and shook her head with a half smile. "Juvenile delinquency?"

He could see that she was simultaneously puzzled and intrigued by the novelty of the idea. "You see," he hastened to explain, "the Erewhon societies continually witness the effects of the ravages of age—of Post Natural Death. People denied Natural Death by medical technology suffer blindness, deafness, insanity and ugliness. They come to fear the process of aging. They come to revere youth and all that goes with it." He watched her. She seemed to be grappling with these strange notions.

"The children," Evelyn said suddenly, "they would be privileged then, like our Red Card holders?"

He pursed his lips, contemplating the question. "Yes, and no. Everybody, including the youth, grows older—nobody gets younger—and it's a perverse privilege that portrays the future as deterioration into living death. But the reverence for youth, the fear of age, is not lost on the young. The youth tend

---

[84] The early Greek Sophist-Rhetoricians (of whom Protagoras was one) recognized that if people could be persuaded to believe that human-made laws are actually *natural* laws, they would obey without question.

to become an elite and apparently they sometimes abuse and mistreat the aged, just as our Senile Delinquents tend to victimize the young."

"And will I be considered aged?" she demanded.

"No, in fact, by the standards of the Erewhon societies you will be considered to be fairly young. They try, rather pointlessly I think, to survive to very great ages. On the other hand, they tend to confuse the characterless appearance of youth with beauty. I'm afraid your own . . ." he glanced at his feet embarrassed, "intelligent, informed beauty will be taken for deterioration. You see, Eve," he said a little sadly, "here one does not chop down a gnarled oak to make room for a newly shed acorn. There it is different."

"Oh, indeed," she groaned.

She laughed at the unconscious irony of the statement and then rose from her chair and crossed the room to stare silently out of the window, down the sloping sides of the jagged Master Med pyramid. She remained for a long time with her back to him. Noel Baker Smyth studied the proud, motionless figure of the woman who had most tried his resolve, for whom he had been most tempted over the years to disregard his responsibilities—the woman because of whom he had most regretted his assignment in life. He sat quietly, letting her assimilate the revelations he had made to her. He contemplated the firmness of her form, the tilt of her head, the subtleness of her curves. He imagined her gentle passion . . . dreamed what might be if . . .

"And so," she spoke again without turning, "now I must decide for myself and the children."

"Yes." He paused, reluctant to release the mental image, then sighing, surrendering once again to reality and to duty. He added, "and for Jim, too."

She swung around. "Jim?"

"Yes, Eve. I know you know where he is. Otherwise you would not have been tempted to violate the computer."

"Jim knows nothing!" She was adamant.

"Eve, you were calling someone." He shrugged his shoulders. "You were calling Jim when the security system intervened."

"Yes, but I didn't reach him. He doesn't know."

Smyth frowned, half sympathetically. "He knows by now more about Lucifer than we can afford for him to know. Moreover, you must see that the very fact that he remains alive and well threatens the Lucifer Myth."

She stared at him in disbelief. "You mean you intend to . . ." She stopped, her eyes begging him not to confirm her fear.

"No . . . no, Eve!"

The impatience in his voice covered the futility and disappointment he felt at her failure to understand.

"Exiled, that's all. Just exiled with you." His voice had risen in anger at her, at Jim Sebring, at himself.

"You'll have to find him first," she threw back contemptuously.

"You must see," he said, regaining his composure, "that it's vital to the Council . . . to our society, that you go to Jim, assure him of his safety and bring him to me."

Eve crossed the room slowly until she stood in front of him.

"You," she said accusingly, "you, Noel Baker Smyth, turned me into an unwitting agent for the Elite Council in my own home." Her face flushed with anger now. "Jim didn't marry a woman; he married a social proposition. I hope I get another chance with him, and if I ever do, I'll come to him as a woman, not as a damned messenger for you and your Council."

"All right, Eve," Smyth spoke sternly.

The depth of her passion unnerved him.

"Very well, you'll have a few hours to decide about the children. In the meantime, you will remain here, incommunicado."

She shrugged her indifference, but the quick flash of her eyes bespoke her contempt. She turned away from him.

"Eve." He hesitated and then took a step towards her.

Reaching out, he clasped her shoulders from behind. He knew he was leaving himself wide open—completely vulnerable. His resolve had gone.

"Eve, there's something I want to say." He spoke quietly, letting his face feel the softness of her hair as he pulled her towards him.

She swung around suddenly, shaking herself free from his hold.

"Yes, Noel, what is it?" Her voice was icy; her eyes were moist.

In her face he read the answer to the unasked question. Nonetheless he hesitated for an instant more. Finally, with a sigh, he poked at the videophone and demanded, "Central Security . . ."

19

RACE AGAINST DEATH

Jim Sebring hesitated for a moment and then pressed the palm of his hand firmly against the Plexiglas screen. He knew that the screen would precipitate a "no admit" sequence and that the door at which he was staring would remain closed. He was taking a considerable risk. Inside the apartment, a computer was at this very moment searching its memory, preparing to inform Noel Baker Smyth as to the identity of his visitor. Jim knew that there was absolutely nothing to prevent Smyth, upon becoming aware of his presence, from alerting Sector Security without even confronting him. If he had misjudged Smyth, the sweaty palm print Jim had left on the screen could easily signal the futile end of his mission.

By now Jim was certain that his death sentence had been lifted. It had been almost two weeks since the crash and eight days since Evelyn's cryptic videophone call to Natasha. Still, the hand that had made the palm print showed not the slightest evidence of radiation damage. The growing euphoria that Jim had felt as each day passed without the onset of the promised radiation sickness had been qualified by the old sadness at the knowledge that each passing day also brought June 7th, Natasha's D. Date, that much closer.

Just as the doubt about Jim's condition had gradually dissipated, so the mystery surrounding Lucifer had grown steadily thicker. Attempts to reach Evelyn by videophone had been in vain, and Jim's concern for her had grown to near panic. The impulse to leave the security of Natasha's apartment and go in search of Evelyn and the kids had been vitiated by the fact that he had not the slightest idea where to look. She was clearly not at home and Master Med denied any knowledge of her whereabouts.

Finally Jim had become convinced that the only way to find out where Evelyn and the kids had gone was to confront the Director of Master Med. He felt certain that Smyth was implicated both in Evelyn's disappearance and in the Lucifer mystery. Indeed, that conviction had taken the edge off Jim's panic because he believed that what he judged to be Smyth's genuine affection for Evelyn would protect her from any real harm. Nonetheless, this morning when Natasha had prepared to drive over to the Northeast Life Conservation Unit for her monthly medical exam—for the last monthly medical exam she would ever take—Jim had asked her to make a considerable detour and drop him off at Noel Baker Smyth's apartment.

Now, as he stood facing the door of Smyth's apartment, he felt a strong urge to run, not from Smyth but from the imagined approach of security guards and from his fear of potential abrupt and final separation from Natasha. He knew the fear was baseless. It was still before eight o'clock in the morning. Thanks to the early hour and Natasha's door-to-door ride, he was fairly sure he had not been spotted on his way over here. And, he had chosen to confront Smyth at his apartment rather than at the Master Med Building precisely because he knew that even if the Director summoned help it would take considerable time to arrive. Still, it seemed as if he had been staring at the door for an eternity.

The door suddenly slid open.

Noel Baker Smyth was standing inside the apartment, just to one side of the readout screen on which Jim's name was plainly printed. Jim thought he saw a faint trace of surprise still flickering across the Director's face, but if it had been there at all, it was gone instantly. Jim didn't speak but stood surveying his antagonist.

Smyth was wrapped in a dark blue robe with wide velvet lapels. There was a shadowy stubble across the lower part of his face, but his thick white hair, like the rest of his demeanor, was unruffled. With quiet self-possession and a casual sweep of the arm, Noel Baker Smyth beckoned Jim further into the room. With a glimmer of a smile, Smyth said, "Jim, please come in."

Jim hated the bastard.

"Very sensible of you; I must admit to being a little surprised though." Smyth regarded Jim grimly and then added quickly, "But of course you must be concerned about Eve and the children."

Jim advanced further into the room. Smyth's easy manner, his preemption of the question, caused Jim's anger to rise. He felt his muscles tensing.

"Let me assure you they're all fine." Smyth indicated a chair. "Have a seat. It's a little early, but you could probably use a drink."

Jim remained standing, but he nodded his acceptance of the latter offer. He admitted to himself that the drink would help his nervousness and while Smyth was about the business of preparing it, Jim had the chance to examine the computer. As far as he could see from where he was standing, there was nothing to indicate that any warning system had been activated. If Smyth had called for security guards, he had done it in the conventional way by videophone. Only time would tell.

Jim took the proffered drink. "Evelyn, where is she?" He tried to match Smyth's calm, controlled voice.

"She and the children are waiting for you."

Jim sat down, taking a sip of the drink. His favorite ingredient, Cannabis, was missing. It was mostly alcohol and some sweet additive that he hadn't tasted before. "Waiting for me? Where?"

Smyth poured himself a drink and sat down next to the videophone. "They're waiting." He paused. "They are in Greenland."

"In Greenland? Waiting in Greenland?" Jim half rose from his seat. "What the hell are you saying?"

"They had to go for their own sakes," Smyth interjected quickly.

Jim sank back. It was vital to Evelyn and the kids and to him and Natasha that he keep his head.

"Eve stumbled on information," Smyth continued, "that would have made life here for her impossible."

"She didn't stumble on anything. You know damned well she was trying to find out about the Lucifer Flights for me." Jim's voice had risen in spite of himself.

"Yes, yes," Smyth acquiesced, "I'm sure she was concerned only for your welfare, but I'm afraid she discovered more about Lucifer than she bargained for."

"And so you sent her away?" He was fighting the impulse to assault Smyth physically. He knew he must not—not yet at least.

"Not precisely." Smyth leaned back, making himself comfortable, but still regarded Jim intently. "In the end, she herself recognized the necessity. She knew she had to go. No one had to compel her." His eyes didn't move from Jim's, but his demeanor was relaxed. "Frankly, Sebring, it seemed to me that her desire to leave had as much to do with you as with Lucifer."

Jim averted his eyes and took a gulp of his drink. So Evelyn had been confiding in Smyth? How could she be that gullible? What else had she told him?

"I take it that everything wasn't well between you two." Smyth gazed at Jim evenly.

"That's none of your damned business."

"Perhaps not," Smyth temporized. "In any case you have the right to know the rest of the matter."

Jim drank from his glass, set it down, and looked Smyth in the eye. "You're damned right I do." He stared at Smyth, hoping the contempt was registering on his face.

"About Lucifer, I mean," Smyth said pointedly.

"Oh, yes, the little matter of Lucifer," Jim sneered. "The Cobalt 57 that doesn't act like it ought to—the deadly gamma rays that didn't kill me."

"Yes, that deceit is a little crude, but quite necessary, I assure you." Smyth seemed impatient. "In fact, your cargo was a vitally important drug concentrate."

Jim laughed volubly. "If you expect me to believe that somebody found it necessary to use the Lucifer Flights as a disguise for the transportation of life-saving drugs, you must take me for an idiot. And what the hell was the microfilm doing there?" Jim drained his glass, enjoying a new feeling of superiority.

"The microfilm contained data relating to worldwide consumption of the drug in relation to population and ecological trends. As for the drug itself," Smyth said, "I didn't say it was life-saving. Quite the contrary. It is designed to be lethal." Smyth reached for the decanter and refilled Jim's glass.

Jim's body tensed. He strove to keep the feeling of shocked disbelief from registering on his face. "Designed to be lethal?" His face remained blank.

"Many drugs," Smyth went on, "are of course lethal, but the Lucifer drug is lethal in exact units." He leaned forward now as he spoke. "It is lethal in precisely predictable circumstances. What you carried on the Lucifer Flights,

Sebring," Smyth paused and let the rest of his sentence flow with slow deliberation, "... was death in doses. Death summonable in response to the necessities of social policy."

Jim's blank facade exploded. "What I carried?" He could hear himself shouting. "There are Lucifer Flights from all over the damned world!"

"The problem of population and consumption of natural resources is a worldwide problem, not a local one," Smyth said emphatically. "The International Commission at Greenwich is charged with maintaining an equitable distribution of population and natural resources between nations." Smyth's face was set with intensity. "It was that or nuclear holocaust. The Commission monitors the computer data from each nation and allocates the Lucifer drug on the basis of an agreed upon formula."

"My God, you mean this country is involved in some genocidal program controlled from Greenwich?" Jim was beginning to understand why Smyth had found it necessary to send Evelyn off to Greenland and to get rid of him. His mind whirled as he tried to fit the pieces together. There was more, he knew now, a lot more.

The urge to hit Smyth, to beat his way through that suave, supercilious mask to the demonic face he knew lay beneath, overwhelmed Jim. He commanded his body to rise, his fists to strike. They did not obey; the glass fell from his hand.

Smyth appeared not to notice. "Hardly. We are full members and we are represented on the International Commission."

Jim's anger was subsiding, giving way to a sensation of horror that caused the hair at the back of his head to bristle. It was as if he were looking through a crack ... no, a rip ... looking through a rip in the social fabric right into a corner of Hell. Death, summonable in response to the necessities of social policy. Jim shuddered.

"How each nation distributes the Lucifer drug is a matter of national, not international, policy. Some nations use it to sustain class and economic systems. Others incorporate Lucifer into a eugenics policy. All must use the unit properties of Lucifer to meet the requirements of international population control and resource allocation."

"Population control? National policy?" Jim forced himself to concentrate. "And our national policy?" he demanded.

"Our national policy is the most benign and the most humane. It is rooted ultimately in a profound belief in the power of persuasion."

"Persuasion . . . death in doses . . . Smyth, you must be mad."

Noel Baker Smyth didn't answer, but rather reached for a fresh glass and offered it to Jim. Jim declined, resisting the temptation. He needed to get back in charge of his body. He knew he was going to act, and soon.

Smyth slowly refilled his own glass and sauntered across to the window. He didn't turn to face Jim as he continued to speak. "Sebring, I doubt you'll understand what I'm about to tell you, and frankly," he turned suddenly to face Jim, "I don't care one way or the other. You will be exiled, so you have a right to know and it's time people like you faced some hard realities."

Jim could see suddenly that his contempt for Smyth was reciprocated. He saw that Smyth was enjoying exposing his, Jim's, naiveté.

"You have no doubt heard of the so-called placebo effect—the tendency of people to be cured because they believe they will be cured. The belief is normally precipitated by some inert substance or other, often in the form of a so-called 'sugar pill'."

Jim nodded cautiously.

"In the old society there was a group of priests who achieved the opposite effect. They literally persuaded people to die by convincing them of the potency of some actually harmless object. It was called voodoo."

"Voodoo?"

"The voodoo effect, in its present form, is death brought about by belief . . . belief in the efficacy of certain rites." Smyth paused to let the point sink in. "Imagine a scientifically conceived ceremony . . ."

Jim's eyes narrowed; his mind was leaping ahead of Smyth now.

The Director continued, "Imagine a ceremony designed to strip the believer of all his connections with life."

"The Terminal Rites," Jim blurted out. He was leaning forward listening, intently fascinated in spite of himself.

Smyth ignored the outburst, "Imagine a ceremony designed to sever all ties with family, society, and material possessions and calculated to produce acquiescence in death."

Jim struggled to his feet. He scowled at Smyth.

"My God," he muttered, "I can't believe all that!" He shook his head as if the action would dispel what he was hearing. "I can't believe it!"

"You shouldn't," Smyth interrupted, staring back at Jim. "It works, but not with sufficient predictability to be the instrument of social policy."

Jim paced unsteadily back and forth across the room twice before returning to his seat. His body was beginning to recover, but he needed more time so that when he hit Smyth, Smyth would know he'd been hit.

"But if you supplement the voodoo effect," Smyth pressed on as Jim sat down, "with a drug which is totally assimilated within seconds of ingestion and which has the effect of producing a peaceful, even euphoric, death at a predictable time and under predictable circumstances," his gray eyes were cold and intense now, "then, Sebring, you could cause spiritual and biological death to occur at a time that makes sense both for the individual and for society. That's the function of the Lucifer drug in our system."[85]

"Those are fancy words, Smyth." Jim's face was flushed with anger. "What you mean is that you poison people at their Terminal Rites."

"I didn't say that," Smyth was ruffled. "The medical authorities are still not certain of the drug's precise action. Some believe it is toxic; others believe that, like the dolls of the voodoo priests, it merely causes the subjects to become overwhelmingly suggestible. I prefer to believe the latter and, either way, it works."

Jim grappled with his feelings. It was vital now that they be concealed from Smyth. Something inside of him had exploded and his spirits had soared. Every nerve in his body vibrated with joy and relief. If Smyth was right, it was not for twenty days. It was forever—it was he and Natasha forever. If D. Date was a myth, then her D. Date was a myth as long as she never went through the Terminal Rites ... as long as Jim could get back to her ... as long as Smyth failed to stop him. He must conceal his euphoria. His pilot training asserted itself.

"It didn't work for Charlie Hazlitt." It was Jim's radio voice, sounding now as if it belonged to someone else. "His death wasn't predictable and it certainly wasn't euphoric."

---

[85] A physician in Great Britain some years ago set off a national debate by proposing just such a solution to the problems of aging, ecology, and population control.

"No, that's true," Smyth said. "Because of an administrative error created by a missing I.D. card, medical life support technology was accidentally used to combat the Lucifer drug. But even with the drug removed by medical intervention, even with the body artificially sustained, you will remember that Hazlitt's spirit continued to acquiesce in death."

Jim forced himself to concentrate. He remembered Charlie's voice directing him to a safe landing at Bradley and felt for the first time that he, Jim Sebring, understood something about the human spirit that was beyond the comprehension of the Director of Master Med. He suppressed the smile.

"Accidents of that sort do happen occasionally." Smyth was speaking more quickly now, apparently anxious to say what he had to say. "And while they are invariably unfortunate for the victim and those close to him, they do serve a social purpose. The horror of so-called Post Natural Death serves to make the Terminal Rites that much more effective."

"You mean you used Uncle Charlie," Jim simulated anger, "for a social sermon? A sermon based entirely on Goras-damned lies?"

"Lies, my dear Sebring," Jim sensed that Smyth was also working against his emotions, striving to seem casual, "have an unwarranted bad name. Lies are, no doubt, the most universal and most effective means of persuasion, and persuasion is the most benign means of social control. In any case, we all lie . . ." He waved his arm as if to include an unseen audience, "despite protestations to the contrary. Our deceptions, as you'll discover, are absolutely vital to the well-being of the people, whereas your petty deceptions," Smyth added derisively, "as I understand them, serve a more selfish purpose."

Petty deceptions? Oh, yes! Smyth was referring to him and Natasha . . . and Evelyn.

Something else the Director didn't understand and never would was Jim's connectedness with Natasha. But, Smyth had somehow come to find out about Jim's affair with Natasha, and that could make things more difficult. Jim had to act soon.

Smyth had walked over from the desk toward the right side of the computer console. From its top he carefully removed two smooth, egg-shaped paperweights of transparent glass. Returning, he handed one of them to Jim. Jim could see that buried at its center was a small, flattened spheroid.

But it was not the spheroid that got his attention, it was the heft of the whole thing. It felt like a weapon. He tensed.

"You won't recognize it, Sebring," Smyth said. "It's a piece of history. A revolution. To you, it is just a pill. To your ancestors, it is 'the pill'. It was the earliest universally accepted method of birth control, used in the latter part of the twentieth century. Of course, it is crude by our standards, but was quite effective nonetheless. By giving women an opportunity to plan when they would have children, it transformed the world.

Smyth placed the object in Jim's left hand. "You hold there the Alpha— man's ability to wrest from God the control of birth."

He handed the second paperweight to Jim. "And this is Omega."

With his right hand Jim took the second glass object and examined it. It too contained a small capsule. He rolled the transparent piece of glass over in his hand, hefting it, waiting for his chance to bury it in Smyth's head. He kept his voice steady.

"This is just the monthly supplement capsule. I've taken these. Everybody has. And I'm not dead yet."

"No," Smyth replied, "far from it. Those capsules you have taken each month are indeed used to eradicate dietary deficiencies, to give immunity from infectious diseases, to provide for birth control. They are veritable elixirs. But that one . . ." Smyth leaned over and pointed to the pill inside the paperweight, "that one is all that and one thing more. It contains a carefully controlled dose of Lucifer drug. It contains your contribution, Sebring."

"Good Goras!" Jim raised his eyes from the object. Fear gripped at his gut. His voice broke as he spoke. "These things are handed out by the P.H.O.'s. Are they part of the whole scheme as well?" he asked in disbelief.

"No, no." Smyth was emphatic. "The true nature of Lucifer is known only to P. Goras, the Elite Council, and the Directors of each of the five regional Master Medical Centers. The P.H.O.'s know nothing of the drug. The capsules each contain a relatively large number of ingredients. The type and quantity of each ingredient needed by any given person at any given time varies."

Smyth was eyeing Jim warily now, but he pressed on. "The choice of a particular medical mixture is made by the computers on the basis of data obtained during the monthly medical examination. There are literally thousands of combinations that can be mixed to order for each patient each month, and it is all done automatically. Ultimately, the computer is programmed to dispense the capsule with the Lucifer drug only at the appropriate time."

The Director of Master Med was edging toward the videophone.

"The P.H.O.'s, though they don't know it, administer the Lucifer capsule at the final monthly medical, and then all that remains to be done is to wait."

Smyth was reaching for the videophone.

"Natasha!" The agonized scream exploded without warning. Jim's left fist, holding the birth control pill, buried itself in the right side of Smyth's face.

Smyth staggered sideways as Jim brought up his right fist, the fist bearing the death control pill. Jim slammed the second glass paperweight into Smyth's weakened frame. Smyth spun a full circle under the force of the blow and fell inert to the floor.

Jim lunged past the stricken form toward the door. His mind was a tangle of hope and fear. His body broke the photoelectric beam, and the door opened just in time to allow his hurtling form to reach the corridor beyond. Not pausing to take the transporter, he reached the stairs and made his way down three and four at a time. He catapulted himself through the main entrance, his mind, like his body, racing. Only one thought propelled him. He must reach Natasha before they gave her the Lucifer capsule.

A few yards down the street, a green E-car, number 81, was hitched to a charging post. Jim reached it in a few strides and yanked out the charging line. Smyth, as soon as he recovered, would alert the Security Force. For Natasha's sake, Jim must get out of the vicinity. He must not be detained at any cost.

He started the motor and without waiting for the indicator to reach moving speed—normally ten to fifteen seconds—he pulled onto the road. The motor complained, but the car moved nonetheless.

Every yard he could put between himself and Smyth's place would increase his chances. He had to get onto the Beltway fast. It would be busy now, he thought, and the traffic would hide him. He wheeled the E-car off the side street that housed Noel Baker Smyth's apartment, doing fifty miles per hour, the maximum speed the E-car would carry. The rubber wheels screeched as he rounded the corner at top speed.

The security vans, which could be mobilizing even now, could reach a speed twice that of his car. Still, there was no sign of them yet, and already three or four other E-cars were around. In another two minutes he'd reach the Beltway. It would be hard to get him then, and they didn't know where he was headed.

Where was he headed? Natasha's place was in Sector R.12. The Northeast Life Conservation Unit was two sectors farther east. He punched R. 10 into the route coder. As he swung onto the Beltway ramp a hitchhiker, seeing his destination, held up her hand in the traditional stop gesture. Since the E-car contained a vacant seat, it was protocol that Jim stop. He floored the accelerator, missing the outraged woman by inches. She would report him for sure, leading him to think that he should have stopped. Now, if they put two and two together, every security man in the city would be looking to stop Car 81. But no, he quickly decided he'd made the better choice. He had to reach Natasha and he had no seconds to spare for hitchhikers.

There was the shrill wail of a high speed S-van on the opposite side of the divided Beltway. It passed him, going in the other direction, and Jim watched in his rearview mirror as the security van exited the Beltway at G.21. It would turn left under the Beltway and go right past the entrance where the woman would be waiting to report his recent outrageous behavior, his number, and his sector destination.

He took a deep breath. There was nothing he could do about it now. There was no way to change E-cars on the Beltway. In any case, the consuming thought in his mind was to reach Tasha in time and to hell with the consequences. If he could just get to her in time, then he could deal with the minor traffic offenses.

A warning alarm started to sound.

"Damn!" Jim swore as he glared at the flashing warning signal on the dash. He was running out of charge. In haste, he had grabbed the car without checking its charge. The warning bell meant that he had only three to five minutes driving time left, which was enough time to get him to a safety island but not enough to get him off the Beltway. There were no charging posts on the Beltway, and so he had committed another violation of protocol.

A safety island swung into view. It was vacant, thank Goras, with no S-vans in sight. He pulled his E-car into the space and jumped out. The red discharge flag had popped up out of the roof for all to see, making him a sitting duck.

His eyes scanned the Beltway frantically. He would have to find a not so public-minded citizen. He was supposed to remain with his discharged E-car until a patrolling van arrived, but that was out of the question. He raised his hand and waved at the oncoming traffic, soliciting someone, anyone, to break protocol by picking up a hitchhiker on the Beltway.

A routine patrol would be expected within minutes. A yellow E-car slowed down as it rolled up to the island, and its door slid open. Jim jumped in without waiting for the E-car to stop, and the grinning miscreant behind the wheel drove back into the traffic.

The driver, looking decidedly triumphant, grinned again at Jim. "Very smooth," he said. "You're obviously an expert at running from the security people."

Jim tensed reflexively and, stroking his cheek in a futile attempt to hide his face, shot a sidelong glance at his savior. Had he been recognized? No! The man was too intent congratulating himself on the neat little pick-up job.

"I am always forgetting to check the damned batteries," Jim said lamely.

The man laughed openly. He had the red bulbous nose of the alcohol addict. His small beady eyes glinted jovially. "Oh, yes, I make that same error myself on a regular basis. Once more this quarter and I become a hike for a while."

"You really took a chance picking me up," Jim said. "I'm grateful." He tried to keep his voice casual—he knew that he mustn't seem too intense.

"Forget it. I'm not giving you much of a ride anyway. I'm getting off here," he nodded at the sign indicating the G.17 exit.

Hell! Jim hadn't noticed his companion's destination. He glanced now at his chronometer in dismay. It was 10:15 already. He could probably get a hike in five or ten minutes but that would cause him to risk being recognized. On the other hand, it might take him thirty minutes to find a reasonably charged E-car in the vicinity of exit G.17.

"Oh, Hell!" This time Jim swore aloud.

His companion stared at him questioningly. "You're in a big hurry?"

Jim nodded vigorously.

"Well," the beady-eyed one hesitated, "I suppose I could let you have this car if it's that important."

"It's crucial," Jim said, jumping at the offer.

"Well, I'm headed only a half a mile from the exit. Take this car. It's still got seventy percent charge. It ought to get you where you're going." The driver, offering another broad grin, swung the car to a stop across from the G.17 ramp.

Jim jumped out, ran to the driver's side, opened the door and extended thanks to his emerging benefactor. He slid into the E-car and swung the vehicle through 180 degrees, past two hikes, who were disappointed to see the G.17 still reading in the window. Jim re-entered the Beltway, simultaneously punching in the R.10 that was his true destination.

He relaxed for a second. He was inconspicuous now, traveling with the rest of the traffic at top speed of fifty miles per hour. He turned his attention to the display panel. A small arrow indicated his current position, and a red line traced the route he would follow to his destination. The time indicator predicted it would take thirty-five minutes. He glanced at his chronometer: 10:25. That would make it 11 o'clock by the time he reached the Northeast Suburban L.C.U. He had no way of knowing how far Natasha had progressed in her examination. She would take the capsule just before the P.H.O. consultation. When would that be?

He toyed with the idea of driving directly to a public videophone but dismissed the notion almost immediately. The medical centers had a prohibition against taking personal videophone messages during private consultations and, in any case, they would never relay an instruction urging Natasha not to take her monthly capsule. Jim cursed the speedometer, which stuck at a relentless fifty miles per hour. The E-car was oblivious.

It was taking too long. He smashed the dash with his fist in exasperation. R.12, the Airstation exit, came into view. He had two more exits to go. Would R.10 never turn up?

Suddenly, from behind Jim came the wail of an S-van speeding up the passing lane he had just vacated.

Jim looked through his rearview mirror. The S-van was gaining on him quickly. Were they looking for him? He thought of using his handkerchief to obscure his face, but decided it was better to brazen it out. If they were looking for him, they would notice immediately anything so obvious. He pulled his hat down a little in front. The S-van was almost alongside him and it must have been doing at least seventy.

Jim could imagine the uniformed occupant on the passenger's side peering intently into the little yellow E-car as the S-van drew momentarily alongside. He could feel a thumping against his chest. His mouth dried. He forced himself not to look over. "Goras, this is it, Tasha!" he said aloud.

But then, they passed him. They were moving ahead of him. Their speed slackened, if at all, only temporarily. They hadn't recognized him and he breathed an audible sigh of relief.

Exit R.10 came into view. The speeding S-van continued straight ahead. Jim merged over and exited without reducing his speed. He was by now oblivious of pedestrians. His attention was devoted entirely to the routing panel in front of him and the road ahead. He ignored the stop instructions that appeared on the panel at crossing intersections. Two or three E-cars screeched to a halt to avoid colliding with him. He kept the accelerator on the floor.

He swerved to avoid a bright orange E-car as he sailed up to the Emergency Entrance of the medical complex. Abandoning the car without taking time to switch off the motor, he dashed through the beam-activated sliding doors and yelled at the man at the reception desk, "Dispensary? Where is it?"

The man regarded him coolly. "It's the other side of the building, near the main entrance."

"How do I get there?"

While the receptionist fumbled for a route card, Jim swung around and dashed back out through the Emergency door. He feared that they'd route him down a maze of corridors and he would waste time; it was best to run around the building on the outside.

He sprinted across the green lawn, leaping a small hedge without breaking stride. He felt no exhaustion, only frantic hope and nagging fear. He rounded a corner of the building and collided with a groundskeeper, sending the man sprawling. Jim ignored the protest. His stride remained unbroken. He vaulted an ornamental wall and felt a sharp pain in his right knee as he did. Forget it. He cleared the three steps up to the main door in one stride, banging against the door as it failed to activate fast enough. Passing through on the second attempt, he staggered up to the Directory board and lunged at the button marked DISPENSARY. As he did, the transporter unit in the corner of the foyer slid open to reveal and disgorge its condemned occupant.

Jim slumped back against the Directory board and uttered a breathless sob. "Tasha!"

And from the city came the distant sound of the Great Clock tolling the hour.

20

JEKYLL PACT

"Call your bloodhounds off or I'll blow the whole Lucifer Myth wide open."

Smyth could not see Sebring's face because Sebring had set it so that the videophone would receive only audio, but the voice was cool and firm. He rubbed his aching jaw. There was no doubt that the Lucifer Pilot was capable of attempting to carry out his threat. He wouldn't succeed. The Lucifer Myth was far too well established for that; no one person could shake it. Still it would make an already difficult situation worse.

"Sebring, I have no bloodhounds to call off. They are a figment of your imagination."

"Yeah, well there are two figments of my imagination guarding Natasha Mollenskaya's apartment right now, but they are guarding an empty nest. The birds have flown."

"I'm not denying we want to talk to you, Sebring; we do. Badly. On the other hand, we intend neither you nor Miss Mollenskaya any harm."

"No harm!" The voice on the other end of the V-phone rose to an almost hysterical pitch. "You've already killed her. You are a bloody murderer, Smyth."

"Hasn't it occurred to you, Sebring, that if you had not left me unconscious yesterday, if you had told me what you had in mind, I might have saved Miss Mollenskaya?"

There was a moment of silence at the other end of the V-phone. Smyth could tell he'd scored. But he knew the victory would only be momentary and he had to press his advantage.

"In any case, Miss Mollenskaya has until June seventh, nineteen days, and I imagine that the two of you want to make the best possible use of the remaining time."

"You're damn right we do, and you're going to let us alone so we can or I will bust everything open."

"I have a proposal that would be better for both of us." Smyth said, playing his ace and waiting.

"Better for both of us? What do you mean?"

"I don't know where you are, Sebring, but I don't imagine Miss Mollenskaya wants to spend her last days in hiding, and I doubt that you want to do that to her either."

Again a moment's silence—another hit. Smyth didn't wait.

"The Elite Council has agreed to let me offer you the use of Jekyll Island in return for your promise to say nothing to harm the State."

"Jekyll Island? What's Jekyll Island?"[86] There was a pause and then an explosion. "If you think you're going to send us to some Goras-forsaken ex-penal colony . . ."

"My dear man, Jekyll Island is anything but an ex-penal colony. In the previous society, it was the exclusive playground of the elite, the ultra rich. It is an island paradise. It is now used solely as a retreat for the Council and those few others who must bear the burden of sustaining the Lucifer Myth. The Council is being very generous."

"And just where is this island paradise?" Sebring sounded somewhat mollified.

"Jekyll is a small island just off the coast in the Southeast Region, accessible only to boat and airplane. You, of course, would fly."

"Hold on." Smyth could hear the buzz of conversation in the background. Sebring was obviously discussing the offer with the Mollenskaya woman.

Noel Baker Smyth's thoughts wandered to Jekyll Island, the place where he had always dreamed of taking Eve. A few miles long and a mile across at

---

[86]There is a vague allusion here to the famous Robert Louis Stevenson novel, *The Strange Case of Dr. Jekyll and Mr. Hyde*—the story of a schizophrenic character who is both benign and satanic.

its widest, the island was surrounded by golden sand beaches. Its beaches were bathed in cool, blue, south Atlantic waters. It was covered with colored subtropical flowers that bloomed riotously. Majestic palm trees presided over its beaches, while Spanish moss-covered oaks dominated its interior.

Halfway up the island, facing east toward the ocean, was an old mansion. It had been built in the Christian era and the Council had faithfully restored it so that it contained no evidence of contemporary technology. Many years ago, it seemed, a hundred of the richest men in the country had agreed to search for a paradise. The Vanderbilts, the Rockefellers, the Macys—historic names redolent of the Christian era—had sent scouts all over the country and those scouts had found Jekyll Island. Controlling as they did one-seventh of all of the world's wealth, this historic elite had encountered no difficulty in making the island their exclusive preserve. A breathtakingly beautiful retreat, it continued to serve now the function for which it had been designed.

"How do I know this isn't some sort of trap?" Sebring's voice broke into Smyth's reverie.

"Sebring, your suspicion and impatience have already cost you a great deal. This is not a police state. I lack the means, if not the motive, to entrap you."

"The hell you do. Then why am I pursued? Why am I a fugitive?"

Smyth sighed. "You are not pursued, Sebring, and you are not a fugitive except from the creations of your own mind. In any event, you will have to trust me to keep my word, just as I must trust you to act with discretion from now until the flight."

"Until the flight? What do you mean? We have no time to waste."

"You will leave Bradley at dawn tomorrow. The plane will be fueled and the relevant flight information will be in the onboard computer. The transponder will be set to 0999. Just turn it on and leave it on until you land. You are to communicate with no one at the field or en-route. Your position will be monitored by the transponder code. The plane will be refueled for your return and you are to use the same procedure, landing at Bradley only to allow Natasha Mollenskaya to disembark." He leaned forward to address his unseen caller. "You will have sufficient fuel to proceed directly to Greenland, to Erewhon Three. Evelyn and your children are already there."

Again there was the buzz of conversation in the background and then Jim replied. "All right, Smyth. We'll be there in the morning."

"One more thing, Sebring," Smyth paused. "This is something personal. How you conduct your affairs is, of course, your own business. It will certainly not matter to you that I disapprove, on Eve's behalf, of what you're doing. What may matter to you is this fact." Smyth spoke slowly. "I have reason to suppose that I, too, will shortly be going to Greenland, and when I do, I want you to know that I intend to take Eve from you."

"So," Sebring's voice was angry, "the gentleman is not a gentleman after all. The facade begins to slip."

"Eve's behavior," Smyth said vehemently, "and I may say my own, too, has been to this point impeccable." He did not wait for a response. "And now I must talk with Miss Mollenskaya."

"What for?"

"I have to assume that anything you know has been shared with Miss Mollenskaya. Obviously, I need her assurances, too. Besides, we must be clear about the conditions attached to her return to Hartford."

"All right," Sebring's voice was grudging. "I'll put her on."

While he waited, Smyth reviewed Natasha Mollenskaya's situation. She had been given the Lucifer capsule at her final medical. Sebring would have told her that the capsule sealed her fate and she would believe him.

But there was one saving fact: Sebring was wrong. What Sebring did not know and could not, therefore, have communicated, was that the capsule was not by itself fatal. Indeed, a careful analysis of the Lucifer drug would show nothing even remotely toxic. Aqua Vie, the ceremonial drink taken at the Terminal Rites, would withstand similar scrutiny. Mix the two together, however, and the outcome was very different. All that Natasha Mollenskaya had to do was to avoid Aqua Vie by avoiding her Terminal Ceremony.

Smyth was grateful now for the punch to the jaw that had prevented him from revealing the whole truth to Jim Sebring. The situation, he mused, was almost Faustian in its implications. Had the Lucifer Pilot learned the rest of the story, things would be even more complicated than they already were.

"Natasha Mollenskaya here."

"Ah, yes, Miss Mollenskaya. Captain Sebring has no doubt given you the details of our agreement."

"Yes, he has."

"You understand that what you know about Lucifer does not change the fact of your D. Date."

"I understand that."

"Good. When you return from Jekyll Island someone will be waiting to escort you to your ceremony."

"I understand." Her voice was matter of fact.

"I recommend that you persuade Captain Sebring to time your return so that you can go right from the Airstation to the amphitheatre. The arrangements you have already discussed with your P.H.O. will be honored. Your Terminal Rites will begin as scheduled at midnight, June sixth."

"All that is quite clear."

"I wish to make one thing more quite clear, Miss Mollenskaya." Smyth wished that he could see her face. "I have examined your medical and genetic records and they show an anomaly in the right hemisphere of your brain. You have probably already noticed that your left hand is not as agile as it should be. The computer predicts that shortly after June seventh you would suffer the first of a series of debilitating strokes..."

"You can spare me the details, Mr. Smyth, I don't doubt that there is evidence to rationalize my situation."

"Just so you understand. That is all."

"Wait, please." Her voice was imperious. "We are not yet finished. I have a condition of my own."

"A condition?"

"Mr. Smyth, men like you do what you do in the name of the common good, and I suspect that your individual victims remain for you faceless. Let's make sure for once that that is not the case."

Smyth's videophone screen lit up and he found himself staring into the intense brown eyes of Natasha Mollenskaya. He did not avert his eyes.

"And your condition, Miss Mollenskaya—what is it?"

"When we return from Jekyll Island, before the ceremony, I want to see that Jim Sebring is out of your hands. I want to see him flying—and free."

"You shall, Miss Mollenskaya. You shall." Smyth jabbed at the videophone and the screen went blank.

The Director of Master Med leaned back in his chair, reflecting for a moment. Then, turning to the videophone once again, he ordered: "P. Goras."

There was a wait of several seconds and then the screen was filled with the huge round face of P. Goras.

"You have made the arrangements, Mr. Smyth?"

"Yes, I have. Captain Sebring and Miss Mollenskaya have accepted our conditions."

"We can expect an early end to this messy business then?"

"I believe we can. It has been a regrettable incident, but . . ."

"The point is," P.Goras interrupted, "the point is to avoid such difficulties in the future. And speaking of difficulties, I have been going over the nomination for your successor. This Leventritt fellow, are you absolutely sure he can handle THE TRUTH?"

"Yes, I believe he can." Smyth nodded.

"Very well then, tell him immediately. I will officially notify him of his appointment to your position at 8 p.m. tonight. He will meet with the Council tomorrow and you will be relieved of your duties at midnight three days from now."

"I understand."

"And tell me one more thing, Smyth." Goras' huge face broke into a cryptic smile. "Tell me, can you handle THE ULTIMATE TRUTH?"

Noel Baker Smyth's jaw sagged as Goras' face dissolved.

21

NORTH TOWARDS EREWHON

James Adam Sebring ruddered the sleek jet northward, heading to Hartford. Beside him Natasha Mollenskaya gazed through the right cockpit window at the fairyland of lights that marked New York City. Inside, the cockpit glowed with the eerie red light that enabled Jim to see the instruments without disturbing the night vision he needed to guide the jet to its imminent landing.

It had been seventeen days since this same jet had cut a low level swathe across the eastern seaboard. Jim had overridden the onboard computer and chosen his own route to Jekyll Island. West out of Hartford until he picked up the Hudson below Albany and then at no more than five hundred feet and at better than two hundred fifty knots, they had thundered down the Hudson Valley.

Natasha had watched fascinated as the sun rising in the east had illuminated the greenery that seemed to completely cover the west bank of the great river. They had flashed out across the harbor, the skyscrapers of New York towering above them on one side and on the other, bathed in early morning mist, the Statue of Liberty. Outside of the harbor, Jim had turned south so as to fly down the coast. A mile to their right, great Atlantic rollers went crashing onto the beaches of New Jersey. A hundred feet below them, a brisk northeast wind whipped the surface of the water into a shimmering diadem. Natasha's eyes had sparkled.

Now the jet was on the opposite heading, racing northeast. The water below was that of Long Island Sound and ahead lay not Jekyll Island but Hartford. Jim pulled back on the jet thrust levers to begin his descent. Beside him, Natasha seemed lost in contemplation, whether of the future or the past, Jim could not tell.

The seventeen days at Jekyll had been the lifetime that Natasha had said it would be and it had also come and gone, as Jim had feared it would, in an instant of time. During the days they walked or sailed or swam or simply lay nude on the beach in the sun. In the evenings they retired to the mansion, emerging occasionally to stroll by the ocean in the moonlight.

Sometimes, in the early evening, they had wandered through the great mansion. Natasha loved to dally in the library where hundreds of books, mostly leather-bound, filled the bookcases that lined three sides of the room. It struck Jim as a cumbersome, inefficient method for storing information, but Natasha loved to peruse the things, especially those having to do with history and poetry.

She enjoyed, too, the two paintings that hung on the remaining wall, one on each side of the sliding doors which separated the library from the great hall. One of the paintings was a modern abstract called *The Great Gorgias*. The other, by its painstaking detail clearly Dutch, showed a group of rosy-cheeked burghers obviously caught up in a lively debate. It was a Jan Steen entitled *Rhetoricians at a Window*. Natasha believed both paintings to be originals.[87]

Across from the paintings in a square niche built into the bookcases was a curious calendar. It indicated the correct month and the correct day, but the year was wrong. The anomaly had puzzled them for several days, but then Natasha had figured it out. This was the old style calendar—one that numbered its years from the supposed birth of Christ. Obviously, when the Elite Council members came to Jekyll to escape the burden of the D. Date Myth, they also abandoned the D. Date calendar.

As Natasha had observed, Jekyll was an island of antiquity set in a sea of modernity. She had reminded Jim that the current system of numbering years had been adopted at the beginning of the D. Date era in response to objections by the Chinese. They had argued that western practice of using the supposed birth of Christ as a starting point was not a reasonable basis for a universal calendar. The International Council had responded by establishing the

---

[87] The Jan Steen painting is to be found in the Philadelphia Art Museum.

present system which was based on the Super Nova in Andromeda that had occurred 2,192 years ago, before the stated birth of Christ.[88] Nevertheless, since the way of arriving at the month and the day had remained the same, the calendar served its purpose for Jim and Natasha. The numbering of the years was quite irrelevant to them. What counted now was the remorseless approach of June 7th—the day when Natasha would die.

Now Jim backed off the jet thrust lever once again, and as the plane's airspeed began to bleed off, he fed in a compensating fifteen degrees of wing flap. Under the right wing lay the hundreds of blue lights that marked Bradley's maze of taxiways. The rotating green and white beacon looked like it sat in a field of blue dahlias. Jim glanced at the on-board chronometer and saw that elapsed time since takeoff was two hours, eleven minutes. They would be on the ground all too soon now.

On the sixteenth night, their last on Jekyll, walking along the beach in the evening, they both knew it was time to talk once again about death. Her time was so short now. Jim felt the old anger begin to seep back. There were so many injustices about which to feel rage—that Smyth had stolen her life, that the system had condemned her, that they had been deprived of a relationship, and that he had failed to save her.

Natasha had reached for his arm, swung him around, and almost fiercely said, "Don't, Jim. Don't." And then more gently, "Life is like a book," she'd said. "One often regrets finishing it, but when it's ended, only a fool would try to drag it on."

"That's not true, Tasha," he had said. "Of course life must end, but yours was not intended to end now."

"No," she said shaking her head "from the beginning my life has been destined to end now. And in any case, Smyth says that were I to live I would shortly suffer a serious illness."

"Illness? What illness?" Jim exploded. "And why believe Smyth?"

"The nature of the illness is unimportant," she said, "and the point is, I do believe Smyth."

Jim had turned angrily from her again.

---

[88]That would render the date by our calendar uncertain, but in any case, earlier than 2192 and later than Orwell's 1984.

After a while, when she sensed that his anger had subsided, she'd tried again to comfort him.

"My dad used to say that society, which insists on sharing every individual's life, can share no one's death. Society is immortal. The old philosophers believed that fear of death is what makes us all moral, but I think it just makes us social. Acceptance of death is what makes us individually moral. That's the sort of moral we've got to be, Jim."

They had walked then in silence until dawn, sharing the beach only with the scurrying sandpipers.

Jim swung the jet into a steep right bank and watched as the star-littered skies spun through 90 degrees. Leveling off and lowering the nose, he pointed the jet down its final glide path to Runway 26. Normally, the tower would break the silence at this moment with the words, "This is your final controller," but tonight there would be no such message. He must guide the speeding craft to its destination without help. He was on his own. Jim knew that for him there would never again be a final controller.[89]

He shivered involuntarily. Natasha reached across and put her hand over his on the jet thrust lever and squeezed. He smiled his gratitude and reached for the undercarriage release.

Perhaps it was because the anger was so futile that it had begun to burn itself out. Perhaps Natasha's calm acceptance of her fate had finally begun to transmit itself to him. He recognized now that Tasha's love of life was partly due to the certainty of her early death and, for her love of life, he was grateful. She had somehow managed to incorporate death into her life and it had lent poignancy to her existence. From death she had learned to love music, poetry, art, and life itself. Jim was grateful, too, because Tasha had willed her vision in these things to him.

He added a little power now as the visual approach slope indicator showed the slight tinge of red that warned that the aircraft was below the glide path. The green lights, plainly visible now, marked the threshold of Runway 26.

It seemed years, not weeks, since he had made the last dramatic approach to this same runway. Uncle Charlie's voice was silent now, gone forever. It

---

[89] If flight metaphorically stands for freedom, then a flight controller limits freedom.

was because of the Lucifer incident, because of the feeling that he himself had been condemned to a seemingly certain early and predictable death, that he could understand Tasha now. But that experience in the end had shattered the D. Date Myth, too.

The plane flashed across the threshold lights. Jim hauled back on the wheel and prematurely reduced the jet thrust to zero. The jet slammed onto Runway 26, bounced once and then settled. He yanked the thrust levers into full reverse and the twin jet power plants roared momentarily. The whizzing, continuous streaks of white light that marked the sides of the runway turned into separate lights as the plane slowed. Jim applied the wheel brakes and simultaneously slewed the jet into Taxiway Tango. Again, Tasha leaned over and placed her hand across his on the thrust levers.

Jim did not trust himself to look at her now. He busied himself with the shutdown procedure as he taxied the plane to a stop in front of the tower. Finally, with the engines silent and only the steadily diminishing sound of the gyros winding down to disturb the silence of the cockpit, Jim turned to her.

"They say any landing you can walk away from is a good landing," Natasha, eyes moist now, said smiling.

Jim rose from his seat and, releasing Natasha's shoulder harness, took her by the hand and led her from the flight deck aft to the lounge. Guiding her towards a narrow leather divan, he turned to the cocktail cabinet and selected a decanter of brandy and Cannabis and two wine glasses.

"I will not even be at your Terminal Ceremony, Tasha."

"It's for the best," she said taking the glass. "Others will be there, my parents..."

"This, then, is our Aqua Vie," he said raising his glass.

She paused for a moment, silent, not ashamed of the tears. It was as if for an instant she might be wavering in her conviction. Or was that an illusion—was everything an illusion? But then she too raised her glass.

"All is well between me and thee, now and forever."

He hesitated, not wanting now to say the words, not wanting to acknowledge aloud his final commitment to let her go. In the distance the Great Clock tolled the half hour; it was 11:30. In thirty minutes the Terminal Ceremony would begin. She stood silently waiting for her release. Finally, he surrendered.

"All is well," he breathed, "between me and thee, now and forever."

They drained their glasses and quickly he reached to embrace her. She came into his arms without resistance and he held her close, but she was no longer his Tasha. She had gone already.

He released her and, with no word or acknowledgement, she turned away from him.

Jim reached over her head and pressed the exit release. The door swung down, putting the steps into place, and Natasha left. He watched her as she walked head high toward the gate, the southwest wind playing once again with her short black hair.

Slowly, he swung the door closed and returned to the cockpit. Fixing his eyes ahead, he taxied out, and without a word to the controller, took off.

He watched for a moment as the flashing lights of Master Med passed under his left wing for the last time. The great pyramid appeared now to lie at the center of a spider's web of cold blue street lights that radiated from it.[90] Banking to the right, he waited until the Polestar centered itself in the windshield and he headed north.[91] North towards Greenland, north towards Erewhon.

---

[90] And so, the story concludes with reference to its central theme. The web—a significant symbol and major motif used throughout the text, yet again hints at the problem of the relationship between the individual and society.

[91] The Polestar is the only star in the firmament which, viewed from earth, does not *appear* to move. It is relatively fixed.

EPILOGUE

Four days later, on June 10th, P. Goras found himself staring at the face of Michele LaTour, the French Director who had worked incognito as a Lucifer Pilot. The face displayed on the readout screen of the Oval Office was intelligent and the hazel eyes were expressive, but he could find therein no clue as to why she had attempted to reveal the ULTIMATE TRUTH to Captain James Sebring.

Goras sighed. It didn't matter anyway. The fact was she had tried, she had failed, and she had been exiled to Erewhon. His immediate problem was to make sure that his nominee to her now vacant position on the International Council would not be capable of the same mistake.

Goras' gaze shifted from the screen to the communiqué he held in his hand. It bore the set of queries that the International Council had addressed to him that morning. He motioned with his hand and then smiled at his new assistant. The short, dark-haired woman returned a half sad smile and then hurried to the computer console to type in his responses. Her agile fingers flew across the console like those of an accomplished pianist, translating his spoken message without hesitation onto the readout screen.

The message read:

DATE: 10 JUNE 2192
TO: INTERNATIONAL COUNCIL, GREENWICH, U.K.
FROM: P. GORAS, WASHINGTON, U.S.A.

1. IT IS MY OPINION THAT NOEL BAKER SMYTH (FORMERLY U.S.A. REGION I DIRECTOR MASTER MED) CAN SUSTAIN AND WILL PRESERVE THE ULTIMATE TRUTH. I HEREBY NOMINATE HIM TO THE VACANCY ON THE INTERNATIONAL COUNCIL.
2. CAPTAIN JAMES A. SEBRING NEVER PENETRATED THE SECRET OF THE LUCIFER CATALYST. HE HAS ARRIVED AT EREWHON.
3. THE LUCIFER CATALYST (AQUA VIE) WAS ADMINISTERED TO N. MOLLENSKAYA 7 JUNE 2192. THE HAZLITT-SEBRING CASE IS CLOSED.

As Goras watched the message rattle onto the screen, a whimsical smile spread across his huge, moon face and, turning to his assistant, he muttered, "Ah Satan's Evil."[92]

---

[92]Readers are left to decipher this last message themselves.

There is no ULTIMATE TRUTH. Each man is the measure of his own truth. That which appears true to a man is true for him; that which appears false to a man is false for him.

Protagoras of Abdera

SUGGESTED READINGS

SECTION I: CLASSIC WORKS ON RHETORIC AND ITS SOPHISTIC ROOTS

W. K. C. Guthrie, *The Sophists*

Only fragments of the works of the Sophist rhetoricians remain. The Sophists are known to us, therefore, largely through the critiques of their arch rival, Plato. They are usually dismissed as professional persuaders who were not above prevaricating to make their point—the "hucksters" of classical antiquity. In fact, theirs was a major system of thought which lies at the basis of any thoroughgoing conception of rhetoric. Guthrie, who does not sympathize with that world view, nonetheless offers one of the few serious treatments of it.

G. B. Kerferd, *The Sophistic Movement*

The Sophist movement gave expression to Athens' greatest age—a period from 450 to 400 B.C. during which intense artistic and intellectual activity accompanied profound political and social change. Kerferd professes to be startled by the modernity of the problems the Sophists formulated and discussed—philosophical problems regarding knowledge and perception, theoretical and practical problems regarding living in societies and above all democracies, questions regarding the nature and purpose of education, etc. Throughout all, two dominant themes emerge for Kerferd—the need for relativism to be accepted without reducing the world to anarchy and the belief that no area of human life should be immune from the understanding achieved through reasoned argument.

Plato, *Gorgias* and *Phaedrus*

The fictional P. Goras in *Lucifer State* is based on the historical Protagoras and Gorgias, two Sophists considered the fathers of rhetoric. Both are the subjects of Platonic dialogues. Plato fairly portrays Protagoras as a serious thinker, but he falsely portrays Gorgias as a dangerously muddled one. In the *Gorgias* Plato conflates rhetoric as a manipulative technique and rhetoric as the analysis of such technique in order to discredit rhetoric as a worldview rivaling philosophy.

Protagoras and Gorgias believed it might be impossible to know the truth; communication for them therefore had to be the process of *persuading* people to accept one's *opinion*. Plato, on the other hand, believed it possible; communication for him therefore had to be the process of first *finding* and then *teaching the truth*. He argues that the only tolerable role for rhetoric is as the *servant* of truth, persuading people to accept the truth when teaching it proves difficult. At best, then, rhetoric for Plato is *cosmetic, enhancing truth* that is present but not obvious.

He accuses the Sophists of supporting rhetoric as the *usurper* of truth and enthroning opinion in its place—rhetoric is a *masquerade, deceiving with appearance*. Ironically, though Plato denounces rhetoric as deception, he countenances its use as a means of controlling the masses ruled over by a philosopher king.

Aristotle, *Rhetoric*

The *Rhetoric* is the single most influential work on the subject in the past twenty-five hundred years. Aristotle is concerned with obviously persuasive situations—the legislature, the law courts, and ceremonial occasions. He sees the major modes of persuasion as being determined by the logic of the message, its psychological appeal, and the ethos of the persuader. Aristotle defines man as the "rational animal," and his rhetoric emphasizes more or less *rational* means of persuasion.

Cicero, *De Oratore*

The most prominent figure in the history of rhetoric, the Roman Cicero was trained in the Greek tradition of the *enkyklios paideia*. In keeping with the philosophical doctrine of his day Cicero held that the perfect orator must be capable of arguing all sides on any question, given that no certainties exist from which to deduce conclusions about right ideas or actions. Testing all sides in debate creates the conditions for reasonably negotiating differences or making decisions in both philosophy and politics. Of course the perfect orator had to be conversant with many subjects to engage in such *controversia*, and Cicero viewed the end of education to be its application to practical affairs.

Kenneth Burke, *A Grammar of Motives* & *A Rhetoric of Motives*

Probably the single most influential modern writer on rhetoric, Burke is profoundly influenced by Aristotle but also by a number of other writers, most notably Marx and Freud. He emphasizes not only apparent persuasive means and situations but also unconscious and covert attempts to persuade. Burke is particularly interested in the broader applications of rhetoric to the problem of social control. As a poet and a novelist, he is convinced that the vocabulary of literary analysis, particularly the "Four Master Tropes"— metaphor, synecdoche, irony, and metonymy—can usefully be applied to social analysis. For Burke, humans are "symbol-using animals," and his rhetoric emphasizes persuasion by strategic *manipulation of symbols*.

Ch. Perelman and L. Olbrechts-Tyteca, *The New Rhetoric: A Treatise on Argumentation*

Certain systems of knowledge (notably science and logic) claim "epistemic privilege." That is, they coerce the auditor by implying that the *method* of arriving at knowledge guarantees its truth. The auditor must accept the findings of such systems or sacrifice the claim to being a reasonable person. Rhetoric, however, has always emphasized the central function of the *audience's* conception of what is true, probable, or plausible. Perelman's *New*

Rhetoric carries this emphasis to its logical extreme. It is a totally audience-centered rhetoric in which *"audience"* becomes the unit of rhetorical analysis.

Richard Weaver, *The Ethics of Rhetoric*

We have chosen to subject the concepts of "security" and "safety" to rhetorical scrutiny. Weaver offers a similar analysis of the term "progress" and in so doing elaborates on the general notion of "ultimate" or "God" terms. In the essay, "The Rhetoric of Social Science," he makes the important claim that much social science is in fact a covert apology for a certain brand of politics.

I. A. Richards, *The Philosophy of Rhetoric*

Richards was among the first to insist that *metaphor* may have a hitherto unsuspected importance to rhetoric. Along with scholars like Kenneth Burke, Stephen Pepper, Colin Turbayne, George Lakoff, Mark Johnson, and Paul Ricouer, he has expanded the concept of metaphor to the point where it is now variously regarded as the fundamental basis for all philosophies, the generative factor in all language, a major heuristic tool, and, of course, a powerful means of persuasion.

Nancy S. Struever, *The Language of History in the Renaissance: Rhetoric and Historical Consciousness in Florentine Humanism*

Like Guthrie, Struever recognizes that rhetoric, relativism, and sophistry are inextricably linked and constitute a major and alternative way of viewing the world. Unlike Guthrie, she sympathizes with the "rhetorical" point of view and clearly shows its contribution to the Renaissance and Humanism. The work is not easy reading, but it is mandatory for any serious student of rhetoric.

Ernesto Grassi, *Rhetoric as Philosophy: The Humanist Tradition*

Grassi perceives a common perspective pervading Greek and Roman rhetoric, Renaissance Humanism, and modern philosophy (whose interest in language has contributed to renewed interest in rhetoric). He argues that a claim to have found truth cannot be established with certainty, since its proof would be circular, dependent upon a system of logical relations established by the claim itself. A claim then is not a timeless, universal truth but an expression of a human need arising out of a specific historical situation, an expression whose persuasiveness is determined by the power and beauty of language.

Humanism is rooted in just such skepticism. Absent sure access to superhuman criteria, Protagoras proclaimed *humanity* is "the measure of all things" and accorded privilege to language as a uniquely human power. Consistent with this view, Cicero and later Quintilian advocated education in the *humanities*, language-based disciplines thought to cultivate in the human being those capacities differentiating it from other animals. Renaissance Humanists sought to revive those capacities (supposed dormant through medieval times) by rejecting theology and returning to poetry, rhetoric, history, ethics, and politics recognized in classical times as the instruments through which humanity exercises its peculiar form of being.

Samuel Ijsseling, *Rhetoric and Philosophy in Conflict: An Historical Survey*

A superb, succinct survey of the quarrel between rhetoric and philosophy from classical to modern times over the nature of human being, the availability of truth, and the significance accorded language.

SECTION II: TOTALITARIAN RHETORIC

George Orwell, *1984*

In this social science fiction classic, Orwell describes a totalitarian state circa 1948 through the lens of a futuristic dystopia. The book is dated in spots, but many would argue that in our world of diminished civil liberties post 9/11, the book is as current as today's newspaper. The message of *1984* is that ultimate rhetoric must not be recognized as such or it will be discounted.

Sinclair Lewis, *It Can't Happen Here*

The title says it all. Americans feel safe, protected by a democratic form of government. Lewis' compelling novel shows how fragile liberty truly is, and demonstrates, step by step, how the citizens of the United States could be persuaded to vote for leaders and support policies that would turn the nation into a totalitarian regime.

Eric Hoffer, *The True Believer*

This is a study of mass movements and the people who comprise them by a highly literate working man. Perhaps because it is highly speculative and non-empirical, it is not much admired by academics. It is nonetheless a provocative treatise which presents a comprehensive model through which we can come to understand how mass movements are generated and sustained. Hoffer makes no distinction between "good" or "bad" mass movements—the persuasive practices of mass movements and the mindsets of the followers is the same, regardless of whether the movement seeks good or evil ends. Particularly important is Hoffer's notion of the importance of a "rhetorical devil" to a movement—an idea that is also supported by Kenneth Burke.

Thomas E. Ricks, *Making the Corps*

Many reject as outrageous any claim that the Marines brainwash recruits; many think it outrageous to believe otherwise. Ricks follows sixty-three men through boot camp on Parris Island providing (like Edwards) material for a variety of interpretations.

Arthur Koestler, *Darkness at Noon*

This is a fine novel by a man who has firsthand experience of the phenomena he describes. The book is inspired by the sensational pre-World War II Moscow Trials which introduced much of the world to the spectacle of hitherto hardheaded men confessing to, and apparently feeling culpable for, crimes they did not commit.

Aldous Leonard Huxley, *Brave New World*

As early as 1932, Huxley sensed the possibilities for a dark compact between Pavlovian psychology and modern technology with a view to the "engineering of consent." *Brave New World* is widely regarded as a masterpiece of fiction but it is perhaps neither a masterpiece nor entirely fiction.

Edgar M. Schein, *Coercive Persuasion*

Overwhelmingly the Chinese "thought reform" movement was applied by Chinese to other Chinese. A few Americans, however, remained in China after the revolution and some of them became "victims" of the same techniques. Schein analyzes the experience of a number of American civilians who were imprisoned by the Chinese Communists between 1950 and 1956.

Robert Jay Lifton, *Thought Reform and the Psychology of Totalism: A Study of Brainwashing in China*

Mao began by exiling Chinese intellectuals to the farms and road gangs because many were trained in the west and were sympathetic with "capitalist bourgeois" ideas. Ultimately, however, he found he needed these literate scholars as teachers and administrators and undertook a program of "thought reform." Lifton's is perhaps the best study of so-called Chinese "brainwashing."

B. F. Skinner, *Walden Two*

This famous and brilliant contemporary behaviorist envisages a much more benign marriage of psychology and technology and incidentally provides material for the commune movement.

B. F. Skinner, *Beyond Freedom and Dignity*

This "best selling" book is a non-fictional defense of the ideas underlying *Walden Two*. Here Skinner offers forthright and compelling arguments for a deterministic view of human behavior. This is the anti-rhetorical stance *par excellence*.

SECTION III: CONSENSUS RHETORIC

Peter Berger, *Invitation to Sociology*

Berger, believing that humans are first social animals, exemplifies the sociological approach to the problems of rhetoric. From this point of view—which owes a great deal to Karl Marx, Emile Durkheim, Karl Mannheim, and George Herbert Mead, among others—persuasion is a matter of the manipulation of consensus. It is about trying to get the group to accept your interest as theirs and vice versa. This is an excellent, readable, unpretentious introduction to a particular view of sociology which underwrites a good deal of a speculation in contemporary rhetoric.

Peter Berger, *The Sacred Canopy* and (with Luckmann) *The Social Construction of Reality*

At a more general level, Berger and his colleagues see our total understanding of "reality" as a "social construction." From this point of view, society provides explanations designed to allay our deepest fears about life, death, dreams, psychosis, the hereafter, etc. These constructions, among other things, provide the rhetor with the "commonplaces," the unquestioned social pieties, which can serve as a basis for any particular persuasive program.

Alan Lightman, *Einstein's Dreams*

Perhaps one of our most cherished consensually validated "truths" is our understanding of time. In this book, Lightman presents thirty fables where time behaves in unexpected ways and we see how humans adapt. The book is profound and endearing. As one reviewer put it, "in their tone and quiet logic, Lightman's fables come off like Bach variations played on an exquisite harpsichord. People live for one day or eternity, and they respond intelligibly to each unique set of circumstances. Raindrops hang in the air in a place of frozen time; in another place everyone knows one year in advance exactly when the world will end, and acts accordingly."

Dale Carnegie, *How to Win Friends and Influence People*, or Norman Vincent Peale, *The Power of Positive Thinking*, or Stephen Covey, *The Seven Habits of Highly Effective People*, or virtually any self-help business book.

These publications might well be called rhetorics of consensus. Implicitly they call upon the reader to adopt uncritically the prevailing social protocols. Explicitly they show how to use consensus to manipulate others and systematically "get ahead."

Thomas S. Szasz, M.D., *Ideology and Insanity* and *The Myth of Psychotherapy: Mental Healing as Religion, Rhetoric, and Repression*

Szasz believes that much of what we term "mental illness" is really only the expression of socially unacceptable ideas using an idiosyncratic idiom— in short, ineffective rhetoric. Correspondingly, he believes that therapy is better thought of not as a medical science but as a *rhetorical art*.

Richard E. Vatz and Lee Weinberg, *Thomas Szasz: Primary Values and Major Contentions*

The authors of one of the critical essays in this volume *(Lucifer State)* provide a useful set of excerpts from the works of Dr. Szasz. Szasz' contentions are not, of course, popular with the "mental health" community. Vatz and Weinberg offer selections from critics of Szasz' rhetorical interpretation of psychiatry and provide responses to those criticisms.

SECTION IV: HIERARCHICAL RHETORIC

Michel Foucault, *The Order of Things: An Archaeology of the Human Sciences* and *The Archaeology of Knowledge*

Both Plato and the Sophists may criticize as deceptive the rhetorical techniques by which claims to knowledge are advanced. But Plato, unlike the Sophists, presumes the philosopher stands in a position privileged by truth, not susceptible to being criticized in turn. Foucault, like the Sophists, doubts such a position exists.

Knowledge claims and power claims are inseparable from one another and from the discursive practices that develop around them, according to Foucault. The exercise of power determines what is known and what is said by whom and how; it generates hierarchies of knowledge and discourse which in turn reinforce the power whose exercise gave them birth. Knowledge requirements restrict who gets power and who gets to speak. Discursive practices effectively limit what may be known and by whom. *Power, knowledge, and discourse* in conjunction then engender what Foucault calls *discursive formations*, basic (though relative and changeable) structures of power and knowledge that shape and are shaped by the language of an epoch.

Study of the past resembles an archaeological dig exposing discrete strata—i.e., epochs defined by distinctly different discursive formations. Investigating past epochs as well as our own, Foucault seeks to give voice to the powerless whose knowledge claims are deemed invalid and thereby reveal their means of resistance and the forces that bring change.

George Orwell, *Animal Farm*

A great deal of rhetoric, of course, either demands or promises equality. According to Orwell, behind such rhetoric lies not the demand for equality but the demand for a different system of inequality—a different hierarchical principle. George Orwell's *Animal Farm* provides an excellent illustration of this process.

Hugh Dalziel Duncan, *Communication and Social Order*

Duncan borrows heavily from Kenneth Burke, who says of himself, "Curse me for a not yet housebroken cur." Perhaps to understand institutions and hierarchies, one must not be "housebroken."

Niccolo Machiavelli, *The Prince*

In hierarchical situations, according to Kenneth Burke, we are continually faced with the problem of persuading our inferiors, our superiors, and our equals. Each of these groups makes different rhetorical demands. Machiavelli's classic work, from this point of view, could be regarded as a rhetoric describing the communications from superior (the Prince) to inferior (his subject).

Laurence S. Peter and Raymond Hull, *The Peter Principle*

Peter and Hull write what the front cover blurb quite correctly identifies as, "The outrageous #1 National Bestseller." The authors announce with a flourish the founding of the "Salutary Science of Hierarchiology"—ignoring the previous and much more sophisticated work of Weber, Burke, and Duncan in this area. For a couple of insights into hierarchy, a few tips about how to get to the top, and an excellent illustration of *The Peter Principle* ("In a hierarchy, every employee tends to rise to his level of incompetence"), by all means read this book.

William Lutz, *Doublespeak: From "Revenue Enhancement" to "Terminal Living": How Government, Business, Advertisers, and Others Use Language to Deceive You*

More than experts doublespeak with forked tongues. According to Lutz, the powerful use language quite consciously as a weapon of social, economic, and political control. Doublespeak, he says, is language pretending to communicate but misleading, distorting, deceiving, inflating, circumventing, and obfuscating instead. It is language seeking to avoid or shift responsibility. Euphemism, gobbledygook, jargon, and inflation are the most frequently abused forms it takes. Believing public awareness the best defense against this frequently funny but at the same time frightening phenomenon, Lutz and the National Council of Teachers of English are countering with weapons of their own. Each year they bestow the George Orwell Award for Distinguished Contribution to Honesty and Clarity in Public Language. They also "honor" with the Doublespeak Award the public figure most worthy of censure for misusing language with pernicious consequence.

SECTION V: INTRAPERSONAL RHETORIC

George Herbert Mead, *Mind, Self and Society From the Standpoint of a Social Behaviorist*

Behaviorism restricts itself to the experimental study of an organism's overt physical responses to stimuli, regarding introspection as unscientific and covert mental phenomena as nonexistent. Mead's social behaviorism seeks to supplement behaviorism proper with introspectively observed phenomena such as "mind" and "self." Mead perceives action as a goal-directed process, commencing with an inner mental phase and completing itself in an outer physical one. He criticizes behaviorism as reductive and materialistic for ignoring the former and fixating on the latter. Mead advocates a *naturalistic* approach to the study of humanity, encompassing the scientific approach of a Skinner or a Pavlov and the philosophical approach of a Laing.

Decades before Laing wrote of the inner tension between conformity and individuality, Mead conceived of the self as an *internal dialogue* between the "me" (internalized social institutions) and the "I" (that which makes a person unique). The "I" expresses itself spontaneously in response to its perceived environment, while the "me" expresses itself by exerting control over the "I." The "I" in turn reacts by altering its response or creating a new response to the "me." Thinking consists in the *internal rehearsal* of projected actions.

Erving Goffman, *The Presentation of Self in Everyday Life*

"All the world's a stage," says Shakespeare, "And all the men and women merely players." Goffman systematically exploits the playwright's insight, treating theatre as a metaphor for life. People are most often engaged not in communicating information but in staging performances, impressing audiences by portraying characters which project various aspects of themselves.

The *self* is a dramatic effect whose credibility is critical. Within social institutions, a troupe of actors may contrive dramas for select audiences. Theatre access is controlled to exclude those for whom a drama is not intended. Backstage access is controlled to conceal cast secrets. When on-stage disruptions or backstage information threatens to stop or give away a show, all involved improvise to save it.

R. D. Laing, *The Divided Self*

Pavlov and Skinner, impressed by the achievements of science, apply to the study of human beings the methods which have been so successful in the study of nature. R. D. Laing, on the other hand, is a product of philosophical schools—existentialism and phenomenology—which take the individual human being as a point of departure. *The Divided Self* is an account of the inner tension created by our desire for security (which can be achieved by *conformity*) and our need to be different from others (our need to establish *identity*). It is as if we all wanted to be *uniform* but paradoxically also individually *distinguished*. This tension is exploited by a wide variety of persuaders—notably in advertising. Laing is difficult to read but worth the time of anyone who has some background in social psychology or who is familiar with the jargon of existentialism and phenomenology.

Robert M. Pirsig, *Zen and the Art of Motorcycle Maintenance*

Sometimes classified as a philosophy text, this novel has little to do with repairing motorcycles—that notion is used as a metaphor for modern humanity's troubled relationship with its own technology. Similarly, the reference to Zen is really an attempt to describe a way of thinking that lies at the very foundations of one conception of the rhetorical point of view. The book constitutes a "novel" introduction to the early Platonic dialogues about the nature of rhetoric, the *Gorgias* and the *Phaedrus*.

Pirsig engages readers in a cross-country "Chautauqua," musing on the maintenance of motorcycles and the nature of reason. From one perspective the machine is rational, from another aesthetic. But the rational and the aesthetic, the technological and the artistic are joined beyond duality (classical and romantic, intellectual and emotional, subjective and objective, mental and physical) in what Pirsig calls *quality*. Such quality, understood by the Sophists as "arête," is what the ancient rhetoricians sought to teach.

Robert M. Pirsig, *Lila*

The sequel to *Zen*, written a decade and a half later, in which Pirsig continues his exploration of quality with a journey on a sailboat.

Robert Bellah, *Habits of the Heart*

Michael Joseph Gross writes that *Habits of the Heart* is "required reading for anyone who wants to understand how religion contributes to and detracts from America's common good. An instant classic upon publication in 1985, it was reissued in 1996 with a new introduction describing the book's continuing relevance for a time when the country's racial and class divisions are being continually healed and ripped open again by religious people. *Habits of the Heart* describes the social significance of faiths ranging from 'Sheilaism' (practiced by a California nurse named Sheila) to conservative Christianity. It's thoroughly readable, theologically respectful, and academically irreproachable."

Harold Bloom, *The American Religion*

As reviewers put it, in this book, Bloom defines "the American Religion" as a Gnostic understanding, focused on an inner self that leads to freedom from nature, time, history and other selves. As Bloom presents it, the American God loves each saved individual in a personal, intimate way, and this trait is the bedrock of our national religion, a debased Gnosticism often tinged with selfishness. Such "faith" is far afield from traditional Christianity, with ramifications that should be cause for concern for the nation and the individual.

Fyodor Dostoevsky, *Crime and Punishment*

First published in 1866, Dostoevsky's description of the inner dialogue of a man guilty of murder is by now a classic. Older notions of rhetoric picture you persuading me. Modern rhetoric pays much closer attention to the process whereby you encourage me to persuade myself. Dostoevsky's hero, Raskolnikov, provides one of the most complete descriptions of internal rhetoric.

Franz Kafka, *The Trial*

Joseph K. is guilty only in the sense that all men are guilty. Nevertheless, he finds himself on trial, convicted and condemned by processes he can neither identify nor understand. Modern persuaders claim to be able to capitalize on this general sense of guilt, this vague feeling of having to prove something—of being on trial.

Joshua Meyrowitz, *No Sense of Place: The Impact of Electronic Media on Social Behavior*

Goffman treats social behavior as theatre, interpreting interactions as performances staged for audiences. Marshall McLuhan argues that changes in social behavior can be induced by changes in communication media. Influenced by Goffman and McLuhan, Meyrowitz maintains that our perception of the stages on which and the audiences before which we perform, and therefore our understanding of the performances appropriate to them, have been disrupted by the intrusion of the telephone, radio, television, and increasingly the computer into every corner of life.

Television especially has dissolved distinctions between here and there, personal and public, immediate and mediated, live and Memorex. The physical barriers that once structured our lives have crumbled, pulling down the social barriers associated with them. Electronic media have left us with no sense of physical and therefore social place. And the new social order makes no sense to us. We stand on new stages and before new audiences both of which demand new styles of performance.

SECTION VII: RHETORICAL FORMS

Wayne Booth, *The Rhetoric of Fiction*

Surprisingly, there has been until recently relatively little study of the persuasive uses of fiction. Perhaps it was assumed that because fiction does not claim to be literally "true," it was unlikely to be persuasive. Booth knew better and offered what remains a classic text on the topic.

Hayden White, *Metahistory: The Historical Imagination in Nineteenth-Century Europe*

White claims to have identified three strategies historians employ to achieve different explanatory affects and four modes of articulating each strategy: *formal argument* with its modes of Formism, Organicism, Mechanism, and Contextualism (following Stephen Pepper): *emplotment* with its archetypes of Romance, Comedy, Tragedy, and Satire (following Northrop Frye); and *ideological implication* with its tactics of Anarchism, Conservatism, Radicalism, and Liberalism (following Karl Mannheim).

A historian's style is composed of a specific combination of modes. Styles relate to one another at a deep level of consciousness on which the historian chooses discursive, narrative, and ethical modes by prefiguring his field of study in a particular way. White names the modes of *prefiguration* for the four tropes: Metaphor, Metonymy, Synecdoche, and Irony (following an interpretative tradition spanning Aristotle, Vico, modern linguists, and literary theorists, especially Kenneth Burke). Ultimately the basis for choosing one perspective on history rather than another is moral or aesthetic rather than epistemological. In White's words, the irreducibly "meta-historical" basis of any historical work is comprised of its dominant tropological mode and its attendant linguistic protocol.

Christopher Norris, *Deconstruction: Theory and Practice*

Deconstruction rejects generic distinctions between types of texts and attendant claims of privilege. Texts are texts, even deconstructive ones. Those supposing privilege systematically seek to suppress all rhetorical elements, but on close reading all texts can be subverted or deconstructed.

Philosophy texts betray pivotal tropes and figures of speech. All texts reveal critical junctures at which paired terms are generated in dialectical opposition with one viewed as superior to or as derivative of the other, but the relationship can always be challenged or even inverted. Plato contends—in writing—that writing derives from speech. Conversely Jacques Derrida contends that speech derives from writing, i.e. from text. Significantly, deconstructive texts admit their susceptibility to being deconstructed too. This reflexive perspective is essential to the rhetorical worldview and as such to *Lucifer State*.

FROM THE THERAPEUTIC STATE TO THE LUCIFER STATE

Richard E. Vatz
Towson State University

Lee S. Weinberg
University of Pittsburgh

Thomas Szasz is the foremost critic of psychiatry in the United States and perhaps the world. For over fifty years he has been warning that the abuses of psychiatry have increased exponentially to the point that in many countries it has become one of the primary components of social control. In fact, he has warned us for years now that institutional psychiatry has become so mystifying to so many people and levels of government that the danger exists of the evolution of a *Therapeutic State* in which psychiatry or some new form of the current mental health structure will be the main and the ultimate source of social control: omnipresent, yet acceptable by definition to the majority of people, for its norms of acceptable behavior are *by definition* the behavior of the majority. Non-conforming behavior seen as "sick" may properly be interfered with (voluntarily or involuntarily) since the goal is "health," an unquestioned good, and the practitioners of this art of the "diagnosing" and "healing" of "sick" behavior are benefiting and will likely continue to benefit from the unquestioned ethos of the medical scientist. Interestingly, Szaszian warnings (and other factors identified below) may have provided a counter-rhetoric, which will ultimately foil his prophecy concerning the emergence of a total therapeutic state.

The possible defeat of the emergent therapeutic state described in this essay may simply pave the way for the emergence of an as yet unknown alternative means of state control. For the choice may not be between a society controlled by a mix of rhetoric and force and one controlled by the masses; the choice may only be among types of control. As the Director of Master Med perceptively explains to Evelyn, in Erewhon One—the Capitalist society, the masses pick their leaders, but come to "choose" what they *must* choose, and in Erewhon Two—the Communist society, the masses do not concern themselves with choosing their leaders, but are satisfied with their belief that their leaders are a part of the masses. In the Therapeutic State the masses will be diagnosed and treated by social/psychiatric doctors. But if this control system is unmasked, what will replace it?

The Lucifer State is in many ways reminiscent of the Therapeutic State of which Thomas Szasz warns throughout his writings. Indeed, for many of the components of Lucifer State there are clear analogues in the still incomplete Therapeutic State. A review of the means by which this state seeks to control people may reveal how the Therapeutic State could in fact develop into the Lucifer State.

Thus, it will be helpful, first, to summarize Szasz's position regarding mental illness and the Therapeutic State. Szasz argues that much of what we call "mental illness" has no relation to illness. Instead, it is simply a label used for primarily two purposes: one, to *discredit* behavior about which we have little understanding or very much disdain or contempt, and two, to *accredit* those whose behavior(s) are socially acceptable as well as those who diagnose the unacceptable, or the "mentally ill."

There are basically three points of view regarding "mental illness." The first, the traditional view, often called the "medical model," which currently prevails, is that mental illness is like any other illness or disease, having characteristic symptoms, causes, pathology, and prognosis. This view is promoted, of course, by the American Psychiatric Association, the National Institute of Mental Health (NIMH), and other voices of institutional psychology and psychiatry.

The second view is that mental illness exists and is indeed analogous to physiological disease, but that it is too often misdiagnosed or too liberally diagnosed. This view allows one to argue persuasively that any patent idiocies in psychiatric or psychological or any mental health practices are evidence of poor practitioners, not poor notions of mental health theory.

The third view, already alluded to and promoted most notably by Dr. Szasz, is that the labels of mental illnesses and the like are used primarily not as legitimate medical notions but to discredit society's nonconformists or deviants, such as criminals, drug users, cultists (devotees of societally unapproved religions), or anybody the labeler finds out of step.

In fact, in 1964 almost 10 percent of the United States' psychiatrists responded to a poll by *Fact* magazine to say that Senator Barry Goldwater (who was then the Republican candidate for President) was psychologically unfit, with many calling him such names as "paranoid," "mentally unbalanced," and "schizophrenic." Senator Goldwater sued the magazine for libel and won his suit. (Had the Lucifer State been in place in the 1980's, might not Master Med and its computers have agreed that Ronald Reagan suffered Post Natural Death when John Hinckley failed?)

From another perspective, it is interesting to note that homosexuality, once considered a mental disease when homosexuality was a more stigmatized and publicly reviled enterprise, was *voted out* as a disease in 1973 by the Board of Trustees of the American Psychiatric Association. This reflected no medical discovery, but simply the increased persuasive power and political clout of homosexual groups. If strange and/or dangerous behavior is not illness or the product of illness, what is it? And why are people so successfully persuaded by the rhetoric of "mental health" professionals?

On the first question, behavior need not be seen as *something*. When we consider behavior that does not offend us, we see it mostly as a matter of individual choice; sometimes, as a choice to be different. In the case of extreme deviant behavior, it, too, is a choice; sometimes a choice to disregard society's rules. Even with bizarre behavior, Dr. Szasz and others argue, purpose can be discerned. This is where people may confuse "senseless" with "insensible." All behavior makes sense to the one behaving (whether the person admits it or not, also a matter of choice). But because some behaviors seem so foreign or macabre in motivation (e.g. violent crime), they are perceived to be without motivation or "senseless" and, therefore, explainable only by reference to mystifying "mental illnesses." In this mode of medical explanation, we justify drugging, violence, and deprivation of people's

Constitutional rights in order to control their behavior and discredit what they do or what they say.

This leads us to the second question above as to how mental health professionals' rhetoric works to create an acquiescent public which will accept their extra-legal interventions in people's lives.

A critical and necessary component of the persuasiveness of the mental illness ethic is the medical-scientific *ethos* which attends it. Because of the mystifying nature of medical science, many people will allow to go unquestioned its propositions, propositions which might create profound outrage otherwise. A major axiom of rhetoric is that the most potent persuasion is not that which adduces the best argument, but instead that persuasion which is so mystifying that it precludes, preempts, or makes seem unnecessary and inappropriate any questioning or counterargument. In the Therapeutic State, when social control is affected by someone's being committed against his will to a psychiatric hospital, it is not seen as false imprisonment, but as "treatment" of "illness." Thus, years ago, *The Baltimore Sun* hailed police who were trumping up charges against innocent citizens because to the *Sun* they were forcing the "mentally ill" to get "help."

What constitutes "help" in the Therapeutic State is also rhetorically controlled. One dominant mode of help is psychotherapy, which Dr. Szasz argues is nothing more than conversation that is seen as medical treatment. Often "therapy" may include more coercive and violent components such as "aversion therapy" wherein heavy eaters are shocked to discourage their gluttony or convicts are forced to undergo torture (not so called, of course) as part of experiments in behavior modification. The seeming medical context and the persuasive language of "help" preclude us from wondering whether an Osama bin Laden is at work as a member of a helping profession. As Dr. Szasz states, "The name of the game is social control." We would add that when rhetoric is successful, people will not know it's a game and will call it by a different name.

In a successful rhetorical or persuasive system, all happenings can be reconciled with the prevailing ideological perspective. Perhaps the most revealing situation in this general regard is seen in a study published in 1973 titled, "On Being Sane in Insane Places." This study, conducted by Stanford psychologist D. L. Rosenhan, involved his sending a number of friends and colleagues to a variety of psychiatric hospitals to try to gain entrance by feigning the hearing of voices (called "auditory hallucinations"—with a diagnostic category, the persuasiveness increases). Once successfully admitted (and all were), they ceased to feign symptoms and were astonished to learn that their behaviors and life histories (all natural and authentic after admission) were never seen by hospital staffs as inconsistent with mental illness. Interestingly, Dr. Rosenhan concluded from his work not that mental illness is a myth or that "diagnosis" of "mental illness" in general is invalid, but instead that the environment of the hospitals made distinguishing between the sane and insane impossible, and that, as he stated in a later feckless observation, "diagnostic reliability in medicine ... has much more going for it than psychiatric diagnosis." Had he said "psychiatric diagnosis" is not diagnosis at all and that it is fraudulent rhetoric, the good "doctor" might have been ridden out of the mental health field. As it was, the outrage was overwhelming (see letters in *Science* following the study's publication).

In the Therapeutic State, in addition to the discrediting function (of deviant behavior) of the rhetoric of mental illness, to maintain control there exists the critical function of keeping the "doctors" in line and potential critics or detractors at bay. Even Rosenhan stayed in line here, perhaps aware of the fact that those who stray risk not only ostracism, but also even implications of *their* psychiatric problems or mental illnesses. (Szasz himself has been "accused" by a fellow psychiatrist of suffering from a new "mental illness," "psychoerynism," a "disease" which consists of interfering with the delivery of mental health treatment to those who need it).

In the Lucifer State one sees many of the components of control anticipated by Szasz in the Therapeutic State. To begin with, just as everybody in the Lucifer State is born into a Death Date, in the Therapeutic State everybody is born into some state of Mental Health. The D. Date can only be affected slightly by the medical team, just as the mental state can usually only be affected slightly by psychiatrists. Basically both are givens. This is why, of course, in the Therapeutic State no one is cured of schizophrenia, for example; they may, at best, achieve "remission." Moreover, in the Lucifer State practically every activity is at least touched by, and usually perceived only in reference to, one's Death Date: birth, marriage, death, and lifestyle in general. In the Therapeutic State we have the analogous or similar centrality of the reference to psychiatric evaluation: psychiatric health in the womb, child psychology, adult psychology, psychology of sex practices, psychology of death and dying, mentally healthy marriages and modes of religion, and, of course, general psychological and psychiatric evaluations of living styles. In her reaction to Jim's growing suspicion about the Lucifer State after his accident, Evelyn attributes his efforts at penetrating the Lucifer myth to his "confused mind" and "amnesia," perhaps subtle reminders of the potential link between two powerful systems of social control. Disconcerting also is the crucial social control role played by the Public Health Officer and Master Med in the Lucifer State.

The other major area in which the Lucifer State is similar to Szasz's Therapeutic State is the inextricable linking of social control and persuasion.

There are some key concepts, which dominate the Lucifer State which are either analogous to, similar to, or perhaps grounded in notions found in the Therapeutic State (and which may make for a smooth transition should psychiatry ultimately be unmasked):

1. Death Date versus Mental Illness: The Central Myths
   - Both are keys to interpretation of behavior
   - Both are key factors in decision-making in life
   - Both are only partially in control of the individual
   - Both are believed to be genetically set at birth
   - Both can be helped, but not fundamentally altered by medical experts
   - Both are legitimate concerns of the state and its functionaries
   - Both are constant concerns of citizens
   - Both replace earlier myths: D. Date replaces the myth of the benevolent creator and mental illness replaces the myth of free will
   - Both provide means for the state to eliminate problematic people
2. Death Date Incompatibility versus Psychiatric Problems: The Arbitrary and Humanly-Created Norms
   - Both may threaten relationships
   - Both are seen as problems requiring counseling
   - Both sets of counselors must possess certified medical expertise in order to define the existence of deviation

- Both are "umbrella" concepts capable of application to all human interactions and experiences
- Both claim a scientific knowledge base for their legitimacy
- Both may involve self-fulfilling prophecies

There are some differences between the Lucifer State and the Therapeutic State, most notably that whereas Jim Sebring and others like him have, at least potentially, the ability to unmask the Lucifer State, the rhetoric of the Therapeutic State allows its critics much less opportunity.

The difference can be explained rhetorically. In the Lucifer State the basis for mystification and persuasion is the diagnosing of individuals' Death Dates and the fulfillment of that prophesy. In the Therapeutic State the basis for mystification and persuasion is the diagnosing of an individual's "mental illness" and the fulfillment of that prophesy. Focusing on death means dealing with an empirically verifiable, unambiguous, and indisputable reality; people are either alive or dead. (Now, we know that some perverse people, particularly readers of *Lucifer State*, are likely to carp about definition of death or brain stem inactivity or whatever, but the Death Date in *Lucifer State* makes no bones about what constitutes death. Other bones, yes, but not that bone.) With mental or psychiatric illness, however, its existence cannot only never be confirmed, but also it can never be *disconfirmed!*

When Jim Sebring's uncle and others do not die as predicted, there must be an explanation of "Post Natural Death," but that is an embarrassment to the Lucifer State which must be rectified and explained away. And the more people who live beyond their Death Date and the longer they live, the greater increase of that embarrassment. Similarly, the psychiatrists who were fooled by Rosenhan sought to explain away that embarrassment. And the ability to reconcile all patient behavior with the doctor's diagnosis offers another embarrassment-avoidance technique to the controllers in the Therapeutic State.

In the Therapeutic State the potential for such embarrassment is not as great as in the Lucifer State and does not involve, at least thus far, all citizens. In the Therapeutic State the diagnosing of mental illness and/or the estimation of "mental health" requires no empirically verifiable reality, such as an actual lesion or other patho-anatomical manifestation. All that is required is a psychiatrist (or other high-ethos source) to make a judgment on behavior. If asked to point to "real illness" or some neurological disturbance, the argument will be advanced that we are not yet sufficiently sophisticated in medical technology to locate the disturbance (here, ironically, is mystification by the claim of the *lack* of mystifying technology. But remember it is the high-ethos source that has convinced you that a problem exists even though he or she has no equipment to certify its existence!). In recent years the fact that medicines and drugs relieve suffering and change some behaviors is used as evidence that therefore they must be curing a *disease*, even though no consistent patho-anatomical evidence for disease is adduced.

The closest thing in the Therapeutic State to a verifiable, unmaskable rhetoric is psychiatric diagnosis or prognosis of dangerousness. If a psychiatrist or any "mental health professional" diagnoses an individual as dangerous, there is the possibility for *confirmation* if that individual commits a violent act, but there is no possibility for *disconfirmation* in the absence of such an act, because there is always the potential (theoretically) for such an act to occur. If a psychiatrist or any "mental health professional" diagnoses an individual as *not* dangerous, such a diagnosis represents the greatest possibility for psychiatric unmasking, for if the individual commits a violent act, explanation and rationalizing would be required.

Two points should be noted here. First, even if the last example should occur, it is more likely that the individual psychiatrist will be unmasked than the Therapeutic State. Remember in the Rosenhan studies mentioned above, the experimenter concluded that the fault lay with the lack of diagnostic rigor of the institutions, not the invalidity of psychiatric diagnoses themselves. Second, apropos of the outcry following the finding of John Hinckley as "not guilty by reason of insanity," the American Psychiatric Association issued a position statement (*American Psychiatric Association Statement on the Insanity Defense*) disclaiming the ability of psychiatrists to predict dangerousness. Indeed this disclaimer has recently received many new adherents in the psychiatric and other mental health professions as the incidence of litigation against psychiatrists who did not anticipate and/or inform victims of patients' latent dangerousness increases. Indeed the only psychiatrist who "treated" John Hinckley prior to the assassination attempt on President

FROM THERAPEUTIC TO LUCIFER STATE

Reagan was sued by three of his victims because he allegedly failed to determine that Hinkley was "schizophrenic" and dangerous. Indeed, the only treatment recommendations made by the psychiatrist were biofeedback and a prescription for Valium. The latter, a defense psychiatrist later testified, may have increased the aggressive tendencies of Mr. Hinckley immediately prior to the shootings. An unfortunate postscript to the Hinckley case is that he has since 2004 been allowed to engage in unsupervised visits to his family despite the objections of Nancy Reagan and the late president's daughter, Patti Davis.

Thus, the Lucifer State and the Therapeutic State are analogous and in many ways similar in the methods of social control which they employ. While the latter seems slightly more rhetorically impenetrable in the short run, it lacks the conscious mendaciousness of the former and, thus, makes the Lucifer State a likely successor. Moreover, the Lucifer State appears to have the advantage (or is it a disadvantage?) of persuasion backed by force.

Finally, both societies present hope for a future where base rhetoric and cynical persuasion has been unmasked. We have seen the beginning of such a counter rhetoric in the Therapeutic State with attacks on the insanity plea, increased stature of Szasz's and others' attacks on organized psychiatry, and the American Psychiatric Association's nervous and defensive changes in its positions. The Therapeutic State may not succeed if Szasz and others successfully penetrate the myth that bad behavior is sick behavior. In the Lucifer State, too, we see some hopeful signs in the dauntless efforts of unmaskers such as Jim Sebring. Yet he, too, perhaps like those of us who live in the current underdeveloped states, fails in his efforts. Perhaps all that we can do is to buoy our spirits by periodically chanting the ultimate hopeful refrain of the canines, "Evil Rover Tailem."

METAPHORS, ALLUSIONS, AND ALLEGORIES IN LUCIFER STATE[i]

Richard Thames
Duquesne University

Though covers are notoriously unreliable oracles, titles almost always are true portents of pages to come. Before *Lucifer State* is ever opened, the title speaks volumes of what a reading will reveal.

What is a Lucifer "State"? The most obvious meaning would be a political body—a nation. The title could refer to a political state ruled by Lucifer. A second meaning would be a mental or emotional condition as in "a highly nervous state." The title could refer to a psychological state induced by Lucifer. Knowing no more than the name of the book, we discover two significant questions to ask of its contents. What *political* role does Lucifer play? What *psychological* reactions do the characters have towards him?

---

[i]This essay was first written in 1983, and has been revised for the new edition of Lucifer State.

Though the name "Lucifer" appears in the Bible but once and not in connection with Satan, popular thought identifies Lucifer with Satan, the Devil, and the ultimate source of evil. Thus, not only does the book's title allude to the Scriptures, but nearly half the chapter headings refer to the Sacred Text. Undoubtedly, the Bible will be the chest in which to rummage for gems of meaning in *Lucifer State*.

Why should the authors make the Bible so central to *Lucifer State?* In a footnote it is noted that the Bible, the works of Shakespeare, and the Greek classics are "rhetorical source books for our society" because they have "shaped so much of our thinking." Given the enormous impact of Christianity on Western civilization, the Bible of all books would be expected to permeate Western consciousness. It is the source of the myth of America as a people chosen by fate to build a model society for all to imitate. America, like Israel of the Old Testament, was to be "a light to the nations."

The Bible exercises its power to shape thought on believer and non-believer alike. Belief or non-belief is not the question. We know without reading Shakespeare who Romeo and Juliet are. We know without reading drama Oedipus' relations with his mother. We know without ever reading the Bible or attending church Adam and Eve and the story of the Fall. Such knowledge is part of the culture. To grow up in a particular culture is to be pickled like a cucumber in a certain set of values and ideas. When the authors allude to the Bible, they do so recognizing the culture readers have soaked up. Atheists, agnostics, Catholics, charismatics, casual Christians, Jews—all have been pickled in the same juice.

So the title of the novel is *Lucifer State*, and it alludes to the "Biblical" Satan. But why not call it *Satan State?* Because "Lucifer" suggests so much more. Lucifer is "the ultimate source of evil" but also "the bearer of light." The name is rich with ambiguity. Generally we associate ambiguity with confusion. Ambiguous statements equal low marks in English composition. But the novelist considers ambiguity a resource to exploit rather than a mistake to avoid. The intentionally ambiguous statement is the diamond that flashes many colors at once.

Lucifer may really be "the ultimate source of evil" pretending to be "the bearer of light." Everyone knows the Devil can quote Scripture. And St. Paul himself warns, "Even Satan disguises himself as an angel of light" (2 Corinthians 11:14). But Lucifer may really be "the bearer of light" libelously

METAPHORS, ALLUSIONS, AND ALLEGORIES 279

labeled "the ultimate source of evil" so that the secrets he seeks to reveal will never be recognized as truths. Lucifer, "lucid," and "light" all derive from the same Latin word. Maybe Lucifer, like Prometheus, angers the gods by bringing knowledge to men. Does Lucifer *deceive* or *reveal*? What is deception? What is revelation? What are we to believe? The title suggests a quandary.

Having studied no more than the title, we can predict that the novel will involve two principal themes—*the "deception-revelation" theme* suggested by the ambiguity of "Lucifer" and *the "political-psychological" theme* suggested by the ambiguity of "state." We can now settle down with *Lucifer State* confident of what to expect.

But reading a book is more demanding than reading a Budweiser label. Having given considerable thought to the title, we will be sensitive to particular ideas in the novel. We will mark them with a pencil, jotting down page numbers for similar images and situations as they appear. By this process we will uncover a series of associations—clues to detecting the meaning of the text.

The beginnings of books are particularly dense with clues. Much may be established on the first page or in the first paragraph or with the first phrase. If we turn beyond the title page of *Lucifer State*, all suspicions created by the title are confirmed. The themes anticipated are announced as primary. We immediately encounter the epigraph, the quote the authors have placed at the beginning of the text to characterize the novel: ". . . a deception in which the deceiver is more truthful than the non-deceiver and the one who lets himself be deceived is wiser than he who does not." The obviously psychological nature of the epigraph is balanced by the obviously political nature of the prologue. There, an International Council instructs P. Goras to report on the extent of James Sebring's "penetration of the Lucifer myth." Goras finds it unbelievable that M. Latour, a member of the Council, attempted to communicate the "ULTIMATE TRUTH" to Sebring and that Sebring discovered as much of the truth as he did. We do not yet know who Lucifer is or what role he plays in the story. But we can guess that *deception is the basic government policy (of the Lucifer state political)* and that *revelation of such deception is a mixed blessing (resulting in the Lucifer state psychological)*.

Having progressed from the title page through the epigraph and prologue, we discover a second major allusion—the cryptic name "P. Goras" which is deciphered in a footnote. P. Goras is meant to be allusive of

Protagoras of Abdera and Gorgias of Leontini, "two Greek Sophists who might fairly be called fathers of rhetoric." Since Gorgias is author of the epigraph, we might be expected to note "Goras" is suggestive of "Gorgias" and ask who Gorgias is. The allusion is not obvious, but books seldom surrender their meanings to a single reading. In this case, the clinching clue is the quote set on the last page to contrast with the quote set on the first. Protagoras is its author. The name P. Goras should be immediately suggestive of the names Protagoras and Gorgias so prominently featured in critical quotes set like bookends at the front and back to support the novel.

We should never forget that *Lucifer State*, entertaining as it may be, is still a textbook written to introduce us to "a thoroughgoing conception of the art of rhetoric." We should therefore expect some reference to the discipline's origins and traditions. The conscientious reader would be obliged to investigate the meaning of "rhetoric" to some degree—hopefully more thoroughly than thumbing through Webster's. We are glad to find some of the basics in the introduction to the book.

Rhetoric can be understood in three ways: 1) a *manipulative technique*, 2) an *analytical instrument*, 3) a *world view*. The first two are often confused, the third ignored. The confusion is due in part to using one term when two are needed. We distinguish between the person who commits crimes and the person who studies him. One is a "criminal," the other a "criminologist." But "rhetorician" can refer to either a practitioner or a professor. The third way of understanding rhetoric also lends itself to confusion between the first two. The Sophists were the first to conceive of rhetoric as a way of looking at the world. As Melia explains, the Sophists believed "it is impossible to know the truth." Communication for them could not therefore be the process of "finding and *teaching the truth*" but of "*persuading* people to accept one's *opinion*." When all communication is conceived of as rhetoric, the point of distinguishing between the act and its analysis is less than clear. If the criminologist claims all acts are criminal, the distinction between the criminal act itself and the necessarily criminal act of studying it is a distinction with no difference.

Though the Sophists believe it impossible to know the truth, most people believe otherwise. If truth can be known, our responsibility is to find and teach it. Rhetoric, at best, is cosmetic. The truth may be difficult to see. But by means of make-up and the proper dress, truth in all its beauty may be made obvious. Or, changing the metaphor, the truth may be difficult to swallow. But rhetoric will sugar the bitter pill that makes us better. Problems arise when make-up is a mask or sugar sweetens cyanide. Then appearance opposes reality and rhetoric takes the wrong side. Appearance is deceptive and so, too, is *mere* rhetoric. Thus the standard interpretation of the claim that all communication is persuasion is that the claim amounts to a license to lie.

The philosopher Plato was a lifelong opponent of the Sophists. He believed the truth could be known but only with difficulty and so only by a few. Most of us are fooled most of the time. Plato, of course, was not; he knew the truth. Therefore, in his dialogues, particularly the *Gorgias* and the *Phaedrus*, he railed against rhetoric and rhetoricians. Unfortunately, most of what we know about the Sophists is through Plato. And given his position, Plato is about as unbiased a commentator on the Sophists as a right-wing politician critiquing his left-wing opponent or vice versa. "Sophist," which translates "wise man," is used ironically by Plato to mean "wise guy." (We today might hear a politician in the same manner dismiss an opponent as an "intellectual.") I should point out that for all the critiques of the Sophists as liars and for all the claims of his own honesty, nowhere does Plato present as honest a discussion of the Sophists' position as this Sophist presents of Plato's in the previous paragraph.

But why bother to be fair? Plato thought the Sophists little more than prostitutes. They were great teachers paid for their services. But to aristocrats like Plato, taking money for teaching was morally suspect. (Unfortunately most college administrators still think like long-dead Greeks.)

Read *Lucifer State* quickly and only once and a Platonic interpretation becomes tempting. P. Goras, Master Rhetorician, and his minions Noel Baker Smyth, Jeremy Leventritt, et al., are such liars as Plato warned us of. But James Adam Sebring and his friends see through their deception. Our heroes, like Michael and his angels, psychologically at least, cast the villains, like Satan and his angels, out of heaven. Rhetoric is stripped away, reality revealed. Smyth is a man who merely follows orders; P. Goras a man who orders genocide. Like an American soldier on entering Auschwitz and seeing evidence of mass murder, Sebring on seeing the truth feels as if he is looking "through a crack ... no, a rip ... looking through a rip in the social fabric right into a corner of Hell."

But who in *Lucifer State* is really evil? For all its stress on Hoffer's notion of the importance of a rhetorical devil, the book never names one. The intentions of the "evil" characters are good. Smyth loves Evelyn. If, as he hopes, they are ever to marry, he wants her to do so willingly. Force is the furthest thing from his mind. Force is the furthest thing from P. Goras' mind, too. A careful reading of the epilogue indicates Natasha is his new assistant. Jim and Evelyn Sebring and Michele Latour are not executed but exiled to Erewhon.[ii]

As for the charge of genocide, Smyth tries to explain to Evelyn and Jim in turn. "Understand," he fixed her with his eyes, "that D. Date is not a gratuitous hoax; it's an essential myth. Understand that the originators at the end of the Christian Era were faced with the collapse of the original myth—belief in a benevolent creator.... Understand that humankind was faced with an exploding population, diminishing natural resources, deadly pollution, terrorism, unsecured nuclear weapons, and that the Apocalypse—war, pestilence, famine, crime—threatened to engulf humanity. Understand that humankind, who had wrested from God's hand control of birth and of longevity, was forced ultimately to seize control of death, too." And later he tells Jim, "The International Commission at Greenwich is charged with maintaining an equitable distribution of population and natural resources between nations. It was that or nuclear holocaust. The Commission monitors the computer data from each nation and allocates the Lucifer drug on the basis of an agreed upon formula." The drug produces "a peaceful, even euphoric, death at a predictable time and under predictable circumstances."[iii]

But the Lucifer drug solves more than the problem of maintaining an equitable distribution of population and natural resources. Thanks to the

---

[ii] The clue for deciphering the last phrase of the epilogue ("Ah Satan's Evil") can be found on the page that immediately precedes it: the last word of the last chapter "North Towards Erewhon"—i.e., "Erewhon" or "nowhere" backwards.

[iii] The Lucifer drug (contained in the capsule dispensed at the final medical exam) is not toxic until combined with Aqua Vie (the ceremonial drink taken at the Terminal Rites). That combination produces "a peaceful, even euphoric, death at a predictable time and under predictable circumstances" only when those Rites have ritualistically stripped a believer of all connections with life, encouraging acquiescence in a "spiritual and biological death" occurring "at a time

drug, says Smyth, death occurs at a time that makes sense for *the individual* as well as society. In the Erewhon Societies, he tells Evelyn, people "try rather pointlessly . . . to survive to very great ages." Those "denied Natural Death by medical technology suffer blindness, deafness, insanity, ugliness, and they come to fear the process of aging." Smyth does not say but implies that if the Erewhonian science of geriatrics were used to prolong the process of dying in the world at large, the population problem would soon get out of hand and the strain on natural resources prove disastrous. The Apocalypse would once more be upon them. But the Lucifer drug makes possible for everyone a healthy, happy life and death with dignity when his time is come. Natasha's D. Date was not determined by chance. Smyth explains to her that he has examined her medical and genetic records and they indicate an anomaly in the right hemisphere of her brain. "You've probably already noticed," he says, "that your left hand is not as agile as it should be." Natasha has noticed and said so to Jim. Smyth tells Natasha the computer predicts that after June 7th she will suffer the first of a series of strokes. From Smyth's point of view, therefore, the Lucifer State is not murderous but merciful.

The Platonic interpretation of *Lucifer State* is tempting but too easy. Besides, Trevor Melia the rhetorician is a Sophist, not a Platonist. He believes it impossible to know the truth. The characters that come in for criticism from him are those who know the truth and demand that others honor it. Evelyn, before she sees the light, slowly chokes the life from Jim. To her his actions are self-destructive, even antisocial, and "social implications never escape Evelyn." Her attitudes drive him to Natasha. The authors open Jim's mind to the reader prior to the lovers' first rendezvous: "Why, Jim wondered, was his world so fragile—so illusory that its truth had to be defended by deception . . . by drugs? Evelyn's world, he was convinced, was illusion, too. But everyone

---

that makes sense both for the individual and for society"—i.e., a "Natural Death." As Smyth argues, the drug is activated by persuasion and its consequent belief—the drug is a placebo. The placebo effect Smyth describes in his confrontation with Sebring can be defined as "the effect of rhetoric on body states." For example, extra-strength pain relievers sold in gelatin capsules associated with prescription drugs are perceived as stronger than over-the-counter medications. Extra-strength products may seem more effective than normal-strength mostly because people believe they are. The drug described by Smyth would be a placebo and a citizen's death following his or her last monthly exam and Terminal Rites would be a placebo effect. Post Natural Deaths would occur because the component of belief was not sufficiently strong.

cooperated in that illusion until it appeared solid as concrete. He shook his head bitterly. He had to defend a truth with lies; Evelyn sustained a lie with truth." When Evelyn learns about Lucifer, she realizes what she has been to her husband: "Jim didn't marry a woman; he married a social proposition." She vows to change: "I hope I get another chance with him and if I ever do, I'll come to him as a woman."

While Evelyn stifles only Jim, Peter Stoneham stifles the city of Hartford. Stoneham, the bureaucrat, is so certain he is right that he will not rest until his regulations restrict everyone. Yet his regulations fail to save Joannah, and when his regulations fail, so does his mind. Evelyn and Peter—both seek to curtail freedom of others for their own good but never understand the good of others is a choice that should be left to the others themselves. No Sophist could be so intolerant. Believing it impossible to know the truth, a Sophist would be most willing to leave individuals to live their own truth so long as that truth does not restrict the right of others to live theirs. Thus a pivotal line in the novel is Jim's as he approaches the runway where he will crash land: "Damn all controllers, everywhere."

We might object that Smyth is as much a controller as Stoneham. Smyth is and isn't. He claims some form of social control is essential. Stoneham represents social control taken to extremes. His regulations are little more than legal tyrants. It may be that Jim represents the other extreme. The end of every control is the beginning of anarchy and anarchy is the greatest tyrant of all. Of the three, then, Smyth is the moderate. Granted the necessity of some form of social control, he opts for the most benign, the most human. The policy he advocates is "rooted ultimately in a profound belief in the power of persuasion." He advocates within the context of the Lucifer myth the myth of democracy. "Democracy is *always* a delusion," he explains to Evelyn. "Control of the masses by elites is always accomplished by persuasion, by force, or by both. Democracy was and is merely the most rhetorical system—the most dependent on persuasion." At least the illusion of freedom is maintained. Psychologically, citizens of Lucifer State feel free, not forced. They are persuaded to do what is necessary. According to Smyth, "Freedom is *wanting* to do what you *must* do."

Smyth rejects coercion in favor of persuasion. At one point he tells Evelyn he abhors violence. When Jim strikes Smyth toward the end of the novel, Jim fails rather than triumphs as a person. It is significant that his violence silences Smyth just as he is about to explain that the Lucifer drug is activated only by a catalyst taken at the Terminal Rites. Were it not for the mercy of Smyth and Goras, Jim's violence would have sealed Natasha's fate. When Jim smashes his fist into Smyth's face, he watches it contort "into its real, demonic shape." What Jim sees is more indicative of his own character than Smyth's.

A great irony may be that Smyth's position is in some ways Plato's, too. Smyth believes in the necessity of a social myth. (Note the spelling of his name!) As is pointed out in a footnote, "the idea of promulgating such a myth as a means of social control is advocated by Plato in his *Republic*." The P. in P. Goras could stand for Plato, a super subtle allusion to possibly the most subtle Sophist of all. Were he convinced of the impossibility of discovering truth and equally convinced that in the world at large that conviction would lead to anarchy, Plato could, like Smyth, advocate a myth for the masses, a myth to be secretly maintained by a carefully selected and perpetuated elite. Plato's entire philosophy of forms could be considered such a myth, cleverly constructed out of the materials of popular consciousness to solve the philosophical problems debated by the learned and thus to be accepted as true.

Whether the social myth is the one supported by Smyth or the one possibly created by Plato, successfully establishing it in the mind of the masses would be difficult during the first generation. But that problem is faced to some degree after every successful revolution. And that problem has been solved in every period of cultural transition from the medieval to the modern world. Once such a myth is established, succeeding generations accept it as true, seeing no difference between the world *not created* by humans (that which we call nature) and the world *created* by them (that which we accept as second nature). What is true is true because the majority says so. Evelyn's world is real, Jim realizes, because everyone cooperates in the illusion until it appears as solid as concrete. "Reality" is, as Leventritt says at one point, socially constructed.

The best way to understand "socially constructed" reality is in terms of fiction. *Lucifer State* portrays an internally consistent world. We know that world is fictional. Most of characters within the novel don't; for them it is real. By willingly suspending disbelief we enter that fictional world. While we are reading we believe it is real. By identifying with characters, we let that world becomes as much a reality for us as it is for them. What is ingenious about *Lucifer State* is that some characters in the novel (P. Goras, et al.) know the world presented is fictional. Yet other characters within the novel don't; for them it is real. And we, as readers, are left to sort it out.

Once we finish the book, can we then toss it aside and blithely assume we have returned to reality? Or is the world to which we return also a fiction? With so many characters waking to the fictional natures of their worlds, how can we not wonder about the reality of our own? But wondering, *we should beware assuming there is some reality to wake to.* The Sophists claim we cannot wake to the ultimately real. We cannot know what is ultimately true. We can escape the books we live but only into other books. At most we realize we live fictions. We may live a book we have written ourselves or written with others. Leventritt says Charles Hazlitt "lives in a world of his own construction." Or, we may live a book others have written for us. Evelyn and Stoneham are convinced that the Lucifer State is real. We may live in full awareness of the fictional nature of our world (whoever has created it), or we may live in ignorance. But we can never live anything other than fiction. Psychologically, we willingly suspend disbelief and enter the novel we have chosen. We open the book and begin to believe.

We may ask, "But what of Joannah? Doesn't she live a fiction?" Yes, she does. But if we watched someone read Victor Hugo's *Les Miserables* then heard him insist the book was actually *The Hunchback of Notre Dame*, we would listen quietly then quickly leave the room. We would have no doubts about the person's mental state. Joannah is something less than sane, because she confuses a fiction constructed by one man and lived by no one with a fiction agreed upon by millions and lived by them all.

We must beware of thinking we can make the world over in our own image. Sentiments such as "if you can imagine it, you can become it" may be lovely sayings which, combined with lovely photographs, make inspiring posters for less than inspiring dormitory walls, but they are little more than sentiments. They recognize no limits to the fictions we write or study. Each of us is limited by sheer genetic endowment. Most of us are limited by the lack of endowments such as are granted to and by the extremely wealthy (though credit card providers try hard to convince us otherwise). Our future choices are limited by past events and present circumstances. Yes, I know that "today is the first day of the rest of my life." But that sentiment does not absolve me of responsibility for past actions. The fictions we create have consequences. They are not as insubstantial as dreams. Sophists are not saying the fictions we live are unreal. They are questioning whether those fictions are grounded in some *ultimate* reality.

The Sophists' position is obviously *relativistic*. The standard criticism of that position is, when relativists make the claim "there is no ultimate truth," they take that claim itself to be ultimately true. Thus relativists contradict themselves. If we are to understand the character of the Sophists' position, the best place to turn is the introduction to *Lucifer State* where the authors allude to the problem. There they acknowledge that there are many problems with relativism, not the least of which "is what may be called the *relativist fallacy. In fact*, it is logically impossible to be absolutely certain of uncertainty; in *fiction*, it's a different story." Sophists do not issue an edict proclaiming "there is absolutely no doubt that all is relative." They speak more tentatively. The sophistical authors of *Lucifer State* say they believe that all is relative but say so within the context of a novel. The context determines the character of their claim. The claim lacks the authority of a pronouncement from on high. Its style smacks instead of paradox and irony. Peter is deeply embarrassed and finally angered by his wife. And yet, ironically, the insane Joannah is closer to the truth than her presumably sane husband when she insists P. Goras is a clown. When the authors claim ironically that all is relative, they are not guilty of self-contradiction, as philosophers suppose. Sophists are jesters. Like P. Goras, when they speak seriously, there is always the slightest suggestion of a smile.

In the introduction it is suggested that philosophers misunderstand Sophists because they are concerned with theories of *truth*, whereas Sophists are concerned with theories of *action*. According to the Sophists we all live fictions but we decide what fictions to live or we allow others to decide for us. As I said earlier, we open the book and begin to *believe*. Our beliefs are actions for which we are *responsible*. Thus, *every moment of being is charged with ethical choice*. Too often, people who claim all is relative do so to evade responsibility. They change their beliefs like they change their clothes, saying what they need to maximize gain and minimize blame. Such people are the very opposite of authentic Sophists. The ancient Sophists were individuals who accepted responsibility. Some were ambassadors representing distant city-states, negotiating on significant issues in an age when one could not phone home for instructions. Smyth is always aware of the enormous responsibility he bears. He could easily argue he only follows orders, but he does not. The Sophist takes responsibility for his or her own beliefs. And, they are tolerant of people who believe differently.

Because most of us believe the truth can be known and, if known, should be acted upon, we have difficulty associating the Sophists' skepticism with their emphasis on ethics. Yet there is an ethics implicit within their thought. If there is no ultimate truth, then "man is the measure of all things" according to Protagoras (quoted in the epigraph that ends the novel). Sophists stand in awe of human achievement. They focus attention on products of the human mind, then on the human mind itself. Culture, civilization, cities—everywhere we turn we encounter our creations, returning at last to their creator—ourselves. The Sophists would be in complete agreement with Shakespeare: "What a piece of work is man."[iv] Every human life should be respected. Skepticism is but one side of the coin; humanism is the other.

Both skepticism and humanism are sometimes misunderstood as necessarily atheistic. But the atheist generally supposes a degree of certainty the Sophist cannot. The atheist *knows* that God does not exist. The Sophist knows nothing of the kind. But neither does the Sophist know that God does. The question of God's existence is left open. The Sophist most often is agnos-

---

[iv]One might also ask with the Psalmist, "What is man that Thou art mindful of him?" Protagoras' proclamation could be viewed as boastful but also as humbling or even tragic. Absent sure access to some superhuman criterion, what measure do we have other than ourselves? Life would prove far easier if knowledge of truth were a guide to action. Without such knowledge, the burden of decision and responsibility is ours alone.

tic; the existence of an ultimate reality (God) being unknown and unknowable. Being a Sophist does not preclude believing in God, so long as *the believer takes personal responsibility for his or her belief and makes no attempt to impose that belief on others.*

The Sophists' attitude toward the existence of God is paralleled by their attitude toward society. Whether or not people believe in God as the ultimate reality, most believe their society is grounded on some ultimate truth. Most are like Peter and Evelyn; few are like Charlie and Jim. Most, like Evelyn, would be troubled by behavior like Jim's, considering it anti-social. These individuals simply live in a style that denies the possibility of other beliefs or other social arrangements. The mere suggestion that there may be other beliefs or social arrangements is in itself considered to be disturbing. As is pointed out in a footnote, though, what each of us takes to be real are in fact socially generated truths, explanations designed to allay our deepest fears about the greatest mysteries—life, death, dreams, psychosis, God, the hereafter. Society is like a shelter constructed to hold out the dark and cold. And to all who fear the dark and cold, the Sophists' position represents a threat.

If there is one problem with which the Sophists are overwhelmingly concerned, the problem is that of *social control.* How does society domesticate the human animal? Peter Berger, sociologist and author of *The Sacred Canopy*, puts the problem differently. How can the continuation of institutions, once established, be best insured? How, that is, can "reality" be maintained? Berger's solution is employed in the Lucifer State. Berger claims institutions should be interpreted so as to conceal their constructed character. Though raised from nothing, they should appear to be based on something existing since the beginning of time (or, at least, the beginning of a particular group). People should forget the institutions were built by humans and continue to stand only with their consent. They should believe instead that, in living out their lives within the institutional framework imposed upon them, they live out their deepest longings at home within the fundamental structure of the universe. According to Berger, then, individuals and institutions should appear to stand on the firm foundation of an ultimate truth. But society will stand more securely when that truth is *known* rather than simply *believed.*

To facilitate social control, the one distinction all Sophists make is blurred—the distinction between *civil* and *natural* law, between *second nature* and *nature* itself.[v] Mere *local* laws are identified with supposed *universal* ones. As Smyth explains to Evelyn, "In the Greenland Societies, the law is obviously man-made. Its justice is therefore disputed." Such laws, he continues are subject to endless debate and are frequently violated. Not so in the Lucifer State. "In our system," says Smyth, "we appear, thanks to D. Dates, to be subject to Natural Law. We don't complain about or evade our social laws any more than we complain about the laws of gravity." The Sophists warn that when humanly constructed law appears to coincide with nature's laws, the merely *historical* is confused with the *eternal*. Society assumes a certain *inevitability* which mortals would be foolish to struggle against. Best acquiesce. No characters in the novel acquiesce more completely than Peter and Evelyn.

Evelyn conditions her son with the sight of "the universally recognized and beloved symbol of Unity in Death" flicking on and off in cadence with the sound of a human heartbeat. She herself has been conditioned to the symbol, "the abstracted figures of a male and female, hands interlocked, heads inclined each towards the other, joined in eternal sleep." Evelyn lives her life in terms of that symbol; she interprets all in terms of compatible D. Dates. When her mind is opened to the reader, there's almost a religious aura to her thoughts. "She had always been awed that out of the infinity of possibilities she and Jim, inhabiting the earth at the same time and the same place, were also destined to pass into eternity together. It seemed to Evelyn to be evidence that the universe intended their union." After four years of marriage when their D. Dates coincided, Evelyn had been ecstatic. She had hung their calendars "in the living room so that their friends could see the incontrovertible evidence of their married bliss. On the first night they had made passionate

---

[v]Sophists differ over what they make of the distinction. Just as the web symbolizing society and its constraints can be viewed negatively or positively, reality as constructed by human beings can be viewed as a conspiracy to be exposed or a creation to be celebrated (the web traditionally symbolizing the beauty and order of creation). Those inclined to the former (e.g., Callicles in Plato's Gorgias) could gleefully turn critical thought into intellectual arrogance, insisting on power as the primary issue and urging a careless rejection of merely human institutions as fraudulent or corrupt constructions, refusing to acknowledge the alternative as anarchy. Those inclined to the latter (e.g., Isocrates) would gravely shoulder responsibility, insisting on the ethical character of all human endeavor and exhibiting a careful respect for human institutions as problematic but still admirable constructions.

love and had melted one into the other, wedded for time and eternity." She "had reveled in her sense of identity with Jim and in the feeling of security and safety that the oneness brought." But Jim's excesses had brought an end to that bliss. "She knew that most marriages underwent periods of incompatibility; she knew that the struggle for D. Date compatibility was what gave drama to most partnerships, but she also knew that Unity in Death gave marriage its ultimate goal." Marriage was "sanctified" by the knowledge that a couple "could hope to live their lives together and then pass into eternity as one." Evelyn seeks constantly to bring her married life into harmony with a mythical "order of the universe."

Perhaps the best example of confusion between the human and the natural order is the Great Clock of Hartford towering above surrounding buildings like an ancient gothic cathedral—the historic "Sermon in Stone." Consider the description of its face. "The figure of the woman pointed dramatically straight up at the number twenty-four and stood facing, and seemingly awaiting, the expectant male now ninety degrees away and moving perceptibly toward her. Once an hour, pointing to each number in sequence, the two figures locked in ecstatic embrace only to be torn apart moments later. Fifteen minutes from now, at midnight, the conjugal pair would finish their day united again. The great bell would announce their achievement." The Clock is the perfect symbol for the Lucifer State, a society "predicated on the belief that time is the universal and fundamental unit of value for human beings." Obviously the Clock tells time, but it also tells citizens how they should spend it. Natural time is social time, not simply passing but ever approaching a person's D. Date—a personal, predictable, and mythical midnight. The Clock preaches the doctrine of the unity of marriage, sex, and death ("dying together" was once a euphemism for simultaneous orgasm)—a doctrine approved not just by society but the universe. Not only does the Clock ticking off the minutes to midnight reinforce awareness of D. Date; so do the personal D. Date calendars. Because the calendars record the number of days until Natural Death, the person who ritually rips off one page daily counts down to the inevitable end of the pages and life. Because unhealthy living styles can shorten the allotted number of days, the D. Date changes. As a person's D. Date changes so too does his astrological sign. The moment of death, not the moment of birth, determines how to read the stars.

The colors of the rainbow also take on D. Date significance. Blue, green, yellow, orange, and red—the natural colors (in reverse of their usual sequence) represent the stages of life in the journey toward death. Each participant wears a black robe trimmed with a band of color announcing in general terms his D. Date. Having described the Clock that tolls the end of the last full day of Charlie's life, the authors describe the participants in his Terminal Rites. "Most of the children wore blue, and occasionally green. The robes of the adults were trimmed in colors ranging from green, for those who looked forward to remarkable longevity, to yellow and orange for the less fortunate. One couple was noticeable for obvious signs of difference in maturity, the man having already lived much longer than the woman. Still, their union, like that of all the other couples, had been made possible by D. Date compatibility so they wore gowns trimmed in like colors—orange in this case. Holders of the Red Card, of whom only two were in evidence at the moment, wore robes trimmed entirely of scarlet.... Evelyn Sebring was dressed in a robe trimmed in bright yellow. The color that framed Jim's neck and ran down the front of his robe was orange, an incongruity that drew more than one furtive glance of disapproval from passersby."

The colors of the rainbow are not just seen. They are also said as part of the "Rainbow Passage," a short paragraph containing in every conceivable juxtaposition all the sounds necessary for communicating with the Master Med computer. The Rainbow Passage, read correctly, gives access to the computer. The computer supposedly gives access to nature.

But nature does not program the computer. The computer is programmed for social control. D. Dates are manipulated to punish "anti-social behavior." As Smyth explains, "Some elite or other always makes the decisions and persuades or compels the rest to acquiesce." In the Lucifer State, as well as in our democracy, the vote "measures not the will of the people but the persuasiveness of the elite.... What the masses decide, the government executes. D. Date technology merely causes the people to want to vote for policies the Elite Council has already decided are most naturally beneficial." When Evelyn returns to work at Master Med the computer informs her that the Aggregate Life Consumption Factor for Northwestern Massachusetts has risen three points in two months. She assumes the information is true. She assumes the rise is due to the overly ambitious flood control project

Governor Sam Orville sold to his constituents "despite warnings from Master Med about possible environmental side effects." Policy dictates "freedom to choose without restraint, and the people had chosen to go ahead with the project." Now, with conclusive evidence of D. Date attrition (supplied, of course, by Master Med), Evelyn knows the project will be quickly abandoned and Sam Orville voted out of office.

Smyth knows that if social control is to be insured, social myths should be confused with natural truths. Smyth also knows the D. Date is such a myth, and yet he seems confused at times. He tells Evelyn that the originators of the myth replaced "an artificial and often corrupt system of rewards with a simple, just, and, above all, natural system.... Nature rewards certain activities and punishes others by giving and withdrawing life. The computer merely speaks for her. It punishes individually, socially, and ecologically unsound behavior."

The totally skeptical stance is almost impossible to maintain. Life requires some belief as a basis for action. As Leventritt says to his colleagues, "No one is totally irreverent; it is a matter of identifying where the reverence lies . . . if not in religion, then in science or philosophy, or art or nature." Smyth has a reverence for *nature* but nature as it is communicated by the *computer*.

Smyth's acquiescence before the computer is an ironic instance of one of the major themes in *Lucifer State*—technological idolatry, defined as the tendency of humans to surrender their decision-making capacity to tools of his own creation. Smyth, who prides himself on taking responsibility for his decisions, ultimately relies on a computer to help him make them.

Not just Smyth, but the entire society is guilty of technological idolatry. The Master Med computer dominates every aspect of life in the Lucifer State. (The example of Sam Orville by itself would be sufficient.) Belief in science and the Master Med computer makes social control possible. During the Birth Rites of Jim and Evelyn's son, Leventritt explains that the Master Med computer integrates the genetic data and calculates the life span precisely.

When Charlie is hurried into the hospital after his accident, the medical technician is at a loss. Without Charlie's I.D. card he is denied access to the computer and the necessary information it would provide—a read-out of the Life Consumption factor, a diagnosis, and instructions for therapeutic intervention. He considers the L.C.F. readout critical because it indicates not only the rate at which the patient is losing time and consequently the seriousness of his illness but also the unit in the medical center to which the patient should be sent. The medical technician is severely criticized for being too dependent upon the computer. Given his obviously serious condition, the patient should have been sent to the equivalent of Intensive Care. The medical problem should have been handled first, the computer second. But when Charlie arrives in the proper unit, the doctor there complains, "No L.C.F., no diagnosis, and no recommended therapy. I'm a doctor not a bloody computer. What do they expect me to do?"

When Jim himself is admitted to the hospital after his own crash, there are no computer problems. The L.C.F. reading is off the scale. When the medical technician is questioned about symptoms he replies there are none. But he does not doubt they will soon appear. Even with a healthy patient in front of him, the technician never suspects that the Master Med computer has told him nothing but lies.

One of the conventions of social science fiction such as *Lucifer State* is that of criticizing the present by writing about a future in which the same problems exist. Aldous Huxley's *Brave New World* is really about the all too familiar old world. Orwell's *1984* is really about 1948, the year the novel was published. *Lucifer State* is no different. The authors are claiming that technological idolatry is not a problem of the future. The temptation to depend absolutely on modern machines is strong today and has been for a long time. As the Public Health Officer admonishes the medical technician tending to Charlie, machines are our servants, not our masters. When Jim flies Charlie to London, he wonders how long it will be before the pilot becomes "backup for the auto-control rather than vice versa." He smiles as he recalls the old chestnut, "In case of emergency, break glass and take out pilot." Jim may be skeptical of machines, but not all pilots are. Having flown thousands of miles in small planes as Trevor Melia's copilot, I have heard many tales—like the one about the pilot believing a broken compass that read due north while flying due west into a setting sun. Such dependence can lead to death. In the Lucifer State death is precisely where it does lead.

A related convention of social science fiction is "extrapolation." The future prophesied is but an extrapolation of the present. What we take for granted is taken one step further. As noted in the introduction, "While

Lucifer State is a work of fiction, every effort has been made to stay within the bounds of what is, if not probable, at least rhetorically and technologically possible. The annotated bibliography at the end provides, among other things, references to factual accounts of much that is presented as fiction here". As farfetched as D. Dates may seem, a present day equivalent exists. Most people would be startled by how accurately an insurance company can calculate a person's life span after a complete physical and an interview. The Master Med computer can probably predict an actual D. Date no more precisely than an insurance company. The Lucifer *myth* is that an exact day can be specified. Given our tendencies toward technological idolatry, how farfetched is the myth?

The great challenge of extrapolation is creating a credible world of the future. If people believed D. Dates could be known, what kind of society would be consistent with such knowledge? Peter explains that in the Lucifer State knowledge of D. Dates "has led inevitably to an increased concern for security. Nothing is more tragic than injury and premature death brought about by failure to take proper precautions." Once humankind "perfected the ability to compute natural life spans—when we learned to know how much time we had coming—we became acutely conscious of risk—we learned to value security almost above all else."

Probably because he himself is an accident victim, Peter is obsessed with security. So, too, is the society. Witness the television debate over proposed regulations prohibiting the use of parks after dark. Peter argues that, given the danger of Senile Delinquents, such regulations would greatly reduce the threat to public security. Levec counters that the regulations' principal effect will be to provide employment for bureaucrats like Peter. If a person were ignorant of the danger, he would probably be equally ignorant of the regulations. The regulations, says Levec, propose to make people safe from their own folly, yet do so at the cost of reducing everyone's freedom. Levec's argument is strong. But the obsession with security is stronger. The referendum is carried by Peter. Ironically, though Joannah votes in favor of his precious regulations, she is not saved by them.

The obsession with security influences public policy not just in the Lucifer State but also in our own. In the name of safety and security, required car inspections are justified. Such regulations provide employment for bureaucrats, insure profits for garages, and increase the turnover of cars to the everlasting gratitude of dealers. There is no evidence required inspections make cars safer.

The most obvious instance of our obsession with security is the American obsession with insurance. We try to insure every aspect of existence—car insurance, boat insurance, travel insurance, home-owner's insurance, theft insurance, fire insurance, flood insurance, liability insurance, accident insurance, medical insurance, dental insurance, unemployment insurance, business insurance, legal insurance, life insurance, social security, and on, and on. Risk must be reduced at any price—and the *price* is high. A novel criticizing our obsession with security would have to be set in Hartford, Connecticut, the insurance capital of the country.

The theme of security, however, is relevant to more than present day America. Any society, we should remember, is like a shelter holding out the dark and cold. Society provides security. Within its walls we feel secure, protected from the threat of madness, dreams, and death. As Levec informs Peter, "No one is more secure than the animals in your local zoo, and no one is more concerned for their security than the local zookeeper." Keepers like Smyth lock us up. People like Peter add more locks to the door—from the inside. The insanity and eventual death of Joannah illustrates *the futility of absolutely insuring either psychological or physical security in this life*. The shelter is none too stable; the locks are none too secure. Yet boards go up and bolts are thrown. Levec points out that in the name of homeland security the most basic human rights have been restricted. Ironically, in the name of security, "armies have been raised, battles have been fought, and men have died."

People like Peter and Evelyn value the warmth, the security of society's shelter. But "freedom is never safe," Levec says. There is a most fundamental conflict between being safe and being free. Charlie always seeks to be free. He lives life in his own way and he spends his final day in his own way, too. Charlie is like a man in Trevor Melia's personal pantheon, Antoine de Saint-Exupery, author of *Wind, Sand and Stars* and *The Little Prince*. Saint-Exupery was a pilot, too. And when he was told he was too old to fly, he pleaded for one last mission in WWII from which he never returned.

Therefore, that Charlie and Jim are pilots is no accident. *Flight is the symbol for freedom and its inherent risks.* When they are in flight, they are free of social control. They test themselves against the elements. Thus the poignancy of Charlie's appearance on the hospital table "suspended in a jungle of wires and tubes, a flyer caught in a spider's web." *The web is*, appropriately, *the symbol for society and its inherent constraints.*

When they say farewell at the end of the book, Natasha tells Jim, "The old philosophers believed the fear of death makes us moral, but I believe it makes us social." Society alleviates the fear. In the Lucifer State with people acutely aware of their Death Dates, society's solace is particularly precious. But, while the fear of death makes us social, the acceptance of death makes us free. The sanctuary society supplies becomes superfluous. Natasha has accepted death. On the flight destined to crash, Jim realizes Natasha has escaped society, broken out of the web. She is flying. She is free.

Natasha could easily have reacted differently to her early D. Date. On that fearful flight, Jim reflects that with her D. Date near "Tasha would be desperately trying to make up for anything she'd missed in life . . . knowing that she'd already paid the price . . . her fate sealed . . . there were for her no more consequences; so eat, drink, and be merry, for tomorrow, almost literally, she would die." He suddenly stops himself, realizing he has described the psychology not of Natasha but of Senile Delinquents. From Jim's thoughts it should be obvious that Senile Delinquency is a logically and psychologically valid extrapolation of the D. Date mythology. Jim again puts it best. When he approaches the runway where he will try to crash-land, his "final controller" comes on the radio. Jim laughs. "What could the final controller do now, beyond direct him to his death, at the appropriate time and place?" Senile Delinquents, having been issued their Red Cards, feel the same way. Their fates are sealed. There are for them no more consequences. They can do as they damn well please. With death imminent, no threat of punishment can deter them. They resent having to die. They resent those who will not be dying with them. So they take out their resentment on society. Not so Natasha. She knows early on how brief her life will be. But she does not turn on society, bitter and frustrated like the Senile Delinquents. They consider themselves free of all constraints, particularly that of responsibility. She, like the Sophist, is free, yet she imposes constraint upon herself, particularly that of responsibility. She tells Jim at the end, "Acceptance of death makes us individually moral."

Senile Delinquents resent death. Natasha and Charlie accept it. After Charlie's terminal rites, Natasha consoles Jim. "You can't live the way Charlie lived if you haven't come to terms with death—prepared for it. Unwillingness to face death—that mistaken sense of immortality—robs life of its meaning. . . . It's a law of economics; what is infinitely abundant has no value. Death is what gives life its poignancy. Charlie knew that—he had to. . . . That's what caused him to wring every last drop out of life and then wring it some more just in case there was something he'd missed." Natasha understands Charlie because she is like him. As she and Jim prepare to part forever, he thinks to himself, "Tasha's love of life was partly due to the certainty of her early death and, for her love of life, he was grateful. She had somehow managed to incorporate death into her life and it had lent poignancy to her existence. From death she had learned to love music, art, and life itself. Jim was grateful, too, because Tasha had willed her vision in these things to him."

Death and the value it imparts to time. Freedom and the conquest of fear. The two great themes are really one in *Lucifer State*. They merge most obviously in the name of Charlie's plane—*Winged Chariot*. The name is taken from the famous poem by Andrew Marvell, "To His Coy Mistress." Never hesitate to love, says Marvell. There's never world enough or time. At his back he always hears time's winged chariot, hurrying. He implores us to clasp life, cast off fear. If by chance Evelyn ever read Marvell, she misunderstood. She is almost obsessed with "optimum living." Leventritt counsels her that optimum living is "quantitative not qualitative; it measures how long we live, not how well." Optimum has a different meaning for Charlie. He has listened to Marvell's plea. When he names his antique biplane, he tells the world that he intends to live his life intensely. He will *fly* time's winged chariot. He will be free.

But freedom is never safe. Flight is the symbol of freedom and its *inherent risks*. Risk is something every pilot is familiar with. On the last return from Greenwich, Jim reminisces about his first flight lessons from Charlie. Charlie has severed "the surly bonds of earth" (the social web) for him. (The authors are alluding here to a famous poem about flight.) Then clear air turbulence strikes without warning. All thought of freedom is scattered on the winds. Jim only gives thought to his jeopardy. Remembering all of Charlie's teaching, he fights to control the damaged plane and survives because he uses his wit. He gets it back to Bradley and crash lands.

In the hospital scene following the crash, all the novel's major themes converge. The scene is *synecdochic*, the *part* of the novel *that contains the whole*. When Peter enters the hospital room, he spots on the computer's video screen the inevitable *security* sermon: "We can't predict accidents; we can prevent them." This particular accident, however, could not have been prevented. Damage from clear air turbulence is a *risk* inherent to flying. Peter is told Jim's L.C.F. is off the scale and his new D. Date but ten days away. Of course, the Master Med computer is lying. But, then, the computer must lie, or else the D. Date myth might be exposed as *deception*—an accident the authorities are anxious to prevent. Like everyone living within the *political* confines of the Lucifer State, Jim feels fine, but he knows he will die, and he knows when. Though Jim displays no symptoms of irradiation, the medical technician is certain that he will because the computer says so—clearly an instance of *technological idolatry*. Jim is uncooperative when Peter questions him. He has translated imminent *death* into *freedom* from society and its security bureaucracy. Still, he describes to Peter what happened when Lucifer broke loose. He saw a small metal canister and a glass vial. What he saw will prove crucial for the rest of the novel. The canister casts doubt on the character of Lucifer. That doubt leads to Evelyn's discovering the D. Date is a myth. That *revelation* so devastates her, and eventually Natasha and Jim, causing Smyth to genuinely fear for their *psychological* stability.

Not only is the plane crash the basis for the synecdochic scene; it is also the genesis of the Biblical allegory, the most brilliant and powerful part of the novel. That allegory draws on the mythology of Satan, a mythology derived from Genesis and Revelation, the first and the last books, the Alpha and the Omega of the Bible.

Revelation 12:7-9 chronicles the triumph of the archangel Michael over the great dragon, "that old serpent, called the Devil, and Satan, which deceiveth the whole world: he was cast out into the earth, and his angels were cast out with him." In Revelation 13:2, the dragon confers its power upon a beast representing the persecuting Roman Empire, particularly in the person of the Emperor Nero. Revelation 13:8 describes the beast as branded on his forehead with the number 666, the total resulting from adding together the numerical values of the Hebrew letters in "Nero Caesar." Revelation 13:11-17 records the appearance of a second beast representing the pagan priesthood associated with emperor worship. (Revelation 19:20 refers to this beast as "the false prophet.") The second beast "causeth the earth and them which dwell therein to worship the first beast."

The allegory is straightforward. (We should beware trying to establish exact parallels for the dragon and the beasts since in the dream imagery of Revelation, the three are sometimes distinct and at other times indistinguishable.) The whole world is deceived by Lucifer, supposedly radioactive cobalt vital in a variety of ways to medicine, but actually a potentially lethal drug. Just as the Roman Empire maintained social control by means of an official religion, so the Lucifer State maintains social control by means of a "secular religion," the mythology of D. Date, itself perpetuated by means of technological idolatry. Within this secular religion a number of rites parody Jewish or Christian ones. Birth Rites correspond to Circumcision or Baptism; Puberty Rites to Bar Mitzvah or Confirmation; Terminal Rites to Last Rites or Communion, depending on whether the person himself is dying or one of his friends. Marriage, of course, occurs in all three religions. The Book of Liturgy is like the Bible. The words of the Terminal Rites are from Ecclesiastes 3.

Technological idolatry is crucial to this secular religion. The citizens of the Lucifer State must be the servant, the Master Med computer the master. The computer requires a special language, a scientific language for the liturgy of worship—Basic Beta Language or BABEL, "a semantically pure language, devoid of ambiguities and, therefore, of puns, of humor generally, and of all traces of poetry." Richly metaphoric language is obscene to the computer. Access requires recital of the Rainbow Passage in a metallic monotone. A rich, well-modulated voice is offensive to the machine. The passage, read correctly, gives access to a false heaven, the home of a false God.

BABEL is an allusion to Genesis 11:1-9. The Master Medical Facility corresponds to the Tower of Babel, a pyramidal temple tower whose summit was supposed to be the gate to heaven. The Tower was built out of a desire to be as God, but the god worshiped at Master Med is a god of the society's own creation (but forgotten as such—as with any idol). This god is "Satanic," the Lucifer of *Lucifer State*, the Devil, the deceiver of all mankind. And the computer is his prophet. "The beast," Smyth calls it. Ironically, in the end the computer does give access to heaven, but heaven is like hell. The Tower enables humans to become like God but to regret ever having wanted to.

The crash of Lucifer Flight Triple Six Lima is the Fall of Satan. Lucifer is loose in the Garden of Hartford, the society of ultimate security, the home of innocents like Eve. The serpent's subtle temptation begins. First, the insinuation of doubt—the metal canister. Then, the suspicion of God's motive—what does Smyth do with the microfilm the canisters contain? And finally, freedom—Evelyn and James Adam Sebring sense they can know the truth, truth that will set them free.

The temptation is now irresistible, not just for Eve staring at the computer, but also for us, the readers of the novel. The psychology is the same. Like Eve, we want the truth to be revealed. We want mystery explained. Eve types into the computer "Genesis 2:17?" The telescreen responds with the ominous warning, "But of the tree of the knowledge of good and evil, thou shalt not eat of it: for in the day that thou eatest thereof thou shalt surely die." The idea of knowledge conquers all caution. Eve types into the machine the text of Genesis 3:4-5: "And the serpent said unto the woman, ye shall not surely die: for God doth know that in the day ye eat thereof, then your eyes shall be opened, and ye shall be as gods, knowing good and evil." Eve shivers involuntarily "at the vision of the Devil calling God a liar," but she knows she is "on the verge of penetrating, if not the mind of God, at least the ultimate regions of the computer." She has a choice. God promises death, the Devil knowledge. She presses the "activate" button. The computer responds, "Request?" She's in. The feeling of guilt is gone, replaced by the euphoria of achievement. She no longer cares what is proper, what is right. She only glories in her triumph. She attacks the console. "What about Lucifer?" she types. And she watches "in amazement and terror as the mighty Master Med computer" disgorges its sinister secrets.

How does it feel, being an accessory to the Fall of Man? How devilishly clever of the novel to twist the plot that we willingly listen to Lucifer and disobey God. What could be more innocent than our hope of enlightenment? But Lucifer is the bearer of that light. Despite all the warnings, despite knowing the ancient story of Adam and Eve, we fall for the same old line: ". . . in the day ye eat thereof, then your eyes shall be opened and ye shall be as gods, knowing good and evil."

But why be so serious? Surely this is the time for jokes about Apple computers. After all, *Lucifer State* is only a book. We just want to know how the book ends. But if, as the Sophist suggests, we live fictions, what is "wanting to know how the book ends" except wanting some ultimate truth, some ultimate explanation? The Devil promises knowledge and we want desperately to understand. We would make the same mistake again, given the same choice, given the same warnings. *We would want to read something like this essay that would bring the mystery to an end.*

So now we experience the Lucifer State—the psychological one. We have sought knowledge and been devastated by what we have found. We have asked to be as gods, knowing good and evil, and we have gotten what we asked. We cannot hide in some corner of the Garden or the social shelter. The comforts of delusion denied to Smyth and Goras are now denied to us.

So, we ask for knowledge, get it, and get guilt as well. But what about death? God said on the day we ate of the tree of knowledge we would surely die. Evelyn mistakenly translates her discovery into her own death warrant. But the punishment is worse than the death she anticipates at the moment because that death is different from the one she will grow to fear. She will be sent forth from the Garden to suffer exile in Erewhon, east of Eden. Outside the social shelter she will be exposed to Marvell's cold "deserts of vast eternity," a soul-freezing existence.

When the Lucifer myth collapses, so does the myth of unity in death. The lovely picture of "male and female, hands interlocked, heads inclined each towards the other, joined in eternal sleep" ceases to comfort. Instead, like a sharp wind, Marvell's words slash to the bone: "The grave's a fine and private place, but none I think do there embrace." We seek for society to tell us otherwise, to say we sleep together rather than with worms. But each of us dies singly and alone and the final bed we will lie upon is the only thing that could be colder than the life we will have known.

Must life be so bleak? No—but at moments it may seem so. Smyth is genuinely concerned for Eve in her moment of discovery, exposed as she is in the rubble of her world. He personally had always contrived to protect her from such catastrophe. Had they married, he would have shared her D. Date, died with her willingly, to preserve the myth and thus the meaning of her life. *The irony is the Lucifer State political seeks to save its citizens from the Lucifer State psychological.* Life would be impossible without something to believe in, even a deception—"a deception in which the deceiver is more truthful than the non-deceiver and the one who lets himself be deceived is wiser than he who does not."

But, the word "deception" too easily implies its opposite, "truth." "Fiction" refuses to surrender quite so easily to dialectic. I prefer "fiction" because I am disturbed by any suggestion of certainty. Too often we are like Evelyn, consumed with the need for explanation. Some things just cannot be explained. Joannah believes in the transmigration of souls. But Joannah is insane. But then the insane sometimes see what others are blind to. As Jim wrestles to control his damaged star-jet, he hears Charlie directing him. But he could be imagining the voice given the stress of the situation, particularly after too many Cannabis cocktails in London. But he did hear Charlie talking him down and later he found Charlie's body at the end of the runway. In his final confrontation with Smyth, Jim remembers and feels for the first time that he understands "something about the human spirit . . . beyond the comprehension of the Director of Master Med."

When Jim flies Charlie to London during the last month of his life, Charlie thanks him, saying he will never be able to repay Jim for the wonder of this last night-flight. He continues, his husky voice now betraying his profound emotion, "I don't know what comes next . . . but I'll tell you this, Jim lad, if there's a life after death and you ever need me, the Devil himself won't keep me. . . ." Jim interrupts to insist Charlie owes him nothing. After all, he says, "It was *you* who taught *me* to fly, and a man never had a better teacher." Jim is lost for words. He and Charlie are not used to talking about the mutual bonds of affection and respect that connect them. Jim blinks away the moisture from his eyes and falls silent.

Death is a mystery each of us must face alone. But life is a mystery we can share. I have written about the novel's intended themes, but there is an unintended one, too—*the power of friendship.* I know the death of a close friend was what moved author Trevor Melia to begin writing *Lucifer State*.

When Jim and Natasha return from Jekyll Island, Jim points the jet down its final glide path to the same runway he had crashed on. "Normally, the tower would break the silence at this moment with the words, 'This is your final controller,' but tonight there would be no such message. He must guide the speeding craft to its destination without help." He is on his own. He knows that *for him there will never again be a final controller*. He shivers involuntary. The green lights mark the threshold of the runway. The weeks since the last dramatic approach seem years. Uncle Charlie's voice is silent now, gone forever. When he takes off again, he will be alone.

Thus the novel comes to its end. It began with the words of Gorgias and ends with those of Protagoras. The prologue contained a telegram that dealt with Jim Sebring's uncovering a deception. The epilogue contains a telegram in which Goras initiates another—that Natasha is dead. The story began with the Birth Rites of Jim and Evelyn's son. It ends with the private Terminal Rites of Natasha. In the beginning a flight arrived in Hartford. Now in the end a flight departs for Erewhon—nowhere. The novel began on the first day of Spring, the moment when the sun, ever racing across the sky, crossed the equator in its yearly journey north. The novel ends with Jim flying north into the Polestar, the only still point in an ever turning sky, the only thing stable is the state of vertigo that shakes him as he leaves Lucifer's country behind. The last thing he sees is the last great image of the novel that draws together all the themes—the great pyramid of Master Med in the center of a spider's web of street lights that radiate from it. He has broken out of the web. He is flying. He is free.[vi]

[vi] Shortly after I finished the first version of this essay, I told Trevor Melia I had failed to mention the final image of rebirth. The symbol of the web appears initially in connection with Charles Adamson Sebring's birth and finally in connection with Natasha's supposed death. Jim reacts with apprehension to its first appearance and apparently with deep resignation to its last. But he flies north into new life noting the web, because the streets at night are lined with cold blue lights—lights which are the color of birth in Lucifer State.

Melia responded to my ingenious analysis by saying it took two to make a work of art—one to do it, and a second to shoot him before he overdid it. The same was true, he continued, of criticism. Still, Melia could not tell me why he mentioned the color of the lights and why he made them blue instead of white, pointing perhaps to something about the process of creation that escapes even the artist's consciousness.

What will happen to Jim and Natasha and the other characters from *Lucifer State?* In the cold light of dawn, July 1st, 1982, after a long and mostly sleepless night on the Atlantic, amidst high winds and steep seas, Trevor Melia and I talked about the sequel, *Escape from Erewhon*, escape by sailboat across a hostile sea.